Waldwick...Driftless

Kenneth Linde

Waldwick Books
www.waldwickbooks.com
McHenry, Illinois

Waldwick...Driftless

Kenneth Jon Linde

Library of Congress Control Number: 2019900112

Waldwick Partners, Inc.
dba Waldwick Books
www.WaldwickBooks.com

July 15, 2019

Printed in Wisconsin, United States of America

ISBN: 979-8-9852613-5-6

ISBN: 979-8-9852-6135-6

WHAT ARE YOU WILLING TO GIVE

FOR

ONE MORE DAY,

ONE MORE HOUR,

ONE MORE MOMENT

WITH THE ONE YOU LOVE?

Driftless:

What a funny word…driftless. Seek out the word in a dictionary and it simply doesn't exist. When one hears or reads the word "driftless" what can you think? A word so unique, so different and almost unheard of in everyday life. For many, driftless elicits thoughts of having no direction or without aim … even concepts of the lack-of-purpose come to mind.

Many confuse "driftless" with the word "drifter," yet there is a profound difference between the two in thought, concept and emotion. While alien to most, there is an area located in southwestern Wisconsin that encompasses a way of life and celebrates the word "driftless" providing meaning, purpose and benefit to those who reside and those who choose to live life to its fullest.

Physically, the driftless area is where nature did not scrape away inherent beauty. Instead, there is a land of rolling, tree-covered hills, magnificent rock outcroppings, quiet streams and patchwork quilts of farmlands that stretch to the horizons, all woven together in a tapestry destined to leave many first-time visitors awestruck by its purity. The land casts its spell upon those who live within and nowhere is it personified more than in the bucolic enclave called Mineral Point. Less than an hour from the hustle and bustle of Wisconsin's capitol, Mineral Point provides a life and lifestyle less complicated, less frenetic and certainly less cumbersome than those of the outside world.

To live or be raised in the driftless area does not make one more or less of a person, just a person with a point of reference to a time and place where life goes by at a slower pace, where many who leave yearn to return, when the speed-of-life makes them breathless and in need of just one thing … tranquility. Driftless is not a secret garden, nor reserved for a few, but a lush veranda, inhabited by people with an easy smile and warm heart who welcome others to come and experience the beauty of life as it was meant to be!

I was born in the driftless area and though my life has moved me away, I continue to make journeys back to the land and people I love. This is yet another story, another segment, another piece of the puzzle I call life.

In the Beginning:

Now that I have shared the entire concept of where I was raised and why I think, feel and believe the way I do, I would like to bring you up to date. One night, as I was sitting alone in our condo in Madison, I picked up the manuscript of my youth which I called "Little Spirit". Many times, I wondered what the word *"Little"* meant. Did it refer to my size? Did it refer to having a small amount of spirit? Was it simply a reference to the Great Spirit with whom I have had the honor of sharing my life? Perhaps, it's all three.

As the light of day turned to darkness, I began reading the entire summary about those magic moments in my life and how they came about and realized I had been blessed beyond comprehension. As the last page turned, I closed my eyes and thanked God for all that was and all that is.

I'm not going to go into all the details of that journal, but felt I did need to share some of it or what transpires here won't make any sense at all. I guess the story all began with one choice ... actually two choices, in the game ... rock-hammer-scissors ... that changed everything that I'll share with you in a little bit.

It is now several years later and I am embarrassed to say, I haven't put pen-to-paper in so long when, in fact, my education was that of a writer. I don't know why I'm peering back now. I'm not that old and yet the memories of all that happened are flooding my soul and begging for reflection and meaning.

Is it a mid-life crisis? Perhaps, and yet, I've been through all that as you will quickly see. Perhaps, all that is floating in my brain is happening out of coincidence. It's amazing how life can get away from you as the day-to-day 'stuff' gets in the way of memories. As life has moved on, little things that were once so important, get shoved to the back as new things take their place.

One day, my wife, Amy and I were talking and she asked me whatever happened to the original copy of "Waldwick" that had been my graduation present from college from my parents. I was embarrassed to think I really didn't know, as it had been so long since I'd seen it. My mind wandered from possibility to possibility as I promised myself that when I found it, it would never happen again. How could I let something so precious simply fade away?

For several days, I pondered the options and then came to the realization, that I knew where it was … in a safety deposit box in the bank in Mineral Point. I drove "home" and went to the bank. They proceeded to ask for the key, to which I had no idea where it was. Normally, this means no access. However, when you live in a small town and know everyone and are also the bank's largest customer, rules are bent and keys are made. My cousin, Sandy, was the Vice President and personally escorted me to the vault. She looked for the authorization card and found it. It had been nearly twenty years since anyone had put their signature on the dotted line and it was that of my dad.

For a moment, I stood as tears welled in my eyes. I breathed deep and swallowed hard. Dad had placed the original in the vault for Tommie and me and we simply let life go on. What had been so important had become inconsequential and I felt ashamed, vowing to place my youthful memories alongside those of my ancestors with the hope that someday, my children would take the time to read what their father had written so that they had a better understanding of who they were and where we had been.

I drove back to our condo in Madison and began reading "Waldwick". It was written by my ancestor I call George the First. Now George the First was no king. George was simply a man with a dream who came to America with a passion for life, liberty and justice, who took a quill in hand and wrote a manuscript, sealed it in candle wax and buried it in a grotto in the wall of the farmhouse root cellar that he helped build. It all seems so innocent and yet, we have come and gone, in so many ways, since those simple days when everyone understood good and bad, right and wrong. It is a wonderful story that filled my heart with love and pride!

As I had written in my journal, I met and fell in love with a woman named Amelia Marie Williams. As I had written, I have a friend by the name of Rodney Whitehorse, who was and remains my best friend, who is the president of the Ho-Chunk nation and married to a woman by the name of Ann. As I had written, we fought together to save a small spit of land in Iowa County, Wisconsin on a farm called Waldwick. Many times, throughout the years, I wondered, was it all really worth it. Yet without it, things would have been so much different in so many ways. But then, that is what this story is all about.

I met Rodney when my three college roommates and I went to the Ho-Chunk casino to get drunk and he was a security guard and that's where the rock-paper-scissors comes in. For those who don't know, you simply have two players and count to three where you extend some of your fingers. Two fingers represent scissors, five fingers mean paper and a closed fist represents a rock. The logic is that a scissors can cut paper! Paper can cover a rock and a rock will break a pair of scissors.

You play the game fast and it's all based on impulse. That night, I lost and yet won! As it was then and is now, Rodney was this huge Native American and I was this little white guy. Our bond was instant and friendship so deep we called each other brother and do so today.

One day, I was driving from Madison back to Waldwick, Wisconsin, which was and remains a distance of 52 miles and lost control of my Jeep and almost my life. I awakened in the hospital in Madison, in critical condition, with so many broken bones, it was incredible. One of my nurses was the woman by the name of Ann, who was from Milwaukee and a member of the Potawatomi Nation. I arranged for Rodney to meet her and they fell in love, got married and have three kids. That could be another story, but not today.

Rodney and Ann invited me to live with them while I was recovering from the car accident, which I did. One day, Ann came home and expressed the fact she had been assaulted and insulted at work in the hospital. I took umbrage and realized the results of Rodney defending his wife's honor could be devastating to him because he could have killed the jerk and was an Indian, while I was this scrawny, accident-recovering, white guy. So, I took it upon myself to "visit" the clown who insulted this wonderful woman. I wasn't certain the idiot realized there were consequences for his actions. It wasn't done to be noble, but out of respect for my friends. Once again, it also changed my entire life.

One of Ann's patients was a woman by the name of Amy, who was being treated for Leukemia. As Ann and Amy became friends, Ann felt lonely me and lovely Amy, might be a good match and set it up in a very clandestine way for us to "run into" each other by having Amy, a UPS driver, deliver a package to the cottage I shared with Rodney and Ann and do so when I was home alone.

I was immediately smitten and asked Amy if I could see her again. She agreed! I smiled! On our first official date, we met in the Capitol rotunda in Madison and I told her, "until that moment, the inside of the Wisconsin State Capitol had been the most beautiful thing I had ever seen. It was and remains, the most romantic thing I ever said.

Amy made certain I realized that she was of mixed race. Back then and I guess, even now, for some people, that makes a difference. To me, I thought I would be cute and told her, while she was half black, I played halfback in high school, which got a quizzical look on her face. I then told her my dad was a dairy farmer who milked 250 Holstein cows who were black and white and so I thought we were pretty much even.

Even after all these years, I still use funny words like ding dong, which I readily admit I am, and got excited when Amy told me her given name was Amelia. Growing up, I had a real passion for

Amelia Erhardt and the first gift I ever gave Amy was a model of Amelia Earhart's plane I assembled when I was 12.

As we were dating and getting serious, I met Amy's parents. I knew they were well-off but didn't realize how rich they were until after we got married, but now I'm getting ahead of myself.

There is a saying … good times, bad times, happy times, sad times, without the valleys, the mountains would mean so little. Where do I begin? For the first thirty years of my life, I went by the name "Q". I was named "Q" as I was George Terrill the Fourth and "Q" sounded a lot better than quad or IV or anything, including George. One day, it didn't seem to fit anymore. I was no longer the son of the son of the son of the son and so on and so on and so on. I was my own man and so I became George.

George isn't a popular name anymore. However, it is my name and I vowed to make certain people respected me for who I am and have tried to earn that respect through honesty, integrity, decency and tolerance. I must admit, I try, but don't always succeed.

The year I celebrated my 35th birthday was a turning point. Amelia and I had been married for nine years and yet, I lived in a house purchased by my wife; wore tailor-made clothes, purchased by my wife and drove fancy cars that belonged to her dad. In my first 35 years, I really didn't feel I had accomplished much, acquired much or matured much and those who called me Mr. Amelia Williams behind my back, were probably right. While every person dreams of wealth, they don't understand that dream can also be a nightmare.

For these past few years, so many thoughts and emotions have lain dormant and now I would like to continue the story. Quite honestly, I've been too busy to write, trying to prove to myself I am more than I am. As the years pile up and memories begin to be buried, I promised myself again and again and again I would put things on paper so my kids and, hopefully someday, grandkids knew a little more about Boppa.

I have taken notes and stashed them away. Does everyone live happily ever after? No! Does good always beseech evil? No! Have I climbed all the mountains I set out to scale? Hardly! Yet, I feel I must continue the story of "Waldwick".

One night, I was staying in our condo in Madison and rummaging through my desk and came upon the manuscript I'd written, which outlined life of fifteen years ago. My God, things had changed. As I read, I could sense my youthful enthusiasm! I could feel my sacrilegious mind set. I marveled at my exuberance! Where had it all gone? What happened to me?

I decided to go for a walk, simply to clear my head and reflect upon the changes that had taken place. I made my way the two blocks up to the Capitol square, which everyone in Madison calls "up" simply because the capitol is built on the top of a hill. I don't think it took a political genius to think that one up.

I meandered into the Capitol and looked at the dome in all its glory, remembering the time Amy and I had our first "date" and smiled a deep, satisfying smile. My mind wandered and a gentle nod reflected my emotions as this was also the spot where I proposed to the woman I love. I walked out the State Street entrance and peered towards the University of Wisconsin campus, glancing at Teddywedgers and remembering it was Amy's and my special spot and the last meal I ever had while working with my best friend, Rodney. My God, times had changed!

I started walking towards campus and with each block, the aura evolved. The profound seriousness of government slowly gave way to the exuberance of youth. I wondered at which point I was in my journey. My mind wandered and I asked myself 'why?' Why had I changed? Why was everything so different?

I came across some high school kids and they were laughing … simply laughing … about something they thought was funny. I had no idea what it was, but it made me feel old. Why is it, that as you age, you don't laugh anymore? Is it because the glee of youth becomes so eroded that all we have are pleasant smiles? Is it because of the responsibilities of life that weren't there? Why couldn't I capture that feeling and put it back into my soul? Perhaps, just perhaps, the layers of worries that cover us all, put a coat of shellac on our minds and we no longer have that joy we once had. I wanted to laugh, instead I thought I was going to cry.

Great Grandfather:

Where do I begin my story about Amelia, Rodney and Ann and all those who were such an integral part of all that changed the course of my existence? I must begin at the death of Great Grandfather. You can read about what happened to me while he was alive and get some concept of why he called me *"Little Spirit"* in my first set of memories. Great Grandfather was the one who imparted so much wisdom that forever changed not only what I became, but who I am as well.

Great Grandfather died on the day the land where his great grandmother's life was saved by George the First, was secured forever from those who wanted it to pass away. At Great Grandfather's wake were members of every Indian nation in the Midwest who came to honor the life of this wonderful man. All agreed, he would be fondly remembered and truly missed! Great Grandfather's remains were placed in a special burial urn. It was agreed his spirit should be interred in the forest co-owned by the Ho-Chunk and me ... the land we fought for and won.

Great Grandfather told me I was the "chosen one". As noted, my name is Little Spirit. In the beginning, I was able to speak through Great Grandfather to the Indian forefathers and believed what they said. With Great Grandfather's death, there was silence, the deafening silence of muted voices, buried beneath the onslaught of today, where yesterday was admonished to trivia, to be forgotten. How sad, children are no longer taught about the past. How tragic dreams and nightmares collide in a world wrought with turmoil and lessons never learned.

On the day of Great Grandfather's funeral, our entire entourage walked from my parent's farm house to the forest. I remember my father cut the hay that morning so the path was clear. No one would ride this day, for the processional journey was sacred, led by the Ho-Chunk Medicine Man, followed by the Chief and my best friend and son of the Chief, Rodney, holding high, the burial urn, as we all walked solemnly behind.

We reached the forest where so many of my ancestors had come and a profound sense of tranquility permeated my body. Once again, I was home! Once again, the silent trees and memories enveloped me, making all that stood between me and complete happiness evaporate. As you read on, there will be more, much, much more about the land. When we got to the spot where Amelia and I first made love, she squeezed my hand, as she knew I felt I was on sacred grounds.

While we had been there before … Rodney, Ann, the Chief and my family that is, this was the Medicine Man's first time and the magical power I had always felt engulfed him, overwhelming his soul so that he too felt the energy of the spirits. I did not know he was also a Shaman and when he stood still, the leaves wrestled in the trees as if there was a breeze and yet there was none. Even in modern times, when most religions are losing their significance, the Ho-Chunk still consider the Medicine Man to be a priest and healer; a spiritual leader who they believe can control natural forces and have nature move him, which meant the land was as special as we all believed it to be.

I watched this mysterious man and trembled as he trembled. He was being overwhelmed by the power of the land. At that point in time, I didn't know why and yet, I revered the passion and emotion that permeated his body, thinking, believing, feeling, it was simply the energy of Great Grandfather within his grasp.

The Nation's members performed ceremonies and rituals to bring about communion with the spirits and they believed the Medicine Man was their avenue to reaching the supernatural world. Rodney admitted both he and the Chief called upon the Medicine Man when they needed advice or solutions for problems facing the nation whom they also called the "Great Spirit" and finally realized why I was called "Little Spirit".

Great Spirit was able to reach to the heavens and speak to the heavens. I, Little Spirit, was given the responsibility of making certain the goodness of life continues through honor, dignity and respect for the teachings that come from the land.

As we entered the glen, Great Spirit looked skyward and there was total silence. The Medicine Man bent down and lit a small fire and I smelled burning sage, the plant used during Native American spiritual ceremonies. At once, the birds stopped chirping, the incessant insects froze in time and space. Great Spirit's face became pale and drawn as his eyes rolled back into his head the way Great Grandfather's had done when we had met so many times. Great Spirit's hands quivered from the energy beneath his feet. I stood and marveled at what I saw. This man was feeling all the energy at once that I had felt in dribs and drabs throughout my life.

Great Spirit dug deep within his body for the strength to continue. He knew he was on sacred ground. He was aware the energy field he felt was far greater than anything he had ever felt before. I believe there was fear within him as the strength of the spirits were so much more than even he could handle.

The Chief motioned to me and pointed so that I put my hand upon Great Spirit's shoulder. I did as I was directed and watched as both of the Great Spirit's wrists met as his fingers and hands remained apart. His hands shook as if the energy flow, which had been growing within him, ebbed and flowed when his body became one circuit. His eyes closed, his hands shook and his mouth opened as his head tilted towards the sky and then the bolt of energy that was within him ricocheted into me and I felt the bright light of eternity beam down upon me.

Like Great Spirit, my body began to quake. As was his case, my wrists involuntarily clasped together with open fingers pointing upwards. My eyes rolled back, back, back into my head as I convulsed as if a thousand volts of electricity were being shot through my body. For the first time, I truly accepted I was fundamentally "Little Spirit" … the "chosen one"! I was the one who had been selected to carry the torch of goodness of those who were gathered, but could not be seen. My God, what was happening?

My hand left Great Spirit's shoulder as my body began shaking and I felt the energy flow within me. All the love and hate, joy and sorrow which had been buried within the hallowed ground upon which we stood engulfed me as my heart pounded and my soul became encompassed in the past. Rodney, the Chief and Great Sprit understood while others stood somewhat aghast, concerned for my wellbeing.

As the trembling softened, Great Spirit passed the urn to me as all the Indians bowed their heads in reverence to me, the white man … the outsider, now on the inside, looking out. What a strange, strange feeling to be the chosen one who felt so ill prepared and so completely, fundamentally, ill-equipped to be what I was chosen to be!

I took the lead as we walked further, passing the withering foundation of Skunk Hollow School where my ancestors had learned so much about life, to the spot where George the First had saved Morning Star's life. It was here where so many tears had fallen by so many people who felt the intensity of survival. I opened the urn and offered a small amount of the ashes to the Medicine Man, Chief and Rodney. They nodded and I placed a small amount between my fingers and thumb. I could feel the power! I could sense the energy! I was absorbed in the pain of death and destruction and yet, at the same time, there was joy, profound, incredible joy that only comes from relief and realization that there was truly a fourth dimension into which all life flows.

The four of us … Rodney, the Chief, Great Spirit and I, looked at each other and a small amount of Great Grandfather's ashes were released. We knelt and mixed the ashes with the soil and then rose and hugged each other. This was the passing of the soul back into the Earth where the spirits lie.

We knelt before the sundial which had been created to place Great Grandfather's remains within the ground. Great care had been given regarding how the sundial would look and where it would be placed. The gnomon, while still a thin, sharp rod which had been hammered from a single piece of brass and etched to look like an eagle feather, that had been blessed by the Great Spirit and placed so that it would accurately reflect, not only the time of day, but the time of year, designed to reflect the passing of the seasons forever. While many sundials, have markings to indicate specific time divisions, Great Grandfather's memorial was left without any markings to infer that the effect one has on others is timeless.

I had learned from Great Grandfather and carried the passionate belief with me that the Earth, together with all life on the planet, must be viewed as a single organism which maintains equilibrium among its various parts ... the atmosphere, oceans and soil ... the totality which has but one goal ... equilibrium. Whether the changes were extraterrestrial, biological, geological or any other way, Great Grandfather had taught me that life responds to them, modifying and regulating the state of the Earth's environment in Earth's favor. Great Grandfather had spoken often that humans were just one piece of the puzzle and Earth and the great spirits of life would always adjust to our intrusion and life, of some form, would go on and on and on.

With Great Grandfather's ashes interred, the Chief was now the elder and Rodney, my best friend, assumed his position as Chief of the Ho-Chunk nation. Never again would Rodney's father be considered the Chief! He was now the elder. The passing of time was upon them ... the orderly, peaceful, transition was taking place ... Great Grandfather, to father, to son, with only Rodney's grandfather missing, when he gave his life for his country … not the Ho-Chunk Nation, but the United States of America.

Great Spirit looked deeply into my eyes and I could see both fear and trepidation. I was not one of them and yet I was the chosen one. Someday, who knew when, my role would change and I would take the place of the Great Spirit. A white man in a red man's world! What did it mean? What would the consequence be? Could I truly, spiritually, lead a nation of which I was not a part?

That day, those around us were but blurs… spectators… almost insignificant relics who came as witnesses, not as participants and yet their presence meant so much. As had been the case at Ann and Rodney's wedding, the dream dancers danced and played the sacred drums. This was not the Ghost Dance so many white people had heard of, where Indian ancestors did the dance which would reunite the living with the spirits of their ancestors and ultimately cause the "white man" to leave, thereby bringing prosperity, peace, unity and the bison back to all of the tribal groups. Today, there is peace, there is the beginning of prosperity and there is unity for my Indian brothers. However, the "white man" remains and it is the Indian who has acclimated to the white man's culture.

At Great Grandfather's funeral, the antique peace pipe used for so many generations was lit and everyone took one breath in memory of Great Grandfather. As the smoke rose, we all believed the soul of this great man was rising with it. Yet I knew his soul did not rise in the wind to be blown here and there. His soul was in the Earth beneath my feet and his energy and that of those who had spoken to me was what nurtured the land and made it sacred. I then accepted that, while he was physically gone, Great Grandfather never left me in many, many ways.

All in attendance that day joined in a circle and held hands. Rodney's father spoke of love and friendship and goodness as we bowed our heads in prayer. I remember feeling as if Great

Grandfather was there with us. I could feel his soft hands upon my shoulders and listened to his whispers in the wind as they entered my ears and my heart …" Little Spirit, you are the chosen one".

After the mixture of ashes and Earth, we walked to the springs. Small ceramic cups were filled with the pure water which came from the Earth and we toasted the people who had come before us and those who would follow in our footsteps. For those who had not tasted Earth's nectar, the intensity of the water took them aback. This was not what came from the tap or even in bottles. This was virgin water from within the Earth … cold, clear and infused with purity as I quietly whispered, "Ashes to ashes…dust to dust. But life must go on. Time heals all wounds and memories fade, but life must go on!"

After the ceremony, we walked back to the house and had a traditional farm lunch the neighbors had brought. Farmers always stick together and while Great Grandfather was not a family member, the neighbors understood. After the legal battle, everyone knew the land was sacred and so was the man and he was considered someone to respect and honor.

So much has changed for the Indians! From humiliation and abject poverty that lasted for many generations, to a situation where wealth was finally beginning to come their way, things had begun to balance out. Big Brother and Ann kept me well aware of the changes and challenges, not to complain, but to explain, all that was happening to their society, their culture and their ways of life.

Today, there are more than 10 million Native Americans living in the United States, and more than half of them are mixed with another race. For all that is good, there is still profound sadness. For instance, it is estimated that more than 28% live below the Federal poverty line or nearly double, all other races. Historically, Native Americans have also been prone to alcohol abuse, and up to 10% of Native Americans are heavy alcohol users, including children and teens.

Native Americans are true Americans, who have played a role in the major wars the United States has been involved in. Great Grandfather explained to me that in World War I, more than 8,000 Native Americans fought for the U.S., and they weren't even considered citizens. 24,000 Native American soldiers, fought in World War II. The most notable of these were the Navajo Code Talkers, who communicated in code that no one, including fellow American soldiers, could understand. Rodney's grandfather gave his life in Viet Nam and Native American soldiers continue to enlist to fight for their country... our country, the United States of America.

While many Americans believe it was the settlers who killed the Indians, it was actually disease. When the Europeans came to the New World, they brought with them a host of diseases the Native Americans had no immunity to, of which smallpox was the most lethal. In the end, 90% of all Native Americans died from disease. Today, the suicide rate among Native Americans is one of the highest in the world. In general, when compared to the entire population of the United States, the suicide rates among Native Americans are three times higher. For those who live on a reservation, it's about 10 times higher, caused by the high rate of poverty, unemployment and domestic violence, along with high rates of drug addiction, alcoholism and sexual assault.

The Ho-Chunk are my friends and I respect all their culture represents. I have come to learn about them and respect them and believe they feel the same about me. Being called "Little Spirit" is a great honor. To be given Great Grandfather's two eagle feathers was the highest honor a man can receive, as eagle feathers can only be worn by a male leader who has earned respect.

I have but two feathers and they are kept in a glass case to remind me of Great Grandfather. The Native Americans who wear full headdresses believe the feathers have spiritual powers because they believe the eagle is sacred, they also believe this power transfers to the headdress. I hope and pray my two feathers give me the power I need to do what I am destined to do. I hope and pray I can do right without doing wrong. I hope and pray the blessings given to me are only used for good and not evil. This is why my life has changed. This is what I must give back! This is where it all will end! I think of Great Grandfather daily and await the time when we will speak again as he promised we would. I miss him and hope that his spirit is at peace.

Amelia:

Amelia made me vow that we remain unmarried until she was officially cancer cured, or ten years from her first treatment. She fought a brave battle against Leukemia and was involved in what, at that time, was an experimental procedure, that saved her life. For five years, Amelia went every month for chemical treatments and had her blood cleaned and T-cells harvested. It has extended her life from a few months to many years. In return, I asked only that I be allowed to become my own man. We both have lived up to our side of the bargain.

Having done well on her LSAT pre-law exam, Amelia elected to earn her law degree from the University of Wisconsin in Madison so she could maintain her cancer treatments. Her goal was to allow us to continue living in our condo on Wilson Street and being "just a couple" fortunate enough not to have the financial worries of others starting out, but humble enough to realize we were blessed with improving health and each other.

For two years, Amelia busted her butt, focusing on corporate and securities law. It was a wonderful time when we were wrapped in each other, thinking of nothing but tomorrow. With Amelia studying, I continued to work for the Ho-Chunk nation heading up marketing and, quite honestly, growing up. While never one to ask, I quickly became fond of the finer things in life … clothes, cars, trips and special perks, which having The Duke as a future father-in-law allowed. My favorite became the custom shoes. Twice each year, The Duke would have a tailor fly over from Italy and we would be measured and fitted for new clothes. In between, the shoemaker from Crockett & Jones in England would fly in with new styles and take our choices back to be custom made. I knew better than to ask the price, but there's something about custom made, English leather loafers that can't be beat.

When it came to Wisconsin football games, I initially acquiesced and sat in a skybox with Dad Williams. He knew I was uncomfortable and purchased four tickets in the stands. Section "T" row 27, seats 19-22…right on the fifty, but outside, where football should be watched. If the weather was lousy, Dad and Mom Williams would go into the corporate box while Amelia and I would snuggle in our seats, decked out in red, watching the Badgers. Going to away-games was a different story and our goal was to visit each stadium. Dad Williams would have the jet pick us up at Truax and we would go and sit in a skybox and be treated like royalty. It's amazing what power and money can and cannot do. It can open doors, but it cannot bring joy and happiness. Happiness is not reserved for anyone.

Each month, Amelia would have her cancer treatment, "bloodletting", as we called it and then a day of recovery. Each month, I would focus only on doting on her. We developed a schedule and a routine. I knew her treatment time was six-to-eight hours. I would drop her off at the clinic and head for Waldwick where my dog-buddy, Jake would be waiting as we walked to the forest to speak to Great Grandfather and see all that had happened in the past month with him and my friends, the trees. Jake must have thought it was odd to have me talking to no one and yet, the energy was so strong, I knew he could to feel it, too. Regardless of the weather, I would take a sip from the springs and feel the warmth of love and say my special prayer and head back to Madison in time to pick Amelia up.

With each passing day, Amelia and my life became more intertwined and we became accustomed to each other. With the passing of her fourth year of phase-two treatments, I had a large countdown calendar printed at Park Printing in Verona that we hung in the kitchen. It was nothing ornate, simply beginning with the number twelve and ending at one to represent the number of sessions she had remaining.

Amelia's prognosis remained excellent, as did her spirits while the months passed and the calendar grew thinner. Finally, it was time for her last session. We both knew she would be in no condition to celebrate the next day. Instead of having the treatment on Friday, Amy moved it to Wednesday so she would be "back to normal" on Friday. Even so, I still needed to remind her of my love. Instead of my journey to Waldwick, I ordered roses and when Felly's Flowers arrived, I assisted in the placement of 10 dozen roses in our condo … one dozen for each year of treatment to remind her of my love and all she had accomplished. As I looked at the roses, I remembered what Great Grandfather said …"Let the relationship open like a rose".

When the last page of the "calendar" stood before us, we took down the little paper and Amelia took it with her to the clinic. She wanted everyone's autograph and wanted them placed on a single sheet of paper. The day was just another "bloodletting" day. When time was nigh, I went to the clinic and waited outside. Normally, Amelia would be brought out in a wheelchair. Instead, with her teeth gritted and assisted by two nurse's aides, my Amelia walked out the front door, followed by Ann Whitehorse and the entire staff, all smiling and applauding. Amelia had made it! Her treatments were done! Assuming the final tests came back negative, she was officially a cancer survivor! Ten years since the leukemia! Ten years since the treatments began! Ten years of life and hopefully, many, many more.

The ride back to the condo was short and she was already nodding off. Like the other 59 treatments, it had taken its toll. I pulled into stall number 805 and helped her out of the Range Rover. She was wasted! When we got to our floor, I picked her up and carried her across the threshold and into her garden of love. Amelia looked at me and a faint, exhausted, smile spread across her lips as she hugged me and kissed me on the cheek. "I love you" she whispered. I simply smiled and put her to bed.

Thursday was like all the other days after treatment. Amelia was weak and mainly slept. I massaged her legs to help ease the cramps and did my best to make her comfortable. By Friday, she was getting back to normal and the fragrance of the flowers filled her with energy and smiles.

Doctor Roberts, the oncologist, personally called with good news. "All clear," the best two words we could ever hear. We hugged and smiled and the inner tension which had been with us for so long simply disappeared. Miss Amelia Williams was now officially and emotionally a cancer survivor. Amy took a deep breath and I could literally see the tension escape from her body. Like a spring uncoiling, Amy's nerves were finally beginning to completely unwind.

"I need to add my final dot." Amelia said with a smile on her face.

Amelia had herself inked with the word *Survivor* on her right shoulder when she began the blood-letting treatments. Starting with five dots for her first five years of medication, every year, she would celebrate by adding a single dot behind the word. This would be the last of ten dots and so it would read *Survivor*.............. To which she said there would be one more "surprise" for me.

That night, I asked if she wanted to go out and celebrate and she said "No," she only wanted to stay home with me and show me how much she loved me. It was our personal way of celebrating the end and yet the beginning. It was quite the evening topped off by Chocolate Shoppe turtle ice cream and chocolate cake.

Saturday meant her parents were coming to Madison to celebrate. It was to be a quiet dinner for the four of us. After the trial that saved the Forest, The Duke remained a member of the Madison Club, although, he rarely went there. When he announced dinner would be there, I was a bit surprised with so many other restaurants in Madison he preferred. I justified it because the Madison Club was only a half-block walk from the condo and so it all seemed to make sense to me.

Dinner was set for seven and at 6:55 Amy and I walked out of the condo and made the short trek. I offered to drive and she said that was silly, especially when it was one of those wonderful Wisconsin June nights with temperatures in the mid-seventies and low humidity. We walked slowly, hand-in-hand, just the two of us.

As we reached the front door of the Madison Club, the doorman asked for identification. I was perplexed! I told him who we were and that we were expected. He asked us to wait outside while he went in to get confirmation. Needless to say, I was a bit perturbed.

After a couple of minutes, the doorman returned and apologized, saying there had been an error and we were to go to room 104 where Mr. and Dr. Williams were waiting. We should have known! We pulled open the door and the word "SURPRISE" echoed from a room full of people. My Mom and Dad, Rodney and Ann, the Chief and Mrs. Whitehorse, Charlie Birdsong and his wife, Amy's Aunt and Uncle from St. Martin, the staff from the clinic, Dr. Roberts and her husband and all of Amy's high school friends, college roommates and spouses were there.

"Oh my God!" was all Amy could say as she looked around the room. I just shook my head and smiled. Everyone who had been part of Amy's support group was in attendance. The people who had walked with her down the path back to good health had joined together to wish her well. The night was filled with smiles, laughter and profound joy. We were celebrating life! Amy's life! Our life together!

As we went from person-to-person, you could see the smiles on everyone's faces. Mom and Dad Williams had done a great job of getting everyone together and still keeping it a secret … including the doorman, I might add. The Williams' owned two jets, Amelia I and Amelia II that were used to bring all the out-of-state guests to Madison, who were staying next door at the Hilton. Some of her college roommates were shocked to find out Amy Williams came from money. She had always been so kind, sincere and unassuming.

Amy's roommate, Sandy, and her partner, had come from New Mexico and were the biggest surprise. Amy hadn't seen Sandy since Amy transferred to St. Martin from John Hopkins for what was believed to be her final throes and both thought they would never see each other again.

I don't know what mom and dad thought of a lesbian couple as the subject never came up and while there had been stories about couples in Mineral Point, it wasn't something openly discussed at the dinner table. Knowing caring mom and conservative dad, I'm certain there was a conversation about it after the ceremony, at which time dad would have said something and mom would have said, "As long as they are happy, what difference does it make?" Little did she know about Amy's past nor would she ever know.

Everyone was seated with both sets of parents at our table and I knew I had to say something. I stood and asked for everyone's attention. I thanked everyone for coming! I thanked everyone for their love and support! I thanked everyone simply for being our friends. I stood behind Amy and put my hands on her shoulders and said, "Bravery isn't only about being in battle, it's also about never giving up, never complaining and never, ever making excuses. My love has shown me courage beyond reproach. My love has shown me generosity beyond compare and my love has shown me the meaning of love, of life and of the profound joy that comes when you sincerely feel wanted, needed and loved."

I looked down at Amy and continued ... "Miss Amelia Marie Williams for the past five years we have kept a promise to each other that we would make no plans of marriage until you were a cancer survivor. Well my dear, sweet love, the time has come that you and I get married!" I knelt on one knee and looked into Amelia's eyes ... "Amy, will you marry me?"

"Yes! Yes! Yes!"

"Hooray!" The entire room exploded in cheers.

The Duke stood and asked for attention. His eyes were glistening. "Amy, George, this is one of the happiest days of my life! You two have come so far together and have shown each other the commitment it takes to make a relationship work through good times and bad, happy and sad, you have stuck together."

Everyone applauded as The Duke raised his hands for quiet, one more time. "Dr. Roberts, can you please come forward." Dr. Roberts made her way to the table. "Doctor, Marie and I cannot thank you enough for all you have done for Amelia. I know, through your efforts, there are many people alive today who otherwise would only be memories. I also know your research needs to continue to help find a cure for Leukemia and to this end, I am presenting you with a check to be used to assist you in your efforts."

Doctor Roberts almost fainted as she looked on disbelief. Her mouth dropped open and her legs began to buckle. The mouths of everyone in the room dropped, including mine when Amy whispered the check was for ten million dollars.

Dad Williams continued. "This is only the beginning Doctor. Let's develop the Williams Center for Cancer Research and see what we can do to help win the war you are fighting."

At first there was stunned silence and then a rousing round of applause. What a night! What an incredible night!

As the clock struck ten, I could see Amy was fading fast. She put up a good front and I nodded to her mom as our eyes met and she too knew it was time for her little girl to go home and go to bed. I took my two forefingers and motioned them in unison. Dr. Williams got the hint. She would walk Amelia back to the condo as mother-and-daughter and The Duke and I would give them some time together and then return a little later.

Each guest made their way to the head table and thanked The Duke for the hospitality as they departed for their rooms in the adjacent Hilton. Each was told the same thing, "We will see you soon at the wedding".

Finally, it was dad, the Duke and me. This was not to be a night of rip-roaring drinking, but a night of celebration, when father, future father-in-law and son could bask in each other's acceptance as we had done on the jet back from the Badger game at Penn State.

"Cheers!" The Duke toasted.

"To Amy's good health," dad replied.

"And to grandchildren," The Duke noted as we all downed the last drink, shook hands and headed our way, dad to the hotel and The Duke and I back to the condo.

The walk back to the condo was strangely quiet. I had no idea what one of the most powerful and influential men in Wisconsin, if not America, was thinking. As we rode the elevator up to the eighth floor, The Duke turned and looked at me with tears in his eyes …" Take care of my little girl!"

"I will. I promise I will!"

"I know, son. I know you will."

After a few moments of future mother-in-law, father-in-law conversation, the Williams excused themselves and walked back to the Hilton.

The following morning, Amy was back to being herself and there was joy in the apartment. She told me her parents were coming at 10:00 and the topic was to be one thing … the wedding. I asked if we could simply elope and the Amelia stare was upon me. I knew better than to make that suggestion again.

At precisely 10:00 the bell rang and mom and dad Williams appeared. They indicated everyone had breakfast and checked out of the hotel except Amy's Aunt Julia and Uncle Frank who were going to explore Madison. The question arose regarding when to have the wedding. Fall seemed good to me but the boss (Amy) said it was too soon. Wisconsin winter meant no! Spring would be a fine time and it was decided that a late May wedding would be great. Warm enough, yet cool enough and so it was agreed.

Next came the venue. I had my hopes and yet, it was Amy's wedding. She already knew what I wanted and so she proposed we have a small ceremony in the forest and then have the reception in Milwaukee. This suited me fine. I only had one request … no tuxedos! Amy had one as well … no gifts. We both got our wishes. Mom and dad Williams agreed!

I asked if it would be OK if I called my mom and dad and asked them their opinion. We called, they agreed and the wedding was set for Saturday, May 21st, a week after my birthday with the reception that same afternoon in Milwaukee. I was concerned about the travel and The Duke indicated he would have two helicopters leased so that the trip would take less than thirty minutes. I thought I had better ask dad if it would disturb the cows and he said he thought they would be OK, but they might be lactating whipped cream. Leave it to dad to come up with a corny joke.

We needed to have a weather plan just in case it rained. The Duke offered to have a white tent placed over the springs and portable heaters so we could still have the wedding outside. The man thought of everything!

Amy told me she had one final pre-wedding thing she wanted to do to celebrate closure to her treatments and made an appointment to have her last dot added. She came home with a smirk on her face and I knew something was up, but didn't know what.

"Remember what Great Grandfather said?" Amy asked.

I shook my head as he had said so many things, asking her "about what?"

"What did you give me on the day of my last treatment?"

"A kiss?"

"What did Great Grandfather tell you about relationships?"

A smile came across my face. She was referring to roses, of course.

"Now, I will have one with me at all time to remind me of you."

I hadn't put one and one together and finally realized what she was inferring to. She had added one more permanent memento to our relationship.

I must have looked perplexed and she giggled her wonderful girlie giggle.

"You're just going to have to find it!"

With a seductive look in her eye, she began undressing. First it was her shirt as she turned around to show me the newest dot and shook her head in the negative. "Not there!" she giggled.

Next, it was her bra, as her breasts became exposed to my glances as she whispered, "Not there!"

She was doing a strip tease in front of me in our kitchen. OH MY GOD!

Slowly Amy unhooked her belt and then began the slow, erotic releasing of each brass snap of her button fly jeans until her jeans were loose and she was holding them up while looking deep into my eyes. "Hmmmm! She whispered. I wonder what comes next?" as she began slowly pulling down her jeans until they were around her ankles.

Stepping out of her jeans, she stood in front of me in only her panties. With a gleam in her eye, she turned around to show me her little brown butt. "Not here!" she whispered as she ran her hands over her butt cheeks. "I think, you need to help me find what I'm looking for!" she said, turning around with a wicked smile on her face.

Oh my God! I was getting anxious.

"Come here, I need your help," Amy said beckoning me towards her.

As I approached, she took my hands and placed them on the sides of her panties and stuck her tongue in my right ear and whispered, "I think you need to slowly take my panties off."

Gulp! I began doing what was directed and slid her panties down. As I was pulling them towards the floor, I saw what it was all about. In addition to the dot on her back, Amy had added a small red rose strategically placed low within her bikini area. My mouth was agape! My fiancée had added a rose tattoo in what she called never-never land.

Amy pulled my head up and said, "That's my way of showing you I love you and saying thank you, George Terrill the Fourth, for all you have done for me. It's saved only for you."

I didn't know what to say except "Thank you." Being the conservative farm boy, I had no ink and yet, I understood the *Survivor* mark and the dots and always thought they were cool because of what they represented. I was honored by the rose and what it meant and particularly all the history behind it … roses, after taking the LSAT; roses when she had her last treatment and what Great Grandfather had always said about rose petals. I smiled a shy smile and kissed her and pulled her into me.

"Do you like it?" Amy asked.

"I love it!" I replied, somewhat lying, yet knowing it was meant just for me. With my second glance, I realized that where it was placed meant that, even if we went to St. Martin and Amy wore one of her teeny-weenie bikinis, the rose would never show.

Let's just say, the rest of that day was spent with me closely examining Amy's newest addition, while I was secretly hoping there would be no more.

The Wedding – Phase One:

That fall and winter, things centered around the big day. We needed a pastor and I asked if it was OK if we used ours from Mineral Point. It was agreed. Amy and I wanted to say our own vows and I asked Rodney if it would be OK to use Ho-Chunk vows and he said yes.

At my insistence, a pre-nuptial agreement was put in place that was 212 pages long. In the end, it simply said that all of Amy's assets remained hers and what was mine, which was nothing, remained mine. Should we divorce or separate, there was no liability on the other side. Amy required clauses regarding death that said, should we have children, regardless of how many, they automatically received half of her estate and me the other half. If I died, the deal was the same. It was all mumbo jumbo to me and, quite honestly, I really didn't care.

The wedding day came and the weather was perfect. Whew! Blue skies, a slight breeze and the ground was firm … no Wisconsin mud on anyone's shoes. Dad rolled the edge of the hay field so we could walk from the house and not worry about sinking in. We didn't think it would be too cool to show up on a hay wagon or ATV's. Everyone thought it was odd Jake was at the wedding, but it was at Amy's insistence. He was my little buddy and meant so much to me. With Ho-Chunk permission, we also made a path from the highway to the springs through the woods for the bridal party and had a raised wooden bridge put in place.

As I entered the woods, I looked at the sundial and knew Great Grandfather was with us. I looked at the trees and even they seemed to be smiling. The force within and the spirits above were all filled with joy. Once again, there was peace in my heart, along with joy.

The best way to describe the wedding was written in the Democrat Tribune, the Mineral Point newspaper … "Mr. and Mrs.

George Terrill IV were united in marriage in a quiet ceremony held on land owned by Mr. Terrill and the Ho-Chunk Nation. The best man was Mr. Rodney Whitehorse and Maid of Honor was Mrs. Ann Whitehorse."

We proceeded to the springs and I was taken aback by what had transpired. The Williams hired a botanist who arranged all Wisconsin natural herbs and flowers around the spring and made it look simply incredible. White chairs were placed on low blue platforms so the chair feet wouldn't sink into ground. Everyone was assured that, within two hours of the ceremony, all would be as it had been before. The goal was to take it back to the way it was as if we had never been there. Everyone agreed this was the way it was meant to be. As the wedding party stood, we could hear the redwing black birds calling and we felt the early summer breeze caress the trees in their splendor.

The attendees included the immediate family of the bride and groom and the small bridal party. Amy had Ann and Sandy who actually wore a dress. I had my brother Tommie and Rodney, of course.

We said our vows where each of us promised to keep them secret until they came from our hearts.

Amy spoke first and quoted from the book of Ruth ..."*Do not press me to leave you or to turn back from following you! Where you go, I will go; where you lodge I will lodge; your people shall be my people, and your God my God. Where you die, I will die — there will I be buried. May the Lord do thus, and so to me, and more as well, if even death parts me from you! This is my life-long vow to you Mr. George Terrill.*"

I looked deeply into her eyes and quoted a personalized version of the First Letter of St. Paul to Corinthians. "*If I speak in human and angelic tongues, but do not have love, I am nothing but a resounding gong or clashed symbol. If I have the gift of prophecy and comprehend all mysteries and knowledge and have the faith required to move mountains, but do not have love, I would be nothing. If I give away everything I own and hand my body over so that I may boast, but do not have love, I gain nothing."*

"Amelia Marie Terrill, love is patient and love is kind and I pledge these to you. My dear, love is not jealous, nor pompous! It is not inflated, nor rude or does it seek its own interests! Love is not quick-tempered, nor brood over injury or rejoice over wrongdoing. Love rejoices with the truth bearing all things, believing all things, hoping all things, enduring all things and so shall I."

I looked down and then into Amy's eyes and continued. *"When I was a child, I would talk as a child, think as a child, reason as a child. When I became a man, I put aside these childish things but still am not whole. Until I met you Amelia Marie Terrill, I only partially knew life and what it meant to live. Now that we are together, I am complete because I know and accept that while our marriage will rely on faith, hope and love, the one that will always carry us on forever and is the greatest of all is love!"*

I reached up and wiped the tears from Amy's eyes as she did mine. These were not tears-of-sorrow, nor remorse, but tears of joy! We were but one! Amy and I turned and faced the small group and smiled, knowing, accepting, reveling in the reality our lives together were now and forever.

Phase Two:

After photographs and such, we all went to the edge of the field and climbed aboard two helicopters and headed for Milwaukee. Drivers had been hired to bring the vehicles and a neighbor friend took Jake home. I think it was the first time in his life Jake had ever been on a leash and he certainly did not like it.

As we were about to land at Mitchell Field, I looked down and there were six white limousines waiting for us. The Duke thought of everything, including hiring a full-time wedding planner who spent six months making certain everything, and I mean everything, was right.

With money comes power. With power comes the right to expect things. When it came to our wedding, The Duke was calling in all the chips in business and politics. It was known he personally asked for little, but when he did, he expected you to oblige. This meant the cream of the crop in local, state and national politics. In addition, there were businessmen including senior executives from all automobile companies Wilco purchased vehicles from, plus lawyers and judges, including two State Supreme Court justices.

The Duke chartered a Boeing 737 for family and friends from St. Martin who flew up that morning and would return after the reception. From my side, The Duke leased two luxury buses and had everyone meet at Jerusalem Park in Mineral Point from where they were driven to the reception. On each bus, were two attendants to make sure everyone had enough food and drink from the bar set up in the back for their enjoyment along the way.

All three of my roommates from college were there and it was fun seeing their shocked expressions when "The Wild Man" as they called me, walked into the room. The Pointer boys, who had come on the bus, were shocked as well as was the staff from Meriter who had taken care of me after the car accident. This was to be a celebration of our lives together and we wanted everyone who had ever made a difference present and they were all there.

The Duke rented the three horticultural domes at Mitchell Park Conservatory and filled them with lush floral elements with backdrops of striking landscapes and winding paths that were all enclosed by the soaring glass terrarium ceilings. The domes were designed by R. Buckmaster Fuller and are the largest geodesic domes in the world. The translucent triangles allow natural sunlight in while keeping the extremes of Wisconsin weather out, making for the perfect venue for our reception. To tie everything together, there were white roses in red vases and red roses in white vases all along the paths in each of the three domes. The wedding planner also set up a bar and hors devours in each dome before the ceremony began.

We wanted to send a message of acceptance to all those who had joined with us. To honor the diversity of our guests, we did so by reflecting the diversity of plants, landscaping and horticultural architecture that were on display not only in the domes but those invited. All aspects brought the same intrigue and beauty while offering their own unique personality where the common bond was one of acceptance ... rich and poor, black and white, young and old, mingling, smiling, laughing and enjoying each other's company.

All-in-all, there were over 500 people at the reception. The Duke hired the Milwaukee Symphony Orchestra for music before and during dinner and for formal dances right afterward. Amy danced with her dad and they did an incredible formal waltz. I danced with my mom and nearly ripped her dress stepping on its edges. Soon, everyone was dancing to the orchestra and having a "nice" time. At first, I thought the young crowd would be bored, but they seemed to actually enjoy it.

After the formal dancing, The Duke got everyone's attention and said he had a surprise and what a surprise it was! The Duke hired

Lady GaGa, who came on stage and sang and played the piano just for us. My God! Lady GaGa for our wedding reception! I looked at Amy and she just giggled her girlie giggle. She had known. I was incredulous and the family and friends were simply shocked as Lady GaGa played for about an hour. To say it was fantastic isn't good enough. It was simply INCREDIBLE! After the wedding, each guest was given a hand-signed copy of her rehearsal CD as an attendance gift.

As she was finishing her last song, Amy took me by the hand. "Come on, I want you to meet her." Here we were, the bride and groom, having our pictures taken with Lady GaGa at OUR wedding reception. I was speechless! Her entire entourage were all such nice people. I was shocked by how generous they were with their time.

"Remember your birthday cake, the first time you were at the condo and we talked about favorite groups?" Amy inquired.

I just shook my head in the affirmative.

"Daddy called some people and made arrangements. She has to leave, but I hope you enjoyed the music!"

"Oh my God! What an incredible surprise!" I could only imagine what it cost.

"Remember how we talked about social involvement and doing what was right?" Amy asked.

Again, I shook my head in the affirmative.

"That's why she came. Daddy pledged money and support to her causes and what she believes in. She is really a good person who is trying to make a difference."

With that, Amy gave me a big kiss and said, "I love you".

With Lady GaGa gone, a DJ set up and the rest of the night was established for dancing. The Duke arranged for a private room adjacent to the reception center where we could meet all the powers-to-be who attended, the governor, both US Senators, two House Representatives, the two state Supreme Court Judges,

Senior Vice Presidents of three automobile manufacturers, bankers and so on. They all laid it on thick and, at first, it was fun listening to the bullshit and then it got a bit boring.

Amy was profoundly aware we needed to meet everyone and so she had the ushers mix in the "common folk" so that they got to say they met so-and-so and we got a respite from the power. Dad Williams did a switcheroo on everyone. While the big wigs were accustomed to having their photos taken for someone to ooh and ah about, The Duke arranged so that photos of them with us were sent to the big wigs. The Duke wanted everyone in attendance to realize and accept the power base at Wilco was shifting from he and Dr. Williams to Amelia and me.

I think my dad got the biggest kick out of meeting all the important people. He told me later that the next afternoon when he went out to milk, he thought of telling the cows the hand that squeezed their teats shook hands with all these hoity toities the night before. Then he chuckled that he should have told all the big wigs that the hand they were shaking was squeezing teats that morning. Either way he got a laugh.

My biggest thrill was having all our friends there who truly were enjoying themselves, along with those who had supported us in our fight over the forest. We had representatives of every major Indian nation in Wisconsin in attendance who had been requested to wear their traditional garb, which they did. Another thrill was having the old couple who Amy and I had met at Rodney and Ann's wedding in attendance. They were there because we wanted them there ... a friend of a friend is always a friend. There wasn't any hotel mini-bar for them to clean out, but they still had fun.

For desert, we had both chocolate and white cake which was served with Chocolate Shoppe ice cream from Madison. There was chocolate and vanilla and our favorite concoction, turtle. Amy, of course, had to smoosh the cake into my face! When we were dancing, I got her back, I pinched her butt. Amy looked at me and said, "I think the rose needs a little watering," and did one of her girlie giggles. By 11:00 o'clock, the party was winding down. The buses needed to be loaded for Mineral Point, the jet needed to depart for St. Martin and those who were staying overnight were given keys to rooms at the Pfister Hotel, where The Duke had rented the entire place, adding extra rooms in case any of the locals had consumed too much Wisconsin brandy or beer and couldn't safely go home.

Amy and I said our goodnight's and snuck up the service elevator to the Presidential Suite where we both collapsed in exhaustion, promising to consummate our wedding when we weren't so tired. The next morning was intentionally set with late plans. We made love ... slow tantalizing love, enveloped in each other physically, emotionally, erotically. Intertwined as two beings morphed into one. The culmination was not the release of pent-up energy, but the profound realization that all that was, all that is and all that would be, was consummated not for an instant, nor a heartbeat, but forever. We lay there, resplendent in each other's euphoric expression knowing we were one, together bonded by love... welded as partners... identical, reciprocal, enmeshed in thought, reason and purpose.

While there was climax, it was not only physical but metaphysical, transcending here and now, forever together, bonded, welded, interlinked in a unity few could comprehend or ever be allowed the euphoric pleasure of experience. I looked at my new wife and shared what I had written only for her. It was my personal vow to her.

My Dearest Amelia:

"What is liquid shall become solid or simply pass away. Whether love or child, what is cannot be without each other. What will be cannot be unless we create what happens to be. Whether passion or oppression, love or hate, these are mutual forces that will not happen, will not mend, bend, or articulate what is until it becomes what it will be. Unlike what was or could have been, ebbing and flowing, restricting or growing, passion is what it is and now that we are one, just one, we will never be altered. With all my love"

My new wife had tears in her eyes. She knew my thoughts came from the heart. She knew all her dreams and wishes would come true. My challenge was now to deliver on what I vowed.

The Sunday version of the Milwaukee Journal reported." The Williams-Terrill wedding reception at the Mitchell Park Domes, included all major political dignitaries in the State of Wisconsin, along with members from all the primary indigenous nations of the State and friends and relatives from St. Martin. Any and all wedding gifts were donated to the American Cancer society for the study of childhood leukemia."

The Honeymoon:

It was time for our honeymoon and we elected to go to Africa on a photo safari. The Duke had the Wilco travel center make the arrangements and we were assigned four travel assistants to go with us. Most people would call them bodyguards, but Wilco called them travel assistants. There were two men and two women, all trained in hand-to-hand combat and all dedicated to one thing, making certain Amy and I were safe at all times. I think they carried weapons, but we never saw them. All I knew was we could call at any time and they would be with us in less than a minute.

Traveling as three couples, no one ever knew who or what they were except Amy and me. We took Amelia II to Atlanta and boarded a non-stop flight for Johannesburg. The Duke reserved the entire first-class section of the plane for the six of us and the flight attendants were told "no visitors". We went through South African VIP customs, took time to call home and went on to Botswana and Tanzania. The scenery and wildlife were incredible, and the few stares seeing a white boy with a mixed-race woman were ignored. My God, will the world ever grow up? The two weeks flew by and it was one of the most incredible vacations we ever took. With 96 elephants slaughtered everyday simply for their tusks and 50% of all living species dying, my hope was that, should we have children, they would be allowed to see the majesty of nature before it was gone.

We returned to Madison where I noticed the condo seemed different. I asked Amy about it and she said The Duke had security scan the place and install a new type of system. Things had been happening, that she didn't want to bother me with and all the notoriety of the wedding was placing additional concern by the security staff regarding our wellbeing. Now I was getting worried.

The wedding and time away made a huge difference and it was time to get back to reality. I called Rodney and he sounded different … more distant … more reserved … more formal than ever before. I thought it was strange and was going to ask, but thought better of it.

The next day, I called Black River Falls and wanted to check in on what had transpired in my absence. I was told Rodney wanted to meet with me. I guess I knew what was coming. They couldn't have the son-in-law of the richest man in Wisconsin on their payroll as it would be too much of a distraction. We met for lunch and sat in the Capitol Park across from Teddywedgers and ate our pasties. Rodney was as nervous as a whore in church.

I asked him, "Do you want me to resign?"

He nodded in the affirmative.

"I understand," I replied, not really knowing why.

"The board voted and they think it's best," he said, looking straight down State Street and not in my eyes.

My realm had changed, as had my world and what once was, would never be again. My only hope was my efforts had made a difference and helped the Ho-Chunk Nation become better, stronger and more capable of walking that fine line between financial security and social identity. Theirs was a difficult challenge … wipe out the abject poverty, make every child aware of the threats of alcoholism and drug abuse, yet retain the integrity of their cultural beliefs.

We stood and I gave him a big hug, "Business is business and friendship is friendship. Because you are my friend does not mean we need to do business together and because we do business together, does not make you my friend. You, Rodney, will always be my best friend, my Big Brother and I understand. It's time for us to move closer to Milwaukee, anyway. We both knew the time would come to end the business part, but let's never, ever end our friendship."

Rodney smiled, it was a sad smile just the same. "Ann and I are moving back to Black River Falls. Dad is retiring and I've been named CEO."

Now it was my turn to smile a sad smile. "You will always be my big brother. You will always be my best friend! You will always be a man who I have come to honor and respect and truly love. There are no hard feelings as I knew this day would come and, yet, I have always regretted its coming. You and Ann will ALWAYS be a part of me. Without you, I would never have become a man. Without Ann, I would have never met Amy! Without the two of you teaching me the meaning of dignity, I could never reach for the goals I now set for myself. You taught me so much about life and about what could be mine. While we will be apart, I give you my word you will always be in my dreams, in my heart and in my spirit. All I ask in return is I remain in yours, Big Brother, and that we share our lives whenever we can."

There were tears streaming down both of our cheeks as the big guy and me, the little guy, hugged each other and walked away, he to the north and me to the south, knowing, hoping, praying we would always be brothers. God, it seemed so strange to think he wasn't going to be just a boat ride away! I went back to the quiet condo and sat in solitary confinement, smothered in sadness. My friend, my only dear friend, was moving away… and life goes on… and life goes on.

A few days later it was announced that Rodney's dad, Mr. David Whitehorse (The Chief) was retiring as President and CEO of the Ho-Chunk nation. The Chief and his wife Rose, announced they wanted to travel extensively in their new Winnebago motor home visiting Native American nations. Mr. Whitehorse hoped to do motivational speaking to children and young Native American adults about opportunity, ability, desire and dedication and the strength and courage it takes to simply say "no" to drugs and alcohol.

Rodney and Ann sold the cottage, kept the boat and moved to Black River Falls, where Rodney began functioning as CEO of the Ho-Chunk Nation. They have three children. One is named George and goes by the nickname "Q". Ann heads up the health program for the Ho-Chunk in terms of medical assistance and drug intervention. Included in the Ho-Chunk social outreach program is a non-denominational and non-ethnic scholarship program for those students interested in careers in Nursing. The book Hocak written by Mr. George Terrill IV, was published and offered for sale at all of the Ho-Chunk Casinos. All proceeds were used to assist Native American children acquire computers for use at home.

I was at a loss regarding what to do with my time. In two weeks, I had already cleaned out the condo "office" and gone back to the farm twice, which made Jake happy, but made my brother's wife, Heather, a bit irritated that I would "just show up".

One morning Amy informed me we needed to go to Milwaukee for the annual Williams family meeting that Saturday. At the meeting, the accountants, lawyers and all kinds of other people would make presentations concerning revenue streams, investment risks-and-returns and net worth. I asked her if I should be there and she looked at me as if I was crazy. "Of course, you're my husband and part of the family".

The day came and we met in the Wilco executive conference room. It was scanned for recording devices, as this was a private meeting. Now I knew The Duke had money, I just had no idea how much. Oh my God! First came reports on the different business segments… legal, automobile, property and property management, the investment company and brokerage firm amongst others. Next came reports on personal investments consisting of stocks, bonds, municipal securities and liquid assets. Next reports on general assets and liabilities such as the boats, planes and several residences.

The Duke had tactfully removed the cost of our wedding and put it into miscellaneous expenses, which totaled nearly ten million dollars. The final report was on net worth. When you added it all up, the Williams family net worth exceeded eight billion … that's with a "b" dollars! Mom and Dad Williams had 50% interest or four billion, Amy had 25% interest or over two billion dollars and there was still the fund for Amy's deceased brother Derrick, also worth in excess of two billion dollars to be designated to charity. Like all Wilco meetings, there was a time limit. In two hours, I realized that I was married to a multi-billionaire. My God!

The New Job:

I was now 29 years old and like it or not, it was time to move on. Amelia's parents asked us to move "home" and help run Wilco. I, at first, refused. I wanted to be my own man and didn't want anyone to think I married Amelia because of her family's money. After much trepidation, I acquiesced, but under the condition I evolve into my own manager at my own pace and only when everyone, including me, thought I was ready for the responsibilities that lie ahead.

The Duke agreed with my terms and conditions with one caveat. He felt I needed an administrative assistant. Rookie-me had no idea what to look for and went through about a dozen young, impressionable, inexperienced candidates. I was about to give up when in walks a forty-something, somewhat rotund, African American woman named Cecelia. If her smile wouldn't have won me over, her intellect, sense of decency and incredible organization would have. Within ten minutes I had a new, platonic, love of my life. Like the Duke, I found the right person to help me through the trials and tribulations of corporate life.

Cecelia started and, as time went on, I turned to her more and more and more for guidance and support, allowing her to make decisions and make certain my work life was completely organized.

The security issue was becoming more prevalent. Times were changing and people were desperate. We were personally at risk. It was agreed we needed "travel assistants". While the Duke had Dennis, who I finally realized was his bodyguard, among other things, Amelia and I realized we were alone, exposed and subject to anyone who thought our incarceration could result in their benefit. Add in the thought of kids and I finally came to realize we were captives of our own achievement, or at least The Duke's.

Amy and I went house hunting and found one on Pine Lake, west of Milwaukee. The rustic house was gorgeous with huge windows and a three-story fieldstone fireplace. I fell in love with it and the fact that the lake, while "public," was rarely used by those other than residents, made it seem perfect. The price was agreed to and a check written. There would be no mortgage as the house was put in the names of George and Amelia Terrill, even though I had done nothing, given nothing, provided nothing towards its purchase.

Regarding security, at first, I thought we should just hire someone like Dennis. I concluded we could start our own security company, bigger, better and more sophisticated than a few random employees encompassing all security aspects of what was needed. I met with The Duke one-on-one and explained there was a lot more profit margin in services than in hard goods, if it was done right. He listened and thought it over, asking me how much seed money I thought I would need. I told him two million dollars. He wrote a check for three. He wanted it to be a free-standing company owned by Amy and me. I refused! And so, it was done! Another segment of Wilco was born! Another spoke in the wheel of fortune ... a company whose function was to provide never-ending protection against the masses, the hordes, from whence I came. For a farm boy, who wanted to be a writer, I was given the task of the start-up. I think I caught on relatively fast and we began structuring all types of security including electronic, surveillance, personal protection and counter-intelligence.

My Minnie Point badass mentality came to the surface one night when three clowns were found trying to sneak onto our property. I agreed to 24-hour security around the house and a "driver". So much for Amy wanting to run around nearly naked! That would have to be reserved for The House-On-The-Hill in St. Martin. Wilco Security was my first leadership role and I knew what I wanted personally ... a second Dennis, who could fly planes, drive cars and kick the shit out of anybody who got in the way. In other words, someone who could develop a team to protect and defend. I guess my imagination got away from me as I dreamed of a super hero with machine guns blazing and all the stuff the movies have in them.

I didn't want just anyone, and I set my standards high. We went through all the applicant profiles. My dream was a Navy Seal and we unsuccessfully interviewed several until Andrew walked in. Quiet, impeccably dressed and very professional in his manners, I let the HR team do all the preliminary discussions and create a psychological profile. The man had to be trusted implicitly.

Andrew's pedigree was simply outstanding. He was a college graduate from Purdue University with majors in mechanical engineering and aeronautics, who joined the marines and, while completing basic training, was chosen as an Honor Guard at the Tomb of the Unknown Soldier. Being 6'4" with a crew cut and incredibly physically fit, he certainly looked the part. I was tempted to tease him about the Purdue name as Amy and I had always called it the *Unidue of Purversity*, but this guy was just too serious for that.

I wanted to start the conversation out casually and let him get comfortable and so we talked about the requirements needed to be an Honor Guard. Andrew outlined the honor guard for the fallen is a very old tradition found in many cultures whose purpose is to show that the living do remember those who have died and respect them for the dedication.

" I am honored to be in your presence," I said.

"I am honored to have served my country, Sir," Andrew responded.

Amy, the kids and I had visited the Tomb of the Unknown Soldier where Andrew had served our country and I remembered the guard walking twenty-one steps, turning and clicking his or her heels and then pausing for 21 seconds, then starting the process all over again in honor of the twenty-one-gun salute.

HR's notes indicated that, upon completing his tour as an Honor Guard, Andrew was accepted into the Marine Corp Special Forces. It was noted that the United States Marine Corps Forces Special Operations Command (MARSOC) is a component command of the United States Special Operations Command or SOCOM that comprises the Marine Corps' contribution to the special forces. The report summarized the Marine Corps Special Forces core capabilities are direct action, special reconnaissance and foreign internal defense.

In bold red letters, the report indicated. "Andrew had been directed to conduct counter-terrorism and information operations **DO NOT** ask any questions about his tour, as he was sworn to secrecy and abides by their directive." Instead, I asked about his training and he shared that he was trained in weaponry and hand-to-hand combat and had a black belt in Brazilian jujitsu.

I asked about Brazilian jujitsu and Andrew said. "Brazilian jujitsu promotes the concept where a smaller, weaker person can successfully defend against a bigger, stronger, heavier assailant by using proper technique, leverage, and most notably, taking the fight to the ground, and then applying joint-locks and chokeholds to defeat the opponent." Andrew indicated he had finished his last tour of duty as an instructor. Heh, maybe he could teach this little shit a thing or two!

The HR summary indicated Andrew was currently a pilot for a regional airline, who was slowly making his way up the ladder, with hopes of working for a major airline. I asked why he left the Corps and his was response was, "Once a Marine, always a Marine," and added that, after eight years he had to choose between a career in the military or a happy marriage and he chose marriage, where Susan, his wife, ran a martial arts facility.

Unbeknownst to Andrew, the conference room was under video surveillance and about forty-minutes into the interview, Cecelia came in and informed me I had an important phone call I needed to take. I excused myself, apologized and went to the viewing room where I watched Andrew patiently sit on the edge of his chair with his back erect for twenty minutes without flinching.

The dude didn't move, which is what I wanted to see. I needed loyalty and the ability not to flinch under adverse conditions. I returned and told him his role was to be my protector, confidant and hopefully, someday my friend. Most important, I needed to make certain what happened was between the two of us, not his wife, mine, nor anyone else, without my approval. If Andrew could handle that, he would live comfortably. If he couldn't, I needed to know. He gave me his word. On a handshake, Andrew became my driver, defender and confidant who, as time went by, also a friend.

The routine was simple, Andrew would pick me up in the morning and take me to the office. He was given my schedule and instructed to identify two others who could take his place with equal efficiency so that he worked normal hours. He had two associates who were also regional airline pilots just out of the military. They were hired and reported to him, but Andrew reported to Dennis when it came to the jets, which was done out of respect for both Dennis and The Duke.

I asked him if he and the other pilots would like to get certified piloting helicopters as well as fixed wing planes and a great big smile came across his face. There would be a lot of downtime while he was waiting for me which he could put to use, expanding his skill set.

Amelia X:

My goal was to grow the total business in any viable manner. While security was one thing, jets sitting quietly at Mitchell Field was quite another. To this end, we reviewed operational hours on Amelia I and Amelia II and realized 95% of the time, the planes sat on the ground. I also knew that, with a little planning, we could turn the planes into a revenue stream which would recoup their costs. We had five pilots on staff and two planes. The family met and the vote was to keep the two fixed wing planes and purchase a helicopter like the ones used for our wedding, which would allow us greater short-run mobility in a niche hardly touched by other flight services.

At first, The Duke was reluctant, until we showed him the use pattern on the planes. He finally agreed, but asked us to add another jet reserved for him. It was agreed and a Citation X+ was added to the fleet which was commissioned Amelia X. The Duke chose the plane because it had a cruising speed of 711 miles per hour or, at the time of purchase, was the fastest private airplane in the world. It also had a flight range of 3380 nautical miles which meant non-stop to St. Martin at an altitude of 51,000 feet, making it impervious to all but the worst of storms.

The Duke was a little disappointed because Amelia X incorporated Rolls Royce AE3007C2 turbofan engines instead of the usual GE. He always wanted to buy American whenever and wherever he could. However, he did like the fact that Amelia X included the high-tech autopilot and fully integrated avionics developed by Honeywell Primus, which meant the plane could literally take-off, fly and land itself if need be.

Even though the twenty-five-foot-long plane would normally hold twelve passengers, Dr. Williams and The Duke spent three months with the interior designers making certain it met their personal requirements concerning color, comfort and convenience as the designers called it. In the end, Amelia X was a spectacular six-passenger plane in every possible way, including the same built-in bed option we used on Amelia II where, at The Duke's and Dr. Williams age, probably meant they could sleep if they wanted to.

I almost choked when I learned it cost $3400 per hour to operate Amelia X. However, when your net worth exceeds eight billion dollars and it's "my baby" as The Duke called her, who could argue with him?

Some people would call it brilliance, others blind luck. I'll go with the second one when it comes to our airplanes. First, we had the expertise of the car business to help us with financing, leasing and all the money parts. Second, we had our own experience regarding why we took Amelia I and Amelia II whenever we could. We quickly realized private flight was based on two criteria ... convenience and ego. While anyone could get you from point "A" to point "B", what really made the difference was how you got the customer there and the entire experience.

Because of the car business and understanding the real money was is in maintenance and service, we began offering maintenance programs to other corporate jets and this led to working on airplanes for regional airlines as well. The realization that only 30% of the total cost of an airplane is the plane itself and 70% came from services and maintenance, provided us with an incredible opportunity. We hired our own maintenance teams who were strategically positioned throughout the Midwest.

When the regional planes landed for the evening, our crews went to work doing anything and everything from routine maintenance, to cleaning the carpets and did so during downtime. This meant the regional planes could be maintained without losing precious air time while those doing the work were our employees and not the airlines, resulting in no additional employment costs such as benefits, taxes and insurance for the airlines, as we covered them all.

Because we weren't tied to any specific airline, we had economies of scale they didn't have. Every morning, the airline's planes were not only maintained mechanically but cleaned, prepped and ready to go.

In terms of our own little airline, we looked at all aspects from pre-boarding to the actual flights and developed a plan. We needed to understand why our competition was so successful and what we needed to do to differentiate ourselves from them. To this end, we zeroed in on repeat customers and this meant learning everything we could about the guests as we called them. We developed detailed user profiles regarding estimated height, weight and whether they preferred sitting up front or in back, at the window, etc. Then we drilled down to what they liked for snacks and drinks including everything from alcohol to even the type of water, newspapers and onboard entertainment they preferred. After two or three flights, their favorite snacks and drinks would be at their seat when they boarded the plane.

As the airline grew, I realized we needed to up the ante and purchased land at Milwaukee's Mitchell Field where we could build our own terminal. We had designers come in and develop a waiting area that was as upscale as any law office in Milwaukee, with deep pile carpeting, leather chairs, a complete bar stocked with the customers' favorite drinks and all types of snacks, even though, most of our guests would want to get going right away. There were huge windows onto the airport tarmac that brought the entire air travel luxury theme home.

If there were children, they would be given entertainment devices that were themed to their age including iPads, coloring books, with a video of the plane they were going on. Everything we could think of to keep them involved.

While other companies made their customers walk out onto the tarmac, our facility was built so that the customers who weren't picked up by our courtesy limo, but drove into our facility, were met by a doorman, who escorted them to the lounge. For those who drove, their cars were washed and stored. If they wanted, we would also take them to one of our dealerships and have any repairs or maintenance done, as well.

When it was time for our guests to depart, the waiting area door opened and the plane was sitting inside a heated hangar with a red-carpet runner with our logo on it, in a building that had the hangar floor polished and photos of all our planes on the walls. As guests, they were met by the pilots who introduced themselves. As the pre-check had already been completed, each guest was given a bound travel manifest concerning the duration of the flight, the weather on the other end, a short biography of the pilots and the history of the plane they were on.

In the back of each seat was a forty-inch monitor that allowed each guest to select what they preferred watching, while in the seat pocket were current local newspapers along with the favorite beverages gleaned from previous flights and the ability to charge any devices and even communicate with the ground.

With our system, the guest was never outdoors regardless of the weather, the guests knew exactly who was flying the plane and the flight plan and had all their favorites at their disposal. We also installed monitors and video cameras that allowed the guest to see the flight and determine our current location. If we were running late, they were offered the opportunity to have us call or text whomever it was that would be waiting for them. If need be, we would even arrange for a limousine at their destination.

With 25 planes in the fleet, we were busy. While Amelia II would always be my favorite. I loved the Badger buses as I called them. These were two Boeing 737's that were painted Wilco red, which happened to be the same Pantone number as the University of

Wisconsin. When we took the Wisconsin teams, we added all sorts of interior Badger details to make certain that everyone on the plane realized we were backing them 100%. In the back of each seat was a video monitor that could be programmed to I-pads that allowed coaches to provide information to their respective players. This made the flight not only go faster but more productive.

We wanted to address the medium charter business for sports teams. While the Boeing 737's were great for larger loads, we also added two Embraer 190 E-Jets to the "air force" as the pilots began calling our flying family. The 190's were narrow-body short-to-medium-range twin-engine jet airliners, that would normally carry up to 124 passengers commercially. We customized both to only handle 80 passengers, so that every seat was first class. Everybody loved them, especially with our premium interior consisting of cream-colored seats highlighted with mahogany trim. As we branched out into plane leasing, we would work with the clients to make certain that every detail in terms of color scheme and facilities fit their specific needs.

I guess assembling my Lockheed plane that sits on Amy's desk sort of put the bug in me. Push-came-to-shove and we stretched our financial neck and ordered two of the Aerion AS2 supersonic business jets. The planes were made almost entirely of carbon fiber composites, just like the Boeing 787 and sculpted to reach a speed of Mach 1.2 or 900 miles per hour without creating a sonic boom. However, when over the ocean, the engines kicked in and the speed would increase to Mach 1.6 or 1200 miles per hour. At first, the government was skeptical of Mach 1.2 over land, but when you have people with deep pockets, they seem to have ways of getting what they want and one of those things is something other people don't have.

At a cool $100 million dollars each, The Duke thought we were crazy until we outlined how we had 80% split-leased them for ten years to a group of clients. The arrangement allowed us to keep

20% of the airtime for individual clients at no cost to the company, who then got the cheap thrill of flying at a little over 1200 miles per hour. This meant that we could make it from Milwaukee to Honolulu in a little over four hours and with a passenger load of twelve people, the additional costs seemed justified to those in a hurry.

The Duke remained reluctant until we took one of the AS2's to St. Martin and made it in a little over three hours. The smile on his face said it all, especially with all the ooohs and aahs at the Princess Juliana airport as we taxied up to the gate. Even so, The Duke and Dr. Williams loved Amelia X as their personal plane. I think it was because Dr. Williams spent so much time designing the interior and making it more like home than an airplane.

One day, we were asked about renting our boats in St. Martin and then another request concerning the yacht on Lake Michigan. We looked into it and expanded into the boat charter and leasing business with the same concept ... high-end service, that pampered the guest and matched their needs. Next, we were asked about renting our condos in Colorado and Michigan and got into the resort rental business as well, while keeping our personal residences there as well. At no time, did the topic of renting House-On-The-Hill ever come up. That was saved for just the family.

We were always professional and completely discrete and as our reputation grew, so did our client list of people who expected to be pampered. These were business executives, politicians and celebrities who realized that owning a boat, yacht, plane or vacation villa cost a lot of money for only a little time used.

The final piece of the puzzle happened by accident when I learned that each Wilco division had its own purchasing budget for supplies, materials and equipment. What this meant was that all of the car dealerships, the law firm, finance organization, security, franchising and property management was on their own when it came to what they needed. While buying multi-million-dollar airplanes was one thing, paperclips was something totally different.

Add in all the other things we needed such as insurance, uniforms, supplies and services and I quickly saw that a lot of money was being wasted that could be saved if we had centralized purchasing.

Amy and I were out to dinner with The Duke and Dr. Williams and I broached the subject. The Duke smiled and said "go for it". I developed a plan that allowed each division to "purchase" from central purchasing, if the cost was equal to or less than what they could get the same product or benefit for on their own. I felt we could fund the entire division on just the savings.

Little did I realize how wrong I was. The savings were incredible! We began negotiating core items such as janitorial supplies and had discounts of twenty to twenty-five percent. Next, we focused on office supplies and the discounts started coming in when everything was put out on bid and finally we added hotels and rental cars used by all employees either on business or vacation.

Soon, we couldn't handle the amount of time needed for the tasks involved and set up a complete division to do nothing but purchase everything from jet fuel to car parts and even oil for the car dealerships. As we grew, we hired professional buyers who had worked in retail stores and knew how to play the game. After we completed the entire consumable aspect, we focused on the benefits programs and standardized all of our insurances, 401K's and retirement plans. Instead of six different programs, everyone was enrolled in one common program with lower employee premiums and better benefits. My goal was to emulate the health insurance I had at Ho-Chunk, but it was really expensive.

By the end of the second year, we were saving over a million dollars a month from what the previous expenditures had been and began offering our services to other companies. We accomplished this while offering better quality products, better benefits and faster service, all of which made the different divisions even that much more competitive in their respective marketplaces and customers more loyal to Wilco. The purchasing division was great, except it was taking up even more of my time.

CES:

The Duke and I got along great and it wasn't long until the real man came out from behind the armor. One of his real passions was anything electronic. In addition, he loved it when no one knew who he was. He could be Doug Williams and that suited him just fine.

The Duke and Doctor Williams had an incredible home theater and The Duke was always buying the newest gadget. One of his favorite junctures was visiting the Consumer Electronics Show in Las Vegas every January. The Duke did not gamble, nor mess around, or at least I didn't think he did. However, he sure liked having fun! One Christmas, he asked me if I wanted to go to see all the new stuff at the show. It would be a short trip and The Duke asked if my dad would like to go too. I thought it would be cool and dad got someone to help Tommie with the cows.

Dad wanted to drive to Madison, but I sent one of our helicopters to pick him up, which was a real treat for an old farm boy. He flew to Milwaukee, got on Amelia X and the three of us hit Vegas. Everything was arranged.

The Duke was a duffer when it came to golf and yet he belonged to the finest golf clubs in America, including Augusta National, Torrey Pines and LaCosta in California along with the Lake Geneva Country Club and Whistling Straits in Wisconsin. His favorite though was Shadow Creek, about fifteen miles north of the strip in Las Vegas. The Duke explained that the course was simply dug out of 350 acres of desert and about three million cubic yards of dirt was moved.

Because we arrived early, The Duke wanted to show us the golf course. I'm certain dad would be figuring out how many cows could be fed off the grass that was planted. We arranged for a private limo for our entire stay and he told the driver to take us to Shadow

Creek. I saw the driver's eyebrows arch when he heard the name as he knew he had either money or a celebrity riding in the back.

When we arrived, The Duke was like a little kid, as he added, "They planted 20,000 trees and there are 200 different varieties that create a lush forest. They put in waterfalls, creeks and ponds, along with a brook, some lagoons and even lakes filled with fish. I come more to marvel at what can be done when you put your mind to it than play golf, but I have met some really nice and very important people here."

As we drove out to Shadow Creek, dad had a worried look on his face. Like me, he had never golfed in his life. We were relieved when The Duke noted he just wanted to show us the place. As we arrived, the doorman immediately recognized The Duke and the red carpet was rolled out as the manager came to greet us and ask if we were playing. The Duke told him "no" he just wanted to show his favorite course to his son-in-law and a good friend of his. It was nice having The Duke call dad his "good friend".

We went into the locker room and met some really rich and famous people. The Duke had a locker with his name on it. I looked at all the other names and recognized about half of them. I learned not to fawn over the rich and famous. When they are at play, they only want to be out of the spotlight and have some fun.

The manager arranged for a young girl by the name of Sherri to take dad and me on a tour of the course while The Duke met with some of his cronies and talked golf or business or both, I guess. After our tour and learning all the details, we made our way back to the club house. I asked how you became a member and was told that anyone staying at an MGM property could play a round of golf where the greens fees were $500 plus gratuity for the required caddie. I thought dad was going to choke. Sherri added that for another $500 per round, you could add drone coverage that would record all of our shots from the air, which I thought would be pretty funny … into the woods left; into the woods right; into the water;

into the bunker; a six-foot tee-shot culminating in highlights of thrown golf clubs and a temper tantrum.

I said "Wow it would cost me fifty-cents a shot to play a round." Sherri wasn't the brightest bulb in the box and I don't think she understood what I was saying … that I would probably shoot 1000. Golf was not my game. Dad got the joke and had a sly smile on his face.

As for membership, Sherri noted that you need to be invited. I thought The Duke had been invited until I learned that he was a primary investor in the club and a major stockholder in MGM. Duh! Of course! I should have known.

As we were riding out to the hotel, The Duke added, "Son you should take up golf, not for the game, but for the people you meet and the business you can do on a golf course. You've got people with undivided attention you can't get anywhere else and it can be fun."

It had been a long day and The Duke had reserved three suites at the Lake Las Vegas Hilton, which was twenty miles east of the strip. He said he really didn't fit in with the strip crowd and liked the property. The hotel was beautiful and, once again, the red carpet was rolled out which, I concluded was because we had reservations for three suites on the bridge that was the most exclusive part of the hotel.

I wondered why we were staying at the Hilton when it wasn't owned by MGM until The Duke let it slip that he was part owner of the investment company that developed the entire Las Vegas Lakes area where the hotel was located. I should have known!

Everyone was tired and agreed to meet at 6:30 at the lobby bar where we sat and had a few … well more than a few and ate a quiet dinner at one of the tables in the lobby and went to bed at 9:30 tired, full and somewhat drunk, relishing another great day.

For CES, everything was arranged with exhibitor badges that got us in before the crowds. I knew CES would be a real marathon.

Boy was I wrong! It was a triathlon at the very least. CES is all about computers and audio and video equipment and virtually every brand of cars there were. So, in addition to the electronic toys, the three amigos bounced around from booth-to-booth-to-booth looking at electric cars and all kinds of neat stuff. It was cool because no one had a clue who Doug Williams was, even though it was printed on his badge.

We all found the 3D printers neat and, as we made our way to virtually the last wall in the North Hall, we turned the corner and I saw The Duke's eyes light up like a little kid at Christmas. Bell Helicopter had a display of a futuristic design they were introducing called the Air Taxi. Dad, The Duke and I sat and listened to the prepared spiel about how much time the air taxi would save, how quiet they were going to be and how environmentally good they were as well. We noticed people were actually being allowed to take a "ride" in the chassis wearing virtual reality glasses.

Like three kids at Disneyworld, we got in line and waited nearly an hour for our chance to see the future as they called it. The spiel said the strategy was to build an interior cabin space that acclimated the passenger to the unique qualities of vertical flight. Bell called it a "comforting, relaxing space." The lady said that if passengers didn't feel comfortable riding in an electric-powered air taxi, they wouldn't go again. The Duke whispered that he thought it was essentially a cross between a helicopter and a drone. By the expression on our faces, the spiel lady had to realize we thought the ride was cool and the demonstration was neat. When it was over and we had disembarked, The Duke looked at me and nodded.

"How many?" I asked

"Six." Was his response.

The Duke wanted to order six of the helicopters on the spot!

What the Duke wanted, the Duke normally got.

I went to the front counter and asked to speak to someone in charge of sales and said we wanted to order six of the air taxis. The girl thought I was joking.

"I'm very serious," I responded. The girl swallowed hard and brought over Mr. Jacobs, who was one of the chief engineers.

"Sir, Beth said that you are interested in purchasing six of the air taxis?" Mr. Jacobs asked.

"That's right," The Duke replied as he nodded his head in the affirmative.

"Sir, these are prototypes only and probably won't be ready for sale until 2025."

"Understood" The Duke responded.

"They still need testing and certification."

"Understood." The Duke reiterated.

"We don't even have prices established."

"I understand that, but I'm willing to make a down payment of a million dollars each to ensure that I get the first six offered for sale."

Mr. Jacobs didn't really know what to do and balked.

"Tell you what, my business partner here" The Duke said, as he nodded towards dad "has his checkbook with him. How about allowing us to write the deposit today. You give me a receipt and then, when the paperwork is completed, you cash the check?" I thought dad was going to mess in his britches. I don't think he even knew how many digits went into six million.

There was a deep sense of reticence from the engineer.

The Duke was used to getting what he wanted and said, "You know what, it doesn't appear that you think I'm serious. Why don't you wait here while I go over to the Toyota display and get one of the executives to come over and vouch for me."

There was one thing you never wanted to do and that was make The Duke appear inadequate.

"Son, you and your dad stay here. I'll be right back".

With that, the Duke was off to the Toyota display and in less than five minutes there was an entourage of five senior Toyota executives following The Duke back to the Bell booth and now it was eight-against-one.

"Mr. Jacobs, these gentlemen are the senior managers of Toyota Corporation whom I happen to know. I have asked them to vouch for my sincerity when I tell you that I want to place an order for six of your air taxis."

I watched as Mr. Tom Yamamoto nodded in a very serious manner. "Mr. Williams is America's largest Toyota dealer and a personal friend. If you will not accept his check, Toyota Corporation will guarantee the purchase in writing."

I could almost read the Bell Engineer's mind … "Holy shit!"

The Duke made his point. However, this was a marketing event and the engineer didn't know what to do, so the Duke called his office and directed them to get Charles Merriweather, CEO of Textron Corporation on the phone. Within five minutes, The Duke was talking directly with Charles Merriweather and we all got to hear one half of the conversation.

"Yes Charlie, I'm standing in front of your booth at CES and I want to make the commitment for the first six of the air taxis that are offered to the public. I offered to provide a check for a million dollars each as deposit but your engineer didn't think I was legit. I went over to Toyota and brought Tom Yamamoto over to vouch for me and Toyota agreed to guarantee the purchase. Now I know Charlie this is a prototype and this is a trade show, but by God, couldn't you have some salespeople here so that I can buy something? Ok, Understood. Got your personal word that I'm getting the first six? Great! I'll have legal work with your people on drawing up the agreement."

The Duke was about to hang up when Mr. Merriweather must have asked another question to which The Duke responded, "No, Jacobs didn't say anything about a cross between a drone and helicopter? The Bell Nexus? Sure, just a minute!" The Duke said, handing the phone to Mr. Jacobs who had probably never met Mr. Merriweather and certainly wasn't on his Christmas card list. We watched as Mr. Jacobs was slid through the wringer with his head nodding as the once self-confident attitude melted like ice cream on a July day in Vegas.

"Yes sir! Yes sir! Right away sir!" was all Jacobs could say, handing the phone back to The Duke.

"Will do." The Duke said. "Thanks … Yes, Marie and Amelia are both fine!"

The Toyota team realized they were now becoming polite intruders and volunteered to end their part of the meeting. The Duke agreed we would re-visit their booth when we were done with Mr. Jacobs to which, we were invited to the Bell conference area where Jacobs, now even more nervous than a whore in church, outlined the Nexus project that consisted of personal drones that would whisk individuals above traffic from one spot to another. Amazing!

We kept our promise and went back to Toyota and their "now-old-fashioned" cars of the future and met with Mr. Yamamoto's team where, what was going to be a quiet dinner that night turned into just what The Duke didn't want … a full-scale ass-kisser as he called them, by Toyota.

Sorry, when you're as important to a company as Wilco was, Toyota took dad, The Duke and me out for one very and I mean VERY expensive Vegas dinner at Joël Robuchon at the MGM Grand. When you're paying $250 for just a steak and $100 a glass for wine, you quickly realize money can get you almost anything you want. I also learned right then and there … don't ever disappoint The Duke.

When we got home, dad asked what would have happened if they would have agreed to take his personal check with the cows on it. I just laughed and said …" Guess you would have needed to get more cows!"

Moving:

The office for Wilco Security was initially in the Wilco building in Brown Deer, on the north side of Milwaukee. My office was small as all I wanted to do was to blend in. This of course did not happen and peering eyes and whispers quickly led me to realize I was Mr. Amelia Williams and not Mr. George Terrill. Money can do that!

I told The Duke I felt awkward and asked if there was another facility available. He had operations look at some property Wilco owned and found one of our office buildings that had open space in Brookfield, just west of Milwaukee. It was closer to home and we had a floor to ourselves. Wilsecure was born and we created a sales and marketing team to first cover Wisconsin and then Northern Illinois, including Chicago. The Duke was concerned about going into Illinois because of the state's political reputation, but we went anyway.

We quickly grew and the Brookfield facility became too small. After one year, we moved into a larger Wilco building and took over the entire facility allowing for surveillance, personal assistants and the counter-intelligence aspect that allowed people to hire our services to learn about others, like husbands and wives and things like that. Next, we moved into crowd control and began bidding on concerts and sporting events, using college students for staffing. It wasn't long until our full and part-time staff exceeded over 500 employees.

Because we needed staff members trained in all different forms of self-defense, we hired Andrew's wife and established a series of exclusive, closed-door training centers throughout the business area that taught everything from weaponry to martial arts, not only to our employees, but those willing to pay for the services. By our third year, we were billing over $15 million dollars per month and profits were incredible. I had just turned 30.

I thought life at home seemed wonderful. Amy was involved in the legal aspects of the company and worked at the law offices. Her driver's name was Karen and they became great friends. While Amy was at work, we arranged for Karen to go to school to become a paralegal. That way, she would not only offer the protection needed, but begin to assist Amy in all she had to do. The drive from Pine Lake to Milwaukee took almost an hour each way and time was valuable.

Happy Anniversary:

Mrs. Terrill was still adding the annual *Survivor dots* to her shoulder and life was good. As our wedding anniversary was nearing, Amy asked me if we could take a long weekend and go to St. Martin to celebrate. I thought it was a great idea!

The devastation from Hurricane Irma had wiped away many of her fondest memories. Gone, were the restaurants where memories were made of including Le'String, where we met up with Rodney and Ann on their honeymoon. I realized Hurricane Irma blew away an important part of Amy's life and I could see the sadness in her eyes whenever we talked about the devastation. I was proud that, after Irma hit, Wilco stripped the interior from Amelia II and used it to transport donated medical supplies to the island. I was also proud that the Ho-Chunk Nation set up special funding and contributed to the purchase of 500 portable generators for use in schools, hospitals and nursing homes. Good people do good things when others are in need!

After the emergency was over and it was time to restore Amelia II, The Duke suggested that Amy and I consider Amelia II as "our" plane and "redecorate" the interior to our liking. I had no idea what to do and so, Amy hired an interior designer and had the plane re-done with cream colored walls and ceiling, medium brown carpeting and over-sized, cream-colored leather seats all highlighted in mahogany wood trim that had high definition monitors for each passenger. The plane looked totally different than it had before and it truly was "our" plane.

After much discussion, we … make that my wife … included the bed option, but designed it as two facing couches that could be slid together in the back compartment. Finally, we upgraded the avionics to meet revised federal standards to the point that, Amelia II could actually take off and land herself, if need be. I never found out what the redecoration cost was, but rumor was, it was more than three million dollars. Ouch!

Amy and I cleared our schedules so that we could take the refurbished Amelia II to St. Martin. We left early Thursday morning for four days on the beach, arriving at the House-On-The-Hill by early afternoon.

The difference in decorum between liberal, Madison and St. Martin can be quite shocking for the first-time visitor. First and foremost, is the speed of life. Things slow-down from hectic Madison and the concept of time is always left at home, even for us, the harried couple. As had always been the case, there was no schedule, other than waking up and going to bed, when we felt like it.

The second difference was/is obviously, the attire. While Madison is known for its liberal *"free spirit"*, it pales regarding what is not only allowed, but accepted on the island. Perhaps it's the French influence. Perhaps, the fact that the nude beach at Club Orient had been established for so long, people came to expect and accept a much higher degree of clothing permissiveness or, should I say, lack-of-clothing permissiveness, than found elsewhere.

While I'm not a prude and had come to accept the ways of the island, it always took me a little time to adjust to the way life is lived and the realization that many of the elements I once found strange, now seemed so natural, normal and in some ways narcotizing to me.

Mrs. Terrill had learned the secrets of spousal enticement and played the game to perfection. The clothes she brought for our days away included the attire from our infamous Devil's Lake bluff hike when she fell and broke her ankle. Included, were the infamous short shorts, that allowed the bottom of her cute little butt to peek out, to which she was oblivious and I remained, shall we say, curious. It didn't matter if we were at the grocery store or even out for lunch, no one seemed to notice, or if they did, didn't seem to care.

The second aspect were her tops. At home, and particularly at the office, Amy always dressed conservatively and did so with a degree of aplomb that included just the right amount of jewelry to highlight her beautiful almond-color skin. I don't think she even thought about packing a bra for this weekend, as she wasn't going to wear one, while the clothes still stored at the House-On-The-Hill mainly consisted of even shorter shorts, tank tops and the almost-there bathing suits, she preferred.

While we dressed in conservative travel garb for the flight, when we got to the house, Amy went to her dresser and pulled out one of her favorite tops … a boy's white, ribbed, strapped undershirt. We called them *"wife beaters"* at the casino, simply because the men who wore them weren't part of the standard socio-economic group we associated with. I always remembered, with a smile that, when one walked in, security would announce into everyone's headsets *"wife beater on the floor"*, which always got a chuckle.

Amy looked at the white top and smiled. Without reservation, she slipped out of her travel clothes and into what had been her primary mode of attire for the year she stayed on St. Martin to recover. I could tell she finally felt at "home" and this was to be her intended mode of daytime dress for the weekend … tank tops, short-shorts, flip-flops, baseball cap, sunglasses and a broad, infectious smile.

I jokingly told Amy, she was wearing Mineral Point "lunar shorts". She didn't get it! I guess it was an old Pointer synonym for "bootie shorts" and so I explained. "When a little bit of butt is showing, it's a quarter moon; when more is showing, it's a half moon and, if the person takes off their shorts, it's a full moon".

Yup! Amy giggled, turned around and dropped trou, (trousers for those who can't speak Wisconsineze), "you mean like this?" as her fully exposed little butt, wiggled in a welcoming way.

As for the tank tops. Well, that's another story! As we made our way here and there, I would look at her and smirk when her two little protrusions became "pronounced". At that point, with no double entendre intended, I would tease Amy by inquiring whether she was cold or simply excited to be with me, which always resulted in the emanation one of her girlie giggles.

Our daily routine was set in stone … or make that sand. Every morning, at sunrise, we walked end-to-end, up-and-down the beach and renewed our wedding vows, watching those who were walking naked, glance elsewhere so as not to make eye-contact, as we walked by.

Long leisurely lunches, highlighted doing nothing more than people-watching, which took away even more of life's tensions. With each passing hour, I became that much more accustomed to the island ambiance to the point of seriously considering purchasing a vacant hilltop home near Amy's parent's residence. With the money we had accumulated, you would think it would have been an easy decision. We had the house on Pine Lake and a condo in Colorado and access to Amy's parent's places in Lake Geneva, Scottsdale and Kuai. However, always-practical Amy, asked the question "why?" when The Duke and Dr. Williams House-On-The Hill was hardly ever used. Case closed. The missus wins again! Those darn lawyers!

Richard Long:

Saturday night was intended to be "fancy night" where we got dressed up and went for the best meal in Grande Case' and probably on St. Martin. Amy's favorite is/was and will always be L'Auberge Gourmande. Unpretentious, intimate and outstanding are words that simply don't do justice for this small, ten-table restaurant.

You **must** have a reservation, if you want to dine there! There are no ifs, ands or buts! The rich and famous won't get in without calling ahead and even then, they had better do it a month in advance. Amy said she had taken care of it. I shrugged, having been spoiled by Cecelia.

We arrived at the restaurant ten minutes early and I went up and announced we were there. The hostess looked at her reservation book and shook her head asking "Are you sure you have a reservation?"

I looked at her in total dismay. I was accustomed to having people fall all over us whenever we went out and responded "I'm certain."

The hostess looked again as she slid her finger down the list, naming those who had called ahead. "Olsen? Johnsen?" she inquired, with me shaking my head 'no'.

"How about Long?" she asked, adding "Richard Long?"

I was incredulous and thought there had been some mistake. I apologized, turned and walked back out onto Boulevard de Grande Case where Amy was waiting.

"Something got screwed up" I announced.

"What do you mean?" Amy inquired, with a scrunched-up nose.

"No reservation!" I replied.

"But I called," she retorted.

"No reservation!" I countered.

A slight smile came across Amy's face as she asked, "What name did you give her?"

"Terrill," I said incredulously.

Amy shook her head and replied. "You never give your real name."

"Huh?"

"No, you always use a fake name," she replied.

"What?"

"Sure, you always use a fake name so they can't trace you if you don't show up," Amy countered.

"What name did you give?" I asked.

"What's the one thing I really am hungry for tonight?" Amy asked. I shook my head, indicating I had no idea, leaving me wondering what was going on.

We walked in and Amy said, "Richard Long" and our favorite table in the front corner was offered. The meal was scrumptious! I had lobster. Amy had grouper that had been innocently swimming in the Caribbean a few hours earlier and both meals were simply outstanding.

I thought nothing of the name Amy had chosen until we got home and Amy snickered. "You didn't get the name, did you?"

I shook my head indicating "no".

"Richard Long?" she repeated, using her hands to indicate I needed to transpose the names. When it all made sense, Amy went about creating a very, very special desert that included whipped cream, just for me.

Sunday was our actual anniversary day and we did what Mrs. Terrill wanted, which was spend the entire day on Orient Beach, where Mr. Terrill allowed Mrs. Terrill to "run around nearly naked" meaning topless, with a bikini bottom so tiny, her little rose tattoo was peeking out. I must admit, there's something macho about having a gorgeous woman that many men ... and, as I also had learned, women covet, knowing she's all yours and the macho realization was splashed across my face in one giant, satisfied smile.

The day was almost perfect. However, when Mr. Terrill was convinced by Mrs. Terrill to be "unencumbered" and we played "up periscope" in the water, I do think she went a bit too far. Fortunately, we were up to our necks in the ocean and no one was near us, as I convulsed in embarrassed pleasure at her overture.

For four days, we did nothing except be together. It was marvelous to simply be enmeshed in each other's existence, relishing thoughts and emotions, as we intertwined in life; creating those things called memories. There was more laughter, more frivolity and more fun than I could ever remember, with or without the woman I loved.

The long weekend was just what we needed. Nine months later Mrs. Terrill gave birth to twin boys … George Douglas Terrill the Fifth, we nicknamed "V" and Derrick Rodney Terrill, after her brother and my best friend.

When Amy announced she was expecting, I finally realized my wicked wife had planned it all and smiled. I can never be grateful enough for those days together and the results she planned. Imagine, not only having kids, but knowing when, where and how they were conceived and the joy that surrounded their beginnings.

Richard Long was gone! Now, nothing more than a sly smile of a time gone by, when we threw caution to wind and simply…had…fun!

What a hoot!

What an honor!

What a thrill!

What a wonderful, wonderful memory!

To this day, I believe God gave us two babies instead of one because of the love we shared for each other that weekend.

Clip, Clip, Here; clip, clip there:

Even though we weren't back at the House-On-The-Hill at the time of the next "event", the excitement of having twins, made us celebrate a little early and nine months later, Mrs. Terrill gave birth to our daughter, Amelia Earhart Terrill at which point, Mrs. Terrill told Mr. Terrill … "enough is enough".

As I lay on the examining table, the lyrics to "Merry Old Land of Oz" sung by five hairdressers and a Cowardly Lion in the *"Wizard of Oz"*, kept playing in my head.

Clip, clip here

Clip, clip there

Fa, la, la, la, la…" as the urologist made certain the number of my off-spring was permanently set at three.

I was 32 years old, had three kids and was managing three companies. I lived in the house my wife bought; wore custom-made designer clothes, she or someone else paid for; drove luxury cars that were her dad's and always knew, behind my back, everyone called me "Mr. Amelia Williams" as the last line of lyrics of the song played over and over in my head…

"Ha ha ha

Ho ho ho

Ho ho ho ho ho

That's how we, laugh the day away

In the merry old land of Oz"

The Next Big Step.

In our next annual family meeting, the subject of investing in assisted living centers and nursing homes was on the agenda. This was another lucrative business The Duke thought we should get into. On the downside, there was a large investment, plus government controls and all sorts of liabilities. Instead, I came up with a proposal to start a service company which allowed elderly people to remain in their homes. Consisting of all traditional maintenance projects needed around the house, such as lawn mowing, window washing, house cleaning, driveway sealing, eave cleaning and snow removal, for a monthly fee equal to what they would probably pay in association dues, homeowners could have all the services found in a condo, without the cost or emotional stress of having to move.

The Duke liked the idea and we had research done where we learned the only reason many elderly people moved was because of home maintenance. By incorporating a program that included payment for all the tasks into one direct-deposit, monthly fee, the elderly, or anyone, for that matter, could retain their residence, friends and neighbors.

I took the project under my wing and began with a staff of five and a small target market. We analyzed costs, subcontracted the work to people willing to wear our uniforms and drive our trucks that were leased from our automobile business. We worked with the banks regarding automatic deposits and opened the doors. With only three outside sales people, business exploded. Once again, another spoke was added to Wilco wheel of fortune that became the WilServ division, with staffing at 50 people in a matter of months.

As we met with residents, we also learned the services could be offered to businesses and expanded once again. As people outside our trading area asked about our company, we elected to franchise and a national franchise division was established. Within 18 months, we hit a million dollars per month in billing. Within three years, we were billing as much as the security division and contributing nearly $500 million to the corporation on an annual basis. I was on a roll. Unfortunately, my time was now being split between the jet business, security, central purchasing and home maintenance and the hours were adding up with me getting home later and later and later.

The Awakening:

The years were rolling by and the time invested in work kept increasing. One night, I arrived home at 11:00 PM totally exhausted from yet another sixteen-hour day which was about the twentieth in a row. Amelia was sitting in the darkened family room. The kids were in bed and it was time for some serious talk. We had become strangers in our own house. The kids really didn't know their dad as he was always at work. Things dads did were allocated to employees.

"I'm not happy!" Amelia said. A word was not needed as I could see it in her eyes. "We are never together and we hardly ever do family things." I knew she was right, but my profound sense of inadequacy kept driving me. The last thing I wanted was for us to be apart. She was my bedrock! I had always felt that Amelia gave meaning to my life! I sat down next to her on the couch and attempted to touch her. She pulled away! This was much more serious than I thought.

"Are you having an affair?" Amy asked.

I was incredulous. "What?"

"Are you having an affair?" she repeated.

I was shocked, dismayed and hurt that she thought such a thing. I responded. "I made a covenant with you Mrs. Amelia Marie Terrill! I vowed you were my wife in good times and bad, happy times and sad and there has never been another woman besides you. I love you more than life itself!"

She looked at me with a great deal of apprehension as I looked at her sadness and continued. "I know we all come into this world programmed to do one primary thing … sustain our genetic heritage and have primal and learned behaviors that transcend the single objective … propagation of the species. You and I have done that. We have three wonderful kids who, along with you, show me love and joy every single day, but there is absolutely no one else but you."

Amy responded. "No one, including us, can expect marriage will be easy, George! It's a very difficult task, and yet, it is the most important job in our lives if we expect to be happy and satisfied. You have shown me time-after-time that there isn't the joy we once had. I've tried to rationalize why and even read a wonderful book on marriage called *"Survivor, Death and How It Saved My Life"*.

Now I was realizing just how deep of chasm had become between us and how she was trying to do everything she could to put the pieces back together as she continued, "the book discusses the seven components required for creating and sustaining a viable marital relationship that I hope and pray remain in ours."

"What are they?" I asked.

Amy answered in an authoritative way, as she had them memorized… "attraction, association, communication, understanding, trust, compromise and forgiveness."

Amy shook her head. "George, the attraction is still there on my side."

I nodded and added, "me too" hoping the short response wouldn't break her train of thought and allow her to continue. I really needed to know what was going on.

"Next comes association and George, we don't do anything together and when we do, your mind is always on work. I want a husband, not a business partner!" Ouch!

I looked down at the floor and shook my head. Amy was totally right, as she continued. "As for communication, we don't talk and I can't tell you the last time we laughed together or even at all. I don't know if you understand me anymore and what my needs are." Tears began to well in my eyes. All I ever wanted was to make her proud of me.

I was demolished. My heart sank at even the thought as Amy continued. "With your absence, there hasn't been any communication and without the communication, there hasn't been any understanding. We are both changing and yet, "we", Amy said, putting her fingers like quotation marks, "haven't changed at all and so my needs and your needs today just aren't being met by the other."

At least she was accepting some of the responsibility, which was a slight beam of light that meant we could work things out.

"Next is trust." Amy continued. "I trust you, but so many lonely nights and so much time away made me believe that you had two mistresses."

"Two?" I questioned almost incredulously.

"Yes two!" Amy responded. "Your job is one mistress who takes you away whenever she calls and I began to feel that because we have become so … so indifferent … towards each other physically, there had to be someone else and I thought about all those greaseballs with their trophy girlfriends." I shuddered as I always looked with profound disdain at those who thought they could justify being unfaithful as they paraded around with someone twenty years younger on their arms.

"Next is compromise!" Amy said, as tears trickled down her cheeks. "I know that I'm not perfect! I know I need to change too! I know that I have my faults and weaknesses, but so do you and all I'm asking is that you try to be a better father and husband by spending more time with us. The kids love you and are heartbroken when you don't show up for their school programs or even go on vacation with us."

Ouch!

"Finally, is forgiveness. George, we must forgive each other when there are errors. We must accept that we are not perfect, as there is no such thing as perfection." I didn't know where she was going with this as she continued. "We both make mistakes, some greater than others, but love is what will allow us to continue to be us."

Amy looked down at the floor and then back at me, taking the back of her hand and wiping away the tears.

There was a pause as I tried to comprehend what Amy was saying and answered, "I agree, marriage is NOT as easy as I thought it was going to be! If this is just the physical thing, I am sorry. While you, my dear, have always been uninhibited and open with and about yourself, I am not. Perhaps, it was the medical treatments for you! Perhaps it was my conservative, small-town childhood for me! We just began at different ends of the spectrum."

Amy shook her head no. This was much deeper than that. This was about making the other person feel special and I was too involved and too busy to almost remember how to do that. I looked at my wife and frowned saying, "I'm sorry."

Before she could respond, I continued, "I'm trying so hard to be worthy of you and your family. Everything we have is because of you. This house! The cars! Even my clothes, aren't things that I paid for. I don't even know our own finances and it makes me feel incredibly inadequate in so many ways. All I want to is to feel like a man... to feel like a husband and a father... especially when everyone calls me Mr. Amelia Williams behind my back."

Amy just shook her head no. Truth be told! My profound sense of inadequacy had finally raised its ugly head for her to see.

I continued on. "Let's go back to what you said we needed in our relationship and talk about attraction. Plain and simple, attraction draws one object closer to another and, in my case, today, I am as attracted to you as much as the first day we met. I am profoundly attracted to you, physically, mentally, emotionally and most of all, intellectually. You, Miss Amelia, simply knock my socks off in every possible way, day after day after day. I don't know how you do your balancing act of wife, mother and leader. Our children are more reliant on us for longer periods of time, than any other species and so susceptible to modification and yet you have the innate ability to raise three wonderful kids who are intelligent, polite, caring, trustworthy, loyal, helpful, friendly and above all else kind.

The kids have been given a lifestyle beyond all but a very, very few children on earth and yet they are well rounded and well grounded, knowing right from wrong, good from bad and realizing they have been given the gift of life that allows them to do more and be more than almost any other child. There is no fear of hunger! There is no fear of danger! There is no fear tomorrow won't be filled with the love and support of their mother and hopefully their father. They have been given the greatest gift of all… the gift of love and you have given it to them."

Amy just looked at me. I don't think she believed I had the feelings in me for anything but work. I continued. "Do I look at other women? Hell, yes! Do you look at others? Of course! It's a natural instinct we can't stop, even if we tried."

My lower lip protruded for a moment and then I closed my eyes and reflected. "I can remember that spring day, at the cottage, when you pulled into the driveway in the UPS truck, as if it were yesterday. I remember the weather and what you were wearing. I remember our conversation. I remember the baseball cap on your head and above all else, I remember your smile and I was smitten. I could verbally paint a picture of you then and I can now. Would it include your breasts? Yes! Waist? Yes! Legs? Yes! Overall body shape? Definitely! Your hair? Of course! Above all else … It was and will always remain your smile! You had me with it and it is still something that lights me up every, single time it happens, which unfortunately, I don't get to see very often, for which I am to blame for many, many reasons.

To this day, I don't know what you saw in me. I hope it was those physical attributes that created a sense of security you felt I could provide which you were seeking. I think they call them "good dad" traits such as gentleness, compassion and sensitivity as well."

Amy nodded in the affirmative … whew!

I continued. "The first time you spoke, I was enticed. The first time you laughed you had me hook, line and sinker! I wanted to be a writer and yet, it was your words that established the parameters of your personality, where your girlie giggle was burned into my soul and every single time I am down or depressed, all I need to do is remember your laugh and it makes me profoundly happy."

Amy was softening and I could see her begin to relax and so I continued, "The final aspect of my attraction to you is the way you smell … except, of course when you fart in your sleep". This got an embarrassed girlie giggle out of her. "When I'm alone in bed and you have been there, I simply take your pillow and breathe deeply and am refreshed because you have made me happy, and made me feel like the man I want to be, who is fortunate enough to be with the woman he loves … his wife, his partner and the mother of his children, for whom he will do anything."

I peered at the ceiling as if to catch a memory and then looked deep into Amy's eyes. "I remember the day at Devils Lake when you fell and broke your ankle. I cherish the day when you and I went to the forest and made love. I still laugh at the silly verbal bantering about you running naked on Orient Beach with your walking boot on. Remember? Das Boot!"

Amy softly laughed as I continued, "Right foot. Club foot. Right foot. Club foot. Right foot. Club foot!" which got another reserved girlie giggle from her, which made me happy. I felt I was winning back the trust of my wife. Thank God!

I turned very serious and looked even deeper into her eyes. "Amy, you asked whether I was having an affair. I am not, have not and will not! An affair is nothing more than lust at its worst possible juncture."

Amy had a frown on her face. She wasn't expecting the intensity of my response and I believe was surprised by my response as I continued, "Salacious though it may sound, lust was the gatekeeper to our love, putting the initial spring in my step and sparkle in my eye, when I was attracted to you."

I looked at her and peered deep into her dark brown eyes, "Do I look at other women? Of course, I do, but it always stops there. Without lust, we might have never found each other and you would have driven away in that big brown van and I would still be sitting on the porch, alone, wondering if there would ever be a wonderful someone for me. While lust keeps us all "looking around," the ones we lust after aren't always the ones we are actually in love with. I got lucky! You see I am married to the woman I lust after AND the woman I love and I sincerely believe it couldn't get any better for me."

Amy's lower lip was protruding. I had hit a soft spot as I continued, "I once read love is expressed as an action and experienced as a feeling. To me, my love for you has an essence which resists defining, in a single way that encompasses compassion, determination, tolerance, endurance, support, faith, and much, much more. I have always felt that my love for you is some sort of addiction, whose feeling I hope and pray never goes away, as I sincerely believe my love is intended to be love for the duration."

I looked down at the floor and then raised my head and took a deep breath and added, "We both have passed fantasy love and entered into real love which I sincerely believe is strong enough to withstand the problems and distractions that come from this thing called life."

Now there were tears in her eyes as I continued. "We have been together twelve years. Twelve years! We have laughed together, cried together, lived together and I hope someday, when we are very, very old, die together. Because we are linked so closely, so many of the things which were once special are now taken for granted. I remember the excitement of our first Christmas, Miles Teddywedgers and Chocolate Shoppe ice cream. This house, my job and your school, the cars your dad provided, events, people! With repetition, these have all become the norm. That's not wrong! It's normal." I said slightly shaking my head.

I gently grabbed her hand and continued, "We both know our passionate love has faded and again, this is normal. Suddenly we both have faults … me, more than you, I believe. I'm certain you have asked yourself 'why has he changed?' Actually, neither of us has changed at all. It's just that we're now able to see each other rationally, rather than through the blinding infatuation and passion which once existed. Don't get me wrong, the passion is still there! It's just in a different, more subdued form."

I slowly pulled back and continued, "Fortunately, at this stage, I hope and pray our relationship has been strong enough to endure my insecurities, where I have attempted to prove to the world I am **not** Mr. Amelia Williams! In working so hard to prove to others who I am, I have been willing to do the unthinkable… ignore my family, to prove I was a man."

Once again, I had tears in my eyes and added, "Had our love not been as strong; had it not been that you have been patient and tolerant; had you not opened up to me and made me aware, all we have could have ended. Fortunately, three things came into our life that changed us, rearranged us and built a stronger bond between us and that's the kids."

"Along the way, you have not only remained my wife, but I have been blessed with the propinquity of you becoming my best friend. Why are you my best friend? Because you are kind, compassionate, intelligent, and above all else, loving. You have tolerated me and my insecurities and allowed me to attempt to define myself in what can only be called a very challenging environment. Being your husband and the son-in-law of your parents is **not** an easy task."

Amy allowed me to ramble on for a long time. As I paused and looked at our massive fireplace that hadn't been lit in, God only knows how long, she picked up the pace and began adding her wisdom to the conversation. "You're so right 'Q'". She called me 'Q' for the first time in years and I liked hearing it. "I love you as much as you love me. After twelve years, the "honeymoon" **is** over, but George you remain special to me ... and I continue to place you in a position beyond reproach, where you remain the light to which I can confidently turn when I find myself in a realm of darkness. This is the real attraction and why, through thick and thin, we will ... no, we must stay together. The challenge is, sustaining the passion of the partnership. We're supposed to eat meals together, sleep together, raise our children together and attend social functions together and, at times, I feel you forget that I am here with hopes and dreams and fears, as well."

She was letting me have it in a very gentle way, as she added. "It's also true, there will be rocky times in any marriage. Outside the home, we lead separate lives and sometimes fail to share the problems we experience at work and with friends. When those issues extend into married life is when there can be problems and this is where we are at."

Another well-timed salvo across my bow, as she continued, "I'm not as strong as you believe I am, for which I sincerely feel sorry. I want to be a good wife and mother. I want to be secure in knowing you want me in many ways. Intimacy is truly an expression of love and devotion that should allow us to know each other more than anyone else ever can. That is part of the reason why our marriage has been sacred and, yet, when either one of us is so tired from long hours or so mentally involved, that the pure joy of physical pleasure is thought to be secondary, troubles begin. You know I am more adventurous than you. I have learned my needs are not your needs. I have accepted this with some degree of regret, as I need more physically than I am getting right now or have received for a long, long time."

It was time for me to pop the question. "Do you miss Sydney?"

There were tears in her eyes and trepidation in what she was about to say. I could cut the tension with a knife as the reservation of thought and word interjected the conversation.

"There are days and times when I do. She drove me, excited me and made me feel important. I have craved those feelings, that sense of excitement and self-worth that have been missing and I'm sorry."

"Do you want me to find her?"

"Not really! She was one person who filled a gap that needed filling. I always thought that if I had you and the kids to do the same thing and then … then you left me!" she blurted out as she started really crying.

"What?" I said incredulously.

"You left me for your job! You left me to show the world you were a man and made me feel as if I wasn't important anymore."

My heart sank as she was gasping for air, as each breath became more encased in remorse.

She put her hand to her mouth. "I'm sorry!" she whispered.

"About what?" I asked.

"I'm sorry! I've been so lonely" she replied.

Reality was creeping into my mind.

"There's someone else?" I asked.

"I'm sorry!"

"Who?" my mind raced in all directions. Another man? Another woman? I was afraid to ask as she looked at me as tears rolled down her cheeks.

"I've been so lonely!"

My heart was broken.

"Another man?" I inquired to which her head shook "no". I guess, I was relieved. Another man would have been profoundly devastating.

"Another woman?" I inquired, to which she bit her lower lip.

"How long?"

The tears rolled down her cheeks, as she wiped them with the back of her right hand and replied, "A little while".

My eyes closed and my mind shot back to when I found out about Sydney. I told Amy then, I was willing to share her if it would make her happy. I never realized those words could open the gates, nor did I realize how sad she had become.

"Do you want to talk about it?" I asked.

Shaking her head "no" she whispered, "I just want you to know, I've been so lonely." as she convulsed in deep sorrow.

"Are you still *seeing her*?" I asked.

Amy shook her head "no" and answered. "It shouldn't have happened. I shouldn't have told you. I'm sorry!"

"Sorry?" I asked. "Sorry about what? I'm the one who should be apologizing. I let you down by taking you for granted. Can I ask who?" I inquired.

"No one you know," she replied.

"Where?" I asked.

"I met her at the health club."

I took a deep breath. "And?"

"We started working out together and then one day, had lunch and, well, it just happened."

"Where?"

"At her house."

I was glad it wasn't here.

"Her husband travels a lot for business and well, we were just both so … so lonely." Again, the tears rushed forward as she took the back of her hand to wipe them away again.

I closed my eyes and didn't know what to say or feel. I was profoundly hurt and wanted to blame Amy and yet, deep inside me, I blamed myself. I put me before we and she simply responded.

I thought back to the day I learned about Sydney and our conversation as we sat upon a hill in St. Martin. In a time of profound introspection, I told Amy to explore, to be free, to follow what she felt in her heart, regardless of what society, culture and people would say. I told her, she needed to be liberated and seek her own plane ... to venture beyond the realm of social propriety and determine what made sense for her, the damaged soul, irreverent and indifferent to expectation. I had not lived up to the words of our marriage covenant and Amy had only followed my direction and simply did what I offered.

"It's over?" I asked, hoping the answer was yes.

Amy nodded in the affirmative adding, "Her husband found out and she said we had to stop seeing each other because her husband wanted more."

"What do you mean more?" I asked in a defensive way.

"He wanted to be part of it."

"What did you say?"

"I said no, of course" Amy replied, almost incredulously.

"Oh my God! Do they know who you are?"

"I don't think so, why?"

"Amy, little secrets like this could really hurt the family and Wilco."

Amy sat erect! I hit a nerve and remorse quickly turned to anger! "Wilco! Wilco? All you think about is the fucking company. What about me? What about my happiness? What about what I want in life? I want to feel wanted, needed and loved and not like I'm just some asset to the company."

"But we could get blackmailed. What if the kids found out?" I replied.

"Found out what? That I like making love with a woman because my husband is never around? Found out that my husband learned about it a long time ago and told me it was OK?" Her anger spewed forth in all its fury. The years of frustration that had been bottled up! The remorse! The loneliness! The devastating feeling of being unwanted, finally had reached the point where her remorse turned to anger and she was letting me have it. I was devastated. The truth hurt and she knew it.

"George, I love you! I have always loved you. When we went to pick up Ann and Rodney and you found out about Sydney, I shared what happened. The only thing I didn't tell you was, I was the one who initiated the relationship and not Sydney. In fact, she was reluctant."

I leaned back in my chair and took a deep breath.

"I also didn't tell you, she wasn't the first."

Holy shit! And now, I realized Sydney wasn't the first or last.

Amy added. "I thought getting married and having kids would be enough, but then you left me, George. You left me!" Amy whispered again and she began to cry. "When Hurricane Irma blew away all the buildings on Orient Beach, it blew away my memories. There's nothing left for me to hang onto. There are no reference points, no stakes in the sand upon which I can reflect" as she was now convulsing in profound sadness.

I realized, for the first time, how sad she was and also how frustrated. I realized I had been so consumed by making myself feel like a man, I had neglected making her feel like a woman. My God, this was a lot more complicated than I thought.

"Do you want to continue?" I asked, hoping her answer would be 'no'.

Amy whispered. "I want you! I want my husband to make me feel special again! I want to feel loved!" at which she began to cry even more. "As the tears trickled down her cheeks, I matched her sadness. My heart was broken. In attempting to become a man, I hurt the only person in my life who made me ever feel like one. I pulled her into me and held her and felt her rasps. She was letting it all out. The years of being second … the instances … so many instances, when I had placed my own perception of who I wanted to be above all else, shoving her into the background, making her feel secondary.

Amy whispered, "All the other things in our lives, including the kids, jobs, social engagements, stress, hobbies seem to limit the time when we can be together and I guess, I should accept it, but I want ……to feel……loved……again."

Bam! An arrow right into my heart! I thought of all the reasons why not … lack of time, too tired after sixteen-hour days, not feeling very sexy or having Amy spurn my infrequent overtures, plus way too much stress, which kept me up at night. My mind continued as I held her. Perhaps, I did hide a deep resentment of her affair on St. Martin or the fact that when we disagree, we never let our anger out, just letting things simmer and go away.

There was a deafening silence, as fears arose within me that had been lost in the bliss of love, which had sadly evolved into the mundane of marriage … taking each other for granted. Questions came into my mind that had never been there before. Would there be more "situations" like this in the future? Would I, could I, tolerate knowing that I had only filled a part of her needs? When and how would I know if there were others and what would I do or feel? My God, once again, the ugly head of insecurity welled within me, shattering both my confidence and the belief that I was the only one.

As we sat upon the couch, I realized that my love for Amy was irrefutable and my ultimate goal had to be to rekindle our relationship, re-engineer the attraction and rebuild the bond, by overcoming the dogma of familiarity so as to mutually compensate for the years of emotional infidelity on both sides. What was done, was done and I had to either accept it or walk away. I knew the answer and pledged to myself to share and love my wife in a new, different and exciting way and to overcome the mundane, familiar and predictable. But how when you are so tired? How, when you are so conservative and she so liberal? How, when all you really want is a good night's sleep, which hadn't happened in months or years?

They say that the two greatest motivators are hope and fear. I had both! I hoped that, by working through this, we could regain the emotional traction we once had. I was afraid that I wouldn't be good enough, strong enough, creative enough to ensure all that had happened didn't happen, again. "Great Grandfather speak to me! Please, please, please speak to me!" I prayed.

As we sat in our darkened family room and listened to the silence of sadness, my thoughts turned to yesterday and the joy we once had and how those joys ricocheted off my heart, plummeting me into the cold, gray, emotional abyss that comes from total singularity. I looked at my wife and quietly thanked her for sitting up and talking with me and loving me while so carefully telling me things needed to change.

"Do you forgive me?" Amy asked.

I replied, "Do you forgive me?"

I tried to hide a yawn. She yawned first! It was nearly three in the morning. I took out my phone and sent a text to Andrew, telling him not to pick me up in the morning. We kissed and hugged and went to bed. I don't remember what time I actually got to sleep, but it really didn't matter. I had miles to go before I slept, to make up for all the nights when Amy had gone to bed alone.

When we finally awakened, the sun was shining. I announced that, effective that day, I would make a point of having breakfast every morning with her and the kids to share their day, knowing there would be nights when I would come home after the kids had gone to bed. However, I also vowed that each night I would be home in time to share my life with my wife.

Off the Wagon:

All my promises lasted a few months. At first it was just one meeting and then one dinner and then we were almost back the way it had been before. I was being torn in two, like the alcoholic who vowed to never drink again and then said he could handle one and then two and soon was back to where he had begun.

Christmas had come and gone and so had winter. Amy and the kids had gone to our house in Colorado skiing while I closed a deal. Amy and the kids had gone to The House-On-The-Hill for spring vacation while I worked on the next acquisition. Amy and the kids had gone to opening day of the Brewers while I was in New York. I was becoming a stranger in my own house… again, but then it wasn't my house, it was Amy's house and they were actually Amy's clothes and Amy's dad's cars. In other words, Amy everything.

Andrew was driving me home one night when it hit me, I had not kept my word. I was almost shocked when security let me in the front gate, as I felt like a stranger in my, I mean, her house. I slipped into the silent kitchen and slithered up the stairs to our bedroom. Quietly I took off my clothes and crawled under the covers. She was awake!

"I'm sorry!" I lamented. "It's just so … so overwhelming!"

"You're not managing people." Amy whispered.

"I don't know how!" I replied as tears welled in my eyes.

Late, the next morning my cellphone rang. It was The Duke. We did our normal family chitchat and then he asked Amy and me to join him to watch the Milwaukee Symphony orchestra with Dr. Williams. Other than our wedding reception, I had never been and even if I had, I still would have said yes. You just didn't turn down an offer from your father-in-law.

The night came and we got all dressed up and met mom and dad Williams for dinner and then the performance. It was really neat and I really enjoyed it. On the way home, Amy asked me what I thought. I told her I loved it.

She said," What part did you like best?"

I thought she meant which song and so I started thinking about all the orchestra had played.

Amy must have realized I misunderstood and clarified her question. "Which instruments?"

I pondered the subject and didn't have an answer.

Amy waited and then responded for me. "I liked the conductor. He probably couldn't play half the instruments in the orchestra and would probably not even make the ensemble, if he auditioned. Yet, he has to understand how they all sound and then how they sound together. Then he has to let each musician play their instrument!" Amy was sending me a message. I didn't need to know how to play all the instruments. What I needed to learn, was to make certain they all played in tune and together.

The next afternoon, I was at the office and there was a special delivery ... a long thin box. Instead of having Cecelia open it, I was instructed to open it myself. Inside was a conductor's baton. The message had been sent. I smiled and realized the orchestra and the conversation was Amelia's wonderful way of teaching me a lesson I desperately needed to learn.

I called Wilco personnel and asked to talk with Dr. Jermaine Washington who headed the division. We had a long conversation and a meeting was set. Management 101! I was going to learn how to manage people. I went to the Wilco offices and was warmly greeted. People all knew who I was and stories of the exponential growth of my divisions were washing away the title of Mr. Amelia Williams.

Jermaine was a tall thin, be-speckled man in his late forties who could have been a college professor. As we sat in his office, I looked at family photos and then one of him with Amelia's mom which I found interesting. Jermaine, as he asked me to call him, outlined what he looked for in a person that had to go beyond cognitive skills such as communication, leadership, creative problem solving and strategic thinking. Then he hit me with the big one. "Employees had to be willing to be part of a team, including the captain or the conductor." With that I gulped! Another arrow across the bow!

Jermaine continued. "Our society is such that when you have a conversation with someone new, one of the first questions asked is "What you do?" This is particularly true of men. By informing someone of what you do for a living, you are establishing a social level. Responding as a professional … doctor, lawyer, etc. results in a completely different set of responses than from saying you work at McDonalds."

I nodded in agreement as Jermaine continued, "We judge people by what they do, not who they are. We have come to identify a person by their job more than by any other aspect except their appearance and this can have profound consequences! Yet jobs are simply power modules where people only have temporary power over others and then, only to the degree they think you need something from them. Take away the perception of need and you erode the power!"

I thought of my mom. She had always been the boss at our house, as Jermaine continued, "The biggest problem today is we are all living in a dichotomous world where we aspire for independence in a system which has stacked the deck against almost all of us. With the way our country is going, very soon only two types of Americans will exist: The ultra-rich and the ultra-poor. America is supposed to be the land of opportunity. This is why so many immigrants have flooded our cities. For some it is simply to get a better job or hopefully, more security. For others, it is to build their dream business."

Jermaine looked out his office window and added, "We have all seen it dozens of times where a creative entrepreneur starts a company and, through the forces of talent, dedication and the ability to inspire others, builds an empire." I immediately thought of The Duke. "It's just like politics, as the company increases in size, so does the founder's ego. Things which were dreams … cars, homes, trips, perks and most of all people catering to them, all become commonplace and the founder's ego begins to get in the way of progress which becomes their undoing. There are classic stories of what can happen when ego gets in the way of the enterprise."

Turning to me with a smile on his face, Jermaine continued, "The reason Wilco continues to thrive is because of Mr. Williams innate ability to see through people and judge them for who they really are. If they are willing to be a team player, they can lead a very, very comfortable life. If they think it's **me** instead of **we**, they will get buried. I've seen him do it so many times."

Jermaine shook his head and continued, "Sadly, most big companies work on the inside/outside concept where you work hard to get on the inside by playing the game so you get the greatest reward for your efforts. Those on the outside are expendable, mere appliances, used until they wear out and are replaced by newer, fresher appliances, which initially cost less to operate. The disaster comes when the insiders impede the outsiders on the fringe because the outsiders are normally the ones who help make a company great. In so doing, the insiders damage the company and impede its growth and vitality."

Jermaine continued. "George, you're on the inside and have done an incredible job of helping the company. The problem is, you're trying to do it all by yourself and it simply can't be done. There aren't enough hours in the day to do everything and do it right. You need to have people you can trust who will help you and that means relinquishing some of your roles and trusting others to do the jobs you're trying to do yourself."

Jermaine leaned back in his chair and picked up a pen to use as a pointer adding, "I can't even begin to tell you how difficult it is today to manage people mainly because of the incredible level of distrust everyone has. Sadly, most Americans today don't trust the government, business or each other and this has created a real paradox in the business world. In 1964, we hit the high spot of trust when 77% of Americans indicated people could be trusted. Today, the number is below 30% which makes managing people a lot more difficult than ever before. What distorts these numbers is that, back then you needed to be a heterosexual, Caucasian male to progress in business and it was just that segment of the population who trusted everybody and everything."

"As a gay, African-American, I wouldn't have had a snowball's chance in hell to get ahead. If you really wanted to be on the bottom of the pile, you should have been a black woman. Regardless of what your skills were, you were stereotyped and there wasn't much you could do about it. Today, thank God, those limits have been somewhat eliminated and nowhere is that more prevalent than at Wilco. We don't even have questions dealing with gender, race or orientation in our employee profiles. Dr. Williams took care of that, for which I will always be profoundly grateful."

The photo on the desk was now making sense as Jermaine continued, "Like everything else in life, for every opportunity, there is a challenge, for every action, an opposite and equal reaction, to the point that we always need to be careful that we haven't reacted too much, gone too far or allowed the minority to control the majority. The social challenges of today are incredibly different than those of even the last decade."

Jermaine was on a roll and I sat profoundly mesmerized by the lecture provided as he continued, "It used to be our accountants reviewed physical capital, such as land and equipment, and human capital, such as knowledge and skills, to determine our corporate worth. Today, we have another completely different component we have identified, which is social capital which is the creation and maintenance of trust amongst and between the employees and our different business groups."

"When my father went to work as head of the house, he, like those of his generation, assumed they would be with the same company for their entire careers and the average length of employment was 25 years, where they built up a sense of belonging and community with their co-workers and the leaders where they worked. Today, the typical employee only stays four years and so the level of community is lost and with it the social capital needed to sustain stability."

Jermaine took off his glasses and put them on his desk as he continued, "What's incredible is the sense of community is eroding throughout society and particularly with whom we call friends." Shaking his head as if in disbelief, Jermaine continued, "In 1985, responses indicated people had three close friends with whom they would feel comfortable sharing important matters. By 2004, the number had dropped to two. Last year, the number of people indicating they had **no one** with whom to talk about things that mattered was **triple** what it was in 2000."

Jermaine added. "High job turnover, reduced levels of important friends and no sense of community! These all mean managing is that much more difficult. Fortunately, Mr. and Dr. Williams saw the handwriting on the wall and understood the criteria needed for comfort and confidence through all levels of our company and that is stability. This is why we have an average employment duration of eleven years, which is skewed young because of all the additions you have done to help with the company's expansion." I didn't know whether to be proud or shirk in embarrassment as 90% of all the new employees were in the divisions I started.

Jermaine shook his head and noted, "I look at our termination rate due to those who have resigned or are terminated and we are at less than 2%, which is incredible. We sustain these numbers because we not only communicate with our employees and incentivize them, but recognize them as well. The money in the annual bonuses and rewards are a small fraction of what it costs to hire and train new employees and yet they provide the impetus needed to keep good employees." I was beginning to see there was logic to the bonus plan and awards meeting that meant more than just handing out money.

Jermaine continued, "Another aspect is who we hire. For the most part, we look at three criteria. First, what is their education level? Not everyone needs to go to college, but they do need some sort of post-high school education to be considered. Second, we like hiring married people. We understand there are always exceptions and yet, there is much greater stability when a person is married. Finally, we look for people who have the education, are married and then have kids and do so in that order."

"While it sounds selfish, we know that by doing things in that sequence, all facts indicate we will end up with employees who are more dedicated and that's why we pay more. This doesn't mean we won't hire someone who isn't married, but we shy away from unmarried mothers and fathers who have had children out of wedlock, simply because of the challenges they have outside of their jobs."

Jermaine leaned back in his chair and continued, "Because of our reputation for generosity, we have a steady stream of applicants. We can tell in a few minutes what type of childhood the applicant had and whether they fit our profile. Kids from traditional families are more stable and have greater abilities at problem solving than those from single-parent homes. Everyone needs to be guided when they are a child, yet those from stressed-out homes, who had discipline pattern consisting of "obey" associated only with threats, won't ever be as dedicated as kids from dual parent families who had discipline consisting of "obey" and then the reason **why**. The net result is kids with intact families have higher levels of social capital and can better navigate the bumps called life, than those without stable families, who are often crippled by even modest impediments."

Jermaine put his glasses back on and leaned forward to make a point. "George, this is the key to understanding how most organizations work and why Wilco is so successful, simply because we do the opposite. We understand that, in time, every position tends to be occupied by an employee who is incompetent or indifferent, who is over-matched for their position and insecure enough to ensure those more intelligent, more creative and more driven are artificially repressed below them in the name of their own wellbeing and then we act."

Leaning back in his chair again, Jermaine added, "As psychologists discovered, the least competent people are usually prone to overestimating their own talents. Our job is to make certain loyal people remain educated and motivated, stimulated and wanting to grow. When we find an employee, who has reached their 'limit' we don't discard them, we find a position which meets their skills, while still challenging them. This is why we are so successful. Mr. Williams is a master at realizing potential and using it for the betterment, first of the person and the good of both the company and other employees."

"Mr.   Terrill"

"George, please!"

"George, my responsibility is to make certain the people who work for you meet those criteria. Your responsibility is to motivate them to do the best they can with what they have to work with."

Jermaine glanced at the clock and I knew that my time was up as he added, "If I can leave you with one basic premise … we look at employees from two basic criteria … attitude and aptitude. Do they have the ability to do the job? Are they educated, motivated and stimulated enough to do the job and do they want to do the job?" This is where managing comes in. You need to develop methods that will allow you to keep people wanting to work and then giving them the latitude needed to do their job without question or interference."

"Unfortunately, it doesn't always work out the way we think it will simply because people change. When is it time to part company with an employee? Just two more words ... incompetence or indifference, which includes the most important component of all ... lack of loyalty to the team and the company they work for. Business is dynamic and people need to change. I'm not saying eliminate people, I'm saying, train people, motivate people and give them every opportunity to succeed but never, ever allow anyone to **not** be a member of the team they are on."

"If you want to manage and manage properly, let people do the jobs they were hired and trained to do. There will be mistakes! If they are honest mistakes, don't make people fear for error when they are trying to grow. If a mistake is made, the key is having people recognize the mistake, admit they made the mistake, learn from the mistake and move on. Insanity is making the same mistake over and over again and only the government is allowed to do that," he said with a smile. "Finally, the most important concept that drives us all is simply to be happy, which comes from sincerely feeling wanted, needed and loved." There were those three words again! Jermaine glanced at the wall clock again and I knew it was time to go. In an hour, he had taught me so much.

Andrew was waiting with the car and we discussed the meeting on my way back to the office and he enlightened me that the key to building a team was the inherent belief that if one persevered, they could get ahead. Bitterness came when there was favoritism or inequality.

I thought back to my days cleaning toilets at the Ho-Chunk Casino and realized he was so right. I wasn't quite sure I could accomplish everything Dr. Washington outlined. However, with Andrew's opinion, it gave me an idea that I put on paper and, after explaining all Jermaine and I discussed with Amy, I asked her to read it. I didn't know if we could implement it, but it did me good to take a swing at it. Amy put the paper down and smiled and then whispered. " Welcome, to the world of management. I love it!"

Peaks-n-Valleys:

Peaks-N-Valleys was a saying at our house my entire life. Mom would say, "You can't enjoy the view from the mountain top without the valley below." When we were young, it had no meaning. As life has progressed, it became apparent she was referring to good times and bad times and when times are good, you should never forget the bad and vice versa.

In six years, I had developed three thriving companies plus purchasing. From a total income of zero, we reached a billion dollars in sales and over $400 million in margin contribution to Wilco. With my compensation and Amelia's income, after our marriage, we created a net worth that exceeded $100 million dollars. This was on top of the two billion dollars Amelia had in her pre-marriage trust, which had also grown to nearly three billion during our time together.

The business success and the money were the peaks. The first valley was the price paid by my family and friends for not having me around very much, as I was gone to so many places and for this I will always be truly sorry. The second and deepest valley is what I am about to share.

Farming is a tough way to make a living. If Mother Nature doesn't get you, the government will. Milk price supports determine whether you make it or lose it. If you want to become a millionaire as a farmer, you better start out as a billionaire.

Dad busted his butt trying to keep the farm going. Add in the weather and all the government regulations concerning nutrition, cleanliness and even genetics, plus the cost of equipment and it's no wonder why every year there are fewer and fewer family farms. However, when it's all you know and what you really love, you keep going.

Dad was a tough guy. He had gnarled, farmer hands which were wider than they were long that could work magic with the animals, equipment and crops. Because times were tough, dad never went to the doctor, always arguing he felt fine and didn't like fingers up his butt.

As communication technology improved, dad was one of the last people to have a cellphone and never did a text in his life. For his 60th birthday mom bought him a plain cellphone, as much for her own peace of mind as his. Dad would go out and plow, plant, fertilize or harvest and when he was heading back to the barn, call mom and tell her he was on his way. This was their routine.

Because the mom-calls were the only ones he ever made, dad was always leaving the phone on the kitchen table. One spring day, dad went out to plant and mom noticed the phone was gone and it gave her a sense of security. As supper time came and went, mom thought dad was simply "putting in an extra few rows" as he called it. As dusk fell and it was becoming dark, mom called, but got no answer. Call it women's intuition, but I think mom knew something was wrong. She went out the back door and told Jake to go find dad. I think Jake sensed a problem, too, and took off to the back forty.

A few minutes later Jake was back, barking like a maniac. Mom called Tommie, who was in Mineral Point and started running out into the fields. Mom saw the tractor as it had veered to the left, but was stopped, yet still running. Mom sensed problems. As she reached the tractor cab, she looked up and saw dad slumped over the wheel with the cellphone on the floor of the cab. Dad died that day of a massive heart attack.

Mom called the rescue squad, but the fields were too wet to take the ambulance out to the tractor and it was too late anyway. They figured dad had been dead for several hours. Tommie came home and had to bring the tractor with dad still in the cab back to the barn. But then, dad would have wanted it that way.

Tommie called me, but I was in an important meeting and Cecelia had been given instructions I was not to be disturbed, except by The Duke or Amelia. Tommie called Amelia and they let me know. Like a fool, I finished the meeting and then went into my bathroom, broke down and cried.

Tommie and mom had to take care of everything. All I did was show up, like a visitor, for the funeral. Amelia came with me and it was the quietest two-hour drive of my life. Wilco sent a huge floral arrangement, which didn't go over too well as it made all the smaller arrangements look out of place and made me look like I was showing off.

Mom was devastated. Her best friend and father of her children was gone. At the wake, the comment, 'he died doing what he loved' didn't resonate too well with me. If he had taken the time or had the money to get a check-up, they would have caught the problem and the "widow maker" wouldn't have taken another life.

At the funeral, Tommie looked at me with disdain. I could sense his anger and frustration and the divide between us had deepened. I was the rich guy from Milwaukee, who didn't have time for his family and he was the farmer from Waldwick, who lost his dad. We buried dad near Grandma. Tommie made a snide remark saying I was probably planning a big headstone. The thought never crossed my mind.

Tommie married Heather the year before and Amy and I were invited to the wedding. We weren't invited to be part of the ceremony. Heather wouldn't hear of it and Tommie acquiesced. They went to the Dells for their honeymoon. I didn't offer the house in St. Martin or even an airplane ride. On our way home, I asked Amy what she thought and she said the question was not if Tommie and Heather would get a divorce, but when.

I knew mom couldn't handle the farm alone and so after a couple of months, I asked her what she wanted to do. She had been a farm girl all her life. She lived in our house for over forty years and everything centered around dad. She just shook her head.

"Things are in pretty bad shape financially" she said.

"Why didn't you say something?" I asked.

"Dad was too proud".

"How much?" I asked.

"$400,000." Mom continued with a forlorn look on her face, "When milk prices collapsed, along with those for grain and other commodities, you just couldn't turn a profit. It's not just us. It's everyone around here and that's hurting everyone in Mineral Point. The grain mill is in trouble, along with the Chevy dealer in Dodgeville and the hardware store. The tax base is eroding and even the church and schools are hurting. It's not just here, Wisconsin lost 500 dairy farms last year and another 150 have stopped milking already this year."

"What was dad doing about it?" I asked.

"He was looking into Chapter 12 bankruptcy."

"What's that?" I asked, not having a clue about accounting.

"It's a program created by Congress which allows farmers to lower their secured debt to a more affordable level." Mom replied, looking out the living room window.

"Was he making progress?" I asked.

"I don't know. You know how proud he was. Like most farmers, he didn't want any handouts."

For most people $400,000 was a lot of money. My mindset was now in the tens of millions.

"Who do you owe the money to?"

"Three banks and the government" mom said with a worried look on her face.

"Give me their names and consider it handled".

"Q, I can't let you do that!" mom said, shaking her head from side to side.

"Why?"

"Because your brother is totally against it," was her reply.

"So, he would rather lose the farm than have me help you?"

"Yes!"

"That's crazy!"

"He has some Chinese corporation who wants to buy the farm"

"What?"

"Yes, they've already purchased two others and will pay top dollar."

"Chinese? What are they going to do with our farm?"

"They say they want to create one of those dairy factories like down by Janesville."

"You mean keep the cows indoors all day and have the entire area smell like cow shit?"

Mom nodded in the affirmative.

"No way! I don't care what they offer, I'll outbid them" My testosterone level was through the roof and I had no idea who I was competing against.

"Q! I lost my husband and I don't think I can handle my two sons fighting each other."

"The farm was my home too. I want to talk to Tommie."

Mom knew it wouldn't be too pleasant, but it was arranged. Two weeks later, I went to the house and even Jake seemed cold. I rapped on the side door and walked in. Tommie, Heather and Mom were sitting in the living room waiting for me, with Heather sitting in dad's leather chair.

"Tommie, Heather, Mom" I formally said. They all nodded. "I had our accountants and lawyers look into the entire situation. The farm is losing between three and five thousand dollars a month, there isn't enough credit to get the equipment repaired and you are two years back on their property taxes."

"How much do you owe?" I asked Tommie.

"That's our problem," Tommie replied with anger in his voice.

"Well I'm still a member of the family and there is still a corporation of which I am a stockholder" I countered.

"I thought you changed your last name to Williams." Tommie retorted. All his anger and frustration were coming to a head and I was the recipient of his wrath.

"Where is your wife?" Heather seethed.

"What's she got to do with this?" I asked.

"Well, it's her money you throw around isn't it?" Heather responded, shaking her head in total animosity.

"So, that's what this is all about! I find a woman, fall in love and THEN find out she's wealthy and you think I married her for her money."

"Your fancy wedding reception and the jets and all" Heather said as her upper lip curled in disdain.

I looked at her and shook my head. "I signed a prenuptial agreement and nothing and I mean nothing, that was Amy's before we married is mine! I have busted my ass to create three viable businesses and the money we have comes from my income from those. Amy's money is in a trust for our kids."

Heather was on a roll and my retort wasn't even recognized. "Big, fancy floral arrangement just to show everyone how rich you are. "

"That was from Amy's parents. Never forget dad and Amy's dad went to football games together and talked on the phone. Amy's parents have been to this house. Amy's parents were expressing their condolences at the loss of someone they considered a friend. Because it didn't fit into your perspective, don't sit there and accuse me of being a social failure because I have more money than you do," I answered, scowling at her insubordination. "I came here to help! I came here to protect mom! I came here to save this farm from what I know is planned that will take what we all love and destroy it. If that's wrong, I'm sorry but I cannot and will not stand by and let this farm fail!" I was royally pissed!

It was Tommie's turn. "I don't want charity. "

"I'm not offering charity."

"I'm not going to work for my rich, little brother!"

"Who said you were going to work for me?"

"If you loan me the money, what do I have to do?"

"Keep farming!"

"Then the money is a gift" he sneered.

"No, the money is not a gift. There will be operational requirements put in place but the difference will be that you will be able to do what you do best ... be a very good dairy farmer and not a very bad businessman."

"What's in this for you?"

"Satisfaction!"

"What, that you showed up your older brother?"

"No! I kept the farm our ancestors started and sustained a way of life that is as pure and innocent as there is and helped our mother in her time of need".

It was the bitch's turn again. "You just want to be the big shot!"

"Heather, I've just about had enough out of you." I said in an exasperated way. "Why are you doing everything you can to divide my brother and me?"

"Because I don't like you and that wife of yours with your stupid ten acres and your stupid Indian friends." Truth be told!

I was now profoundly pissed and said, "The deal is off the table. When you go broke, I'll simply buy the place. If you think this battle is over, you are sadly mistaken. You want to see the power of money? You want to be an adversary? You got it. Mom I'm sorry, but I sincerely tried." With that, I stood, walked out the door, got in my car and headed for home. Along the way I called Cecilia and told her I needed to see Mr. Raskin from Wilco law first thing in the morning. I think she was shocked by my demeanor as, for the first time, I didn't ask, I simply told her to have it done. Ten minutes later, as I was driving past Blue Mounds, my phone rang and it was

Raskin. After the pleasantries, I told the lawyer the same thing. He said he had a conflict. I asked at what time was the conflict and he said 8:00. I told him I would be in his office at 6:00 AM. From the tone of my voice he knew this was serious.

I didn't sleep that night, which was nothing new, and arrived at Wilco law at 5:45. Raskin was already there. I outlined what had transpired and asked for guidance. He seemed reluctant.

"Do you want me to go to The Duke and get his approval?" I had never hidden behind The Duke before, but this was important.

There was a pause I didn't like, as if he was daring me … trying to show how important he was. I pulled out my phone and punched in the security code.

"Hi, dad! No Amy and the kids are fine."

I proceeded to lay everything out. "Yes sir, he's sitting right across from me," with that I handed the phone to Raskin.

"Yes, sir! Yes, sir! Yes, I understand, sir. Yes, I was not treating your son-in-law the way I should have. Yes, sir! Consider it done, sir! It won't happen again, sir!"

Raskin handed the phone back to me, but was not smiling. The Duke had ripped him a new one. Cross him off the Christmas list!

The Duke added. "Son, I liked your dad a lot and think your mother is a fine lady. Consider it handled."

"Thanks dad."

"Give my love to Amelia and the kids and I'll see you Sunday."

I intentionally repeated the message. "Yes dad, see you Sunday. Thank you."

I had Mr. Raskin's attention and made a statement, I was no longer Mr. Amelia Williams in his eyes.

Fifty Additional Miles:

It was nearly my birthday and also the anniversary of the death of Great Grandfather. I knew where I needed to go. I should have stopped when I had the meeting with Tommie, mom and that woman, but I didn't.

After work, I headed for Madison, took the south beltline and then down 18 and 51 through Verona until I was entering Mineral Point. My mind wandered the entire drive. I was on mental autopilot, even at dead man's curve, as we began to call the spot where I wiped out in my Jeep and caused so much in my life to change.

When home was Madison, I could come back to Waldwick often, to mom, dad, Jake and the forest, to wash away my frustration and rekindle my spirit. Now it was so rare! Fifty miles! Just fifty additional miles and yet they could have been 1000! When I was in college and when I met Amelia, it was all so easy. Fifty-two miles from Madison to Waldwick! Come home, go to the forest, relax, refresh and remind myself life was good.

Our marriage had added distance between my life and my other love … my forest, for which we had fought so hard to save. Just fifty additional miles! Sadly, what used to be a short jaunt, became an infrequent journey.

I looked in the rearview mirror and realized I was turning 35. 35! My God, what had I accomplished? What had I become? Would I, could I, ever come out from beneath the enormous shadow under which I had begun to live … a shadow so deep and so intense, few could escape? To many, this was the ideal life, wealth, power, love, all wrapped up in a world of finery. Yet, I felt as if I had accomplished nothing, become nothing, done nothing, but lived up to what was expected as the husband of Ms. Amelia Williams, son-in-law of Douglas, The Duke and Doctor Williams. My God, they had been good to me! My God, they treated me like the son they had lost! My God, what most men wouldn't give for half of what I had and yet there was yearning for more and simply to be me!

On those nights when just the two of us would go to dinner, Amy would sit across from me and we would look at each other and words were rarely spoken. I began to look around the restaurants to see if I could tell if it was just us or all married couples. It wasn't long until I could see those seats filled with people sitting side-by-side, smiling in each other's eyes, whispering and giggling, where every thought, word and evocation was so important … and were reserved for those who weren't married. Alone together, alone apart, sitting, staring, wondering, wanting to peer into our phones for any respite … that was marriage. I made a vow and promised the hole in my heart would not be filled by another. My only hope was that Amelia felt the same way.

For my birthday, Amy knew I only wanted to do one thing … to visit the forest. I needed to go home to my primeval enclave and clear my head. It had been a few months since dad's funeral and two since I went to visit Tommie and mom and didn't have time to go into the forest. I made my way down Shake Rag Street and out to Waldwick. Heather and Mom were at work and Tommie was in the fields. It had been a late spring and he still had planting to do.

As I pulled up next to the house, my buddy Jake saw me and his head rose up from his spot in the shady spot on the floor of the screen porch. Age was taking its toll and my buddy was relegated to the porch for his own good. I opened the door and Jake had a doggie smile upon his face. Just like Old Ed in what George the First had written, there was a bond between Jake and me that went so deep as to intersect each other's heart and soul.

"Wanna go to the forest?" I asked my canine friend.

Slowly he arose and tried to walk over to me. His tail slowly wagged hello. It was a sad wag as we both knew it wouldn't be long until he would be up on the hill with all those who meant so much to our family.

There was no way he could walk the mile out and back and so I knew it would mean a ride in the cart behind the ATV.

"You stay here little buddy. I'll come and get you." Either he understood or was simply too weak to follow. I went to the barn and hooked up the cart to the ATV, put an old blanket in the bottom for a bed and came back to the house and picked up my little buddy and gently placed him in the cart. I took it slow and looked back to watch the gleam in his eyes for he knew where we were going and I knew it meant as much to him as it did to me.

We went back to the forest amongst the trees where I hoped they would whisper to me simply the answer to my question, "Why"? Why had so much which had been so good, gone awry? Why had I, who had been such a free spirit, become enmeshed in the tangle root of commerce, forgetting the feeling of freedom? I looked up at my ancient friends, but there were no answers, only the whispers of melancholy. How sad, incredibly sad, to have everything, but nothing, to sit and stand amongst the oaks and allow tears of remorse to stream down my cheeks and not know why.

Jake and I slowly walked to where the Skunk Hollow school foundation had been. Even in the early evening darkness, I could see the moss had tumbled yet another stone from the withering foundation, relishing yet another morsel of yesterday into anonymity … slipping it, sliding it from its abode where it had stood for nearly 200 years.

I quietly walked to where ashes-to-ashes had been mixed with dust, when all that mattered was tomorrow. I wandered to the spot I had chosen to have a small obelisk with the two feathers on the brass plaque placed within the ground and my mind swung back to a time so long ago and wondered was I really Little Spirit.

In reality, what had I done? What had I accomplished? What allowed me to sustain the power and the integrity invested in me when I had given so little and taken so much for such a long, long time? I stood in the silence of singularity wondering whether Great Grandfather's trust in me would come again. The stoic silence was deafening. The calm air enveloped me in melancholy. I needed a sign ... something, anything to remind me of all that was bestowed. No one had ever come to visit me since that day so long ago when Grandfather's spirit was lifted into the heavens and there were no signs. Perhaps I was oblivious, caught up in the maelstrom of achievement where goals were measured in dollars and not in lives. Had I become so introspective in the concept of me, I had overlooked the entity called we?

A full moon rose and I stood by the small brass marker, illuminated only by the moonlight, I saw him from the corner of my eye. Could it be? Was it really the deer of so long ago? As I gazed at him, he gazed at me and there was tranquility. The still leaves of the trees began to rustle, although there was no breeze. For the first time in ten years I felt the spirit and knew my destiny stood before me. This was to be my legacy! This was to be why God brought me home. Once again, I was to become a warrior, a proud brave willing to do battle against wrong in the name of right. But what was wrong? What about answers about how and when and most of all why?

I walked to where the water dribbled from Mother Earth and cupped my hands. The cold, clear liquid, so resplendent with purity, sanctified all that had been. Once again, I was baptized in the name of the Father, Son and Holy Spirit.

Humility, generosity, compassion and forgiveness ... forgotten for so long, rushed back through every cell in my body, flooding me with the intensity for the good I had once relished. How did I ever forget? Why had I gone astray? Would my journey take me back? Could I make amends to all whose lives I touched in an indecent way? "Our father who art in heaven, forgive me, for I have journeyed far and only ask guidance to the path of righteousness." I fell to my knees and caressed the spot where

Amy and I consecrated our commitment to each other. My Amy! Would she, could she ever forgive me? Could I ever forgive and forget her transgression or stop blaming myself for their existence? My hand covered my eyes and I could hear her laugh. I breathed deep and could smell her scent. My God how could I have been so wrong?

I turned and looked at the trees watching me, judging me, wondering where I had been. The feelings of long ago, so conveniently forgotten, came rushing forward as I trembled in the mystic madness realizing I had transcended and was becoming spiritual.

I walked back to the clearing as the white light of the moon ricochet off the dark earth, pointing fingers at the blackness in my heart. Were these scars? Was this nothing more than a road map to show me all the places I had been where goodness should have been happened?

Moonlight:

As Jake and I returned to the spot where George the First saved Rodney's Great, Great, Great, Great grandmother's life, I saw him. At first, I didn't recognize who it was and then I realized it was the Ho-Chunk Medicine Man, except his hair was totally white! Chills traversed my body!

"The Great Father said you would come tonight!" he said without looking up at me. "The Great Father is calling you home! Little Spirit, your time has come!" With that he looked at me. My surprise must have caught him off guard, when I realized his face was covered with paint. I hoped it wasn't war paint. It was not.

He had aged and yet the gentle smile that only comes from internal peace radiated from his lips and put my mind at rest. This kind, gentle, man had come to help me, for which I would always be grateful.

Rodney taught me long ago that Native Americans considered the Medicine Man to be a priest and healer; a spiritual leader who could control natural forces. I learned that the word medicine means "mystery" to Native Americans. They did not address their spiritual leader as "Medicine Man," but more as a deity or Great Spirit, willing and able to impart wisdom on those who would open their minds and heart to what he shared. I stood in awe of his presence and the aura that surrounded him. I was praying his appearance meant resolution from the demons within my heart as emotionally, I was walking on egg shells when it came to Amelia and her leukemia, our marriage, my job and the farm. While it was a warm night, chills percolated through my body, shaking my soul and making me afraid of tomorrow, unlike any time before in my life!

I knew that the Medicine Man sensed my turmoil and said, "Sit with me," as I sat on the edge of the remainder of the ancient Skunk Hollow school foundation. "You are the chosen one! I will abide" he said. "The spirits have spoken to me and instructed me to teach you all that I can about our life," he said as I shook my head in agreement with Jake nestled next to me.

The Medicine Man took a stick and made two marks in the soft Earth … "We all have the same two points … our birth and our death. It is the path we follow between these points which matters most and our belief in the consequence of our existence. Along that path, we need to develop many things … a concept of self, in terms of our relationship with others; a concept of right and wrong, and therefore good and bad and finally a concept of permanence and our temporal existence, which is where our spirituality lies."

The gentle man looked down at me and his words surprised me. "I have read the Bible many times Little Spirit, and always hold it to my heart when I read the Old Testament, especially the Book of Wisdom. I did not need to memorize these words, because they have been placed within my soul and here is what the Book of Wisdom says …"

"Resplendent and unfading is Wisdom, and she is readily perceived by those who love her and found by those who seek her. She hastens to make herself known in anticipation of their desire; whoever watches for her at dawn shall not be disappointed, for he shall find her sitting by his gate. For taking thought of Wisdom is the perfection of prudence and whoever, for her sake, keeps vigil, shall quickly be free from care; because Wisdom makes her own rounds, seeking those worthy of her and graciously appears to them in the ways and meets them with all solicitude."

The Medicine Man continued his biblical oratory, looking once again, deep within my soul. *"What wisdom is and how she was born, I shall now explain; I shall hide no mysteries from you, but shall follow her steps from the outset of her origin, setting out what we know of her in full light, without departing from the truth. Envy is no companion for me, for envy has nothing in common with Wisdom. Within the greatest number of the wise, lies the world's salvation; in a sagacious king, the stability of a people. Learn, therefore, from my words and the gain will be yours."*

I sat, incredulous. The Medicine Man had evoked an entire passage from the Bible aimed directly at me.

He beckoned me to follow and I stood and began walking, stopping at great Grandfather's memorial. The Medicine Man looked down and bowed his head in reverence to the man who had preceded him. "Great Grandfather has instructed me to teach you the spiritual way of our people and I have come for you, "Little Spirit". Who selected this spot for the marker of the eagle feathers? He asked.

"I did," I replied.

"Why did you choose this spot?"

"Because it felt like the right spot to honor Great Grand Father." I replied.

With that, he nodded in the affirmative and stretched his left arm out to point me in the direction he wanted to go. "Come let's walk to where the water is pure. You must count your steps as we make our way."

I thought this was an odd command and yet did as I was instructed…."One, two, three…." I continued until I neared the mouth of the spring and my last step echoed the number 35. Chills ran up my spine!

"How old are you little spirit?"

"35!" I answered.

"And so, you placed the marker exactly 35 steps from the springs?"

I nodded in the affirmative even though there had been no consideration.

"If you were to walk from where life springs from the earth, back to the marker, do you believe you would also walk 35 steps?"

"Yes! Of course!" I replied.

"Do you see your footprints in the soft ground?"

"Yes"

"Let's walk back to the marker and count your footprints."

As we walked, I counted and was amazed…there were only 31! I had counted out loud and yet four steps were missing! I shook my head.

"Let's walk back to the springs and count your steps again!" the Medicine Man instructed.

"One, two, three….35!" How could I have 35 steps towards the springs, but only 31 going back? I glanced at the Great Spirit with a perplexed look.

The Medicine Man looked deeply into my eyes. "Did you ever learn about the senses of your body that allow you to realize where you are?"

"Sure! … Sight, hearing, taste, touch and smell!" I replied.

"How many is that?"

"Five!"

Quickly doing the math, I added them to 31 and arrived at 36. Either my math was bad or this wasn't what he was talking about.

"It is through the five senses we create a perception which allows us to realize not only where we are, but who we are, yet we take them for granted, unless they are gone," the Medicine Man stated.

"But we are only missing four." I reiterated.

He smiled and continued. "There are many other senses such as temperature, pain, balance, vibration, hunger and thirst, but those are just physical. Your perception was there when you walked to the springs, but, as you can see, your perception was missing, as you walked to the spot you selected to honor Great Grandfather. My people believe there are four additional senses … the sense of being, belonging, purpose and the sense of humor. These are not autonomic responses, nor intellectual, nor do they come about from reasoning. These responses manifest themselves only in the spiritual self, which can lead to our one true goal – happiness, not only for ourselves, but for others. To become Little Spirit, you must gain these four senses which will culminate in a true sense of being. From that sense of being, you will then be able to accept the fact that God has placed you here to do good for many people and not just my people and make life better."

The Medicine Man stopped and looked right at me. "You, Little Spirit, are like a whirling dervish. You have so much energy and yet, you never stop to think about what has transpired. There is a method called mindfulness, which I believe will help you better understand who you are."

My look must have given away that I had no idea what he was talking about. The Medicine Man looked deep within my soul again and said, "while I am the Medicine Man within the Ho-Chunk Nation, I also have a regular job outside our world."

My look of surprise must have motivated him to continue. "I am a clinical psychologist".

Now I was really taken aback.

"Mindfulness is about achieving peace within yourself by being present in the moment and looking at your thoughts with self-compassion instead of judgement. You, Little Spirit have spent the last few years judging yourself, doing everything you possibly could to prove to yourself and only yourself, you are worthy of all you have … money, power and love … things most people strive for their entire lives and never acquire."

"If I can teach you one thing tonight, it must be a method that will allow you to let go and become comfortable with what is happening in your world! While this sounds like an easy task, it is not. In fact, how you view and react to your own thoughts is an extremely challenging task that will take time and practice to achieve."

"Please, sit on the ground," he directed, as I sat down. "Close your eyes and begin to notice each breath as you inhale and exhale. When a thought enters your mind, notice it and bring your focus back to your breathing and let the thought go, doing so without judging, dissecting or acting on it."

The Medicine Man continued, "To practice mindfulness is actually quite simple. First, breathe deeply through your nose while counting from one to four. Next exhale through either your nose or mouth while counting backwards from four to one. While you are doing this, focus on the change in your stomach and chest as the air comes in and goes out. See how simple it is! Now repeat the process five-to-ten times focusing on your breath while you erase all other thoughts. Relax! Relax! Relax!"

I breathed deeply and a sense of relaxation began to take over my body. As thoughts entered, I did as was told and attempted to erase all beyond the breathing. At first, my thoughts were about what was happening and then Great Grandfather, then they turned to Amy and how she had explained the beauty and value of Wim-Hof and the Japanese forest bathing, whose name I had forgotten long ago. Soon, my mind was clearing and all that transpired was my breathing… in, hold, count-to-four, out! In, hold, count-to-four, out! In, hold count-to-four, out! I could feel the tension evaporating from my body and with it the stress of life.

The Medicine Man added, "The goal is to focus on the events of your life as they truly are, instead of ruminating about what could have been or what might still be. From this, you will begin to achieve internal peace, which helps both the body and the mind and may be especially beneficial for people like you who are under tremendous levels of stress, simply because they can't accept their achievements and wonder why it is all happening to them."

He continued, "The practice of mindfulness has been a part of our culture since time began. Mindfulness has shown it can actually slow the aging process simply because you will be rewiring your brain to support present-moment awareness, while weakening pathways which make you contemplate things that are normal and natural, yet beyond your control."

I did as I was told as he stood in total silence watching me begin to relax. Within a few minutes, I was at peace. The Medicine Man reached down and grabbed my hand and helped me up. We paused for a moment face-to-face and then proceeded to the springs as Jake slowly walked ahead and licked the cold, clear water as if it were a tonic. I could sense the energy entering his body as his curved back became straight and his tail began slowly wagging. For a short instant, it was as if he were three again, instead of nearly fifteen.

We each took a long drink from the cold spring and it was different than ever before. We looked in each other's eyes and the Medicine Man's head tilted towards the sky. He was seeking wisdom and the ability to speak from the heart. For the first time in a long, long time, I felt the peace that had been eroded by my own insecurities. Tears streamed from my eyes. It was like having a long, lost friend suddenly appear with a smile of acceptance on their face and I knew, I really, really knew right then and there, that I had returned to the place that meant so much to me and had done so, not only physically, but spiritually, as well.

We went to a fallen log and the Medicine Man had me sit again. With clear mind, I was to be his student and he, the teacher, as he added, "Little Spirit, today you are confused and disappointed with life. All the dreams you had, have not turned to reality. What you thought was forever, was only the beginning. You are still moving from being a boy to becoming a man. If you are to be a great leader, you must realize this is normal and all that is happening is a part of life. Your wife loves you, but in a different way. The winds that blew away her memories on her island, where she went to heal, have left an open wound upon her heart you need to mend. To do this, and become the man Great Grandfather knew you would, you must understand your spirit. You were not named Little Spirit on a whim. You have been chosen to transcend from a mere mortal to a one capable of leading many people and doing much good."

There was a slight smile on the Medicine Man's face as he continued, "I know you are troubled. I know you have many questions you want answered. You are not alone, Little Spirit, as long as man has been able to escape his here-and-now in both time-and-space, the questions of who, what and why, have always lingered."

The Medicine Man continued, "I have studied many things in my life… anatomy, physiology, psychology, philosophy and the great religions of the world. I have taken what I have learned and blended it with the history and beliefs of my people. In doing this, I believe I am a better person, a better man, a better husband, a better father and a better friend to all who have befriended me. I now share with you, my learning with the hope that what you hear will become what you feel and what you feel will allow you to lead not only our people, but all people to greater happiness."

I sat, feeling totally overwhelmed. All Great Grandfather said would happen, was about to begin.

The Medicine Man began again," While the science of the human body is based on, for the most part, cause-and-effect, the perceptions of human existence are not. Instead, we end up with many different ideas that are not a soliloquy, but a symphony; not a mandate, but a set of alternatives; done so, not as fact, but as an interpretation from which one and one alone can deduce their own conclusions. I will share with you my thoughts and my interpretation of our beliefs. You must take them and add them to your own. When you have mixed the stew of righteousness, you will become a great man who understands what goodness means to all."

And so, the Medicine Man began. "Beliefs of my people were shared for generations by simply verbally passing them to each generation, adding-or-subtracting, increasing-or-decreasing thoughts and values to fit their needs. So too was the case of the white man. I quoted the Bible and yet wonder what the books removed by the church centuries ago reflect?"

I sat feeling profoundly inadequate as the Medicine Man outlined things in my own religion, I did not know and continued, "What was written has been controlled by man and not by God. It is based on man's interpretation. As an example, Roman Catholic and Orthodox Christians include all the Apocrypha in the Bible, except for the two books of Esdras and the Prayer of Manasseh. Beyond that, there is even a rumor there was a book for Mary and perhaps, somewhere it says that Jesus was married. Man has interpreted what happened and altered it to fit their own beliefs and conclusions. Mary of Magdalene is a classic example, as it wasn't until Pope Gregory determined she was a prostitute, that the subject ever arose."

I shook my head in disbelief. I sat before a man of a different faith who was teaching me more about my own religion than I ever thought or knew and the Medicine Man continued. "In order to understand the profound premise of the philosophies of the spiritual self, one needs to understand all that has transpired and you must realize so much of what has happened to man has taken place simply because of man's concept of himself and how he relates to others!"

The Medicine Man beckoned me to look up as I followed his eyes into the night sky. "Come with me, back to the time of the Greeks and their concept of introspection regarding where humans fit in. From Plato and Aristotle, through all the great thinkers, the question has always remained "Why?" Is this not the question you asked yourself as you drove here tonight?"

Shivers ran up my spine. How did he know that?

The Medicine Man looked at me and added, "While I am an Indian, I live in the white man's world. While we have our beliefs, like the wind and snow, I cannot stop how the world has changed and melded my people into what we are today. While my ancestors were not unified and worshiped many Gods, the white man's evolution of human spiritual philosophy has moved from a disorganized set of beliefs to a structure that binds mankind today to moral and ethical values which establish right-and-wrong and good-and-bad, many of which my people have also followed."

A slight smile crossed his lips as he pondered his next words. "As we sit here tonight, we are not alone and are certainly not limited to what lies within ourselves. The energy of our body does not stop at our skin. It is an aura that radiates beyond ourselves that we, as individuals, must be comfortable with. This energy is neither fixed, nor stagnant, but vacillates like the ocean's waves upon the shore and can be transferred to another being. Your love of your dog has given him new energy. Likewise, this energy transfer can come from any other body… the sun, earth and even the air… things my people have believed forever. You see, while we did not have those who wrote it down, we have accepted, for thousands of years, the belief that what individuals consume to create their own energy, is a method of energy transference available from one entity to another."

The Medicine Man crouched before me and petted Jake's head. "While it is our assumption this energy is exclusive to man, the fact is, this marvelous transition happens to all bodies alive and inert, to the point where each entity accepts or repels the pulsations of others in the form of harmonic existence, vacillating with the circumstance. Listen to the birds as they call to each other. Watch as a leaf responds to your touch and you can see the energy of all living things acting and reacting to changes! See how the wind erodes the sand. The gravestones in your cemetery are but two hundred years old and yet, the wind has smoothed them, erasing the name of the person whose body was transformed."

My teacher stopped petting Jake, rose and looked down at me. "Energy pulsates to address any spectrum of imbalance and returns it to tranquility! It doesn't stop with living beings! We obtain energy from what we consume and the vitamins and minerals which are stored in what we eat. This, Little Spirit, is the first lesson you must learn! Life is about the energy within us, around us, between us and it is the sharing of that energy which can make a man great! For some the aura will not be noticeable, for those who have harnessed their internal energy, the aura can be spellbinding and life changing for those who come in contact with those who have a profound aura, which is something Little Spirit, you must attain."

The Medicine Man was now expounding and, as had been the case with Great Grandfather, there was no need for note taking. What he was saying was going to both my brain and my heart.

"Lucretius, the Roman philosopher noted, like the stump upon which you sit, wood decayed. Yet, the seed of that stump has grown into another oak tree, made of similar wood as the wood which has already decayed."

The Medicine Man put his hand on my shoulder. "Lucretius basic question was: "Why has everything in the world not yet decayed and how can the same materials, plants, animals be recreated again and again? Lucretius placed man in the same group as everything else … carbon based … and therefore, he argued, there was no reason to think the Earth or mankind occupied a central place in the scheme of things. He concluded man therefore, was no different than all other living things and this must be your second lesson. We are all just a part of everything, no greater, nor any less and we must respect all that is around us with piety and equity, nothing greater, nothing less."

I watched as the Medicine Man's eyes dug deeply into my soul, searching for a spot to deposit his wisdom. "Lucretius postulated, that time does not have limits. Time isn't something with a beginning and an end and therefore no fixed points, no references and certainly no limits."

Slowly, the Medicine Man removed his hand from my shoulder and looked off into the distance. "Lucretius belief was there was no single moment of origin and all livings things evolved through trial and error, over a period of millions of years, not from a period of peace and tranquility, but from millennia filled with primal battles for survival which manifested itself in the core craving for one thing … security … to live in peace. Something mankind has incorrectly postulated could be enhanced through greater wealth, fame and power. In so stating, Lucretius proposed the universe was not created for or about humans and his entire theory matches that of my people … we are just passengers along for the ride like everything else and someday mankind and Earth shall perish."

I leaned back and took what he had said in and melded it into my heart, bowing my head in reverence to the thoughts he had evoked. The Medicine Man looked at Jake and then at me and continued. "With this core tenant, my people's beliefs completely match with those of the Greeks and those of your faith. Human beings should simply conquer their fears and accept the fact they, and all things they encounter, are temporary and transitory … composites of energy, temporal in nature … beings who consume energy until they too shall become an energy source for something else."

I sat quietly listening and a profound feeling of humility enveloped my body as he continued, "In so doing Lucretius noted, people should embrace the beauty and magnificence of the world and accept that a world in motion is a world not rendered insignificant, but made more beautiful by its transience, energy and ceaseless change, where the sum was, is and will always be the same… zero! This is the next important lesson you must learn Little Spirit. To acquire wealth for the sake of wealth does nothing, means nothing and accomplishes nothing, unless it is used to make the world better in some way."

The Medicine Man's hands slipped to his sides and his palms opened … "Finally, it was Lucretius' position, as it is my people, that wonder and therefore religion, does not depend on gods or demons and the dream of an afterlife. Like the seas and the stars and all living beings, including human existence, everything is made from the same components and we are no greater nor less than anything else. Lucretius believed gods were meaningless and people are without any form of soul that would carry on, after life itself had departed, because all energy would be transferred to some other form."

I was about to interrupt and disagree, but the Medicine Man poked his finger into the night and continued … "If this point is accepted, there could be profound ramifications, because all the concepts of heaven and hell would be dissipated and with them the premises of good and bad and right and wrong, for there would be no consequence. With Lucretius realization came the acceptance that all humans and all living beings have only one life and one existence and nothing more, which is something you, me and our people completely disagree with."

"Lucretius stated 'Death is nothing to us. When you are dead and the particles that have been linked together to create and sustain you, come apart, there will be neither pleasure nor pain, longing nor fear, it will simply be over!' We all believe this is true for the body, but not the spirit. The spirit lives on in all those who follow."

I was beginning to understand the logic as he continued … "From this, Lucretius stated …'The same passage you made from death-to-life, without feeling or fright, you will make again from life-to-death. Your death is part of the order of the universe; it is part of the life of the world. Death is nothing to us. To spend your existence in the grip of anxiety about death, is mere folly. It is a sure way to let your life slip from you, incomplete and un-enjoyed."

Now my head was shaking in the affirmative as the Medicine Man continued ... "Our people believe that, while living, we absorb and then, when we are no longer a receptor, we simply become a source of energy for other components ... ashes-to-ashes, dust-to-dust, with or without the remaining soul. Great Grandfather's ashes have mixed with the soil to give life to something else. His spirit has risen and yet his soul is here today, sitting with us, listening, watching, sharing and caring about you and me and the people whose lives we touch! You must believe he is here, Little Spirit, if you are to become the spiritual one. You must also accept that one day you and I shall move on. With this premise in hand, can you then see there are no dividing lines ... no marks in the sand ... no points of reference between who and what we are in relationship to all other elements ... only degrees of density?"

Once again, my head shook in the affirmative and asked, "The big question then becomes ... where did the atoms came from?" The Medicine Man smiled, realizing that his point had my rapt attention. No one had ever spoken to me like this as he continued ... "Immanuel Kant asked how the universe could be explained through some sort of cause, when it embraces all causes. He noted 'that which causes all, cannot itself have a cause.' In the end, everything is simply a form of energy which is either consuming or eliciting. Even today with all our knowledge, Einstein's theory regarding energy and matter are interchangeable and have never been refuted."

"Little Spirit, when humans focus their energy, they gain more power than when it is dissipated, for better or worse. Sadly, our minds are normally most focused when we are angry, upset, afraid or worried, which are all antithesis of spirituality. Tying spirituality to health, we can conclude anything that enhances a sense of intimacy, community or connection, with any form of living being, which then makes us feel like we are part of something larger than here and now, will make us happier than being alone and isolated."

His face was but a few inches from mine and his eyes glowed with wisdom... "As you can see, Little Spirit, this entire philosophical exercise has no end. The spiritual self is the establishment of relationships from man-to-man and God-to-man.

Through man's belief in something greater than himself, God is reflected in his relative position within the absolute order, not only of mankind, but the universe as well. In so doing, spirituality takes into consideration all forms of these relationships by creating a set of parameters which address right-from-wrong, good-from-bad and what is expected by our family, society, culture and God."

I was being overwhelmed and made to feel incredibly inadequate as the Medicine Man continued, "The spiritual self goes beyond the rational self to address those questions of "why" the Greeks pondered so long ago. Why do I exist? Why must I act the way I do to be accepted? Why am I doing what I do and for how long will I do it? Finally, what are the consequences of my actions? You must understand goodness begins and ends with giving ... of oneself, so those whose lives you touch are better."

"This is the final point you must accept. We are all here physically just once and we must make the most of it for ourselves and for others. We must bring good to the Earth and our fellow living beings and from this, our spirit shall continue for eternity. When our time comes to join Great Grandfather and all those who came before us, we must open our arms and accept the fact and ask ourselves ... will I be fondly remembered and truly missed?"

As he looked off into the woods, the Medicine Man summarized all that he had said. "Tonight, there are many thoughts swirling in your head. In the stillness of one, you will need to reflect upon yourself and see these consequences. You must ponder who you are and delve into your spiritual self to create a form of manifest destiny which provides a pathway to the accomplishment of a single objective … true happiness … not only your own happiness, but that of others, whose lives you touch, by determining a physical, mental, emotional and rational sense of wellbeing!"

"I sense your sadness! I feel your frustration! I understand your loneliness and yet, I also see beyond the horizon that this was what Great Grandfather needed you to see, yet feel the journey you are about to begin will have more meaning and more value than you can imagine. It is only when you are deep within the valley that the mountain tops look the highest. It is only in the darkest hours that the first rays of sunlight have meaning. You will climb that mountain! You will see the brightest sunlight and, in the end, you will have the power and strength Great Grandfather saw in you. It will not come easy! It will not take place in a few days, weeks, months, or years, but it will happen!"

He turned and looked directly at me again, "The critical precursor is that life and happiness are already within you and are readily available. It is only the question of learning how and when and where to open up your life to broader horizons that will allow you to reach a higher plane of individual, social and spiritual security and satisfaction so that you have a more profound sense of wellbeing and consequence."

Shivers of fear went up my spine. The Medicine Man looked at me and asked a rhetorical question, "How does one achieve a sense of wellbeing?"

Once again, he answered his own question … "What are our boundaries? Where does our personal aura end? Or does it? At what point have we traversed beyond what is considered normal? How do we, as social animals, create and maintain a set of parameters by which we can interact with those around us from whom we need acceptance and social approval? These are question we must all answer and from this we will develop our own conscience."

"What is conscience?" I asked.

There was a pause as the sound of an owl filled the still night air.

Without directly answering my inquiry, the Medicine Man said, "Come let's drink again from the spring."

As we dipped our hands in the cold water, he looked at me and said. "The second phase of transition revolves around the people you meet who open their hearts and share their innermost thoughts and emotions. Thomas Kuhn's book, '*The Structure of Scientific Revolution*' points out that all humans have a really difficult time dealing with infinity and the universe due to its extreme complexity and profound vastness. What people do to fathom this concept, is reduce it down into smaller segments or portions to the point they develop theories, structures and opinions of the world that Kuhn calls paradigms which he defined as 'universally recognized scientific achievements that, for a time, provide model problems and solutions for a community of practitioners. Such things as a flat world or the Earth being the center of the universe, were all paradigms that now seem quite quaint. However, when people were burned at the stake by the church, for believing in something which was not popular, it became quite serious, especially to them."

I was instructed to close my eyes and think of infinity. It was a difficult task and then it was there! The Medicine Man continued, "First were the stars and the space between. Where did they come from? How did all of this start? No matter where you stop, you can keep going back and back and back to yet another source to the point of incomprehension and wonder where it all began."

I leaned back and thought of Amelia and how she opened my eyes to the Caribbean, not only the warm weather and the sun, but the stars, sand and all she had endured which healed her body and her mind. I read an article about astronauts who said space was a religious experience that makes one realize how small we all really are and how great the universe really is. We think of stars only at night and yet, in boy scouts, we took the tube which paper towels came wrapped on and pointed it at the daytime sky and saw the stars were there, even during the daylight. Our scout leader noted "God wasn't only there in our hours of darkness, but on our brightest days as well."

The Medicine Man sat with Jake's head in his lap and continued, "I was once an alcoholic. As my life began unraveling, I took time to study the primary religions of the world to learn what lies at their roots. In all instances, there is a God or supreme being. In all instances there is a focus on the unexplained, which revolves around death and what happens after we die. Most primary religions came from some sort of myth or story shared from generation to generation. Christians, Muslim's, Hindus and Buddhists all believe in a life hereafter that will be determined by what we do during this life. The beginning of time almost always is perceived as a point when great chaos achieves a sense of order, such as in the Hindu religion. Some religions believe that, with an infinite past and an infinite future, there would be no beginning. The Bible differs from most religions in that there was an absence of an initial state as is outlined in the Book of Genesis."

There was a gentle smile on the Medicine Man's face as he added, "Christians believe they will lie in waiting for the return of Christ. Muslims believe if you have lived by the faith, you will go to heaven. Hindu's feel you will be reincarnated over and over and over until you lead a good life where you will be finally freed to go to heaven. Buddha taught that you are reincarnated and are a basically good and it is your errors in life which determine if you need to have a do-over. My people believe goodness comes from the spirit of life."

I looked at the night sky as the Medicine Man continued, "What is remarkable is all the religions seem to teach the same four basic tenants ... humility, generosity, compassion and forgiveness, as personified through their prophets ... Jesus, Moses, Mohammed, Buddha or whomever. In all cases, their lives and their teachings center around these basic elements. Can you see all religions are formalized interpretations set down by people? There is no direct communication with some form of omnipotent being, even for me! I feel things, but there are never conversations."

He continued, "Lucretius concluded all religions were superstitious delusions where humans projected concepts of power, beauty and security that they aspired to achieve. Humans created gods to personalize those aspirations. Everyone is subject to feelings that generate dreams which wash over them when they look up at the stars and start imagining beings of immeasurable power or when they wonder if the universe has any limits. We all marvel at the exquisite order of things or experience an uncanny string of misfortunes and wonder if we are being punished. My people do not believe this, nor in my heart do I think you do either. You are a man of faith and from that faith there is the goodness I can feel ... goodness that will allow you to give to the world what God has chosen for you and why Great Grandfather realized you truly are Little Spirit."

There were tears in my eyes ... tears of joy, tears of excitement and tears of regret about so many things and yet there was hope, hope that all the Medicine Man said was true and my life did have a purpose, direction and meaning which would make life fulfilling to not only me, but those whose life I touched.

The Medicine Man stood and looked down at me. "You are called Little Spirit for a reason and I hope you understand spirituality is the quest to discover that which is sacred to all people. Do not look for a meaning to the word. Spirituality is a sense of awe, a sense of wonder, a sense of profound unity with the universe that can only happen when we sincerely feel what is transpiring is good ... good for us ... good for others ... and good for the universe in which all beings live."

"Little Spirit you are at an apex where you will change, then and only then, will your spiritual self be at rest. Then and only then, will there be a fulfillment of your dreams! Then and only then will the tranquility of self-satisfaction permeate all that lies within you so that you bask in a realm of contentment, bathe in the cool water of internal peace and know your being has purpose and true meaning."

"From your spirit will come character predicated on the establishment of a set of criteria based on one profound aspect ... Respect! For others! For all things great and small, to which a person is both dominant and subservient! But most importantly, respect of yourself, which, I hope you now realize, has been profoundly lacking. You are a man with the potential for great character that begins when the little things in life are tested, revealed and further developed by the decisions you make in the most challenging times. It doesn't come from following a set of rules, regardless of who has made them, but from the small acts of responsibility you take upon yourself every single day."

"In order to have spiritual character, you must know right and wrong and choose what is right. This is how character is developed. By facing tough decisions and choosing the right ones because you are honest, forgiving, trustworthy, understanding, reasonable, thoughtful and individually accountable for your actions, so that you act in a way which is important enough to be right. In the end, it's not what we do, but how we do it, that really matters!"

We stood by the springs as the Medicine Man continued. "Our spiritual character, is the sum of our personal integrity, where integrity is doing what we do when no one is watching and doing the right thing even when we could get away with something that is wrong. Spiritual integrity is critical to every single thing we do because it is the foundation of trust in our own eyes and those around us. If you do not have personal integrity, you cannot truly love yourself or others. This then, is what is formulated in our spiritual self ... that point in our brain which understands right from wrong, good from bad and inhibits our transgressions."

"The beauty of spiritual integrity is that it is blind to all other things ... age, wealth, fame or social circumstance. From the moment you were born, only you have been able to determine whether you will be a person of integrity and it is not something to which there are levels ... either you have it, or you don't. You, Little Spirit, can garner profound spiritual integrity simply by changing from within. However, this means you must first recognize and admit you need to change. This is a profoundly difficult thing to do. Few sane people believe what they are doing is wrong, even when it is. There is always some justification for our actions to make it right within our own mind and this is what makes it so difficult."

"At the end of the day, it's not your reputation which matters, it is what you honestly, sincerely and, in an unbiased manner, think of yourself. It is your spiritual self that will make the decision. All any religion does is create a conscience. I see a great battle that lies ahead which will take all of your strength and all of your stamina. This battle will rage for many years. In the end, it will be your character against the power of others. I do not know if you will win the battle. I do know the Great Spirit has put you on this Earth as a mighty warrior. However, like Great Grandfather, I also believe you will do your best for all those whose lives you touch. Little Spirit, the time has come. Walk with me and count the steps."

There were 35 steps back to the little marker and tears in my opened eyes. Great Grandfather had come forth through the Medicine Man to teach me ... to move me ... to help me understand life is not about getting, but about giving. Darkness was upon us and yet, the world before me was bright. My eyes were opened wide and I knew my role was not to be Mr. Amelia Williams, it was to take what was good and make it better.

I slowly stood as the Medicine Man put his hands on my shoulder. I looked at Jake. He had departed and joined Great Grandfather. My dearest friend! My little buddy had gone home! There were more tears and yet I knew he was in heaven! Slowly I carried my little buddy back to the cart in which we had come, where he loved to ride. I turned to say goodbye to the Medicine Man, but he was gone, nothing more than a shadow amongst the trees on a cold spring night.

The Farm House:

I made my way back to the farm house deep within my thoughts. It was nearing midnight and yet the lights were still on. Farmers don't stay up late as milking always comes early.

I walked to the front door and knocked. This was no longer my house or our house, but mom's house. My brother, from whom I was estranged, was in bed resting up for another day. Mom opened the door and a weak smile came to her face. I looked at her and she at me and she saw the tears in my eyes and felt the sadness in my heart. Mom knew Jake was gone. I held out my hand and she grasped my arm and pulled me into her grasp. The sobs came as I wretched the anger and hate which had accumulated day-after-day, week-after-week, year-after-year within my soul about my brother, about how distant I had become, about dad's funeral and all.

"I'm sorry!" I whispered to which there was no reply. Mom just held me and let me cry until the sorrow within me had run its course. This was her way of sharing my sorrow about Jake. Nothing else had changed.

Finally, I pulled back, looked her in the eye and repeated, "I'm sorry!"

Mom opened the door further and I stepped into yesterday. Like an old pair of well-worn jeans, I slid into familiarity and the memories came crashing down, smothering me in what had been. I took a deep breath as mom pointed to the couch with nary a word said. I slid down upon the soft brown leather and allowed its warmth to envelop my sadness. Mom turned and walked into the kitchen. I sat with my head in my hands, wallowing in regret that I had allowed so little become so much.

When mom returned with a glass of water, I said, "Thanks, Mom". It had been so long, so very, very long and there was so much to say of calls and visits not made and Christmas cards not written … of days and events and circumstances when we should have been together. Instead we sat in total silence, alone, engulfed in everything.

I drank the water and asked to use the bathroom. It was now her, Tommie and Heather's house! She nodded and I made my way to where I had been a thousand times before and, once again, the memories rushed back, exploding in my mind, filling me with sentimentality. I did what I had to do and turned to wash my hands. As I did, I looked in the mirror and stared at what was looking back. How could it be? It wasn't me! That night, my brown hair had turned silver white! It was still my face peering back. In an instant, I had changed. Was it the forest? Was it the deer? Was it my profound sense of remorse? My trembling hands went through my mane and it was real. This was not an illusion. I closed my eyes and Great Grandfather stood before me smiling. I heard him whisper. "Little Spirit, your time has come". My hand slid to my mouth and I realized that all which had been told was about to come true.

I walked out into the living room and looked at mom. She arose from dad's chair next to the fireplace and we hugged again. I pulled her close and then retreated slowly, quietly, walking to the front door. As I reached the jamb I opened the door and looked back.

"I'm sorry!" I whispered as she slowly nodded, following me, only with her glances, as I entered the darkness that surrounded me.

"I'll take care of Jake" I said. I knew he would join so many others who had been such a wonderful part of our life. Not once did mom mention my white hair.

I went out to the tool shed and got a lantern and a shovel. It was around 1:00 AM and yet, I knew where so many had been buried, nothing but memories of lives long gone. I carried Jake's body to within the limestone fence and dug a grave. As I was digging, mom came with Jake's bed and a blanket. "These were his favorite," she said.

I lowered my little buddy into his final resting place as tears roiled in my eyes. He was now but a memory of a friend gone by. With each shovel full of dirt, his outline disappeared. With each shovel of dirt, another memory cascaded in my heart. With each shovel of dirt, another thought, another sense of profound remorse, clamored within me until the disturbed Earth was back in place waiting for the warm sun to carry forth yet another day as if nothing had happened.

Mom and I walked hand-in-hand back to the shed and then the house.

"Your brother does love you. It's just he is under so much pressure these days," she whispered. With that, I gave her one last hug, got in my car and drove into Mineral Point and went to where our little church had stood. It was long gone, ravaged by age and destroyed by fire. I looked to the spot upon the hill where Pointer the dog had stood for so many years. He too looked alone, cold and sad, now just a memory for some of us whose lives had become too fast to be looking at a statue of a dog tarnished by time. Once again, I thought of Jake and dad and more tears came to my eyes.

It was nearly three in the morning and my ride back to Madison was singular as few headlights flashed at me while I rode in total silence engulfed in regrets, compounded by self-stated promises of rectification. I would make it right with Tommie, Amelia and the kids, if any of them would have me.

I pulled into parking slot 805 in our little-used condo and thought of not turning off the engine, just letting the car and me run until we were both out of gas. Instead I turned off the car and went up to the cold, dark, emotionally-empty apartment which had been ours that was once filled with so much joy and so many firsts … the birthday cake and ice cream, the long hot showers together, the love! My God, what a fool I had been.

I peered out at the blackness of Lake Monona and wondered what it was like to really drown and not just in regret and sorrow. The first vestiges of sunlight were streaking their pale pink fingers across the water as I went into Amy and my bedroom and slowly took off my clothes and crawled into our bed and tried to remember her scent. I had forgotten its purity as my turmoil had negated its goodness. For the first time in so very long time, I craved having her next to me so I could listen to her breathe and smile at her smile. Would she? Could she ever forgive me? Would she realize my words were true when I said, "I love you!"

I lay there half asleep and wondered "which was worse, to have everything or nothing?" I felt that it was worse to have everything as there was nothing left to acquire, nothing left to achieve, nothing but nothing before me and yet, how could it be? How could I, who started with nothing and now had everything, have such a profound sense of nothingness wrapped in a world filled with what others could only dream.

After a couple hours, I arose and looked in the mirror at my white hair and wondered what would people think or say. It was my birthday. I drove home and sat alone in our empty house waiting, waiting, waiting for my family to return from their days of doing whatever it was they did. When everyone arrived home, I realized no one said a word about my hair.

As my birthday progressed, the obligatory congratulations and condolences from mom and The Duke and Dr. Williams and everyone who was important to me, came in. That night, the kids handed me homemade birthday cards, which had more value than any other gift I could possibly have received. Amy brought out a birthday cake and the kids all sang. I closed my eyes and made one wish…to simply be happy again.

Obligatory condolences were shared by Amelia and the kids. Derrick asked if Jake would go to heaven. I told him he was already there and that he and grandpa were probably already out for a walk. This seemed to appease his imagination.

After the kids went to bed, I went into the bathroom and looked in the mirror again and my hair was still white.

I came back to the family room and asked Amy, "What color is my hair?"

She gave me a quizzical look and responded, "Brown! Why?"

She must have thought it odd or something strange had happened. No one ever asked another person what color their hair was. I didn't know what to say. I just kissed her goodnight and went to bed, exhausted by a day of sadness, overwhelmed by grief and succumbed by a profound sense of regret. As I closed my eyes, I prayed to God, asking for nothing more than allowing me to heed the words of the Medicine Man, to be a better person.

For the first time in a long, long time, I slept a deep, deep, sleep, unencumbered by thoughts of business or feelings of inadequacy. I was who I was and no longer needed to prove to the world or myself I wasn't something more. I dreamt of Great Grandfather and awakened startled, realizing it wasn't my reflection in the mirror I saw, it was that of Great Grandfather! At first, the dream gave me the chills, until I realized Great Grandfather's spirit was now within me and the reflection I saw was his way of letting me know he was there.

Washburn:

The first point on my resurrection docket was making things right on the farm. $400,000 was not that much. A man's pride was worth much more.

That afternoon I met with security and accounting and contacted our PR wing. Security was instructed to determine what was going on between Heather and Tommie. I smelled a skunk in the woodpile. Accounting was told to determine where the money was owed and the real value of the farm, along with the name of the Chinese company who had purchased the other two farms and at what price. PR was told we needed to work with our legislators to block the creation of another dairy factory on whatever grounds they could. The goal was to determine who was buying, what they were buying and what the value would be when the milk factory did not happen.

It was easy to find out the name of the company wanting to buy the farm. It was Hongshe out of Changzhou China. They were buying land all over the world to meet the growing demand for dairy products at home and, like most big businesses, intended on cutting out all the middle-men so that their profits would be greater.

Security began tracking daily habits of mom, Tommie and Heather. This included what time they left the house and where they went. After two weeks, security had already placed GPS transponders on all three vehicles and hidden video cameras in the yard, barn and machine shed. None of them could fart without us knowing what it smelled like.

From our offices in Milwaukee, we could watch the comings and goings as Heather and mom left for work and Tommie worked around the farm. Mom's schedule was pretty basic as Monday through Friday she went to Spring Green to work at Lands' End.

Tommie normally went to town on Wednesday afternoons. Heather was a different story, with a completely different pattern.

With a basic degree from Southwest Wisconsin Community College in Fennimore, Heather had a job in Dodgeville with a small accounting firm. Using the GPS tracker, a pattern was developing where every other Wednesday she was leaving Dodgeville at noon and driving to Madison. In the olden days she could have been making deposits, but nobody did that anymore. What was crazy was she would drive to Madison, park her car in the ramp between Wilson and Doty, just east of ML King Drive and leave it there for three hours.

Security asked for the right to do a tail. I agreed. Two weeks later they came back and said Heather kept the same routine. She would drive to Madison, park in the parking ramp, go to the Bank of Madison, walk back to the Hilton where she would spend two hours, go to her car and head back to Waldwick.

Security had some "friends" look into her bank account and found she was depositing money under her maiden name. There had been an initial deposit of $100,000 and then subsequent deposits ranging from $5,000 to $30,000 periodically. All totaled there was nearly $350,000 in the bank.

Our team followed her into the Hilton where she met with a man named John Washburn, who happened to be the realtor handling the offer for the farm. Washburn and Heather looked around the lobby and then went to the elevators. Gee, I wonder what they had planned? About two hours later Heather walked out of the Hilton, got in her car and drove back to the farm.

Two weeks later, the same routine was enacted. Depart from Dodgeville, make a deposit at the Bank of Madison, walk down King Drive to the Hilton, meet with Washburn, go up to a room and well, I think you get the idea. Heather was skimming from Tommie and mom by under-reporting income and taking the embezzled funds and depositing them in her maiden name. As Tommie's wife, our legal team could see the handwriting in the wall. Embezzle as much as possible. Force Tommie to sell the farm. Divorce him. Take half the cash and be gone.

We inquired regarding who the Ambassador to China was and found that he had once been in business and was an indirect friend of The Duke. We had began discussions with him, which weren't going too well, until our investment team looked into his stock portfolio and noticed he was reaping some very big rewards from Chinese companies doing business in the States. While not illegal, it certainly wouldn't look good on an otherwise pristine business record.

The Duke gave him a call and asked whether he would be coming to the States soon or should The Duke personally fly to Beijing to meet face-to-face. This was a tacit way of saying there was some serious shit going on. Needless to say, our second conversation went much smoother and a plan was implemented.

Hongshe was a very large, publicly traded company and this meant there were formal minutes of all board meetings. We bought 50,000 shares of stock in their company and acquired their financial statements. The Ambassador did a little research into the board records and learned Hongshe had been willing to offer $1.6 million for the farm. Our accountants dug a little deeper and found a payment of $250,000 to a Mr. John Washburn as a consulting fee for learning the price Tommie was willing to take for the farm was $1.2 million. All this was legit, except for the fact Washburn and Heather never reported the income to the IRS.

Knowing the CEO of the corporation that owned the downtown Madison Hilton, was all we needed to do some "maintenance" on the room Washburn and Heather would have for their next tryst and see what their plans were. Listening devices were planted. It was illegal as hell, but no one would ever know. The front desk at the Hilton was informed Washburn was to be upgraded for loyal service and a suite provided.

After the normal chitchat, we heard Washburn tell Heather they needed to close the deal and added pressure was needed to be put on Tommie and mom.

Heather asked for guidance and Washburn said he felt that high repair bills on farm equipment could push Tommie over the edge. Washburn said he had already contacted an implement service man named Homer who would sneak into the machine shed and fray the hydraulic lines, which would destroy the hydraulic pump. It wouldn't happen right away, but within a few hours of use, the tractor would need repair beyond what Tommie could do himself.

Tommie wasn't trusting me, but then I hadn't called him either and so it was another two weeks before we learned the tractor repair bill exceeded $3,000. We also had the video of Homer slicing the lines while Tommie was in town.

Heather made her regular journey and reported the event and felt one more circumstance would be enough. Washburn asked when all three would be away and Heather said the three of them went to church on Sunday. Washburn said he would instruct Homer to slit one of the rear tires so it would be flat in a couple of days.

We had the time and knew what was going to happen. I wanted one more bit of evidence and so we taped Homer in the act … trespassing and criminal damage to property which, we thought, would be enough to get him to sing like a canary.

Now it was time for the final act. We went back to the hotel and tapped into the hotel elevator and hallway video security system and put video surveillance in the room.

I learned people are so stupid when it comes to being predictable. Here comes Washburn and Heather and they're making out in the elevator. Then, as they're walking down the hall, he grabs her ass. It was time to make our move.

Andrew had the chopper ready and I hopped on board and took off from our helipad to Mineral Point. Arrangements had been made to use the conference room at Farmers Savings Bank and we had a wireless feed from the hotel all set in case we needed it.

Bank of Madison records indicated Heather had embezzled $270,000 from Tommie and mom and added the $100,000 on top of that. When they sold the property for $1.2 million, less selling expenses there would be about a million left. The divorce would give Heather another $500,000 and she would walk away with nearly a million dollars and Tommie would be broke. The more I looked at it, the more anxious I was to nail her.

Legal had already informed the FBI and because it had been happening for nearly three years with no reported income, the IRS had also been notified. There was embezzlement, bank fraud, and failure to pay taxes. We had two from our security team, two FBI agents and one from the IRS ready and the entire five-person team was treated to lunch next door at the Madison Club, as they waited for Heather to show up.

It was agreed that the team would let Heather meet Washburn and go to their room. The group would go into the Hilton and when Washburn and Heather had their proverbial pants down, we would give the signal for the entourage break in.

Tommie's attitude would determine whether he witnessed the entire event or not. If there was anger or doubt or any animosity, the show would be broadcast to him. If he was amenable, the idea was to save him the pain and humiliation.

Because we had GPS on Tommie's truck, we knew where he parked in town. Security had filled in Sheriff Fred Balrude about Homer, who would be arrested while we were watching the fall of Washburn and Heather. The plan was for Balrude to keep an eye on Tommie and when we were situated at the Farmers' Savings Bank, meet Tommie at Farmers Implement store where he was trying to extend payments so that he could get the tire replaced, as rear tires for the John Deere were about $1500 each.

Balrude noted later that Tommie was shocked he was there and surprised when Balrude asked Tommie to come with him and pissed when he correctly surmised I was involved. Fred noted, he told Tommie I was trying to help him, not hurt him and, by the end of the day, he would be thanking me.

Tommie was led into the conference room at the bank and saw the entourage consisting of three people from our security company, two from our legal offices, one from the Wilco accounting team, another FBI agent, Andrew and me and all parties were introduced.

"What's going on?" Tommie asked.

I had been coached regarding what I could and could not say and with everything being recorded, I had to be careful. "Tommie, as a board member of Terrill Farms Inc. it has come my attention illegal acts have transpired which are causing the demise of our corporation."

Tommie just shook his head and sneered at me. "Bullshit!"

"This is Frank from the Wilco Accounting offices who has been auditing our financial records for the past three years and found numerous irregularities."

"I don't need to sit here and listen to this crap" Tommie responded.

"Yes, you do," IRS Agent Larson responded, which took the wind out of Tommie's sails.

"It appears Terrill Farms has been under-reporting its income to the Internal Revenue Service for the past three years for a total exceeding $200,000," Larson continued. "Mr. Terrill, we believe you were unaware of the situation and, unless proven otherwise, will be held harmless unless other information implicating you is discovered. Can you please tell me who has been completing your financial documents and maintaining your financial records?"

Tommie was calming down. "My wife, Heather."

"Are you aware Mrs. Terrill maintains a separate savings account at the Bank of Madison in Madison and is making regular deposits to the account?"

Tommie shook his head in the negative.

"Are you aware Mrs. Terrill is doing so under her maiden name?"

With this Tommie's mouth dropped open. "How much money are you talking about?"

Agent Larson slid a copy of the bank statement across the table and Tommie saw the $370,000 and his heart sank.

Larson added, "You will note, deposits have been regularly made every-other Wednesday, including one for $5,000 two hours ago."

Tommie's head tilted forward as Agent Larson continued. "Please note the initial $100,000 deposit. Records obtained indicate these funds were paid as a consulting fee for the potential sale of your property by the Hongshe Corporation of Changzhou, China."

There were tears in Tommie's eyes and yet there was still a tremendous level of disdain towards me.

Ted from security interjected, "Here is an audio recording of Mrs. Terrill with a Mr. Washburn four weeks ago at the Hilton Hotel in Madison which outlines some of the other events taking place." With that, the tape was played and Tommie listened to Heather and Washburn plan the damage to the hydraulic lines.

I nodded and the video screen came on as security continued. "Here is the gentleman by the name of Homer, slicing your hydraulic lines in your machine shed."

"How did you get that?" Tommie demanded.

I responded. " Tommie!"

Tommie stood and pointed at me. "Who gave you permission to come on MY property and put up video surveillance?"

Johnson from legal responded. "As a stockholder and part owner, Mr. Terrill has all the right in the world to be on the farm and protect his investment."

This infuriated Tommie even more. "It's MY farm! You traded a lousy ten acres for any rights to the rest."

Johnson continued. "While there was a verbal agreement, there is nothing is writing. At no time has Mr. George Terrill interfered with the operation of the property, nor expected any compensation. However, he does have the right to protect his investment, which includes the right to visit the property as he sees fit."

Tommie just shook his head. "Lawyer talk and then all this about Heather. It's all bullshit."

I looked at Ted from our security team and simply nodded. His assistant sent a text to our security people at the Hilton and the video screen came alive with Washburn and Heather in bed making love.

"This is happening right now Tommie!" I offered.

Now Tommie was really getting riled up.

I nodded at Agent Larson and you could hear the crew at the Hilton pounding on the door. Heather almost jumped out of her skin as she pulled the covers up under her chin.

Washburn refused to open the door as he attempted to put on his pants. Using a jimmy key, the agents were in the room in less than 15 seconds.

"What in hell is going on?" Washburn demanded.

"Francis Washburn, you are under arrest for bank fraud, embezzlement and extortion. You have the right to an attorney and anything you say may be used against you in a court of law."

Heather tried hiding under the covers. A police matron read her the charges ... "Heather Terrill, you are also under arrest," as she was read her rights.

"Turn it off!" I directed and security made the screen go black. "Tommie, Heather was embezzling money from the corporation and provided information to Hongshe that you were willing to take $1.2 million when they were ready to pay $1.6. For this Heather and Washburn received $250,000 of which Washburn kept $150,000." I slid the meeting notes across the table.

"Beyond that, here are copies of payments made by the U.S. Government to Terrill Farms Incorporated. You will see they do not match any of the deposits at the banks." Again, receipts were provided.

"Tommie, the farm is our heritage … yours, mine and mom's. You can hate me for what I have done, but what I did was catch a thief. Her goal was to steal as much as she could, have you sell the farm for the lower price, divorce you and take half the cash. Washburn had already purchased a condo in Scottsdale and the two of them would be gone. You would be unemployed, have no farm and our family history would be over. Mom would have nothing. You would have nothing and a dairy factory would be placed where our memories are and I couldn't allow that."

Tommie slumped in his chair. He was beaten and he knew it. "What's going to happen to Heather?"

Mr. Johnson responded, "Heather will be tried and with the evidence in place, certainly convicted unless she pleads out of it. Because most of the money was embezzled from the corporation, it will return to the corporation. You can file for the $100,000 retainer, but her legal fees and yours will eat most of that up."

I interjected. "Tommie, you are my brother. We have not seen eye-to-eye on a lot of things, but one thing we have is the same mother and the same love for our land, just for other reasons." I opened my briefcase and pulled out a cashier's check. "Here is a check for $1.6 million dollars. Add this to the $120,000 from the bank account and you're at $1.7 million. Deduct the $400,000 owed in back taxes and you will have the $1.2 million you wanted."

"Then what?"

"Terrill Farms continues!"

"And you're my boss?"

"No! Mom's the boss, as she always has been" which got a slight chuckle out of him.

"You mean, everything continues?"

"Almost everything!"

I saw the hair beginning to stand up on his neck. "You're a great dairy farmer Tommie, but a lousy businessman. Instead of Heather keeping the books, our accounting department will do them. All we ask is that, on expenditures greater than $5,000, accounting be appraised so that they can see if they can get a better price. In addition, you will be living in the house we grew up in. I have personally signed a waiver allowing you to participate in all the benefits we offer Wilco employees except the stock options. This means health insurance, 401K, paid vacation, everything and yet you will report to no one."

He was beginning to relax and inquired," What about mom?"

"Mom will be moving into a new condo we're building in Dodgeville. She's going to have a huge garden and a great kitchen and plenty of space to have her grandkids come and play."

"Does she know about all this?"

"Mom has been involved since day one. I called her the day after I left the house with my first offer and told her my concerns. I kept her in the loop on everything except the Heather-Washburn situation so as not to embarrass you. If you want anyone to know, it's up to you. If you want to stay married to Heather, that's up to you." There was a strong negative response to that option, which made me feel good. The bitch! "On the first of the month, mom is changing jobs. She is going to be general manager of Terrill Chevrolet in Dodgeville."

"Terrill Chevrolet? She doesn't know anything about the car business!" Tommie replied.

I answered, "Mom is smart, gracious and above all else, honest. We have over 150 dealerships and a complete training platform which will teach her the business and provide her with all the support she needs. Also, being the mother of 'Mr. Amelia Williams' as you have called me, has some perks. Don't worry, she won't fail and yet, I'm also going to make certain she is proud of her accomplishments. "

I looked at my watch. It was 4:00 PM. Heather was in the Dane County jail. Tommie had a big decision to make and 250 cows to milk. "Well Tommie, what do you think? I will always be your little brother. You will always be a dairy farmer and we can always keep Waldwick."

Tommie looked at me and shook his head. "I came in here hating you, despising all that you were and yet you have shown me what dad said about you was totally true … you are Little Spirit … you bring goodness into people's lives and I will always be grateful to you." With that, Tommie took the pen and signed the papers.

I responded as I handed him the check. "I ask only one thing in return … no more chastising me about being a millionaire because you're one too." This brought a slight smile, to his face. In the matter of two hours everything in his life had changed and it would take a while for the pain to wear off.

"One last thing." I mentioned.

"What?" Tommie responded.

"When we buy the farms Hongshe purchased, will you be able to run them, too?"

This got a shit-eating grin on his face. "How are you going to do that?"

"Trust me, it's already in the works. We have to save family farms, even if it's one at a time." (Little did I know, it wasn't going to be as easy as I thought) "Now let's go downstairs and make the bank manager's day with the biggest deposit he's ever seen and then you have to go home and milk those cows!"

We walked downstairs, brother-and-brother, just like old times. Tommie got in his truck and went home to Waldwick. I got in the helicopter and looked at my phone. 216 emails, 36 texts! I shut the damn thing off and watched as we flew over Waldwick and my precious forest, on my way home and for the first time in a long time, I simply smiled.

Christmas:

When you've gone from being a farm boy in Waldwick, Wisconsin to having virtually everything you could imagine … clothes, cars … lots and lots of exotic cars, first class travel all over the world, you do get a bit jaded. Perhaps it was because the number of hours invested in work had cut so much into the number of hours invested in my family, I felt this Christmas needed to be special.

Amelia and I needed it! After our discussion, our marriage was still solid, but we were still taking each other for granted. Those special moments we had when we were young had all evaporated like the puddles on the sand in St. Martin. I realized the Medicine Man was right and blamed myself for much of what was happening. The question became, what to do about it?

I was thumbing through a magazine in the doctor's office as I waited for my annual, mandatory Wilco physical and came across an article about space travel aboard hypersonic planes and a balloon which would take us to the edge of the atmosphere. I began reading about one journey into space and how you would get there. It seems the initial technology, which created the entire idea of a hyper-sonic airplane began in the 1960's with the Boeing 2707 which was developed as the first American Supersonic Transport or SST.

After winning a competition for a government-funded contract to build the plane, Boeing began development. Unfortunately, because of high costs, the project was cancelled in 1971. The SST concept lay dormant for decades until new engine technologies determined the plane could be economically feasible as the first hypersonic commercial jet capable of speeds up to 2300 miles per hour, or Mach 3 while carrying 295 passengers to the edge of space. While the SP2707 sounded really cool and was put in my bucket list, I wanted more than a three-hour trip to the other side of the world. As I was also about to learn, my decision was one of those which completely changed my world as well.

The same article referenced Voyager 1, the spacecraft, launched in 1977. The article said, "Based on Voyager I, a deep space balloon was built by a company called 'Stratospheric Flight Company' known as World View, that was designed to ferry 10,000 pounds of equipment to the edge of space. From altitude testing, to experimental craft, there were a surprising number of scientific hurdles that needed to be overcome, but the experts had done it. I was so enthralled that I wanted to go with them to the edge of space.

I waited a couple of days to see if my excitement would wane and when it didn't, I had Cecelia contact World View to see what the requirements were to go as passengers. The company e-mailed all the criteria, age, health and affordability. At $250,000 per person, based on a load of six, this wasn't like getting on a city bus.

I had our legal department review the formal risk statement to see if there was anything out of the ordinary. They thought I was nuts and sent the warning to one of our scientists who wrote the following report. *"Freezing temperatures aren't the only danger posed by the stratosphere. The atmospheric pressure there is about 1/1000th of what is typically experienced at sea level. While differences in pressure turns out to only mildly affect humans, it can cause electronics to seriously malfunction."*

Legal heard back from World View who outlined the fact the designers helped create the International Space Station and Mars expeditionary vehicles. They then outlined the test protocol which included four days in temperatures of 80 degrees below zero and the fact that all systems worked as planned. They noted the balloon material was the same as used in modern spacesuits and it was the balloon-like lining which maintained air pressure around an astronaut. They also noted that polyurethane foam would be sprayed on World View's External Tank keeping the fuel from getting too hot. The company sent a video showing how, once we arrived at our 80,000-foot elevation, an inflatable space habitation module would open, providing not only more room, but a place to eat, sleep and view the world below.

I looked at our schedule and realized we had blocked two weeks for a vacation. The trip was for five days. I told Cecelia to book the entire ship. This was to be Amelia and my trip of a lifetime and it was just for us and the two-million-dollar investment in our marriage.

For Christmas, the house was its normal resplendent self, where professional decorators had come in and did their magic. Long gone were the popcorn and paper chains we made for our first Christmas. So much had changed and, in some ways, I yearned for the old days, when all of it was so much simpler.

Christmas morning, we went through the typical mayhem of the kids getting too much of everything. When they were done, I handed a handmade card to Amelia. She opened it and looked perplexed as all it said was. *"Come with me to the edge…to the immense nothing and share the joy of a bright blue something and you shall perceive the magnitude of my love for you!"*

The kids wanted to know what it said and Amelia read it to them. Mela, as we called our daughter, was our resident expert on everything and even she was baffled. Instead, she simply asked Echo our artificial intelligence monitor what the card meant.

Echo responded. *"Immense nothing, probably refers to outer space and the bright blue something therefore referred to the Earth."*

Again, Amelia looked perplexed.

I looked at her and smiled. " You and I are going on a five-day trip."

"Where?"

"Around the world!"

"Boat, plane, ship, train?" were Amelia's guesses.

I laughed. Think again and pointed upward as Amelia got a quizzical look on her face.

"Outer   space!"

"What?" she inquired.

"Yup! It's all booked. We will fly out to Phoenix and get on the space balloon World View that will take us to the Kármán Line, which is the legal border of space at around 80,000 feet."

Again, Amelia looked at me like I was crazy. "You and I are going into outer space?"

"Yup! Actually, only fifteen miles up, but high enough to see and experience something less than 600 people have done before."

"Outer space in a balloon?" I'm certain the kids were thinking of the kind they had at their birthday parties.

"Yup" For the first time in a long, long time I heard the girlie giggle that I always loved as she sat totally, profoundly, incredulous.

"What do I pack? What do we wear?"

"Not what you like to wear on St. Martin." I snickered. "World View provides everything … clothes and space suits. If you want, we can even go on a space-walk."

Amelia just sat and shook her head. "Outer space? A spacewalk? 80,000 feet?"

"What do you think?" I asked her.

"Oh my God!" she responded and I knew she was excited.

"We needed to go somewhere different and I thought outer space would be neat."

The kids just looked at Amelia and enjoyed her excitement. Of course, they wanted to know if they could come too. I told them they had to be at least 21 years of age and promised that, when they graduated from college, they could go. They were disappointed, but reluctantly understood and it would give both grandma's a chance to spoil them rotten.

Blessed Are the Curious for They Too Shall Have Adventures:

Plans were made and we set our schedule to allow for the pre-trip orientation which included a complete physical exam, stress test and psychological review. Three days in a balloon could be rough on someone with claustrophobia. Our classroom work was almost as interesting as the trip itself I believe because we learned about space travel and astrophysics.

While we thought it would be cold all the time, one instructor pointed out, "In the stratosphere, the curvature of the Earth and the blackness of space are both visible and gorgeous. What isn't visible, though, is weather. With around 80 percent of the atmosphere's molecules below it, including most of the world's water vapor, the air of the stratosphere lacks the right stuff for any real cloud formation. Winds zip along at speeds of 100 miles per hour or more, making it ideal for space balloons. But, oddly, the stratosphere is not entirely cold. The absorption of ultraviolet rays by the ozone layer means the stratosphere gets just a bit warmer as you go higher."

We were informed the balloon would orbit the Earth eighteen times in three days and each orbit would be ten degrees less than the previous. In that way, we would see virtually the entire planet from the poles to the equator and everything in between.

As we neared our departure date, we both were like kids again. I really don't know who was the most excited. Amelia II was arranged and we flew to Phoenix. On the plane were just Amy and me. We hadn't been alone in a long, long time and I really regretted the infamous airplane bed hadn't been put onboard so we could have relived that memory too.

While I am a man of many words, I cannot express the experience we had. It was beyond anything we hoped or dreamed about. The World View people were a bit taken aback when it was just Amy and me. To smooth things out, each instructor was remitted a bonus and it wasn't long until they all realized this was a very special event in the lives of some very wealthy people.

We met with Captain Luke Arnold, who was to be the pilot. The first words from Captain Lucas Arnold was "No, I am not Luke Skywalker," as this gregarious man won our hearts. I learned Luke had been a Navy pilot and was a retired flight instructor. He always wanted to become an astronaut, but never made it. When we got home, I Googled him and found out he was actually Dr. Lucas Arnold who had a PHD in astrophysics from Stanford. It sounds like a funny thing to say, but he was one of the most down-to-Earth guys I ever met.

It was departure day and all of our training was done. Extra ballast was added to compensate for the four missing passengers and we were launched. To look down on the world from above was simply a religious event. To see the incredible blue and white sphere below us as it stood out from the blackness of space was truly all we had hoped it would be.

We were awestruck. The experience altered us in an instant by electrifying our emotions. Both Amy and I were simply overcome by the feeling of something so vast and beyond our human scale, transcending anything either of us had ever seen, felt or experienced before.

Facing our planet and referencing it to the deep dark space surrounding us was like being in church with a starry cathedral. We both realized we were simply a very small part of something much larger, where our small blue dot looked so tiny against the vastness of all that enveloped it. While the two of us had gone as a couple, there was still a profound transition from me-to-we, first encompassing ourselves and then all living beings. Captain Luke smiled and quoted Einstein. "Awe is the source of all true art and science," as he continued functioning as pilot and philosopher who shared thoughts about everything from religion to physics to environmental awareness.

At times, the silence was deafening. There was no noise, except the sounds of beating hearts. As we were looking down at Mother Earth, Captain Luke reflected, "We all tend to think that the things we humans create have been the most profound creations ever. However, since the beginning of time we have relied on Mother Earth's bounty for food, medicine, warmth and light."

"This balloon is nothing more than a tool that gets us from there to here and yet, some of our most powerful and influential tools that have allowed us to escape here-and-now have come from Mother Earth's own tool box."

"Mankind is not a creator, only a facilitator of things that have always been there that took time and energy to identify, modify and implement to make them useful in our daily lives while, at other times, creating things so deadly and powerful as to threaten all living things Mother Earth carries in her womb."

Both Amy and I shook our heads in agreement. Man was the great and powerful Oz, and yet he was also the monster whose madness was taking and reshaping life, constantly honing the precipitous edge upon which the balance of existence of all living things was perched making it ever more precarious.

Captain Luke continued. "Mother Earth is sometimes tough, sometimes dangerous, and sometimes surprisingly fragile, providing all living species with uncounted treasures that we have twisted and turned, molded and shaped, until we have the power to both harm and heal. As we look down on the profound beauty and tranquility that lies below, we cannot, must not, should not ever forget what we see and what we feel consists of equal parts mystery and revelation and accept that we are all just visitors at Mother Earth's abode and we should act as such ... temporal, careful, never forgetting that man's time is but a speck of dust on the mountain of eternity."

Whew! I had the chills! This man could have been a preacher, but then perhaps he was and Amy and I were simply blessed to be his congregation, if only for a moment in our own time that we would never, ever forget.

After circling the Earth a few times and looking down at all the things we could point out, including the Great Wall of China, Florida and even the Great Lakes, things were beginning to get familiar and it was time to go for a space-walk to which there was some trepidation on Amy's part. We did it and it was simply incredible. We were floating in a splendorous sea of tranquility looking up and down and all around. I looked for God and realized He was all around us. My entire perspective on life changed and I realized and recognized what Great Grandfather intended for me was more than just the people of the Ho-Chunk Nation … so very, very much more! This was not a denigration of these wonderful people or the value I placed on their friendship. This was a sincere belief that, by helping all, I would be helping them as I honored the dignity imparted in my soul as I learned, accepted and profoundly believed in the values they had taught me about the dignity of life for all living beings.

As the laps accumulated, all types of topics arose as Amy and I sat transfixed in not only the beauty, but the wisdom shared. When we were over eastern Africa, I mentioned my passion for Amelia Earhart and paralleled my feelings for her as she crossed the Indian Ocean. Captain Luke was surprised I knew Amelia Earhart and Fred Noonan were the first people to ever fly from Africa to India.

Captain Luke looked at Amy and said. "Most people know Amelia Earhart was a legendary pilot who mysteriously disappeared during her most daring journey. But the aviatrix was much more than that. In every aspect of her life, she fought against the strict gender roles of 1920's society. The fact her disappearance was never solved is only one of the fascinating facts behind this record-breaking pioneer."

My Amelia was mesmerized by Captain Luke's dialogue as we floated over Australia, pointing out Sydney which brought back memories of the other one, which quickly were forgotten as Luke pointed down at the blue Pacific. Luke continued, "After the stop in Australia, Amelia and Fred continued to New Guinea, arriving there on June 29, 1937, where they took off for Howland Island, which was 2200 miles away. Sadly, they never arrived. The nation was utterly shocked by Earhart's disappearance. It seemed impossible. Most people believed she got lost, ran out of gas, and crashed into the ocean, but the theory has never been confirmed. Without a concrete story for her disappearance, conspiracy theories ran and continue to run rampant. I've heard everything from she was captured by the Japanese to having her bones found in 1940, which were then lost before DNA testing could be done. I don't think anyone will ever really know, but then that's part of the incredible attraction."

Amy and I looked at each other and smiled. Now we hand a first-hand perspective and the story of Amelia Earhart and the little plane which sat on Amy's desk. The plane, assembled by a twelve-year-old boy, who admired the first Amelia and loved the second one more than life itself and why the little plane now had more meaning than ever before.

Ley, Lady Ley:

We floated over 2,000 miles during Luke's dissertation and when we refocused on the sights below, the Captain offered us pairs of special magnetometer goggles to wear. "With these you will begin to see that the surface of the Earth is more than just water. I hope you also see that land and space aren't as empty as you thought they were." the captain said.

We put on the goggles and looked down at the Earth. What had been this beautiful blue and white sphere turned into a dark brown ball with red and yellow lines intermittently etched upon its surface.

"What are the lines?" Amelia asked.

"They are called Ley lines" Captain Luke responded.

"Are they named after Lae, New Guinea." I asked.

"No, it's spelled L-e-y and most people haven't heard of them. Yet, after today, you will never forget them." Luke replied and continued. "The core of the Earth consists of molten iron. Above that, sits the gooey asthenosphere, which is a semi-liquid layer of magma and partly melted rocks which is then covered by what is called the lithosphere. As the Earth spins, centrifugal force is taking the lithosphere and cracking it creating what are called the tectonic plates. In so doing, the sub-mantel allows a much higher level of electro-magnetic energy to be present along the cracks, creating literal rivers of focused energy."

The captain was on a roll and his audience, namely Amy and me, were mesmerized by what we were learning. Luke continued, "Ley lines not only exist on Earth, but in space, as well. Look out into space and you will see." Sure enough, there appeared to be faint rivers of red light. "These have been likened to the veins of our body because, like your veins, energy flows through them. As you can see, they not only exist on Earth, but in the universe as well and many of us believe in the megaverse, which our universe is simply a part of."

I must have had a look of apprehension on my face that caught Luke's eye as he added. "A lot of people have shaken their heads in disbelief when I talk about the megaverse. I think this is because the megaverse is an area so large it is beyond human comprehension. While we look into the blackness of space and then at Earth, we think we can see it all which is only because what we are seeing is so much more than what we are accustomed to. Before airplanes, if a man stood on the ocean's shore, the farthest he could see was three miles to the horizon. Even with the Hubble telescope and radio frequency astronomy, what we see in space is just like standing on the shore and believing we are seeing everything."

Captain Luke smiled and added, "We already have distance learning, but now we are acquiring what is called immersive distance learning which allows astronomers to listen for certain radio frequencies which correlate with the big bang theory and the beginning of our universe."

Luke continued, "Based on these measurements, most astrophysicists believe the universe is about fourteen billion years old and began from what they call the "big bang". Imagine all you can see up here and all you can't that makes up this universe, being condensed into a ball as small as the dull end of a straight pin."

I shook my head in disbelief as Luke added, "Then kaboom, it began … growing and growing and growing, while constantly cooling and creating the one-hundred billion plus galaxies in our universe today."

"Here on earth, as the Greeks looked up into the sky and saw a milky patch they called galaxias kyklos, which meant milky circle. A few hundred years later, the Romans called it "via lactea," which translates to "road of milk," which we call the Milky Way."

Captain Luke was excited and animated as he continued, "There, amongst the millions of stars of the Milky Way, stands a small but powerful star, we call the sun … burning, burning, burning, letting off heat and light and all kinds of energy that is emitted to the planets. The little star, whose energy and gravity are so great that former asteroids were pulled into orbit around it with Mercury, Venus, Earth and Mars being amongst its satellites. The sun, where the total sum of all the planets in the solar system make up less than five percent of its mass and yet, the sun is considered just a little star!"

Luke continued shaking his head in disbelief, "We look at the universe from a macro perspective because of its magnitude. However, one must realize there is also a micro perspective which keeps everything in place, such as the right balance of gravity and velocity to keep earth and all of our sisters in the same orbits going round and round and round the sun in elliptical circles. To tell you how intricate space is, all earth would need to do is speed up to 1.4142 times its current speed and it would reach what is called 'escape velocity' and go hurtling out of the solar system, taking all life forms on earth to their demise."

Looking out the window, Luke continued. "Here was earth, this little sphere, and, for some unknown reason, it evolved through the combination of energy and gravity and life began. At first, it was a single cell that started to mutate into multi-cell organisms which continued the process to create different species who adapted over millions of years, until about two hundred million years ago when earth was dominated by the dinosaurs."

Luke was getting even more introspective about what he was saying. "They had it really good for about 135 million years and then, about sixty-five million years ago, a ten-trillion-ton asteroid smashed into what is now the Yucatan Peninsula and obliterated more than seventy percent of all living organisms … flora, fauna and, of course the reptilians who, at that time, considered our mammal ancestors nothing more than lunch."

Luke continued, "As the world evolved and the competition narrowed, one big-brained branch of the mammals evolved to dominate and, in many ways, destroy the balance of what had been. As this branch of all living beings evolved they began to stand erect, with their head on their shoulders, which allowed them to intellectually evolve to the point they began to have sufficient intelligence to think abstractly, not only about the earth upon which humans exist, but the origin and evolution of the entire universe."

"In the past century, the science of mankind has done profoundly good and incredibly terrible things to all living species and to Mother Earth herself. Man has taken what we know and measured our universe to the point we have defined its end, where light from all luminous objects in all directions loses its energy before reaching us. At this point, the concept of our existence has reached what we consider the spherical edge and a finite point, for which we currently have knowledge. What lies beyond the edge, no one knows. Man does not have the technology, nor the hypothesis to even imagine what lies there and it is thus called the "unknowable" applying not only to astrophysics, but to so many things in life.

Luke sat back in his chair, let out a long sigh, and let what he was saying sink in as he continued. "Who really knows? Perhaps our universe is nothing more than one atom in the megaverse. Something had to start it all … a force greater than all others … a source from which all else has come. But then, where did that start and where did that little pin head come from? There has to be something!"

I was beginning to sense this trip was more than just seeing the sights. It was truly becoming an extension of the religious experience the Medicine Man had alluded to in the forest where, instead of teaching us about our relationship with others and having God stand as judge of right and wrong, there was a sensory stimulation that could only be described as a profound feeling of surprise and fear, which Amy and I would carry with us the rest of our lives.

Captain Luke said once you have been touched, you always carry a sense a reverence and admiration for where we exist. I sat with my chin in my hands and measured my emotions … reverence, respect, dread and wonder, all rolled into one, as I sincerely felt the hand of God reaching down and touching my soul. For an instant, I was beyond myself, carried, buried, enveloped in my sense of insignificance that no one could ever take away. I thought the social, political, economic mess that floated below could simply be resolved by taking those who perpetrated injustice and have them witness how small we all really are and how great things could be if only they would feel a sense of wonder that did not include themselves.

My mind snapped back as Captain Luke continued. "Concepts of focused energy are not a new phenomenon. Ancient civilizations believed the stars were major sources of magical energy. They felt the sun was the node point of our existence. They felt this way because, even then, they realized energy only flows out from the sun and not into it. Ancient drawings have shown that people before us believed that, at the precise center of each star, sits a small pinpoint that intersects with a concept called non-dimensional space, where the 'Ancient Ones' are being held."

"In other words, heaven?" Amelia asked.

"If that's what you want to call it, yes!" Luke nodded as he shared his appreciation that his two students were comprehending his ideas and beliefs. "Solar and lunar events provide erratic spatial lines of energy. In areas of intense gravity, such as black holes, pulsars and other 'warped' stars, Ley line energy tends to pool to a much greater degree. Ley lines in space tend to loosely follow the demands of gravity, but they have been known to do really strange things and nothing prevents them from running through a planetary core, underwater or even through solid objects."

Luke looked at me and asked, "Do you remember the movie *'Back to The Future"* and the scene where Doc talks about a flux capacitor?" Amy and I both nodded in agreement. "A flux capacitor would be one way to increase or decrease magnetic energy and use it for propulsion. Christopher Gale's book and research had him on the cusp of technology no one really understood and yet, what he used in his book and movies makes all the sense in the world."

Luke pointed down at mother Earth. "Ley lines on Earth tend to form a web of fairly consistent paths around the planet where they are literally 'rivers of energy' which not only flow through the Earth but, as many scientists and the ancients believe, flow between worlds and universes." I began to feel the Captain was speaking again in a metaphysical sense.

"Depending upon the location, Ley lines can either support life or be detrimental to it. Sometimes the lines are weak and never attach to others and eventually bleed off into the environment. However, in some cases, weaker lines attach themselves to stronger lines, becoming permanent additions to the grid, or 'web-work' as some people call them, which is what you are looking at below … a network of connected energy channels."

I was getting the heebie jeebies!

Luke added, "What is incredible is how much the ancients knew about Ley Lines and how important they were to them. As an example, when the Druid pathways were mapped in England, at the beginning of the 20th Century, they all appeared to connect one ancient holy shrine to another throughout the entire country. Such places as Stonehenge and Druid burial grounds were all placed on top of strong Ley lines."

"This structure and development wasn't just in England! The ancients of each civilization knew the paths of the Ley lines and how to amplify the already abundant energy and use it for healing and religion. Native cultures in the Americas called them Spirit Paths. The Chinese understood them to be a balance between yin and yang and the Aborigines of Australia called them Song Lines."

Amy and I shook our heads in amazement. We both knew so little about what they knew so much.

Luke continued, "Our European ancestors, who settled America, often traveled pathways alone. Yet, in countless journals they outline they often felt most comfortable when they were riding atop a Ley line as it provided communion between their physical, mental and spiritual being with the Divine. The settlers knew when these energies interacted with the body's physical makeup and they often experienced a feeling of enhanced self-awareness and a sense of centered spirituality."

"The entire energy concept continued throughout the middle ages and the Renaissance, including the Catholic society. As an example, the Cathedral of Chartres in France, has a spot where the priest stood while addressing the congregation that is a sacred crossing of two Ley lines and is where the priest received the Earth's energy through his body and transmitted it to the people." I thought about why I felt the way I did whenever I was in the forest and believed there had to be a Ley line beneath the land.

Luke continued on. "How did the settlers know where these lines were? Because, we all sense the energy intuitively and logically, even though we can't see it. As an example, when a magnet attracts iron filings, we can't see the cause, yet we can see the result and in turn, know the energy exists."

"While much of the Earth appears inert, it is actually a dynamic, living being and many of these invisible forces the Earth emits interact between human beings and the planet, making us better or worse. This is because all electrical energy flows in the form of a sine wave and you can have both positive and negative strengths depending upon where the line reaches the Earth's surface."

We were floating over the Rockies as Luke continued. " When energy levels were measured at the Temple of Salomon in Jerusalem, researchers discovered the same kind of energy intensity in the absolute center of the Holy of Holiness room, where the arc of the covenant is located. This grid is called the Sacred Grid."

My mouth was agape with an incredulous awareness which had been beyond my own consideration.

Luke added, "All energy is not positive. In fact, there is a grid called the mummification grid, which has the opposite energy of the sacred grid and consists of a drying and emptying energy. When the pyramids of Giza and Sakara in Egypt were measured, researchers found negative Ley lines in the center of each pyramid." I was getting the heebie, jeebies again.

So much of what Great Grandfather had spoken was now making sense. His religion and that of the Native Americans was amplified in my head as my conversations with Rodney about humans being a part of nature was coming into play. I began to better understand why Indian children were taught to live and act on the Earth impeccably. I began to sincerely appreciate why they were instructed not to disturb either the harmony, balance, nor beauty of the environment and to listen and understand the world around them such as the sun, stars, wind, forest, rivers, lakes, animals. Finally, I realized the meaning of being taught to follow the laws of nature throughout their life and why violating these laws causes unnecessary pain to the living.

From fifteen miles above the Earth, little things like crossing a river, walking forest trails or swimming in the ocean, unencumbered as Amy had once said, began to become important to me. I, too, felt as if I was one with the wind, water, mountains, birds and no more important than trees swaying in the wind, clouds floating in the sky, squirrels frolicking in the trees or fish swimming in waters.

Amy asked Captain Luke if he had ever heard of the Wim Hof concept. When Captain Luke said 'no,' to which Amy explained, "The entire Wim Hof concept is based on human evolution where, over time, humans developed a different attitude towards nature around us and we actually forgot one thing called 'inner power', which is the relationship between our physiological mechanisms to adapt and survive and our natural environment, which is direct and effective."

"Like the Indians," Captain Luke added.

Amy continued, "Because we wear clothes and control the temperatures at home and work, we have changed the stimulation on our body, thus the old mechanisms related to survival and function are not in order. As these deeper physiological layers are not stimulated anymore, we have become alienated from them, thus our bodies are weakened and we are no longer in touch with our inner power. The inner power is a force accumulated by fully awakened physiological processes that also influences the very core of our self."

Luke nodded and smiled in affirmation

Amy added. "I began practicing Wim Hof a few years ago and added the Japanese activity called shinrin-yoku or "forest bathing" which consists of purposeful walks for meditation. With three kids, I don't have the time I used to, but I love to walk and periodically sit down to do deep breathing and use all my senses … sight, touch, smell, taste and hearing to refresh me."

Amy continued, "Until this trip, these were intentional activities. Now, I can see things I normally would not see and sincerely believe I will hear things I would not normally hear, smell things I normally would not normally smell and sense things I normally would not feel and for this I am in awe. This trip has been like taking a beam of light and running it through a prism so all the different colors are shown. They were always there, but we never take the time to look at them individually. For the first time in my life, the statement 'people who believe they are ignorant of nothing, have neither looked for or stumbled upon the boundary between what is known and the unknown, for it is this boundary that keeps man striving for more,' make sense." I smiled at Amy's soliloquy.

Luke added one final profound thought. "The universe continues to evolve and every one of the atoms in our bodies is traceable back to the big bang and we are simply stardust. God gave us the power to figure out who we are, what we are and where our destiny lies and, in my opinion, we have only just begun."

I smiled. The trip was worth every dime we paid. As I looked at my wife and watched her expressions change from amazement to surprise-to-acceptance, I fell deeply in love once again. For the first time in many years, there was a sense of serenity and joy which bonded us together as one. The initial excitement and ecstasy of the trip was morphing into a much deeper bond between us and I sincerely felt love for my wife grow. There had always been my admiration, trust and acceptance but, for the very first time in a long, long time, there was also a sense of optimism that tomorrow would certainly be better than today.

I smiled at Amy and she at me and the joy of the experience transcended the day-to-day travails which had wallowed our existence and almost shattered the very thing we held dear. This was, by far, the most important event in our lives, after our children, resulting in the acceptance of each other for what we were, a team devoted to each other and to those who made our lives together seem all worthwhile.

Luke continued. "While I was in the Navy, I always wanted to go into space, but never made the cut and so, after my military career, I was offered this position and began making these voyages. To date, I have been here over 40 times and yet, I am still in awe as my spirits are rejuvenated and my belief in God becomes greater. I can see and actually feel the rhythms of energy and accept all living things emit these unseen influences." I was beginning to feel as if Great Grandfather was speaking to me once again.

We were floating over central United States and I imagined what all the people in our lives were doing on a typical Wednesday while Amy and I soared by in what was becoming one of the most important experiences of our lives as Luke added, "Because Ley lines don't normally run parallel with each other, they periodically intersect at what are called nexus points. Those points, where the combined energy is strongest are called Earth Energy Vortexes. This combined energy can be positive, neutral or negative. How strong or weak the energy field depends upon what type of energy field is being emanated by each Ley line at the point of intersection. Positive/positive creates the highest amount of positive energy; positive/negative cancel each other out; negative/negative creates the greatest amount of negative energy."

"There are even a few spots on Earth where three Ley lines intersect where the relationship can have even different sets of permutations that can be so strong that, in some cases, such as in Scandinavia, cows will not lactate near nexus points unless they are wearing a copper harness around their necks. The forces of nature do not discriminate. He who has the knowledge, holds the power, whether it be of the dark side or the light. Ancient people knew wherever the Earth's energy gathered in a vortex, was a sacred place. These strongly charged areas of the globe are places where people have chosen to build churches, temples and other centers of spirit and learning."

Luke peered out the window and continued, "The ancients knew how to work with a vortex to achieve a better understanding of self and spirit. They also knew vortex energy held the potential to help heal the mind, body and spirit. As I noted, places like Stonehenge, the Pyramids of Egypt and Easter Island, are not the only religious structures built on Ley lines. Sacred temples of the ancient world around the Mediterranean were all found to be located at powerful vortices. What is really amazing is cartographers have drawn lines between the temples and the vortexes and realized that their locations create geometric patterns, of which most are triangles." Now Amy and I were really getting amazed.

"The Indians in both North and South America, located their cities and roads on or between vortices and ley lines, which look like so many spokes and hubs. The Chinese practice the ancient science of geomancy. "The Olde Straite Pathes" of England, the location of Stonehenge and its relationship to the Great Pyramids, Glastonbury and the myth of Avalon all correlate to vortices and I'm sure there are many more examples throughout the world."

"The power and strength of a Ley line and vortex is a personal thing which can affect an individual in a lot of ways or not at all, and is not something that can normally be measured. Those who are affected often sense a level of spirituality, where the Ley line and its force is the conductor and the person's mind is the translator. Not everyone feels a change, but those who do can be profoundly affected."

Luke added, "Our ancestors and the Native Americans knew that ley lines and vortexes were energy sources and centers and were to be considered holy, which supplied their physical needs, cured their ills and balanced their spirit. They respected the strength of the unseen powers and knew these were places to heal physical, emotional and spiritual pain. Used as a place of communion with the Creator, our ancestors knew these energy points uplifted one's consciousness and fortified the soul."

Captain Luke continued. "Before I began doing this, I was like everyone else … in too big of a hurry to realize where I was until my first visit here when I realized I am but a part of something so much bigger, so much more powerful and so much greater than mankind."

Now I was really getting spooked. What Luke had shared was exactly what happened to me every time I visited the forest and what the Medicine Man talked about. My mind was going 100 miles an hour as I was beginning to realize why I was chosen as Little Spirit. It was not to work with the Ho-Chunk on an individual basis, nor to be their Medicine Man. I was chosen to take the land that had so profoundly affected some of us and have it become not only a spot of religious consequence, but a spot for learning ... a location where we could take our resources and use them for the betterment of all people regardless of gender, race, orientation or religion.

Luke continued and another part of my life-long riddle, was about to be solved. "Anthropologists who have studied the Ley lines, have found something else. Under every valid sacred site there is water. Now, if you dig deep enough it wouldn't seem like such a big deal. However, there are two types of water and one is called 'primary water' that is created in the bowels of Earth as the by-product of chemical reactions which create hydrogen and oxygen that is then is forced, under tremendous pressure, towards the surface of Earth until the water hit's a layer of rock or clay."

"How about lead?" I asked.

Luke nodded in the affirmative "Yes, lead, of course!" and continued. "The pressure then forces the water out horizontally through cracks and fissures in the rocks and becomes virgin spring water and you have the combination of high positive energy and Primary Water, which has been used for baptisms for centuries."

Now, I was getting the chills.

Luke continued, "You can find primary water under virtually every valid ancient holy site because, people of religion realized when these veins of water reached the surface, they were places of healing and spiritual contemplation."

Amy looked at me and we both just shook our heads. I was almost hyperventilating.

We were somewhere over Nebraska as Luke continued. "You're from Milwaukee, correct?"

"Yes" Amy concurred.

"If you look ahead you can see the outline of Lake Michigan. Now follow it toward us, almost to the Mississippi River and then a little south. Do you see where three bright red lines intersect and the glow around their intersection?"

We both saw what the Captain was referring to and responded in the affirmative.

Luke continued. "That vortex is in southwestern Wisconsin, where three very strong positive Ley lines intersect. There are only a few other spots like this have been identified in the world…one in China and one in Africa. I don't know if you have ever heard of a little town called Mineral Point, but I have been told the vortex is just southeast of town."

I was getting goose bumps as Amelia squeezed my hand and tears welled in my eyes.

I responded. "You're talking about a little town called Waldwick. I believe the spot where the lines cross is located beneath ten acres of primeval forest and has a small spring flowing on it."

The captain looked at me in total surprise. "How do you know?"

"Because it's on the farm where I grew up. We co-own the land with the Ho-Chunk Nation. This land has been in my family for over 200 years. It is a primeval forest where my ancestors saved the life of an Indian girl who was the ancestor of my best friend and that I

have gone and had numerous religious experiences throughout my life where I have gone many times to find peace and tranquility. It is also where a man, dear to my heart, who was my mentor, is buried."

Now the captain was in awe!

The trip had been a gift for Amelia and yet I was the one reaping the greatest reward. All of my questions were being answered. All of my dreams and nightmares were being resolved! All of the wonders which had been buried within me were being explained.

Great Grandfather had been right and it was not part of my imagination.

As we floated, one last time, over the Atlantic Ocean, we removed our goggles and peered down at the blue and white Earth below as Luke explained in almost in a religious way… "We all take Earth for granted and don't realize our planet is a dynamic being which is giving off energy that can't be seen, tasted or have an odor, but the effects of the Earth's energy can be experienced in all of those ways. It isn't loud, but it can be heard. It can't be touched, but definitely can be felt. When you are aware, then you can begin to sense the internal peace we all strive for."

I knew for the first time why the forest meant so much to me, as I explained to Luke about the land and how we had to go to court to keep it from being developed. "We fought for and won the right to keep the land, as it is so that it has become a point of religious experience for many of those who come, where the energy of life springs forth and goodness prevails. We have established it legally so that it will always be for the good of man as he reaches out to God and asks for guidance and forgiveness. When you drink the water, which comes forth from the ground, it is like being reborn and the trees shelter the spot and keep it pure."

Luke sat back in his chair and we in ours. There was nothing left to see, nothing left to feel and nothing left to do but end our journey knowing that we had changed. In our studies, Amelia and I learned many of the astronauts who witness the vivid blue of our planet come back with an altered perspective — about themselves, the world and about life. We were not alone!

We sat in total silence as we traversed the globe one last time. As we neared set-down, Luke noted. "Researchers call your emotional changes the 'Overview Effect'. While it has always been unclear whether the cause was physiological or cultural, the effect is strong enough many astronauts have turned to lives of charity, religion and transcendental meditation after their return from the void. Personally, I am a totally different person today than I was when I started this job. I am much more attuned to mother Earth and mankind and feel I am a better person for it. While I believed in God before, I am now certain he exists and we, mankind, are simply one component in an incredible tapestry called life."

As we were about to be tethered back on earth, Luke added, "Steven Hawking once said. *'Remember to look up at the stars and not down at your feet. Try to make sense of what you see and about what makes the universe exist. Be curious. And however difficult life may seem, there is always something you can do, and succeed at. It matters that you don't just give up.'* Hawking also said *'Never give up work. Work gives you meaning and purpose, and life is empty without it.'* Finally, Hawking said. *'If you are lucky enough to find love, remember it is there and don't throw it away."*

There was no way I could have said it any better. Like the astronauts, Amelia and I were profoundly affected. Like the astronauts, our lives and our outlook changed. Like the astronauts, all that had been was now behind the demarcation of all we had seen and experienced before.

After we went through re-adaptation to gravity, Amelia and my earth-bound, bond rekindled. We were once again a team, once again equal partners, who had experienced something, shared something and done something, neither of us would never forget and were profoundly changed by.

We said a reluctant goodbye to Captain Luke and accepted his thanks and offered to take him to the forest if-and-when he came to Waldwick. Amy and I both agreed, when you have all we had acquired, the time had come for us to look to the stars, knowing and realizing life would never be the same again. Little did we realize how big of change was about to happen.

Resignation:

We boarded Amelia II and headed for home. Looking out the window now seemed anti-climactic as I watched as my Amelia's eyes closed with a soft smile on her face. Andrew brought along a copy of the Milwaukee Journal for me to read. I perused the sports page and then found an article in the "life" section, about health care and how much it cost for middle class people to simply have insurance and try to get better. Was this coincidence or another way God was sending me a message?

The article said the median annual family income in America was $50,500 per year or $4208 per month. It said the average mortgage payment was $1434 and the average car payment was $439 per month. Add the two together and you had $1873 per month, for an average house and average car without utilities, gasoline or insurance.

What got my attention was the fact the average annual cost for health insurance for a family was $28,166 of which $19,481was paid by employers and nearly $725 per month paid by the employee. Sadly, costs were rising by about $100 per month and had been doing so for ten years and was the reason why deductibles and co-pays were increasing every year and there was such a burden on families. I realized why mom and dad had struggled to continue to keep farming. If you had a decent job with average benefits, you still paid half of what you pay for your mortgage for health insurance. As we landed in Milwaukee and Amy awakened, I knew what my goal in life was to be … to help people afford to be healthy. In the car on the ride home, Amy read the article and looked at me and smiled. She also knew the trip had been more than sightseeing. It had been life changing, just like everyone said it would be.

The kids were excited to see us and wanted to know if we brought them anything from space. This put a smile on my face as there wasn't anything there. Instead, they all got small models of the balloon and shirts which said, "My parents went into outer space and all I got was a lousy t-shirt."

Amy and I knew what needed to be done. We asked for a meeting with The Duke. It had never been that you just "showed up" even at their house, even though, I was their son-in-law. Amy and I arrived and there was a look of concern on her parent's faces. I'm certain they thought there was something wrong with one of us or the kids.

We all went out on the patio to look at Lake Michigan and I began the speech I never thought I could give. "I would like to resign from Wilco." The Duke's mouth dropped open.

"Before you respond, may I please finish?" I asked. The Duke's head reluctantly nodded in the affirmative.

"I've been reviewing the entire structure and the area which has my greatest concern is our charities. We donate millions of dollars per year and yet, we don't seem to see any results. I would like to start a research team funded by Wilco. I would like to look at ways to improve the quality of life. I know there are many fine organizations, but Amelia and I believe we can generate a higher return-on-investment if we have our own organization."

With this Amy nodded in the affirmative.

"How much money do you think you will need, son?" The Duke inquired.

I responded, "I'm not certain, but I am willing to donate five million dollars of what I have saved to start things off and would like permission to develop a business plan we would bring to the board for approval".

The Duke stood for a moment and looked at Dr. Williams. His head nodded down and then he looked at Amelia and me. "When would this take place?"

"As soon as we can develop a transition plan concerning running my divisions." I responded.

The Duke answered, "Son, I'm ready to retire. You and Amelia have done everything I could possibly expect from both a daughter and son-in-law and a loyal employee. You have shown intelligence, dedication to a fault and the ability to accomplish things beyond my expectations."

"I can't accept your resignation from Wilco. What I can do is make you CEO and surround you with top management in all areas of the company. This will free up your time and allow you to focus on what you want. You two have made incredible sacrifices these past ten years. When others might have taken the resources they had and lived the high life, you have worked as if you didn't have a nickel to your name and made our company stronger than ever. If this is what you want, then, if it's all right with Marie, it's certainly all right with me. However, instead of developing some form of loose organization, I propose we build a world-class medical research facility and go from there."

I was shocked. My idea was having a few scientists and the Duke's idea was a complete medical research center, established and operated as a division of Wilco.

"We're all in, son. If this is what you and Amy want, you know we are behind you 100%."

"If it's all right, I'll begin by making my recommendations concerning who should be running my departments."

"There are a couple more things," The Duke noted. "We have always maintained Derrick's share of the net worth of the company and planned on donating it to charity in his name. Would it be all right if we start with some of his share as the initial seed money and you call it the Derrick Williams Center for Medical Research?"

My mouth dropped open. In the matter of a few minutes what had been a question I had been dreading to ask was turned around and we had over a billion dollars to start the facility. Instead of being unemployed, I was offered the opportunity to be CEO of Wilco. I looked at Amelia and she at me and the passion which had been worn away by the years of work began again. I smiled. She smiled and it was as if were standing in the Capitol Rotunda in Madison and the most beautiful thing I had ever seen in my life just walked in the door. I looked at Amelia and had an alternative offer.

"Sir, I appreciate the offer and vote of confidence, but believe there is someone more qualified to be CEO than me. The person is articulate, intelligent, compassionate and driven. My recommendation is to allow Amelia to be CEO and allow me to be totally committed to medical research. In addition, through your generosity, money is not and will never be an issue. Instead, sir, I would like to take a salary of one dollar per year, allowing my income to be used to bring in more talented people who can actually help us achieve our goals."

I think the Duke was stunned by my counter offer. For a moment he stood looking at Amelia and me and then said, " Amelia, what do you think?"

Amelia replied as she looked at both Dr. and Mr. Williams. "Dad, Q and I are really committed to helping people and allowing him to focus completely on the research division would allow this to happen. It is what I hoped he could do. I believe with your guidance, I can achieve what you have begun, but will only do so if you work with me to teach me so much more than I already know."

"Mom, you know a working mother means sacrifices for the kids. I know this means a greater time commitment on my part and I will need your help in showing me how I can be as good of mother as you have been. I hope you and dad can work with us to help us raise our kids in the manner you have raised me so that when the time comes that George and I want to retire, our kids will be qualified enough to be considered to keep the Williams tradition going."

Both parents smiled and in the matter of a few moments tectonic decisions were made which were going to affect the rest of our lives. Dad went into the wine cellar and brought out a bottle of Krug Clos d'Ambonnay, which Amy told me later was one of the most expensive bottles of champagne in the world. The cork was popped and we toasted the new CEO of Wilco and the new division having the goal of helping mankind.

It was only a few months until the annual employee meeting and so it was decided to wait until then to make the big announcements. This gave us time to work on the transition plan regarding who would be responsible for the different divisions. There were some surprises. In the end, those chosen had earned their spots through ability, desire, dedication and loyalty.

I was certain Amelia being named CEO would not come as a surprise as even the most jaded assumed she was next in line. Me becoming a divisional president would meet with the normal snickers and many thought the reason I married Amelia was to weasel my way into the fortunes. Little did they know!

The Annual Meeting:

February came fast and a mandatory senior management meeting was scheduled for the morning before the general session. The hushed silence of gossip throughout the company was deafening. As we gathered that morning, all parties were asked to give their cell phones to security. There was to be no recording to ensure the announcement came as a surprise to all employees at the same time as the Duke wanted it to be a family affair.

To really ensure the message remained a secret, the entire executive team was sequestered until the company meeting and was then seated on chairs on stage so there would be no whispers. The program went as it did every year with performance statements followed by the awards ceremony. When everyone thought the meeting was about to end, The Duke rose and asked for everyone's attention. The room immediately went quiet.

"I have a few announcements to make." There wasn't a sound in the room.

"Marie, will you join me here on stage?" Everyone knew Dr. Williams and so this was no surprise, just a little out of the ordinary. The Duke did something he had never done in any meeting before when he took Dr. Williams' hand in his. "As you all know, there comes a time in life when you realize the challenge is more than you have in you and I have reached that point! It's time to hand the reins of the company over to someone else. Over the past 30 years, we have grown together, prospered together, laughed together, cried together and even been angry together. In the end, you have been the glue that has allowed our company to grow and for all of us to prosper."

"Last winter, George and Amelia Terrill came to Marie and I and George offered to resign from the company. George wanted to take his passion for life and see if he couldn't help people by developing a medical research program. I refused to accept George's resignation. Instead I offered George the opportunity to start the Derrick Williams Center for Medical Research. While there are many wonderful research projects taking place all over the world, in many instances, the administrative costs eat up a large percentage of the dollars invested. For this reason, George offered to head up the division with a salary of one dollar per year, which I accepted."

"This new division will have as its goal, the identification and implementation of methods by which diseases and cures can be identified that help improve the quality of life. This is an exciting opportunity for our company to give back to the world and do so with the same financial efficiency we have implemented to allow our company to prosper".

"Initially, I had hoped George would assume the role of CEO of the company, but he had a better idea … an idea which I shared with my staff, to determine their opinions. Today I am happy to announce that effective immediately, Amelia Terrill has been named CEO. Amelia's degrees in business and law and her ten years with the company have given her the insight needed to carry on in your behalf. I will remain on the board of directors and will work with her to assist whenever she feels she needs my help. Amelia has shown the capabilities needed to manage a company such as ours and I trust her judgment completely. In addition, she has shown the passion and compassion for the people of not only our company, but those with whom we come in contact with that has allowed us to become a leader in every phase of business we are in."

The Duke paused for a moment and then continued, "This morning, we had an executive meeting and announcements were made concerning changes that are about to take place. These changes were considered for the past several months and each division has been placed in the capable hands of someone we believe will allow the company to continue to grow and prosper. While there might be surprises in some of our choices and I am certain, some disappointments, each and every decision made was done with one critical thought in mind, the wellbeing of you …our employees and then our customers and clients."

Again a pause and then The Duke quietly added, "This will be my last meeting with you. Marie and I could not be prouder of all of you and what you have accomplished. We cannot thank you enough for all you have done for us and for our family. Yet, when it's time to go, it's time to go."

There were tears in everyone's eyes. Tears of joy! Tears of sorrow! Tears of sadness and tears of gladness! The Duke was stepping down. The man who had made it all, was walking away. With that, he waved goodbye and he and Dr. Williams walked, hand-in-hand, out the door, to the thunderous applause from those whose lives he touched.

Amelia waited for the room to quiet and then began naming the new presidents and why they were selected. With each affected division came a round of applause. When all division presidents had been introduced, Amelia asked all of managers to step forward and join her as she paused for a moment and noted there was one additional thing. "Each person will receive an envelope as you leave. In it is a token of appreciation from Dr. and Mr. Williams for your loyalty consisting of $5,000 for each year you have been with Wilco". There were gasps as each person did the math in their head. For some, this meant checks of $150,000.

"We are a team whose goal is mutual trust, mutual respect and mutual reward. Through your efforts and commitment, we have been able to accomplish a lot. Through your continuing efforts, we can accomplish a great deal more. Thank you for coming" to which, we all clasped hands, raised our arms and bowed. The place went crazy!

Reality:

As the waves upon life's ocean's calmed and reality set in, Amelia and I realized our lives were changing too. Her intellect and expertise, along with the six-month transition period, made her first Monday as CEO go as smooth as if The Duke was still there. For me, it was a different story! For the first time in years, Monday was not met with an onslaught of what needed to be done. There were no meetings! There were no deadlines! There weren't people clamoring for my time, attention or thoughts. With the kids in school, those first few moments found me drowning in the deafening silence of reality. My God, what had I done?

It was late morning when I jumped in my truck and headed for Brookfield Square. I needed to buy some clothes. I walked past the Brooks Brothers store and made my way to J.C. Penny. I walked in, went to the men's department, but at my size, I probably could have stopped in the boy's area, and bought three pairs of jeans and six T-shirts. I drove to a DSW shoe store and bought two pair of tennis shoes.

As I was driving west on I-94 to the 287-mile marker, I headed south on Highway 83 to Wales, instead of North towards home. It was noon and I stopped at LeDuc's and had a hamburger, fries and chocolate custard shake. As I sat on one of the park benches, I thought of the kids, as this was their favorite spot in the entire world. The boys loved chocolate custard with marshmallow topping that we called the regular. Our daughter, Mela liked strawberry shakes, while Amy and I ate whatever they put in front of us because it was all so good.

Next, I went up the hill on Highway 83 to Wales Lawn and Garden, which was a gas station that sold lawn and garden equipment. I hadn't purchased gas in ten years, as my cars were always washed and filled every week.

As I was pumping my own gas, I spied what I really wanted, sitting on the showroom floor … a brand-new Simplicity Broadmoor lawn tractor with 40" mower deck. I went inside and talked to the guy behind the counter and asked the price. We dickered a little and I agreed to buy it. I said I would pay him one-hundred dollars more if someone would follow me home and deliver the tractor right away. I thought the guy was going to choke on his cookies, when I paid him in cash.

We filled the floor model with gas and I bought a five-gallon gas can and a kid loaded my new toy onto a trailer and followed me home. After showing me all the ins-and-outs, I gave the kid a hundred-dollar tip and sent him on his way. Needless to say, I made his day, as I spent the afternoon playing on my new tractor loving every minute of it.

That night Amelia came home and saw the shit-eating grin on my face. She knew the little kid had come home. The next morning, I got up, took a shower and put on jeans and a tee-shirt. I thought Amy and the kids were going to have heart attacks. "Sir George" as they called me behind my back, looked like a real dad for a change. About 8:30, I called the gardener and told him he wouldn't need to come anymore as I would be mowing and blowing myself. I think he was shocked, as no one and I mean no one on Pine Lake, mowed their own lawns or plowed their own driveways.

By ten o'clock I was restless. By noon, I was anxious! By the time the kids got home from school, I was going insane. Life's pace was profoundly different! It was 4:30 when I called Andrew and asked him to meet me for breakfast the next day. My respite was about to end. Andrew asked where. I told him to come to the house.

While I was offered an office in my old building, I wanted to work from home until I was ready. Cecelia was still at the old office and I was texting her ideas and thoughts for her to organize. I knew we couldn't stay there. I knew my travels initially would be extensive.

I wanted a new place which was convenient for her. It would be small! It would be nice and yet, it also needed to provide some sort of social structure that would allow her to sustain her network of friends.

That night, I asked Amelia what she thought and she indicated an office near the house made sense. Wilco had property, which included several offices in western Waukesha County and one was vacant. After the breakfast I proudly made for Andrew, we went to see the property. It was in with a group of lawyers and was quiet, dignified and somewhat elite. I called Cecelia and asked her if she wanted to come and visit. I think she was excited to get out and have something to do. Andrew and I met Cecelia at Kopp's on Bluemound Road in Brookfield and had their huge hamburgers and chocolate shakes. Cecelia was shocked to see me in jeans and a tee-shirt and I was loving it.

We went to the offices. There was an anti-room, four offices and a conference room. The former tenants had simply skipped out on Wilco and left everything in place, including all the furniture and pictures on the walls which I called "early lawyer" in design. It had been a long time since I saw wallpaper, but it was there with an off-white background and thin maroon stripes which accentuated the light beige carpeting. The carpeting was thick and the walls were insulated, all in lawyer style. After the hustle and bustle of the old place, I think Cecelia was a bit shocked at the tranquility.

"Cecelia, what do you think?" I asked.

Cecelia knew better than to beat around the bush.

"It's nice!" she replied.

"Nice? Like in too nice? Nice, like in boring? Explain nice, please."

"Awfully quiet!" was her response. But then, after the mayhem of our last place, I think a train station would seem quiet.

"Too quiet?" I inquired, to which Cecelia shrugged her shoulders.

"Look, you're the one who will be here all the time, not me! I want a place you like and will feel comfortable in."

"Is there a dress code?" Cecelia asked.

"Most certainly," I responded with a very pregnant pause. "Absolutely no bathing suits!"

That got a chuckle out of her and Andrew as I added, "We are here to build a foundation! What we wear isn't going to mean a damn thing to those we help. You can wear whatever you want. My only request is that, when we have someone important, we look like we are important, too, which means keeping a change of clothes in the closet in case there is a surprise."

I could see her concerns were dissipating.

"What about you?" I asked Andrew who looked at me with a surprised look on his face. "You want to be on the team or would you rather keep your old job?" There was a grin on Andrew's face. "I can't do this without the two of you!"

I don't think they understood and perhaps I was doing a lousy job of communicating. "Look!" I said "Besides Amelia and my mother, you two are the most trusted people in my world. I want you both to work with me and help me build the foundation. Right now, you don't see much activity and yet, if I can do what I want to do, you will be very busy."

They both smiled and nodded in the affirmative. We were still a team as I added, "All right, who wants the fancy office?" They both looked at me as if to assume it would be mine continuing, "I'm only going to be here every now and then and so I want you, Cecelia to take it. Andrew, you've never really had an office and so you get that one," I said as I pointed to the next largest. "I'll take the smaller one."

"Let's call central purchasing and order the phones and equipment you need and then contact personnel and hire a receptionist. Andrew, check with the FAA and see if we will be able to land a chopper in the field next door. If we can, call and have it designed for paving and lights. Better yet, see if it's big enough for two choppers. I think Amelia should be flying to the office instead of wasting all that time in a car. We'll use mine when we need to go to the lab."

This caught them both by surprise as they had no idea what was going to transpire. All they knew was the stressed-out workaholic they had reported to was like a kid at Christmas opening presents. They were in for a very big surprise! "Let's all meet here next Monday. Take the rest of the week off! I've got to go home and wax my truck and get dinner ready for the kids." I said with a big smile on my face.

IMVR:

The following Monday, we showed up at the new offices. Everything had been installed and Andrew noted we not only had FAA approval for the helipad, but Wilco owned the land. I outlined my concept of wanting to create a research campus and how I hoped my brother wouldn't mind if we took a small slice of Waldwick next to the forest to create it on.

Andrew said he had another idea and outlined a concept that was so intriguing and made so much more sense that I could have kissed him … not on the lips mind you, but my God, was he spot on.

"Why do researchers need to be all in the same place?" he asked. "Couldn't they live wherever they want and work wherever they were and still contribute?"

"How?" I inquired.

"Through IMVR" Andrew responded.

"What?"

"Immersive virtual reality!" Andrew replied.

I scrunched my shoulders. "What's that?"

"Immersive Virtual Reality is simply having the person wear virtual reality glasses while also controlling the sounds they hear. The entire concept is one of 3D visuals and surround-sound. This combination, immerses the person both from a visual and auditory perspective and they feel they are at the site they are viewing."

Andrew added, and continued. "Our brains are wired for the incorporation of both visual and auditory senses, but only our vision is working with regular virtual reality, so the overall effects are reduced. With IMVR, you not only see the image in front of you, but you are immersed in the image both visually and acoustically. Such things as small echoes in a room, add as much sensory depth as shadows do to an image. In the end, when done properly, all the stimulation of having a person or group of persons in the same room, are overcome."

"How do you know so much about IMVR?" I asked.

"We use it for flight simulation and training. It saves time and money and, if the student makes a mistake, there is no physical consequence. It used to be just the visuals as if a pilot was looking out the front window of the plane, but all that changed when IMVR came along because you add auditory and visual spatiality to the equation and there is a much higher sense of reality."

Andrew continued, "If we incorporate IMVR, instead of coming to an office, the person can work wherever they are and then 'jump' to the site for research, meetings and interactions with others without really being there. Now, instead of traveling from place-to-place, you jump in when you need to or when you want to just like flipping from one web page to the next on the internet."

I must have had a weird look on my face as Andrew kept expanding on the concept.

"A basic form of IMVR has been used in schools and education for years helping students develop emotional, interpersonal, intrapersonal and spatial intelligence, giving them an incredible diversity of skills. Imagine a room with researchers residing all over the world at the same time!"

Andrew added, "From my perspective, IMVR would eliminate the need for large research facilities saving facility, energy and maintenance costs and eliminate downtime. Imagine taking a project and having a team around the world working on it in segments, twenty-four hours a day instead of one lonely researcher in a lab, working on a project all by themselves."

No huge building! No major costs for relocation! No funds needed for utilities! My God, what a great idea!

"Why hasn't this been done before?" I asked.

"Because the internet was too slow and the bandwidth too narrow to carry all the information at the same time. The net result had been lousy pictures or lousy sound to the point the receptor was never even close to what they could see and hear outside their headset."

"Why now?" I added.

Because of what is called 5G or fifth generation transmission technology." Andrew replied.

"What's that?"

"5G is the transmission technology that has erased the differences between wired and wireless networking to accommodate the growing mobility of network users while also increasing transmission speeds up to ten gigabits per second or one-hundred times faster than 4G did."

Andrew could have been talking Greek for all I knew and I guess it showed as he continued, "Remember when the Internet first started and you had dial-up which went through your phone lines?" I nodded with a bashful smile. "The system was slow and clunky and it took forever to download anything." Again, a nod in the affirmative.

Andrew continued, "When the first commercial 4G networks were rolled out in 2010, it changed the way users thought about wireless communication. People didn't have to wait until they were on Wifi to download files or stream music and movies. They could do it from basically anywhere they had a cell signal. The leap in speed between 3G and 4G was massive and opened new doors for everyone from app developers to content producers to pursue boundary-pushing ideas. The problem was it required one end to be, what I call static or recorded, simply because there wasn't enough bandwidth."

I could tell Andrew was into what he was talking about as he continued, "5G's transformative potential is affecting every type of institution from business and government, to doctors and caregivers being able to provide therapeutic treatments through virtual reality. Even things like parking sensors, which would indicate empty spots and security systems that create smart cities which are adjusted in real time, are possible. Add to this, the ability to create and communicate instantaneously seems almost hard to believe."

"Another incredible advantage will be for manufacturers who will able to create intelligent factories and provide services unlike ever before."

Andrew was on a roll, "Let's say your furnace or air conditioner needs to be repaired. The way it has been until now is that a technician comes to your house and does a diagnostic to determine the problem. With 5G, all your appliances will have sensors built-in that automatically diagnose the problem and contact the servicer and let them know what the problem is. The servicers will contact you and set a time when they will come and replace the broken part. This means one less service call and no mistakes on what's wrong."

"In the past, the service company would have a warehouse full of parts and if they were missing what you needed, you would have to wait. With 5G, your appliance will contact the service company's computer and their 3D laser printer will make the part so the servicer doesn't need to have a huge inventory of things no one needs laying around. This is exactly what the car manufacturers have done with the Wilco car dealerships and why you are seeing less inventory in your back rooms. In addition, your customer's cars are constantly 'talking' to your service departments, telling them what's going on and this information is then being directed back to the manufacturers so they can see where potential problems are going to arise if the problem census gets too large. This will allow manufacturers to determine recalls before they become a big problem and actually make running changes to everything if a problem is identified."

I shook my head in amazement and asked how this was applicable to what we wanted to do and Andrew answered. "With 5G, we can create virtual reality in real time. If you ever watch the news and see the delay between the anchor person and the reporter in the field, it's because of transmission delays. With 5G that will simply cease to exist, allowing for interaction anywhere two people are connected. With IMVR our researchers would be able to simply put on headphones and have meetings regardless of where they were?"

The points he made were spot on and now I was back, not even to first base, but one step off home plate, in my thought process.

"Where would we find someone, who could set all this up and how much do you think it would cost?"

Andrew replied. "I know who, but I don't know how much it would cost."

"When do I get to meet the company that could set all this up?" I asked.

"It isn't a group of people, it's one person."

"You know somebody?"

"Yes! I believe so."

"Who?"

"My brother, Peter!"

The message from the Medicine Man hit home!

Peter:

An appointment was made for later that week aa I was anxious to meet the guy who could save us millions of dollars. It was agreed we would meet at our offices at 10:00 AM. I was there in a coat and tie, Cecelia was dressed to the nines. I looked out my office window and saw this guy on a motorcycle in jeans and no helmet pulling into the parking lot. This wasn't just any motorcycle, but a vintage Harley soft-tail, fat boy with raised handles bars.

Soon there was a knock at my door and Cecelia had a look of trepidation on her face. "There's some kind of biker out here who says he has an appointment!"

I stood up and went out to the lobby. The Biker was Peter. His hair was almost shoulder length and he had a long Foo Manchu mustache and was wearing a blue jean jacket, jeans with a big chain on it and heavy boots. I could see the tattoos on the backs of his hands. My God!

"Peter?" I asked.

Peter nodded in the affirmative.

"Welcome!" Cecelia's eyes were as big as quarters. I don't think there could have been any way he would be more different than his brother.

"Come in," I said, beckoning him to the conference room. "Would you like some coffee or something to drink?"

"Water would be fine, unless you have tea." He responded.

Peter's voice simply did not fit the image. I was expecting something rough and tumble and those first words were articulate.

"Cecelia, can you please make Peter a cup of tea?"

"Do you prefer white, green, herbal, black or oolong?" Cecelia asked.

Peters eyebrows raised in anticipation. "Do you happen to know if the Oolong is Chinese or Taiwanese?"

This was not the way I thought the meeting with a biker dude would begin.

"Chinese" Cecelia responded.

"Great! Chinese Oolong is a bit sweeter and my favorite." Peter replied.

I looked at this guy and could see the resemblance to Andrew … same color hair, eyes and distinct chin.

"Andrew told me you know a lot about computers." I noted.

"Yes sir." Peter replied.

I thought we were about the same age or at least within a few years and so I asked him not to call me sir.

"OK sir!" he responded with a smile and continued.

"Why computers?" I asked.

"I really enjoy critical thinking," Peter responded as he looked deeply into the surface of desk as if memorizing where everything was placed and continued, "critical thinking is actually the basis for all computer computation, and that's why I got involved with computers."

I had no idea what he was talking about regarding critical thinking and asked him to explain, which he did with an answer which simply floored me.

"Critical thinking is the disciplined process of conceptualizing, applying, analyzing, synthesizing, and/or evaluating information gathered from or generated by observation, experience, reflection, reasoning or communication. It is used as a guide to belief-and-action, based on universal intellectual values which transcend subject matter to include clarity, accuracy, precision consistence, relevance, sound evidence, good reasons, depth, breadth and fairness interwoven from modes of scientific, mathematic, historical, anthropological, economic, moral and philosophical thinking."

I must have had a bizarre look on my face, but then who wouldn't as Peter added, "Critical thinking varies according to the motivation underlying it and is never universal to one individual. While I love to debate and from debating learn, I also must accept that everyone is subject to episodes of undisciplined and irrational thought where the quality of thought is typically a matter of degree, dependent on, among other things, the quality and depth of experience in a given subject or with respect to a particular class of questions or interactions the person has. I think when the mind is stretched, it has a difficult time going back to its original form."

My frown must have caught his attention as Peter continued, "when you go back to something you either have done before or even pondered previously, the entire thought process is easier and you become more comfortable with what you are doing or thinking at that moment. To me, this means that continuing to expand my intellectual horizons will allow me to function that much more efficiently on things that are either redundant or commonplace and will result in greater intellectual efficiency."

I had no idea what Peer just said, but nodded my head because it all didn't matter. The dude had already shown me he was way, way, way above my intellectual grade and it made me excited.

Peter concluded, "No one can be a complete critical thinker! It's impossible! People can only critically think to a limited degree because we all have natural tendencies of bias which affect insights and create blind spots that warp our reality and skew tendencies towards self-delusion. For this reason, the development of critical thinking, reasoning skills and dispositions are life-long endeavors and why I love computers, because they don't have bias built in and can use the knowledge provided in its purist form, to derive a conclusion."

I countered. "Isn't a computer limited to the knowledge provided and therefore the limits and bias of the person who programmed it?"

Peter replied. "In the past, that was the case. Today, it's no longer true. Artificial intelligence is allowing computers to become critical thinkers with the ability to reason and conclude and do so without emotional bias."

"So, you are a computer geek?" I questioned.

"I've been enamored by computers since I was a little kid. I've not only been involved in the software side, but built my own computer and got involved in what were called computation competitions where you build the computer and then try to see how productive you can make it in terms of computational capabilities such as memory and speed."

"Where did you go to college to learn all this?" I asked.

"I never went to college." Peter responded. "In fact, I never finished high school."

My facial expressions must have given my surprise away as Peter continued. "I wasn't very good at following orders from teachers about things I knew more about than they did. It wasn't ego or anything like that. I would read what they wanted read and then would dig a little deeper in the subjects I liked and sincerely felt they were holding me back."

"So, you quit school?"

"Not quite!" Peter said with a bit of a squeamish look on his face.

"What then?"

"I was arrested and convicted of a felony."

"What?" I asked in a surprised manner.

"Well, being a real computer nerd, I was studying physics and quantum mechanics and got involved in competitions to see who could break into the most secure websites. It was a stupid thing to do, but the challenge was there. Fifteen years ago, things weren't as sophisticated as today and so I got into bank websites and 'borrowed' a few thousand dollars to pay for more equipment. I took the money and built a more sophisticated computer and my own software and was able to breach the NSA's internal site."

"You mean the National Security Administration?" I said incredulously.

"Yes! One day as I was digging around, two FBI agents showed up at the door and I got arrested. When I went to trial, I was offered a plea bargain if I would tell on those in the competition. The problem was word had spread. Everyone used an alias and they were gone. I was sentenced to five years in prison and because I was eighteen, it was in Waupun."

"My God!"

"It wasn't that bad! I got my GED."

Peter looked at the floor and then at me. "There are some consequences to being a convicted felon. The net result of the conviction is I can't work for a bank or the government or join the military. And, because of my record, I'm not allowed in casinos or I would have played poker professionally. I thought of becoming a professional bridge player, but it's a tough gig. I play chess whenever I can and enjoy all three."

"Peter, where do you live?" I asked, meaning which city.

Peter looked down at the floor again and I could tell he was embarrassed. "I live in my parent's basement with my girlfriend, Cindy. Because of my record, her parents have disowned her."

"Did your brother tell you what we might want to do?"

"Yes, that's why I'm here. I think I can help, if you let me. All I want is a chance do things right. I learned my lesson the hard way and realized it the first night the cell door clanged shut. While I was in prison, I helped create computer classes for the inmates, taught guys how to play bridge and started the chess club. My claim to fame was playing six games of chess at the same time, while blindfolded. This got the warden's attention and the next thing I know I was paroled after three years, two months and three days."

I looked at Peter and saw someone who needed a break and asked, "Why the hair and the look?"

"My way of showing my independence, I guess!"

"The problem is you are pre-judged."

"I know and it has kept me away from the status-quo. But I want to be judged for who I am and not what I am."

He hit the nail right on the head! Bango! Everything Amelia and I had been going through our entire marriage!

I looked him straight in the eyes. "Look, your brother said you are an incredible person who only wants a break. In the few minutes you've been here, you have knocked my socks off. However, we are funded by a very big corporation which is incredibly conservative. I would love to have you meet with our human resources people and, if it works out, head up what we are doing when it comes to computers. We all have to make sacrifices and pay our dues. You did it in prison and I wonder if you are willing to do it again. I don't care if you are an ex-felon. I really don't care how you dress! I don't care about tattoos. In fact, my wife has one," (carefully omitting any reference to "my" rose, strategically placed in never, never land). "What I care about is building a team of talented, dedicated people who can help us help people."

There was a smile on Peter's face as I added. "However, in order to do this, I need to make you get through the front door, which means following a few rules of engagement in the beginning."

The smile was gone.

"Nothing major! How about some conservative clothes and a slight trim of the mustache? I would like to have you meet with the head of human resources and get his opinion."

Now the head was cocked.

"If he has the same opinion that I do, we will hire you and give you complete control over building our computer system from the ground up. This is a non-profit corporation and we do watch our pennies, but I can offer you a starting salary equal to what people with your skills are paid in the rest of the corporate world, plus benefits including an annual bonus, insurance, profit sharing and a 401K."

The head was back level.

"Do you think you want to meet with him?"

Peter slid back in his chair. "I get my mustache trimmed and wear standard clothes and go for an interview with human resources?"

"Yes"

"OK!" Peter said with a slight smile of relief on his face. "You'd hire me?"

"Certainly. You see, I see a lot of me in you. It's just, I was given an opportunity and took it."

Cecelia brought in the tea and I invited her to sit down as I introduced Peter. Cecelia's trepidation began to wane as she saw a young man who was profoundly intelligent, articulate and polite sitting across from her.

As the two finished their tea, I smiled and said. "Cecelia, we need to get hold of Jermaine Washington in HR and set an appointment for Peter to meet with him."

Cecelia nodded in the affirmative.

"Peter, what are your plans for the next couple of hours?"

Peter responded he had none.

"Cecelia, will you drive Peter over to Brookfield Square, unless you want to ride on the back of Peter's Harley." This got a smirk out of Cecelia and a smile out of Peter. "Go to The Duke's store and have him pick out some job interview clothes. Please put them on my account and tell the tailor we need the work done while you and Peter are having lunch." Now Cecelia knew I was serious as I added, "I'll call Jermaine and set up the second round."

With that Peter and Cecelia were out the door. I called Jermaine and filled him in on Peter, his background and what I wanted to do.

Three hours later, Peter and Cecelia returned. I was taken aback! The foo Manchu was completely gone, along with the long hair. In my doorway stood a young man in a Navy-blue blazer, grey slacks, white shirt and silver-and-blue necktie. I smiled.

"Do you want to borrow a car?"

Peter shook his head in the negative.

"Well, you better get back into your biker duds as you will look pretty silly riding in that get up."

Off the cuff, I asked, "What do you do in the winter to get around?"

"Take the bus" Peter replied as I shook my head and smiled.

"Cecelia, call Jennie in capital goods and have someone deliver a loaner to Peter's address from the Hartford dealership and tell them I'll sign for it."

I think Peter was in shock.

I added, "Dr. Jermaine Washington heads up our executive search team for the company. I have set an appointment for you for Thursday morning at 9:00 AM. The process will take most of the day. Is that convenient?"

There was a huge smile on Peter's face. He was being accepted for who he was.

Time flies when you are swamped and the entire realization Peter was going through 'the process' slipped by until Friday. Shortly after lunch, Jermaine called to inform me that Peter was there at exactly nine and went through the entire process with five interviews and four hours of intelligence and psychological tests.

Jermaine noted everyone was simply blown away by the intellect and also the humility Peter had. Jermaine noted Peter took a fifty-question math test and was instructed to answer as many questions as he could in five minutes and there wasn't any special order he needed to follow, but to do as many as possible.

This was a trick!

The questions were mixed between difficult and easy and the idea was to see if the person taking the test would skip around and only do the easy ones and then go back and do the more difficult questions. If they did, it showed they weren't as diligent as someone who progressed sequentially. Jermaine noted that Peter not only got the questions answered correct, he did them all and completed the test in less than five minutes.

"I've never had anyone complete all fifty questions in five minutes!" Jermaine noted. "Then to get them all correct was unheard of."

"In other words, a smart dude?" I asked.

"Brilliant!" Jermaine added. "Not only mathematics, but vocabulary, spatial reasoning and logic, which puts him in the top one-tenth of one percent of anyone who had ever taken the tests."

"Social skills?" I asked.

"There are some issues caused by his intellect. When you are thinking ten steps ahead of the person you're talking to, it can be a problem."

"Did he talk about his childhood?"

"Yes, of course and he was open about the mistakes he made." There was a pause on the other end of the line. "George, we all make mistakes when we are young. I was a gang banger until Dr. Williams helped save my life. Without her and the opportunity she provided, I would have probably been in prison with Peter or dead."

"Hire him?"

"Of course! But, let him run his part of the show and don't hold him back!"

"Did you talk compensation?"

"No! With your new division I don't know if you are on the same scale as everyone else or not."

"What would someone with his skill set earn in the real world?"

"Six figures!" Jermaine replied.

"Does he still owe the banks he borrowed from?" I asked.

"Yes"

"How much?" I asked.

"$42,000," Jermaine answered.

"Make it his signing bonus. Write up the offer and throw in the car and the benefit package."

I went out and told Cecelia we had the fourth member of our team who would head up all artificial intelligence. She smiled. It seems the three hours away from the office had done her as much good as it did Peter. I called Andrew and gave him the good news. His brother was being entrusted with developing the entire computer system for our group and, if it worked out, the entire corporation, some day.

Day One:

Andrew and Peter came at precisely 8:00 AM the following Monday, but then I would have been shocked if they hadn't. It was day one of our little team. Andrew had taken a set of employment papers for Peter to complete at home. Peter had scanned them and emailed a copy to Cecilia, who, in turn, sent them to personnel. No time was wasted settling in.

We directed Peter to his office and asked him to get set up and we would all meet at 10:00 AM. I saw an Amazon speaker and was afraid we would be inundated with some kind of heavy metal music. Instead, soft instrumental music came from his office and we all frowned. We had a brilliant, biker dude with tattoos, who listened to soft piano music.

Cecelia came back with a smile on her face. Peter told her he was a big believer in music therapy as a way of being more creative and productive. I didn't have a clue what she was talking about. All I knew was that the soft sounds filled our offices with warmth and friendship.

Peter noted, "I am certainly no scientist with any profound revelations. However, studies have repeatedly shown music can have a tremendous effect on your body and psyche. Today there is a growing field of healthcare known as music therapy, which uses music to help cancer patients, stroke victims, children with ADD, and others including those incarcerated, to simply calm down. Leading hospitals are beginning to use music and music therapy to help with pain management, ward off depression, promote movement, calm patients, ease muscle tension."

"How?" I asked, literally forgetting this guy was a walking Google.

Peter continued. "Humans are electro-mechanical devices, which means we have a small current running through our bodies which is created by the chemical reactions taking place within us.

This electrical energy can be measured and the average frequency determined. Music is based on what are called harmonics, which are nothing more than multiples of the frequency. When there are harmonics, we find the sound pleasing. When the frequencies are disjointed, it's called noise."

Ceclia just shook her head and smiled as Peter continued. "Research has shown music can stimulate brainwaves to resonate in sync with faster beats, bringing sharper concentration and more alert thinking and a slower tempo promoting a calm, meditative state. Music can also be used to bring a more positive state of mind, helping keep depression and anxiety at bay by preventing the stress response from wreaking havoc on your body. In other words, the right music can keep both creativity and optimism levels higher, blood pressure lower, while boosting immunity and easing muscle tension."

Peter added, "Noise is disturbing while the music a patient or employee loves can relax them. 75% of all people listen to music to ease tension and stress. I personally like soft piano or stringed instrument music and hope it doesn't upset or offend anyone."

We all just shook our heads that it didn't. Music! Music! I smiled. We were becoming a classy joint in our jeans and T-shirts. I couldn't wait to tell Amy.

We got back to business and Andrew said he thought about our goals and wondered if we could develop a mission statement. After extensive discussion, our mission statement became ... *"The goal of the Derrick Williams Medical Research Foundation is to enhance the quality of life through the reduction or elimination of maladies detrimental to a living being's existence."*

We initially used the word human but realized some of the research might be applicable to animals and other living species. We all sat back and pondered what we had written and nodded. We concurred our goal was not to extend life, but simply enhance it.

Peter surmised, "We are looking at ways to improve life from a qualitative perspective and not from a quantitative manner." Like so many other points he made that day and every day, he had a bead on what we wanted to accomplish.

I outlined, "Regardless of how much money a company has, you still need to be cognizant of expenses." I pointed out that our goal was to get the biggest bang possible for the buck, while our administrative costs were targeted to remain under 5% of our total operating expenses. I indicated we wanted to hire the best researchers we could who were leaders in their fields and pay them an equitable wage. I indicated, based on Andrew's idea, we were willing to invest in the latest technology to ensure we had a comprehensive global team.

Peter leaned back in his chair and smiled. "I think I have a way we can get researchers to work for free."

I think my head must have jerked back six inches as I questioned, "How are you going to do that?"

Peter replied, "By giving them access to something they all want, but can't afford and trading their time and talent for what we have to offer."

"What's that?"

"Greater access to more intelligence than they can possibly ever get on their own or through any medical, educational or research organization they are affiliated with."

I frowned as Peter continued, "Most researchers are limited to their access to the ever-growing information about their subject matter. This is because the organizations they work for can't afford to provide either the computer they need or the time required on the net to harvest all the data in their fields. I think I have a way which will allow those researchers to have virtually unlimited access to all the data in the world and do so on a daily basis."

My mind was already spinning as I asked, "How?"

"By linking a series of IBM Watson binary computers to one quantum computer, which harvests everything on the global internet every six hours and deciphers the collected data into applicable files or folders, which is then transferred categorically to the Watsons to which the researcher would have access."

"Huh?"

"With this structure, the researcher would simply log in whenever they wanted to and download all the data which had been harvested on his subject. Because we would be linking the Quantum to several Watsons, the macro data could be correlated to eliminate redundancies and only provide new and pertinent information to that specific researcher. In other words, they would be more efficient and productive and remain current with any and all information applicable to their research on a daily basis."

"What about language, if you are talking about global researchers?" I asked.

"That's easy" Peter responded. "We just download every language and cuneiform on Earth."

"What?"

"Sure, we download all the languages and then whatever language the researcher is most comfortable with will automatically convert the data for them. We can even program it so that, in real time, they can either speak or write in their native language and have it translated into a language of choice, which also can be written or spoken."

"You can do that?" I inquired.

"I can't, but the computer can."

I just shook my head in amazement and thought of the term 'Global Village' coined by Marshall McCluen in the 1950's, as Peter continued. "Concurrent with the individual reports, I think we can develop a form of artificial intelligence which will take harvested data and combine it with information from other researchers and create daily integrated reports on the subject matter. Whenever there was a change, advancement or breakthrough on any selected topic, we would have a written report that day. Add in the IMVR for conferences and interaction, and it would be like having everyone in the same building."

Peter sat back in his chair and smiled as Andrew, Cecelia and I sat dumbfounded by what he proposed.

"Do you think this would work?" I asked.

Peter nodded in the affirmative as I smiled and shook my head as he added, "A/I is already being integrated into transportation, financial services, retailing, agriculture, eco-friendly manufacturing, along with health and medical care and so, I see no reason why we can't proceed."

"How much do you think this all will cost?" I asked.

Peter replied, "From what I know, Watsons run about three million each and we would probably need six of them, if we are going to differentiate into categories and provide both back up and security. Today there are two primary companies with quantum computers…IBM and a company called D-Wave with Google coming on strong. I believe IBM would rather have us lease space on their quantum, which would be correlated to the amount of time we use it. My idea is creating a source at a fixed cost with variable operating expenses. I think this would be most attractive to researchers because they would not be limited and their information would be secure. If we decided to buy a D-Wave 2000Q quantum computer, it would be about fifteen million dollars. The D-Wave has a capacity of 20 qubits or 2 to the 20th power, while the IBM unit has a 50-qubit processor."

"Why not the IBM?" I asked.

Peter replied, "Initially would be over-kill and I think I could probably modify the D-Wave, over time, to reach 100-qubits if we need the space."

Andrew added, "When we get going, we can also add one of IBM's new Project Debaters to the family. It will allow the researchers to debate with the computer to determine if their hypothesis is correct."

"You mean there are computers which can do that?" I asked, shaking my head.

"Just in the start-up mode," Andrew replied. "Today, the sheer rate and pace of technology has made the amount of information available to researchers almost overwhelming. To have an unbiased source which would allow differing opinions be presented from both sides of an equation in a factual, well-written manner, makes all the sense in the world to me."

"But I've already got my wife and she is tough enough to debate!" I interjected.

This got a polite laugh from the boys who didn't comprehend the reality of my statement.

I got serious. "In other words, you're talking thirty-three million for computers?"

Peter responded, "I think IBM would give us a discount if we purchased six Watsons and then, if we have IBM and D-Wave competing for the quantum, we should get a discount there. I'm thinking we could get all the equipment for around twenty-five to thirty million plus tax."

Cecelia interjected. "No sales tax. We are a registered non-profit foundation." Her planning just saved us over a million dollars.

"There's another aspect that needs to be addressed." Peter interjected.

"What's that?" I inquired.

"Quantum computers make errors when they get hot and so they need to be constantly cooled."

"So, we buy an air conditioner?" I responded.

"They need to be kept at one-degree Kelvin, or one degree above absolute zero, or they start making mistakes, which means liquid nitrogen or helium is needed."

"How cold is absolute zero?" I asked.

Peter had forgotten he was talking to a non-scientist. "That's 459.67 degrees below zero."

"Almost as cold as the heart of an IRS agent!" I joked.

Peter continued without even an acknowledgement for my lame attempt at humor. "Around twenty years ago, physicists observed what they called the Bose-Einstein Condensate, which is a fifth state of matter that exists within a sliver of absolute zero, at which point individual atoms overlap so much they collapse into a single quantum state where they act as a single entity."

I had no idea what Peter was talking about but thought it dealt with the computer and the fact that, at one degree Kelvin, quantum computers were able to do two things at once that wouldn't be lost in the electrical noise that heat can create.

Peter added, "And so we will also need to build an inert facility that can sustain the environment and cool the computer with helium.

"Helium? Like the stuff in kid's balloons?" I asked

Peter responded. "First, you need to understand helium is used in much more than party balloons. Helium is the second-most common element in our solar system. Unfortunately, most of it is on the sun. The helium found on Earth was created over millions of years by the decay of metals and elements underground. When helium gets cold, it can glide friction-free, through narrow tubes and sustain currents for long periods of time that allow it to flow up and over a container's sides. The stuff is so applicable that scientists call it a super-fluid."

"What's also really neat about helium is that can't catch fire and will get much colder than other gases, so it's very good at keeping sensitive equipment like large medical machines, welding equipment and NASA's rockets the right pressure."

I stopped and scratched my head. In the matter of less than two hours, the entire concept and structure I had been mulling over seemed so antiquated and archaic and this made me smile as I added, "Peter, none of us, except Andrew and particularly the board, understands a thing about binary and quantum computers and what they do and how they work. Can you take some time to develop a write-up and power point we can present?"

A few days later Peter walked into my office with the following report.

For the past seventy years, the world has come to rely on what are called binary computers for all of its computations and storage capabilities. A binary computer uses a system of 'gates" to do nothing more than reflect either a one or zero, which are called bits.

With binary computers any question asked requires the computer to proceed in an orderly, linear fashion to find the answer. In this manner it is like opening and closing doors. If the door is open, the search continues to the next set of doors until one is open and then the next and the next and so on. All of this takes time!

A quantum computer marries the sciences of quantum physics and digital computing into one device. To do this, it takes the same idea of one and zero but looks at them in two slightly different universes at the same time thereby seeking possible answers in two different universes. When this is the case, a single quantum, called a qubit, can be in two states at the same time and can therefore perform two calculations simultaneously. Now instead of one door opening you have two doors which can open four doors which can then open eight and then sixteen and so on. The D-Wave 2000Q incorporates a 2,0000 qubit, niobium chip which performs at a speed of two to the 2000th or 1418 followed by 599 zeroes which represents more calculations than there are atoms in the universe and does so all at the same time. The IBM unit expands the processing capability to 50,000 qubits or two to the 5000th power or greater computational capability than the estimated number of atoms in the universe as computation speeds become proportionally faster with each qubit added.

With this capacity, quantum computers have the capability of solving problems in seconds which would take conventional computers centuries to answer. The D-Wave 2000 is very effective with so-called optimization problems such as selecting the most efficient route through different destinations. With quantum computing, we can provide more knowledge and do so a higher rate of computation speed than ever before.

However, there are challenges with a quantum computer which go beyond the initial cost and programming. The greatest being not only heat build-up, but a profound sensitivity to vibrations and electromagnetism. To solve this, the D-Wave 2000 uses niobium loops which become super conductive at ultra-low temperatures and are cooled to nearly absolute zero by using liquid helium to cool the loops and represents the rationale for the additional expenditure for the Watsons. Using a quantum computer would allow the foundation and its researchers to handle multiple conditions at one time through superposition and do so at a rate currently unheard of by those involved in the project.

Incorporating IMVR glasses will allow for 3D modeling so that researchers will be able to actually "look inside" things as small as individual atoms to determine not only structures but variances and even sub-atomic nuances and do so at a rate of one to the ten-millionth power. In so doing, the computer can serve two primary functions. First it will sweep the entire global internet for specific data four times per day, adding any new pertinent information regarding specific research projects to the database where the information will then automatically be transferred to one of the binary computers to be checked for redundancies and anomalies against the already stored information. From there, the binary computer will create a written update on the subject matter and communicate it to the researcher in their native language, as it is applicable to the field in which the researcher is studying.

Second, the computer will be able to work with virtually all individuals on Earth as a medical resource regarding allowing researchers to establish personal medical profiles and create more effective drugs, more finite in their capabilities of assisting in the specific compensation of the malady of the individual instead of the current generalized application methodology.

Finally, the computer will be able to work with researchers in determining how diseases develop and do so on a micro instead of macro perspective, while taking into consideration all other heath factors including genetics, lifestyle and the environment of the specific patient. While the initial expenditure is great and operating costs extremely high, the reward will be profound and will immediately position the Foundation as a global leader in medical research and wellbeing.

I read the report, put it down and read it again. Then, I set it aside for a day and read it a third time and realized this truly was the core ingredient to our future.

Two days later, Peter poked his head in my office and asked my opinion. I just smiled and shook my head. I was in awe! That night, I tried explaining everything to Amy and she could feel my excitement. Little did I know it was just the beginning.

Mark:

Friday, Peter stopped by again and asked if he could introduce a computer-nerd friend to me. It seems his friend had a concept which could be applicable to what we were doing. I said, "Of course" and the next Tuesday another meeting was set.

As was the case initially with Peter, in walked this initially awkward, "free spirit" with long hair, jeans and a black tee shirt carrying a small backpack, as we all entered the conference room.

Peter made the introductions and I could tell his friend, Mark was extremely nervous.

"Sir, would all of you mind signing an ND/NC before I share my ideas?"

This caught me by surprise and I looked at Andrew and Peter and my brow drooped.

Peter interjected. "Mark has been working on this for five years and the last idea he presented was developed by the people he shared it with and he got screwed."

I could sense the sincerity in both Mark and Peter and asked Cecelia to run copies, which we all read. It only said what Mark was about to show us was his idea and the ND, or non-disclosure part, was to make sure we wouldn't share it with others. The NC, or non-compete aspect, simply stated we would not take Mark's idea and create products of our own. As a foundation, until that moment, we had never thought of creating products.

Cecelia had been involved in these before and nodded it was OK to sign. We all signed on the dotted line and once again, our little foundation was about to make a dramatic turn.

Mark neatly folded the four signed documents and placed them in his back pack and pulled out a pair of gloves. I thought "My God, what is this, some sort of nut job?"

"Mr. Terrill, will you please put the Medi-gloves on?"

I took the gloves and slipped them on. They felt just like normal cloth gloves except the finger tips had a vinyl cover on each end and there appeared to be a small battery pack on the back of each wrist end. I raised my hands to show the group I had the gloves on.

Mark opened his laptop and turned it on. Within a few seconds, a screen appeared. On it was a blood pressure, body temperature, pulse and oxygen level readings. In other words, all of the key components called "vitals" doctors use to determine overall health.

"Whose readings are those?" I asked, already believing I knew the answer.

"Yours!" Mark replied.

I smiled.

"Just a moment, Mr. Terrill, you will feel a slight prick in your right pinkie finger." I did.

"Is there going to be blood inside the glove? I asked.

Mark looked at me as if I had just asked the dumbest question of the day and responded. "No sir, we only went through the epidural layer of skin and so there will be no blood, no chance of infection and no injury."

With that, a second screen appeared and there were more results that Mark explained.

"The episodic review people get from the current health care system is what is called 'sick care,' where people only go to the doctor when they need medication or modification. What people really need is 'well care' which will keep them healthy in the real world."

Mark continued, "Today, we have a process called 'digital therapeutics' which can be implemented to help treat diseases by modifying patient behavior and providing remote monitoring to improve long-term health outcomes. The first phase is remote diagnostics and that's what the gloves are all about." As he turned on the computer for all of us to see and continued. "The first report is your complete blood count, or CBC which measures the amounts of red and white blood cells, platelets and iron in your blood and can detect anemia, inflammation, infections and bleeding disorders. The chart here indicates that, for a man of your age, you are within the range of what is considered normal." I was glad it wasn't doing the mental part!

Mark continued, "The second report is your basic metabolic panel, or BMP, which measures how much glucose and calcium is in your blood, and whether you have the correct number of electrolytes and minerals, which are used to detect diseases such as diabetes, cancer, bone disease, kidney disease and other disorders. Again, you fall in the range for someone your age."

"The third report consists of enzyme tests which determines whether you have damage or disease in various organs of the body. I included a creatine kinase, or CK, test to determine if you've had a heart attack, which you have not. We also administered a creatinine test to measure kidney function and a liver enzyme test for liver disease. In addition, we added a PSA test for prostate cancer and your PSA number is less than 2.0 which is great."

My mouth was agape.

"In other words, by wearing these gloves, you have given me a complete physical?"

"Not quite. However, we did check all your vitals. You would still need to periodically see your doctor. However, by wearing the gloves once a month, you would build a complete medical record which would show any changes in the formative stages instead of at an advanced stage."

I was incredulous as Mark continued, "When we are done we will also be able to take a DNA sample to build your profile and record your finger prints eliminating the need for medical forms. All you would need to do was put on the gloves. If this was integrated with your insurance records and a credit card, the entire medical process including billing and payment, would be seamless."

I leaned back in my chair with the gloves still on and asked. "In other words, a person sitting at home could acquire this information, have it uploaded and sent directly to their doctor?"

Mark nodded in the affirmative and added, "The information would go into your personal database. Only when there was any change beyond prescribed parameters, would you be notified and be asked for permission to send the data to either your physician, or, if Peter and I think we can do what we want, have the computer do a complete diagnostic to determine the root cause of the changes."

Continuing, Mark added, "Using the computer, Peter said you are considering buying, we could also incorporate up-to-the-minute medical data, which would take all the permutations of your test, parallel it with your genetic data and health history and provide the physician with, not only the symptoms, but prescribe specific actions to alleviate your condition. By paralleling your age and genetic profile the system could even make recommendations regarding treatment, including prescriptions, which would then be cross-checked with those you were already on."

I sat shaking my head in disbelief and asked "Won't this put doctors out of business?"

"Hardly" Peter responded. "Today's physician is simply overwhelmed with data about patients including, not only their prognosis, but different treatment options. By having a resource which codifies all the medical algorithms and provides options instead of decrees, the methodology becomes an asset and not a liability to any physician."

Mark added, "Our goal is not to use artificial intelligence to replace doctors, but simply to personalize the care given to make sure it is not only contemporary, but specific to any changes taking place within your body that need attention."

"In other words, my doctor would receive my information only if there was a change and would also be given specific recommendations concerning treatments, which were virtually up to the minute and individualized?" I asked.

"Yes!" Mark said with a broad smile on his face.

"People going to doctors or are waiting to be released from hospitals because they are waiting for nothing more than their vitals to be checked, could do so from home?" I continued.

"Yes!"

"But how much would a pair of gloves like this cost?" I asked, waiting for an astounding figure.

"We believe, mass produced, they could be offered for $50.00," Peter interjected.

"$50.00?" I asked in disbelief.

Both nodded in agreement. "The user would need to purchase four AA batteries about once a year unless they forget to turn the gloves off. However, I believe I can actually modify the software so the gloves would turn off whenever there were no fingers in them."

"What about the software?" I asked.

Peter added, "We have everything done on our end. All the user would need is a router at home or even at a clinic. If they have a camera, they could also use it to connect directly with the doctor and never go to the doctor's office."

"In other words, virtual care?"

Again, both nodded in agreement.

Once again, I shook my head in amazement as Mark continued, "Imagine having a specialist from anywhere in the world helping you. Imagine what this could mean in underdeveloped countries. Gone would be the time and distance needed to make and keep a traditional doctor appointment. Using a team of trained individuals, we can put specialists virtually in everyone's home or clinic, or anywhere, and do so as frequently as needed, simply by monitoring a person's health and making real-time diagnoses and treatment adjustments. By simply putting on a pair of gloves, any individual would have all their personal data at the fingertips of those who needed the data to make a decision."

I sat, with my hands still in the gloves. Marked looked at the screen and smiled. My heart rate had increased. I was excited.

"Mark, we are a non-profit foundation, why didn't you take this to some medical company?" I asked.

"Because I want to help all people, not make a few people rich!"

"What's in it for you?"

"Satisfaction! My passion is to change the future, rather than falling victim to it. Financially, I would like a royalty of one dollar per pair when sold and be involved in the development of the entire project. In addition, I would like a base salary, which would keep me out any more debt until the gloves and the project are in place."

"How much money do you have invested right now?" I asked.

"A little over $30,000." Mark responded, as I almost choked in glee.

"And the software is done?"

Mark looked at Peter, "Here's the guy who did it!"

Peter added. "We're 90% there, but have complete confidence it can be achieved in a few months.

"Tell you what," I offered. "The foundation pays off your debt, you become project manager at the same salary as Peter, we sign a royalty contract and you begin next week?" There was a broad smile on Mark's face. He was working for a non-profit foundation which gave him control and the resources needed to finish his project and was working with his best friend.

That night, I went home whistling as I drove. If this was as big as I thought it was going to be, we would have the funding needed for as many computers as Peter ever thought of owning. I walked in the house and explained the entire process to Amy. She too, was excited and called her mother.

Two days later Dr. Williams met with our team and I watched as tears rolled down her cheeks at Peter, Mark and Andrew took her through the entire process. "All my prayers have been answered," Dr. Williams said. "All my prayers! Imagine going into villages and offering these to people and having the computer do a complete workup. Imagine how we will improve the health of so many people throughout the world who currently can't afford medical care or have no facilities close to them. Thank you! Thank you, Mark and Peter."

Doctor Williams looked at me with her broad St. Martin smile and for the first time ever, gave me a great big hug saying, "Thank you, George!"

I was honored, but hadn't done much except find two geniuses who had a passion for life. I looked at my two feathers in the glass case and the conductor's baton and hoped and prayed this was what they both were leading up to.

The MadCity Boys:

The following week, I went to the Wilco building and we developed a business plan. The gloves would be sold for $60.00 per pair of which $10.00 would go to fund those who could not afford to pay for them. Mark would get his dollar a pair which would make him a millionaire in a very short time and we would charge $1.00 per month subscription fee to all users, which would be covered by insurance and Medicare in the U.S. and social programs in other countries.

No one was to be denied access and yet the money generated would be used to improve and enhance the services offered, including our own medical team. We were on a roll. All we needed were the computers and a facility to keep them in.

Now having hardware and buying great big computers are one thing, but getting them to work is another and that required integrated software. To this end, Peter told me Madison had become a bastion for the next generation of software geniuses. While everyone thought it would be cool to work in the Silicon Valley, they all knew the cost of living was so outrageous, the quality of life simply wasn't there.

Madison offered an ideal spot for growth and development. The city was big enough to have everything to the point that, with the aid of the U.W., it was considered quite cosmopolitan. Yet Madison was small enough to be able to use what the city had to offer. In addition, Madison was still economical enough in terms of housing to afford to live there. The metro area had exploded and major software companies had set up suburban operations that attracted the newest and brightest minds in both computer programming and medicine.

Peter asked if we could begin interviewing people in Madison. I agreed. He said he would commute from Milwaukee. I told him he didn't need to and arrangements were made for him to use our condo. It wasn't long until Peter and Mark were established in MadCity and I realized our apex of power had shifted back to the city I loved.

After about six weeks, Peter called and said he had some candidates and wanted to make a presentation about what they felt could be the next step. I agreed and the group came to the office. With Peter and Mark were two individuals, Matt and John. Both were of the same demeanor as Peter and Mark, long-haired, free-spirited, geniuses who delved in a world where I had absolutely no idea what they were doing.

Peter made the introductions, as he was alpha male. Matt was the quiet one and began, "Mr. Terrill (God that made me feel old!) our team believes we can develop software which will be more productive, efficient and accurate than most human researchers. We have examined the parameters regarding Mark's invention and with Mark's involvement, believe we can go deeper into achieving a goal than initially thought possible."

John chimed in. "We believe that, by incorporating artificial intelligence into the base programming, many of the challenges faced with what researchers are manually doing, can be automated, with results developed almost instantaneously."

I heard the term artificial intelligence again, but wasn't quite certain what they were talking about and asked them to explain to which Peter responded, "Artificial intelligence is based on the hypothesis where every aspect of learning or any other feature of intelligence can, in principle, be so precisely described that software can be developed to simulate it. While the process of artificial intelligence has been around for decades in such things as digital personal assistants, it has only been the past few years with the evolution and development of what is called 'deep learning' that artificial intelligence in true capabilities have been comprehended.

Matt added. "Deep learning or deep neural nets, or simply nets, as we call them, is simply developing computer software which is self-teaching."

John included. "Rather than programming for every conceivable permutation and combination, as had been the case in the past, deep learning looks at all the possible scenario and teaches itself."

Back to Peter. "The incredible thing about deep learning is that all it takes is a programmer feeding an algorithm into the system, which is nothing more than a step-by-step procedure for solving a problem. To do this, we have developed software which can not only read all words and cuneiforms in any language, but also has voice and visual recognition as well."

My mouth dropped open as Peter continued. "This has allowed us to harvest hundreds of thousands of images and words and years of speech samples that are all related to medicine and used the data to teach the computer how to teach itself … or write its own software. The net result is we have a database which not only encompasses all current knowledge on anatomy and physiology, but chemistry, physics and math as well."

It was Mark's turn. "My gloves are literally sensors which have basic artificial intelligence built into the software. What these three have done is move beyond traditional logic into what is called machine learning, which will allow our computers to continually improve themselves as they experience the functions they are asked to do repeatedly."

Matt again, "Our goal was to develop software capable of deep thought. With Mark's sensor gloves, the same pattern is repeated over and over and over and with it, the same data is collected. With our program, the computer will begin to differentiate and narrow its parameters as the system is used repeatedly. Instead of macro perspectives, the computer will begin looking at all possible scenarios on an individual basis, first from a micro perspective and finally, from literally a molecular or even atomic perspective. In so doing, the data collected will be able to look at any aberrations in a much more finite manner than any human ever could."

Back to John, "We have developed a prototype for what we call a deep neural net. It has the ability to start from a macro perspective and keep digging deeper and deeper and deeper whenever it identifies anomalies in the person being evaluated. We have also been able to develop a reverse program, you might say. If the results created seem to be inaccurate, the neural net will send messages back down to the subsets so that all the lower neuron-like units retune their activations to improve the results."

Peter again, "We're not there yet, but we are working on what we call unsupervised learning. With it, all the data from the internet harvested and even Mark's gloves, are unlabeled and will automatically activate a search, where the software looks for recurring patterns. When we have this done, our computer will be able to not only harvest all forms of data, but delineate, correlate and disseminate the information to the appropriate parties."

Back to Mark, "Because of the anticipated wide use of the Medi-Gloves and the information gathered, we actually will be building what is called a "genome-wide association study" of GWAS that will house a huge amount of information that can then examine specific maladies predicated on genetic dispositions. Because the database will be dynamic and continue to grow with each new applicant, we will be able to decipher genetic maladies and develop what are called polygenetic scores or probability levels for certain types of maladies predicated solely on the genetic make-up of the person involved."

"As an example, there are over 100 different types of cancer. With our software and the use of a micron microscope, the computer will not only be able to determine the type of cancer but, by correlating it to the data collected on the patient, determine not only what type of treatment would generate the greatest success, but where, when and how it should be administered. Instead of using a curative paint roller, physicians will be able to use single strand of treatment hair to paint the most detailed picture possible."

John added, "What's really cool is that our software will be able to seek out any anomalies which are identified as precursors to the beginning of cancer and notify the physician the signs are there. With this, physicians will be looking at pre-stage cancers instead of waiting for other signs indicating the cancer cell has spread to stages one, two, three or four."

I sat shaking my head in disbelief.

Peter continued, "In addition, by simply storing data on the individual patient in a micro-environment concerning the results of the cancer treatment, the computer will be able to determine the treatment's effectiveness. Based on imaging of the entire physiological make-up of the patient, the computer will be able to determine the cost/benefit ratio of the treatment options, while examining what other drugs or courses of action may assist or impede the curative rate in like situations."

Back to John, "What's neat is that instead of looking at just a few symptoms, our database will look at over 100 different permutations within each patient sample and examine all the possible curative options to determine a root cause of any change."

I sat in total disbelief as Matt added. "Once we finish this, we want to combine deep learning with reinforcement learning, where our computer will update all of the values it has 'learned' and do so every millisecond. This will ensure our information is not only capacious, but dynamic in nature. In the end, we feel we can develop software for the Q2000 which will be able to not only examine patients, but do so on such an individual level that all treatments and analysis will be personal down to the genetic level, thereby improving life from the qualitative perspective you have established as the foundation's goal."

These guys were excited and they had a reason to be as Cecilia, Andrew and I began to applaud. Smart-ass me looked at the foursome and said. "So, what did you do in your spare time?" to which the reply was, "play video games!"

The Next Addition: Ever since Amelia and I returned from space, I couldn't get Captain Luke out of my mind. His passion and inspiration changed the two of us and I didn't know if it was the person or the event that made him stand on a pillar above almost everyone else.

Amelia and I discussed the experience a dozen times and yet, I yearned for more than just memories. One afternoon, I called Phoenix and got Captain Luke on the phone. We shared updates on his continuing trips and I invited him to come to Waldwick and go to the forest.

At first, I believe he was reluctant and then agreed. I asked Andrew to take one of the jets and pick Luke up and let him sit in the right, or co-pilot, seat so they could talk. The day was set and Andrew took off from Mitchell.

Andrew and Luke returned from Phoenix and I had a driver take Luke to the Pfister where we reserved a suite. Andrew called me from his car and simply said, " Holy shit!". In other words, he liked the dude.

When I picked up Luke a little later, he had a similar expression on his face, except it was about the hotel. Over 125 years old, the Pfister was designed with Romanesque Revival architecture. I remember thinking "huh?" until a brochure outlined that "the style was characterized by massive, articulated walls, round arches and powerful vaults that are all highlighted by an incredible ceiling fresco in the Pfister lobby". The place is so cool that, each year narrators and artists compete to chronicle the hotel's many stories and highlight the world's largest collection of Victorian art. Luke just shook his head as I produced a proud grin, knowing that he, like so many others, had a "Holy Shit!" moment when he realized Milwaukee was a whole lot more than Oompah bands, brats and beer.

To really knock Luke's proverbial socks off, dinner arrangements were made for the VIP table at Sanford Restaurant for Amelia, Luke and me to re-visit all we had seen and done. The dinner was splendid and we laughed and joked about all we had experienced. It was getting late and Amy had to get up and run the company, besides being a mommy, which meant a five AM wake-up call, as we still always ate breakfast together.

Luke knew we had money, I just don't think he knew how much. After dinner, Amelia went home and Luke and I went back to the Pfister and into the bar, where I outlined the next day. I told him Andrew would pick him up at 8:00 am and drive him out to the office. From there, we would take the helicopter to Waldwick. I had called Tommie and informed him of our visit and schedule and he wanted to know what he could do. I asked him to keep the cows quiet and have two ATV's and helmets ready for Luke and me. While Andrew was becoming my friend, this was to be a one-on-one experience to determine if Luke felt the way I did in the forest.

The trip went as planned. Luke was impressed that Andrew was certified in both fixed wing and helicopters and loved the ride. Luke had never ridden in an Airbus H135. Andrew explained that the chopper, was called Q-II and had twin engines and was rated as a civil, light utility helicopter that could reach a maximum speed of 259KM or around 180 MPH, with an operating range of 620KM or 385 miles. Andrew also noted that Q-II was capable of flight under what was called Instrument Flight Rules (IFR) while being outfitted with a digital Automatic Flight Control System (AFCS). I just sat there knowing this was meant for safety, but the two could have been talking Lithuanian for all I knew.

The real reason I love Q-II, was the design. The exterior was gloss black, just like Amelia II, while the interior matched Amelia II's cream and mahogany color scheme as well that Amy chose as it reminded her of Hermes. I liked the company, Hermes because of who the real Hermes was ... god of trade, heraldry, merchants, commerce, roads, thieves, trickery, sports, travelers, and athletes and also the son of Zeus, god of the sky and thunder and king of all other gods in Greek mythology.

I let the two jabber on as I sat back and looked at the land below that I had seen a hundred times, but never got tired of looking at. Our flight plan called for a little sight-seeing, where I outlined the whole history of the Driftless Zone and how it affected people and what I thought was the reason why.

We landed on the farm helipad, which consisted of a mowed hayfield, and there were two ATV's and helmets waiting for us. I smiled. To my delight, Tommie and I were a team again. He had divorced Heather and was back to being his own self. Tommie came with the truck and introductions were all around. He and Andrew left and Luke and I put on our helmets and rode out to the forest.

As we parked the ATV's and got off the bikes, Luke's hands began to tremble. As we walked to where the foundation for the school had been, his mouth was agape where, "Oh my God!" was all he could say. He too was feeling, what I felt every time I visited my friends the trees.

I took him to the spot where George the First had saved Rodney's great, great, great grandmother and told him the story of all that had transpired and how Rodney and I bonded. We walked to the spot where the Medicine Man had recited the portion of the Book of Wisdom and Luke simply shook his head. I proceeded to the obelisk and shared the entire story of Great Grandfather and me and the Ho-Chunk history and how we spread Great Grandfather's ashes in the forest.

As we reached the small springs, I knelt down and took out two small tin cups we kept in a small box and offered a cup of water to Luke where I indicated, "I am called Little Spirit by the Ho-Chunk Nation. I was bequeathed the name by Great Grandfather, who said I would become a great leader someday. Until Amelia and my trip with you, I had no idea what it meant or what was intended by the great spirts. When we returned from our trip, I realized everything had changed, just like you said it would. I gave up my position in our company and am focusing completely on medical research. I am surrounding myself with people who have the knowledge and talent to do so many great things and yet, I need someone like you to help put all the pieces together."

Luke looked at me and the smile I had seen in the balloon as we traversed the earth, came across his face, as I continued. "I brought you here today to see if what I felt, you would feel. I brought you here to allow you to see and feel the majesty of this place called Waldwick and ask if you would like to be a part of it. I know it's space, but in the space of time, I sincerely believe you will soar higher than you ever thought possible, reach higher than you could have ever imagined and feel more rewarded than you could possibly ever comprehend."

Luke stared at the ground and then at me with tears in his eyes and said, "I have circled the Earth and seen it's majesty and always felt there could never be anything which could move me, inspire me or affect me as much as space has done and yet, in a few moments on a small spit of land, you have made me feel more than I have ever felt before. I have looked into the heavens and thought I had seen the majesty of God, but I never felt it until now."

Luke shook his head and looked deep into my eyes. "Yes, I will walk with you! I can already sense greatness lies just beyond the horizon and I want to be with you, Little Spirit as you fulfill the dreams of Great Grandfather. I have but one request."

"What's that?" I asked.

"I am allowed to visit the woods whenever I need to?"

"Of course! The woods aren't mine. They belong to God and even if you didn't join with us, you are always welcome here whenever you want to."

There was a broad, effervescent smile on his face as we shook hands.

"What do you want me to do?" he asked.

"I need someone who can coordinate everything. I need someone to be our spokesperson, who can relate to people and get them to understand our mission. I need someone who can help develop the facilities we are going to need, to allow what we want to do and make it actually happen."

I dipped the cups back into the water and we drank again. "To our success!" I toasted.

"To our success!" Luke replied.

I put the cups away and we began walking back to the helicopter. "We will provide you with a compensation program equal to your current wages and I believe you will see our benefits program is second to none. If, or when, you are certified to fly one of our planes or choppers, you can take it whenever it's available."

"How planes many do you have?" Luke asked.

"Around twenty-five." I responded, shrugging my shoulders and continued. "You will be able to maintain your flying hours and use the planes, with reasonable prudence, for your own convenience. In addition, you will be offered use of our homes in Telerude, Colorado, Lake Geneva, Wisconsin and St. Martin for vacations, along with any of the boats we own, if they are available."

I stopped and looked at Luke. "None of what is happening would have begun, if it weren't for you."

Luke just shook his head in disbelief as we climbed onto the ATVs and headed back to the helipad.

Tommie and Andrew had seen us coming and were waiting.

"Tommie, I want you to meet the newest member of our team...Luke Skywalker!"

Tommie's head jerked back as Luke formally introduced himself and they shook hands.

"Let's head back to the office and then Andrew can fly you back to Phoenix."

"When do you want me to start?" Luke inquired.

"As soon as you can."

"What about relocation?"

"We will make arrangements for a temporary residence for you and your family until you get settled."

"I'm a widower and have no kids" Luke replied with sadness in his eyes.

"I'm sorry!" I responded.

"My wife had Leukemia. It's been a while, but I still miss her badly."

My eyes closed, head drooped and all I could think about was Amelia and how lucky we were. I wondered if the half-million dollars it cost for Amelia's treatment would have made a difference for Luke's wife, as we boarded the chopper and waved goodbye to Tommie.

The trip home was uneventful as we were all deep in thought. Andrew set the chopper down on the office helipad and Cecelia was waiting with a wrapped package. As I got out, she handed it to me and I, in turn, presented it to Luke. "Reading material for the trip" I said, as I handed him a copy of George-the-First's accounting of the beginning of *"Waldwick"* and my rendition of "Hocak".

Luke looked at the books and then at me and smiled.

Andrew had clearance at Mitchell field for the chopper and lifted off as he and one of our corporate pilots would fly Luke back to Phoenix and I would drive home.

That night, I shared the entire day with Amy. I told her about how moved Luke was by the forest, where George the First had saved Rodney's ancestral grandmother, Great Grandfather and the obelisk and then the water. I said Luke accepted the job, without even knowing what the pay was going to be and his wife had died and he had no children. I didn't mention what she had died from. It was the only thing I didn't share with my wife that night.

The next morning there was already an email from Luke. "I read Waldwick on the plane. You have shown me dignity and grace. You have proven to me there can be heaven on Earth. My commitment is more today than yesterday and I am ready for the challenge."

I contacted Jermaine Washington in HR and told him I had made a decision. Luke Arnold was to be considered the group Vice President of the Derrick Williams Medical Research Group responsible for the integration of technology and research, along with facilities management. Luke was to receive a compensation package which included all the benefits of a Wilco group vice president. Jermaine asked if we need to discuss it. I told him, there was no discussion on this one. I had met the man I was to trust the most in terms of bringing all the pieces together.

Later that morning I received another note from Luke. He tendered his resignation from World View and noted they countered with more money. He indicated, he told them it wasn't about money, but about mankind and the satisfaction of knowing the feelings he had experienced in space could be used on Earth. It would be two weeks until he could end all that needed to be done, but he was set to go.

Cecelia and I met and I asked her where she would recommend we have Luke live. I had initially thought Milwaukee, but with all the talent living in Madison, she recommended there. I wondered if he could temporarily live in our condo with Peter. Cecelia asked for some time and we agreed to meet at the end of the week.

As the days flew by and I was involved in so many other things, I didn't give it any thought. My calendar had Cecelia and I down for a 9:00 am meeting on Friday. As I was sitting in my office, she walked in with a sheet of paper and a big smile. It seems the old lady who had asked me if I was living with the "colored girl" in the condo, a long time ago, had passed away and her family had put her condo up for sale. Our real estate group had surveyed the property and made an offer, which was accepted. We would have our second condo in the same building on Wilson Street. Our property management team said they would go to work and have the entire place redecorated.

Luke came to Milwaukee and I laid out our plan … using artificial intelligence to gather, evaluate and disseminate medical research data to a team of international researchers we wanted to develop. I pointed out that the first step was to keep the Mad-City boys moving forward on the appropriate software while finding a location stable enough for the quantum computer. I also wanted Luke to meet Rodney. I felt we had a direct responsibility to help the Ho-Chunk Nation in any way possible even though, with the revenue they were generating off their gaming interests, those needs certainly didn't mean money.

Luke arrived as planned and we spent the first week doing nothing but brain-storming. I took him out on Lake Michigan in the boat and had him out to the house. With Andrew there, we made quite the trio and quite honestly, probably drank a little bit too much of Peter's favorite New Glarus Staghorn beer.

After the weekend off, Luke came to the office and I offered him the opportunity to live in Madison. He thought it was a great idea. We were expanding our staff and I didn't want to have the same issue with our next addition and a thought came to my mind and I called Cecelia into the office. "Cecelia, please have real estate find out who owns Capitol Towers. Perhaps we can buy the entire property."

Cecelia nodded and said "Already done." She was always one step ahead of me.

A month later, we purchased the entire building. This gave us control of who resided there and the inside track on any people wanting to move out. We sent notices to all the residents, we were the new owners and would pay top dollar if they elected to move. We noted we were not forcing them out and would maintain and upgrade the building and the monthly dues would not increase. We just wanted to quell the nerves of those who lived there.

It wasn't long until another elderly couple wanted to sell and move to Florida. It seems the combination of winter, Madison real estate and Wisconsin income taxes made Florida seem like a better place to live. I remember dad calling Florida 'heaven's waiting room' and chuckled.

We purchased the old couple's condo, had it remodeled and Peter moved in. Luke remained in ours until another tenant wanted to sell and we moved him there. Finally, Amelia and my condo was empty and back with us. It would become my home away from home whenever I was in Madison. The second bedroom would be my office. I think both Peter and Luke were a little disappointed to be moving from the penthouse, but they still had a great place to live for free with a next-door neighbor they worked with.

While Luke was organizing everything, I worked with The Duke on building stronger political ties in Wisconsin, New York and Washington DC. I knew the time would come when we would need a stronger alliance. I proposed we begin looking at a lobbying group in Washington that would match the company we used in Madison. The Duke agreed and he and I spent the next couple months commuting to Washington and New York, having him bridge the gap between the Foundation and the politicians.

For the most part, I found the people we met with … CEO's, company presidents and politicians, to be relatively interested in what we were doing as long at The Duke was involved. My concern was what would happen when he was out of the picture. To this end, we developed a regular routine where The Duke would begin the conversation and then turn it over to me. I would go through what our objectives were, the costs involved and then, when I was certain, all the big boys thought we would hit them up for a donation, The Duke would step back in and tell them the entire foundation was being funded by Wilco. We assured everyone that, until the time we could no longer afford to maintain the operating costs, we weren't going to ask for any money from anyone, including the government.

The closer was always the same. "Can we count on your support for our project?" With nothing to lose, we had a 100% commitment. The Duke was a master politician and knew half the time this was bullshit and so he brought along a camera and took a picture of the CEO with me. When we returned home, a copy, along with a confirming letter, was sent to that person, politely reminding them they had agreed to support our undertaking.

In the end, The Duke and I met with over 50 different politicians and business leaders and felt we had laid the groundwork for our endeavor. During this time, I got to know the man that much more and he got to know me. I was the son he lost and he was teaching me how to work with those in power.

One day he said "Ask for little, but expect a lot! When you ask for a favor, make certain it is something that can be provided. Half of what you've heard these past few weeks has been bullshit, but the log you kept will go a long way in helping us when you need it. Trust me, the time will come when you will need friends in high places. What you want to do is revolutionary and will affect a LOT of people in ways they don't want changed."

I guess, in my exuberant naiveté, I had overlooked Newton's third law … *for every action, there is an opposite and equal reaction.* What this wonderful, powerful, gracious, caring man was doing was making certain the power of the reaction wasn't so great as to destroy what we were doing. I also didn't realize how steep the slope would be to accomplishment.

The Final Product:0

In a matter of months, Peter and Mark had the Mediglove prototype and software completed. They were like proud parents, to say the least.

Amelia let me know all kinds of companies would be coming after us with knock-offs and so we hired a great New York patent law firm who ended up with 27 different patents applied for. The boys were concerned about the costs and I assured them the investment would be worth it.

I thought we were set until someone asked if we had FDA approval. The thought never crossed my mind as I believed the FDA only dealt with drugs.

We were progressing on the technical side but needed to understand the timetable and steps required to get any medical device approved by the government. I called Dave Raskin in legal and he said it was outside the auspices of Wilco Legal. He indicated he would make some calls and determine the right law firm who could assist us. A week later Dave called with the answer. It was a firm based in Atlanta. Cecelia called them and made an appointment for Peter, Mark, Luke and I to fly there, along with Attorney Goldberg from our patent lawyers to show them first-hand what the boys had done.

We went through the preliminaries and Mark auditioned the glove. To say they were impressed would be an understatement. Goldberg outlined the 27 patents and why each one was applied for and you could tell the Atlanta team realized we had done our homework.

I thought the day was going well and it would be a slam-dunk, which for a little guy is a real accomplishment, until the Atlanta team began. The lead attorney was a gentleman by the name of John P. Morgan. Someone, who I sensed right away, knew what he was talking about. I had been informed the process would take years and wanted someone who was not only knowledgeable, but personable with whom we could deal.

After pleasantries, Mr. Morgan began his explanation. "The first question you must ask is whether the product is a drug or a medical device. Based on your product description, it was determined the gloves are medical devices and, as such, if they are marketed in the United States, are subject to the regulatory controls in the Federal Food, Drug, and Cosmetic Act better known as the FD&C Act and the regulations in Title 21- Code of Federal Regulations (21 CFR) Parts 1-58, 800-1299."

I had no idea what he was talking about and simply nodded my head in the affirmative as JP, as he liked to be called, continued, "Because these medical devices incorporate human electrical signals, there may be another area of consideration. Here, medical devices that emit radiation are also subject to regulations for radiation-emitting electronic products cited in 21CFR Parts 1000-1050. If that isn't complicated enough, some requirements apply to medical devices before they are marketed, called premarket requirements and others apply to medical devices after they are marketed called post-market requirements."

I sat shaking my head in disbelief. All we wanted to do was help people.

JP continued. "Before offering your products, you must follow several steps prior to marketing a medical device in the United States. The initial step in preparing a device for marketing is to find the federal regulation which classifies your device. A medical device is defined by law in the section 201(h) of the FD&C Act, and the classification, which may be found in the Code of Federal Regulations, determines the regulatory path and regulatory requirements for your device which our firm does on a daily basis."

Peter told him his personal computer could do it in a matter of seconds as he opened his laptop and punched in a code. I think Mr. Morgan thought it rude to see Peter punching keys until a topic came up and Peter reiterated every single salient point JP had outlined with points and sub-points to the nth degree. That's when those who already didn't realize how intelligent Peter really was, found out that he could actually do two things at once and have total recall of both!

JP continued, "While the FDA will officially classify your medical device when reviewing your premarket submission, it is helpful for us to identify the classification. This will allow you to select the correct regulatory submission path and become aware of the level of control necessary to assure the safety and effectiveness of the medical device."

"Medical devices are categorized into one of three classes, based on the degree of risk they present. The classes are as follows:

Class I – Lowest Risk, such as a manual toothbrush, which are subject to general controls.

Class II – Moderate Risk, which include items such as non-invasive blood pressure monitors, which are subject to general controls and special controls.

Class III – Highest Risk, such as a heart valve or perhaps your gloves because they penetrates the epidural layer of skin, which are then subject to general controls and premarket approval."

I let out a loud "Whew!" in exasperation, as JP continued, "It gets more complicated. If your product is a combination product - a medical device plus another FDA-regulated product (e.g. drug, biologics, etc.) we will need to contact the FDA's Office of Combination Product where, based on the gloves primary mode of action, the OCP will tell us which FDA Center we need to contact in order to market the product."

"This is just the first step?" I asked incredulously.

Mr. Morgan continued. "After device classification, you then select one of the four premarket submissions required for that regulation. Some Class I and most Class II devices require a

510(k). In a 510(k), you need to demonstrate the new device is "substantially equivalent" to a predicate device in terms of intended use, technological characteristics and performance testing. Obviously, what you have developed is revolutionary and won't fit in here. Some Class I and Class II devices are exempt from 510(k) if they do not exceed the limitations of exemption stated in 21 CFR xxx.9, where xxx refers to 21CFR 862-892. For example, an elastic bandage classified under 21CFR 880.5075 is exempt from premarket notification, provided it does not exceed the exemption limitations stated in 21CFR 880.9."

I shook my head reiterating, "All we want to do is help people!"

JP continued. "Most Class III devices require a PMA. A PMA is the most stringent type of premarket submission. Before the FDA approves a PMA, the sponsor must provide valid scientific evidence demonstrating reasonable assurance of safety and effectiveness for the device's intended use and this is where I hope your products will be classified."

"What do you mean, hope?" I asked.

"There is another class called De Novo. De Novo provides a means for a new device, without a valid predicate, to be classified into Class I or II, if it meets certain criteria and this can get complicated."

"You mean expensive?"

"Yes!"

JP continued. "There is one more and here is where I would like to begin. It's called HDE. HDE provides a regulatory path for Class III devices, which are intended to benefit patients with rare diseases or conditions. In order for a device to be eligible for an HDE, a sponsor must obtain designation as a Humanitarian Use Device (HUD), which is granted through application to FDA's Office of Orphan Products Development or OOPD."

"Then we get to offer the product?" I anxiously asked.

JP responded, "No, you've only accomplished two of the five steps needed for approval. You need to go to step three. Once we have selected the correct premarket submission type, we will need to prepare the appropriate information which will be required. In this section, the FDA identifies resources for assistance and information they will consider when preparing the premarket submission."

I looked at Peter and asked, "Can you do this?"

Peter nodded in the affirmative.

JP seemed somewhat suspect and added. "The FDA has developed several types of resources to help you prepare your premarket submission. Here you need to realize there are design controls on all Class II and Class III submissions under the Quality System Regulations. Then, when the designs are approved, you will probably need nonclinical testing, which is determined by the device classification, mechanisms of operation and technological characteristics, from which labeling must comply with the Good Laboratory Practice. Because the gloves are so unique, they will require clinical evidence. Here, prior to initiating a clinical study, we will probably need to obtain approval of an Investigational Device Exemption by the FDA. The study must also be approved by the appropriate Institutional Review Board and comply with all applicable IDE regulations and Good Clinical Practices."

"Then are we done?" I impatiently asked.

"Hardly!" JP responded. "The labeling for a device must be written according to labeling regulations and included in your premarket submission. Then, we can send the Premarket Submission to the FDA and interact with FDA Staff during Review."

"After a premarket submission is received, the FDA conducts an administrative review to assess whether the submission is sufficiently complete to be accepted for substantive review. While a submission is under review, FDA staff communicates with applicants to increase the efficiency of the review process. If and that's a big IF, we pass all these steps, the foundation will need to register itself and the manufacturing facility along with all of the devices."

"Then we're done?" I asked.

"If the products require premarket clearance or approval prior to marketing, you will have to wait until you receive FDA clearance or approval before registering and listing."

"Then we're done?" Yup! Me again.

"Normally, yes, but registration of a device establishment, assignment of a registration number or listing of a medical device does not in any way denote clearance or approval of the establishment or its products by the FDA."

"How long do you think all this will take?"

"Three to five years!" JP answered.

"We don't have that long." I responded.

"Nothing you can do about it." Was the response.

"Nothing!"

"Shit!" We needed to call in some favors and soon!

The Duke pulled strings all up and down Pennsylvania Avenue and lo-and-behold, Medi-gloves were given high priority. It pays to have friends in high places, especially when their house is painted white and has an oval office.

I learned, it's amazing what a few million dollars in political contributions can do! Because the product was so unique and really didn't do anything more than a modem, the boys in Atlanta pulled a rabbit out of a hat and applied for and received FCC approval instead of the FDA simply because the gloves transmitted a signal.

Like magic, the FCC gave their approval that superseded the FDA. In so doing, the gloves were classified as a broadcasting product and not a medical device and we got the go-ahead, to which a lot, and I mean a lot, of Spotted Cow beer was consumed.

Structure:

It had been a while since I had seen Rodney and called to see when we could meet with him. I wanted him to "meet the team" and share our vision. A day was set and, having been there before, knew we would need to take the chopper. Black River Falls is 52 miles from La Crosse and 55 miles from the Eau Claire airport and I readily admit, I am spoiled. The day came and Andrew and I took off and landed at Truax to pick up Peter, Mark and Luke. From there, it was a quick forty-five-minute flight and we landed behind the Ho Chunk corporate offices.

As the blades stopped, my dearest friend popped his head out the back door and I saw his big shit-eating grin. My God, it was good to see him!

We entered the building and were treated like royalty. After the typical how's the family questions, we got down to business. Luke and Rodney hit it off right away and so I sat back and let Luke outline what we had in mind.

"We would like to develop an eight-segment research group," Luke offered, "which looks into different areas of integrating artificial intelligence with anatomy and physiology." Rodney nodded and smiled as Luke continued. "We believe we can take some of the resources Q's family has offered and develop a dynamic, global research group that looks at ways to improve individual health. The core of the program will be purchasing a quantum computer, along with a series of satellite IBM Watson computers. The quantum computer will scan the global internet four times each day and harvest any and all data concerning identified subjects, which will then be delineated by category to the eight Watson's, where the data will be summarized and provided to the appropriate research team."

Rodney sat back in his chair as Luke continued. "The eight categories are anatomy, physiology, biology, chemistry, engineering, mathematics, physics and computer science."

Rodney had a questioning look on his face and asked. "Mathematics, physics and engineering?" to which, Peter leaned forward, quietly responding as if it were top secret, "We not only want to have the quantum computer serve as a source of medical information, but believe we can take the entire concept of artificial intelligence one step further." Rodney was incredulous, shaking his head in disbelief.

Looking at me, I could tell Peter wanted approval to share all of our dreams. I simply nodded. If I couldn't trust my best friend, who could I trust? With that, Mark opened his briefcase and took out the sensor gloves as Rodney's eyes squinted creating burrows of incredulity across his forehead.

"Put these on, please," Mark requested, as Peter opened his laptop and booted it up.

As directed, Rodney put on the gloves and Peter spun the laptop screen around so Rodney could see the instantaneous data.

Mark instructed, "Your little finger's fingerprint has been recorded and you would be identified by it in the computer. By using it as a biometric and then having your physician have the same imprint, we believe no one's medical data could be hacked. While the government uses fingerprints for such things as enhanced security, we take it one step further by including DNA data, which would be mined from the epidural layer of your ring finger, creating a complete summary of your genetic make-up."

Peter added, "At one time, scientists believed your DNA was fixed, but recent studies have shown it can change. However, when we combine your fingerprint and DNA and have them matched to specific computers who have downloaded the same biometrics, the chances of theft are miniscule and the probability of duplication is less than one in ten trillion."

I proudly added, "Once you are identified and matched, your middle finger will transmit your vitals...heart rate, blood pressure, oxygen levels, etc., while your index finger will read your blood through the epidermal layer, without being invasive."

Rodney's mouth dropped open.

Luke continued. "The guys thought about creating a wrist band, but feel the gloves allow for more information, without any chance of error due to dirt and sweat."

Mark added, "With the glove, we have the ability to do a complete medical work-up in the matter of seconds. With the patient's permission, they would simply push the button on the back of the glove and the data would be fed into the quantum and stored. When needed, you would be asked to put the glove on again and in a matter of seconds, the new diagnostic would determine any changes. Should there be none, you would be notified. If there was a change, not only would your physician be notified, but a treatment recommendation based on your history would be provided to the doctor as well."

"This is fantastic!" Rodney responded looking at me and smiling.

Luke added. "Our first goal is implementing the glove and testing it to see if it functions as a method of analyzing a patient's overall health. Because our research is dynamic, we also believe, as new treatments or drugs are introduced, everything can change. If everything is linked properly, we can establish a network where physicians can make decisions without going to conferences or even download the input of pharmaceutical companies who want doctors to have patients buy their drugs."

I added. "Due to the personalization of treatments and the ability to actually measure chemicals within the body, the MadCity boys believe we can also provide individualized treatments instead of macro-treatments. As an example, drugs can be prescribed in specific milligrams instead of pre-measured amounts which might be too little or too much."

"And this is just phase one?" Rodney asked.

We all nodded in unison.

Mark continued, "There is a new development in cancer treatments called immunotherapy. One of the pharmaceutical companies has developed a drug which, when used with chemotherapy, has been able to extend the lives of people with a common form of lung cancer, while cutting the risk of death in half. Our goal is to eliminate the chemotherapy aspect altogether."

"How are you going to that?" Rodney asked.

Peter responded, "We eventually want to develop nano-fish which are one micron thick that can be implanted in the brain. The chip would be programmed to communicate with gold colloid nodules one-tenth the size of a grain of rice, which would be magnetically directed to the primary organs of the body, along with the soft tissue within the spine."

Now Rodney really had a perplexed look on his face as Luke added. "We believe the addition of the nano-fish and colloids will allow the brain to improve communication with each organ to the point that any dysfunction, including rogue cells, would be addressed by the brain itself, who would then send the proper chemicals needed to regain the initial balance the organ once had within the body. In other words self-induced immunotherapy!"

Rodney was shaking his head in disbelief, as he added. "The body would heal itself?"

We all smiled as big brother leaned back in his chair, shaking his head and smiling.

I added. "We're getting way ahead of ourselves, but believe, through artificial intelligence, we can have the body naturally stop the development and spread of cancer, while eliminating or reducing the effects of several diseases such as dementia, Alzheimer's, Parkinson's and MS."

"What about alcohol or drug addiction?" Rodney asked.

Luke replied. "We haven't got that far, but think we could possibly control those as well."

"Where do we fit in, Little Brother?" Rodney asked, sliding forward in his chair and putting his elbows on his desk, even though I think he knew the answer.

"We need to do some beta-testing and wondered if Ann would like to work with us in identifying twenty-five people who would like to test the glove." I replied.

"Why us?" Rodney asked.

I responded. "First, you are my best friend and leader of an entire nation. Second, because you are a nation, your citizens have certain freedoms non-Indians don't have, including being involved in trials which won't require government approval."

Rodney smiled. "I can't answer for Ann, but personally, I don't see why not."

Perhaps, it was all a pipe dream, but we were all like little kids, excited about what we thought we could do as I added. "Right now, we are still a long way off, but I wanted to share with you what we are working on. We still need to build the facility for the computers and program the software. We have a team in Madison already doing that, and we have a really long way to go and hope to build a facility next year."

Rodney smiled and asked, "What can we do to help?"

"Be patient and understanding," I replied.

Rodney discretely glanced at the clock on the wall and with that the meeting was over. We all stood and Big Brother gave me a huge hug. "Great Grandfather was so right! You are Little Spirit who has come to help my nation!" I was humbled by his words and challenged at the same time.

We walked out to the chopper with Rodney's hand on my shoulder. As we stopped, he looked at Peter, Mark, Luke and Andrew and said. "Thank you for joining Little Brother's team. He is a great man who will bring much goodness to the world." We got onboard as Rodney walked back to the door, turned, smiled and waved goodbye. God, it was good to see him!

Location, Location, Location:

We needed to find a spot which was geographically inert and yet convenient. Madison was too cosmopolitan and real estate was really expensive. The more we looked, the more frustrated we got. Finally, Luke suggested Waldwick.

The more I thought about it, the more logical it seemed. Rural, quiet, tectonically stable. The big issue would be getting approval from Tommie, Mom and Iowa County. After a great deal of discussion, the thought of building the facility adjacent to where Skunk Hollow school once stood came to the forefront.

Because the forest was co-owned with the Ho-Chunk, I called Rodney and asked his opinion. He said he would bring it up to the council. A week later he called and asked that plans be developed, which delineated where the facility would be and how much of the forest would be taken.

I responded in the affirmative and indicated that none of the forest would be affected, as the Terrill family would donate the land from adjacent property. Even with this being the case, I offered to have a member of their nation sit in on all meetings. Rodney volunteered to be that person, which put a smile on my face. Big Brother and I would be working together, once again.

With the failure of Hongshe to acquire our farm, they couldn't do what they wanted. Instead we went to them and offered to purchase both Wisconsin farms at the original purchase price, plus the costs incurred in the entire Heather deal. At first, they said "No" and then realized the deal made sense when our friend, the Ambassador, had conversations with high ranking members of the party. In the end, we added nearly one-thousand acres to Waldwick. This allowed Tommie to expand the dairy operation on nine-hundred acres, reserving ten acres, next to the forest, for our development. We also offered, and it was accepted, that a small park called Terrill Park, dedicated to the memory of my dad, be added to the county roles, which we would develop and maintain with the county's approval. I believe, there was a collective sigh of relief throughout Mineral Point when people learned farm land was being sustained for farming the traditional way.

Big Brother and I had a long conversation and we both agreed, not a single tree would be removed from the forest. Instead, we developed a plan for a driveway from the road near Tommie's house that would stop at the edge of the forest. By having it curve adjacent to two fields and then reach the parking area, Tommie maintained his privacy and we had access. It was decided everyone could park and walk down a path 100 yards to the facility. It was certainly a lot less than the mile my ancestors walked, but more than you would normally find on an office structure.

Rodney and I outlined what we wanted … a very natural design integrating limestone, wood and glass which opened into the woods. We envisioned a design similar to the Prairie Designs created by Frank Lloyd Wright and used the Unitarian Church in Madison as a model. This way, everyone who worked at Skunk Hollow or came to visit, could share in the beauty of nature, while those affected by the Ley Lines could walk the path to the springs and drink from the water. We both agreed to add a small bench next to the obelisk and a series of brass plaques that outlined where George the First saved Rodney's so many great grandmothers and the story of Great Grandfather.

We had geologic studies done and were assured the bed rock was such we could build our facility and not have to worry about Earthquakes or vibrations. We contracted with a specialty architectural firm who developed nuclear reactors and began our plans. Luke informed the architects that we wanted a facility that would have no environmental footprint, which meant solar power and geo-thermal heat. We also added the caveat that our operation could not affect the forest or the primary water in any way.

In the end, the architects developed a small pod with a conference room which was to serve as the center of the compound where the computer would sit below. Radiating from the pod would be glass hallways that would branch out to eight additional pods, which would be placed in a circle around the main pod and designated for each of the sciences. By arranging the pods, you could walk to the pods to your left or right or go through the center or main pod to get to the other pods. Using a lot of thermal glass for the walkways and leaving the grounds natural, made it always feel as if you were outdoors.

It took nearly six months of planning. During that time Luke was on site almost every day and issued a report to Rodney and me on a daily basis. In so doing, he and Tommie began to bond and, with mom living in Dodgeville, managing the car dealership, Luke began bunking with Tommie at the farm. It was cool seeing two guys from such different backgrounds become good friends.

For communication, the MadCity boys, developed a hyperbolic dish which maximized communications regardless of the season. The dish was linked with a communications satellite that was launched by Luke's old company that was geo-positioned and exclusive to our network, which the MadCity boys also developed. The entire design was so intricate that all signals were scrambled and could only be decoded by a dual-wave system they also developed.

Luke developed a geographic concept that he felt would allow for round-the-clock research. For this, he examined international data points and set Waldwick, Britain, India and New Zealand as reference points from which we could collect and disseminate shared information. The team felt that the amount of data collected could be massive and it was determined that the maximum number of researchers would be 18 per reference point, or a grand total of 72.

This meant everyone would be working in teams, where someone working on a project in the U.S. would hand off their daily accomplishments at the end of the work day to their research partner in Great Britain, who would work on the project and hand it off to their teammates in India, who would repeat the process and hand it off to their teammates in New Zealand, who would do the same thing back to the States. By having the teams six hours apart, it allowed for linked teams to interact in a live mode and have discussions, simply because it would be late afternoon at one spot, while morning at the next facility.

We started calling the daily transfer of information "batons" as each team would hand off data, just like they did in relay races in track. By using the IMVR glasses, the teams could discuss the progress as if they were in the same building. We set up satellite offices and met with IBM and took it upon ourselves to install smaller mainframes in each of the baton offices so that we had regional data and insurance in case something happened to our system.

Upon completion of the building, our quantum computer was delivered with serial number three on the face plate. The MadCity boys wanted to have a naming contest for the new quantum computer. After much good-natured bantering, the name S.I.M.O.N. or Simon, came into being, referring to Super Intelligent Miner of the Net. The guys liked the word miner in the title as it reflected the Mineral Point heritage. From that day forward, our quantum computer was simply called Simon, although Simon certainly wasn't simple by any means.

With the MadCity boys in place, we felt we had phase one of the research team up and running and drinking an awful lot of beer, I might add. Now it was time to move forward with the rest of the team. We knew when it came to anatomy and physiology, we needed medical researchers.

Things were progressing rapidly and we realized just how far we had come in such a short period of time. It was decided, we needed to have an open house and so we had a small party at the new facility hosted by the MadCity gang with Ceclia, Luke, Andrew, Tommie, Amelia, The Duke, Dr. Williams and mom all present. We had a pig roast, drank lots and lots and I mean lots of beer and smashed a bottle of champagne on the cornerstone, which included an engraved list of all those who had worked so hard to have everything fall into place. The brass plaque on the building said, *"To Derrick Williams, who could not be here, but will always be in our hearts."*

The Good Doctor:

Using Simon and the internet, the MadCity boys began harvesting names and locations of the top medical researchers in the world. It was neat to find several of them working in Madison where they were doing research at the Carbone Cancer Center at the University of Wisconsin. Better known as the UWCCC or CCC, the Carbone Center brought together nearly 300 physicians and scientists from 55 UW departments and nine schools to conduct research and translate laboratory discoveries into new patient treatments. In other words, … a really neat place.

We learned that, UWCCC research scientists, academic faculty, and clinicians worked together across eight research programs: cancer control, cancer genetics, chemoprevention, experimental therapeutics, human cancer virology, imaging and radiation sciences, nuclear signaling, and tumor microenvironment, to advance the study of cancer. We had hit the sweet spot!

This left one field still open, which was biology. As we dug deeper into the field, the same component kept popping up … Immunology and one name appeared over and over again … Dr. Tanalai Hsu, who was a chair of the biology department at the UW. I told the boys to contact Dr. Hsu and tell him I would like to have a meeting to discuss what we were planning on accomplishing. Cecelia called and was informed Dr. Hsu was a very busy person and didn't have time for meetings. I told her to call back again. She did and the response was the same. I called Wilco and asked who they knew at the UW who could break the ice. It seems, when you are donating two million dollars a year to a medical school, you do have some leverage.

Wilco called back and said they talked to the Chancellor's office and Cecelia should call again. This time, the response was totally different. Money does talk and a meeting was set for lunch for Dr. Hsu and me.

Reservations were made for a private room at the Madison Club and I was expecting an elderly Asian gentleman. Andrew went to pick up the doctor and bring him to the Club. I almost fell off my chair when this young, vivacious, Chinese woman walked in.

I stood as she entered and I smiled. She seemed distant and hassled because she had been forced to meet with me.

"Sit down please," I offered, as she looked around the room.

I could read the contempt in her facial expression. She didn't want to be there and was offended I went over her head, as she sat down across from me.

I nodded to Andrew who left the room, so it was just the two of us.

"I'm certain you are wondering why you are here."

She nodded in the affirmative.

"I'm certain you think I'm some rich guy or have ulterior motives." She looked at the plates on the table.

"My name is George Terrill, I am heading up a research project we believe will help all living beings enjoy a better quality of life." There was a look of distrust in her eyes as I continued. "I have invited you here today to share our dream and explain why we would like you to join our team."

Dr. Hsu leaned back in her chair as I outlined that we were a non-profit organization whose goal was to develop a method of minimizing the effects of cancer by assisting the body in fighting the malady. With that, I opened my wallet and took out a photo of Amelia. "This is my wife Amelia. She was diagnosed with Leukemia fifteen years ago and almost died. She was offered a position in a trial program at the UW and is alive today because of the efforts of people like you."

I could see her edge was beginning to soften. "We have the financial resources needed to do research and develop comprehensive programs which will enhance cancer research and assist people like you in doing the tremendous work you are doing."

Dr. Hsu took a sip of water as I continued, "We have purchased a quantum computer and have the ability to survey the entire global internet four times each day to harvest data specific to all fields and have, as part of our project, identified … anatomy, physiology, chemistry, engineering, mathematics, physics and computer science and probably the most crucial segment, biology or anything you feel is appropriate."

"Dr. Hsu, I have read your resume and am profoundly impressed. Bachelor of Science and Master's from Stanford and a PHD from Harvard. From there, you came to Madison and continued your education and received a second PHD in Veterinary Medicine, where you did your thesis on…I apologize, but I need to read this part."

I picked up a piece of paper and read it to her. *"The complement immune system is the major humoral component of the innate immune response which is a biochemical cascade which attacks the surfaces of foreign cells, destroying them before they can do damage to the body of most mammals plus some plants, fish and invertebrates. Containing over 20 different proteins, the compliment system is named for its ability to "compliment" the killing of pathogens by anti-bodies."*

I looked at Dr. Hsu and smiled, proud that I made it through what would be child's play for her, as I added, "I also know your work has been published in numerous books and magazines and you are considered an expert in immunology."

This got a shy smile on her face.

Finally, she spoke. "You've done your homework."

I nodded and continued.

"I was really interested in the fact you are a proponent of what is called the "unified theory" which draws upon research from genetics, immunology, microbiology, epidemiology and evolution as it applies to leukemia. The entire premise that we have become 'too clean" for our own good, is intriquing. Being a kid from a dairy farm, the entire idea of eating dirt, has been part of our family diet for generations."

This got a brief smile from the doctor.

"Dr. Hsu, we are a small team which currently consists of yours truly, Andrew, who you met, who is my associate; Dr. Luke Arnold, who is coordinating the entire project and four of the brightest, weirdest, most creatively wonderful computer programmer misfits you could possibly imagine. All of us then report to Cecelia, who I say is my administrative assistant, but we all know is the real boss."

This got a bigger smile out of her.

I continued "We want you to join our team. Your pay would be one dollar per year" which made her frown. "You get to keep your current job. In return for working with us, you get complete access to Simon, the quantum computer and use of one of our IBM Watsons, which is designated exclusively for biology. The computers have been programmed with deep learning capabilities including reading words, photos and images. In addition, all the computers have been downloaded with 6,809 living languages in the world, including all words and cuneiforms."

"Our programmers call themselves the MadCity Boys. They have developed software which will allow you to communicate with anyone in the world either through typed or spoken communication including real time visual interchanges. In addition, we have IMVR sets, providing immersive virtual reality, as well."

"With our capacity, each day the key words you tell us or even images from your electron microscope can be scanned across the entire internet from which you will be provided a comprehensive report on what was found. You retain complete control of all your information and research through a double lock security system predicated on your own fingerprint and DNA script."

Dr. Hsu sat in suspended disbelief as I continued. "While I know you have a lot of assets at your disposal at UWCCC, we believe we can make your time more productive, research more comprehensive and results even more profound than what you already accomplished." I hoped I didn't sound like one of those guys doing an infomercial.

Dr. Hsu sat back in her chair and for the first time spoke. " You need to understand my field specialty is in epithelial cancers, or those that start in the linings of organs."

"We are aware of that, and that you are a brilliant researcher seeking answers."

"And you want to offer all this to me?" she inquired.

I nodded in the affirmative.

"Why?"

"Because you are the type of person we want to work with … kind, generous and humble."

"And there are no strings attached?"

"A couple"

Her back arched.

"First, you have to put up with us. Second, once each month, you would need to submit a one paragraph summary of what progress you made for presentation to the entire team."

"Progress on what?"

"Well that's the secret, and the only way I can let you in on it is by demonstrating what we have accomplished already, which would mean visiting our facilities."

"Where?"

"A little town in southwestern Wisconsin."

"Which one, may I ask?"

"A little, dinky town called Waldwick"

"I've heard of Waldwick. A Chinese conglomerate attempted to purchase a farm and create a milk factory … one of the most inhumane ways to treat animals I can think of and a family farm was saved!"

"That's our family farm."

A broad smile came Dr. Hsu's face as she completely relaxed, "I have a deep love for animals which is why I got my degree in biology and thought I would teach veterinary medicine. I needed to write my dissertation and stumbled across the entire process of immunology and have been hooked on it, not only for animals, but humans as well."

"We know, that's why we need you on our team," I offered.

The waiter brought our food and we spent the next hour talking about our families and dreams. I found Dr. Hsu, not only profoundly intelligent, but incredibly humble. Dr. Hsu indicated she had a hard stop at 2:00 PM and, as our meeting was nearing its end, it was time for the big question.

"Will you visit our research facility and let us show you what we are up to?"

She looked at me as if I was nuts. "Of course!" she replied, which generated a huge smile of satisfaction on my face reminding me, once again, why I always lost at poker.

Both of us checked our schedules and a Saturday was set for ten days later. I discretely tapped the call button on my watch and Andrew appeared.

"Andrew, can you please take Dr. Hsu back to her lab?"

Dr. Hsu politely said she could call Uber and Andrew could take me elsewhere. I told her there was no need, as our office was less than a block away. Little did she know, it was the second bedroom in Amy's and my condo.

I walked back and called Cecelia, asking her to make all the plans. In Luke's and my meetings, we had drawn up different color-coded scenarios concerning what we would do at Skunk Hollow. Depending on different levels of importance, a code red, meant someone was snooping around and we wanted to show as little as possible. Code white meant a polite overview. Code blue, was only for VIP's and people we wanted to join our team and included the works. This was definitely a code blue.

I called Tommie and asked if the day would work for him and he said yes. I called the MadCity boys and told them what was going on. I called Luke and relayed the message. Finally, I called Amelia, filled her in on all that transpired and asked if she and the kids could join us as they could go horseback riding and then visit with grandma in the afternoon. I wanted this to be a family affair to show Dr. Hsu we were all in this together. Amy suggested I invite Ceclia and I thought it was a brilliant idea. She was part of the team and it was time to show her what we had accomplished.

When all was set, I sent Dr. Hsu a text outlining the day. She responded in the affirmative, asking if it would be all right if she brought an associate. I concurred and asked to let me know a convenient time and place for Andrew to pick them up. She offered to drive and I said absolutely not as I had another idea.

The Big Day:

We had a driver pick up Dr. Hsu and her associate Dr. Indira Patel and bring them out to Truax and the helipad. I think they were surprised and somewhat excited. Amelia, the kids and I were already onboard and Andrew was our pilot.

The day was planned where mom and the kids would go horseback riding in the morning while we visited Skunk Hollow. After lunch, mom was taking the kids to House on The Rock, while we toured the farm and talked business. For the grand finale, we planned a picnic dinner and a bonfire for the kids and me too, I must admit. The goal was to show Dr. Hsu we were just a normal family and wanted her to join the team.

I wanted to make a big impression and so we brought the Air Bus ACH175 chopper called Q-III that had the same design as Amelia II and Q-II, Amelia sat midship. 'V', Derrick, Mela and I crawled in back. Dr. Hsu sat up front and Dr. Patel sat next to Amelia. We quickly learned, neither of them had ever flown in a helicopter before. With that knowledge, Andrew called in a revised flight plan, which took us over the Capitol and University, before heading for Waldwick. On a normal day, the thirty-mile trip was fifteen minutes at 200 miles per hour. Andrew kept the speed down so both ladies got to see some of the sights.

Andrew radioed Tommie and he, mom and Luke were standing by when we touched down. I don't know whose mouth dropped open the farthest when the two doctors got out, Tommie's or Luke's. They were expecting a couple of old guys in white coats.

I introduced mom and explained that she lived in Dodgeville where she managed one of our car dealerships. Then I introduced Tommie and he didn't know whether to shake hands with the ladies or simply tip his head. Being the shy one, Tommie nodded his head. I introduced Cecelia and her husband Johnnie and saw both doctors melt as they realized this was a family and not a bunch of scientists who were inviting them to join the team.

Finally, it was Luke's turn. "Doctors, I said, I would like to introduce Doctor Luke Arnold, better known around these parts as Luke Skywalker."

"Are you a physician Dr. Arnold?" Dr. Patel asked.

"No, I've just got my degree and please call me Luke."

"What's your degree in?" Dr. Hsu asked.

"Astrophysics," Luke replied

"He's being very humble." Amy interjected. "Captain Skywalker was a Navy pilot and our pilot who took "Q" and I into space."

"Space?" Dr. Pattel inquired.

"Yes" Amy added. "Captain Luke piloted a balloon for us at 80,000 feet and gave us the trip of a lifetime … a truly religious experience."

"Incredible!" Dr. Patel added.

"V" and Derrick took after their mother, quiet, polite and introspective. Mela, my Mela, well she took after her dad. I called her Mighty Mouth and you never knew what was going to come out of her four-year-old brain.

When the noise of the helicopter waned, Mela looked at Dr. Patel and said, "You're brown like Rodney and Ann. Are you an Indian?"

Dr. Patel politely replied that yes, she was Indian.

Mela asked, "Do you belong to the Ho Chunk too?" This got a chuckle from everyone, as the good Doctor tried to explain her parents had come from India before she was born and she was not Native American. Mela didn't understand and so Dr. Patel explained we were all God's children, which was good enough for Mela.

Mom and the kids rode with Tommie to the stables, while our entourage got in a Suburban and headed for the research center.

"We have three farms and milk over 800 head per day." I noted to no one in particular. "We keep the herd segregated for health and genetic reasons, have our own infirmary and nursery and a vet on staff. In addition to the cows, we have somewhere around 200 pigs, plus chickens and eight horses. We now farm nearly 1,000 acres to raise corn, soybeans and hay, plus mom's garden, of course. With milk prices as low as they are, we purchased our own cheese factory and all of our milk is converted into twenty-three different types of cheese."

I think the ladies were pleased as Dr. Hsu responded. "I majored in biology, because of my love for animals. Many are much more human than people." I immediately thought of the MadCity boys, but didn't reply.

When we arrived at the complex, I heard a small gasp. I don't think our guests were prepared for what we had developed. The brown wood buildings with glass walls shimmered in the warm Wisconsin summer sun. The quiet whisper of the breeze and the call of the redwing blackbird pierced their ears as they stood surrounded by trees and grass and the small stream running through the complex.

"The facility is completely self-sustaining with no carbon footprint. We harvest sunlight with our solar panels and use geothermal energy for both heating and cooling," Luke noted.

The MadCity boys were ready! Peter remained the alpha leader and took it upon himself to make all the introductions. Luke then took everyone on a tour, showing them the "outer ring" as we called it, with the separate research pods for the different groups who work in teams.

After making the entire circle, Luke took them to meet Simon, where they saw the cooling tanks filled with liquid helium. Then we all walked upstairs to the conference room and took our seats where the MadCity boys put on quite a show, talking about Simon and his capabilities, using programming words like neural nets and how Simon and the Watsons were programmed for deep learning.

Peter continued, "We taught all the computers to teach themselves and each other by simply feeding Simon a learning algorithm and exposing the Watsons to terabytes of data, including hundreds of thousands of images and years of speech and written samples in every language on Earth. When this was completed, Simon had his core knowledge and is now allowing the IBM computers to figure out for themselves, how to recognize desired objects, words or sentences."

Luke added, "One of the problems our team faced is called unsupervised learning. Virtually everyone has been using supervised learning where the neural net is trained with labeled data. What we have done is determine how to create unsupervised learning … much like the MadCity Boys, I might add. Here, we simply show Simon unlabeled data and ask him to look for recurring patterns. In other words, Simon is like a child, who is teaching himself minute-by-minute, hour-by-hour, day-by-day, but doing so only in the areas we want him to learn. Simon is then taking what he has learned and sharing it with the appropriate Watson."

Peter continued, "Now we are working with Simon on what is called reinforcement learning, which is a way of learning algorithms. This will allow software agents and Simon to automatically determine the ideal behavior within a specific context and maximize not only Simon's, but the Watson's performance. Reinforcement algorithms are not given explicit goals; instead, the computers are forced to learn these optimal goals by trial and error. To do this, we have created an operating system that not only functions at an optimum level of performance today, but, as we grow, Simon and the Watsons will not be overwhelmed by all the things we hope to have going on in their brains."

Peter continued. "Doctor Hsu, you are involved in immunology, correct?"

Dr. Hsu nodded in the affirmative.

"This morning, we had Simon scan the internet for anything we thought was applicable to immunology including some key words, phrases, and articles. In the end, we harvested over 20,000 pages of information."

"WOW!" Dr. Hsu exclaimed. "How long did that take?"

"Because the harvest was scientific, 90 minutes." Peter replied.

"You scanned the entire universe in 90 minutes?" Dr. Patel asked incredulously.

"Yup!"

Luke jumped back in. "No one can read 20,000 pages of information and so Simon gave the material to Watson Number Four who, as of today, we are calling Hsu, who has been programmed for the subject. Hsu took the data, scrutinized it, redacted all duplication and wrote a summary, that she transferred back to Simon. Simon then checked it against the harvested data for duplicity, accuracy and whether it was comprehensive and sent it back to Hsu, who printed out a five-page report."

"If tomorrow, we did a re-scan, the same process would take place and the report provided would only include what was added or changed since today's scan. Because we are not in your field, we simply put in a few words. Experts like yourself would be able to include more words, terms, images or subjects and get into greater detail."

Dr. Hsu asked to see the report and began to read as she nodded her head in agreement.

"I'm impressed!" Dr. Hsu interjected.

Luke added. "As you can see, we have the ability to gather all available data on any topic, and condense it into a working content level and do it simultaneously. This capacity will allow researchers, such as yourselves, to have an up-to-the-minute information resource. While this alone would seem like a worthy addition, the MadCity boys have programmed Simon and the Watsons to do a lot more."

Dr. Hsu and Patel just shook their heads.

Peter continued. "What's really neat is, we can personalize the data to address specific individuals and their maladies. As an example, if there is a need to improve their immune system for any reason, other than hitting their Hayflick limit, Simon can help. To do this Simon, would take all the data concerning possible treatment options and chemicals and develop personalized prescriptions for a person, plant or animal."

Luke added. "With Simon, we will also be able to read x-rays, MRI's and CT Scans more rapidly and accurately than radiologists. We can also diagnose cancer earlier and do so less invasively, while looking at all the possible combinations and permutations in developing better and more effective pharmaceuticals."

"Dr. Patel, your field of study is cancer research, correct?"

"Yes, that's correct."

"You use an electron microscope?"

"Of course."

"You then look for differences in samples, correct?"

"Yes."

"Imagine being able to digitally transfer those images to Simon and, in a matter of seconds, have him identify any changes and diagnose not only what the consequence of those changes are, but provide treatment scenarios."

Dr. Patel put her hands to her mouth. "You can do that?"

"Not yet, but that's where people like you come in. We can develop the software, but we need to teach Simon what to look for."

Dr. Patel added. "You could save hundreds of thousands of hours of research every year."

I smiled and said "That's why we're here."

There was a VERY pregnant pause.

Luke handed both doctors pairs of IMVR glasses and we all put them on, adding, "Welcome to our world of immersive virtual reality. With the glasses tied into Simon, you will be able to not only have conference calls with anyone in the world and do so in both visual and auditory three-dimensional planes, but look at data, even slides for closer examinations. All parties will be able to speak in their native languages and Simon with instantly translate what is said into the receptors selected language. If for example, Dr. Hsu you are speaking in English and are talking to someone in China and the Middle East, they will receive your real time message in Mandarin and Farsi and when they speak to you in their native language, you will hear it in English."

"As our team of researchers grows, all parties will be provided with the lenses. Because we are in the alpha stage, we want to take you on a tour of Madison." With that, we all visually walked through the Capitol, around the square during farmer's market, went out on Lake Mendota, watched the sun rise over Lake Monona and sat on the fifty-yard line during a Badger football game." In Amy and my seats, I might add, wondering how in hell they did that.

Everyone thought the tour was neat.

I added, "Now, let's show you one of the projects we've already developed."

The Glove:

The lights dimmed and Mark walked into the room with a big smile on his face. Luke introduced him and relinquished the floor to him.

"Good morning, I would like to share a bit of the future with you." Mark said.

Mark pulled out the pair of his, not-so-famous, gloves. "These are sensor gloves. Will one of you please put them on."

Dr. Patel abided and slipped the gloves on.

"Please push the button on the back of each wrist. Do you mind if we share some data with you?"

The doctor agreed to sharing and did as she was instructed. With that, the projector turned on and a split-screen appeared. On one side was a set of readings with blood pressure, body temperature, pulse and oxygen levels showing while the other side remained blank.

Both doctors looked at the gloves as Mark explained. "The sensor in one finger has scanned your fingerprint and the report is now exclusive to you. For security, a second finger completed sampling your DNA, while your third finger measured all your vitals and the small pressure you felt on your index finger was an epidural blood count from which, we were able to acquire data without drawing blood. From this, we have your vitals … temperature, blood pressure, pulse and oxygen levels, along with your CBC, BMP and enzymes and have also looked at your genes for any risk factors."

Dr. Patel's mouth dropped open. "This is incredible!"

Mark continued. "If we tied this and your genetic imprint into Simon, we would begin building a personal and secure medical database, which could only be unlocked when the physician on the other end matched the fingerprint and DNA to that which they had on file. Once your file was opened and revisited, Simon would look for any variances. He would then report not only changes, but treatment recommendations, including updated options, such as pharmaceuticals, in specific dosages apropos to the wearer, which would then be shown on the right side of the screen. Because the gloves can be tied to any router via Bluetooth, they can be worn by anyone in the world and the wearer can get expert diagnostics via the computer or a specialist, who could also be located anywhere in the world.

Dr. Hsu repeated the process and her vitals were read. She shook her head and leaned back in her chair and exhaled loudly as she looked at Amy and me and said, "And I almost didn't come to lunch!"

Mark opened the presentation to questions and we spent the next hour talking about accuracy, communication capability and liability. We outlined we had FCC approval and this had expedited the process in terms of the FDA. We also noted that, until that approval was completed, we would incorporate Simon simply for medical research, by enlisting researchers around the world who wanted to share knowledge, by acquiring knowledge.

It was close to noon and the meeting adjourned as we all got into the Suburban and headed back to the farm house not realizing that Dr. Patel was still carrying the gloves.

Lunch:

Tommie had constructed a large, screened gazebo near the house so people could eat outside without the bugs. When we arrived at the gazebo, it was all set for lunch. Cecelia assumed she would be helping but I told her, she was our guest and to sit back and enjoy the day.

Mom and the kids were back from their ride and so the first topic of conversation was where they went and what they saw. "V" and Derrick talked about their horses. Mela, of course, had to talk about the pretty flowers and all the neat things she saw while riding her favorite horse named Buckwheat she called Bucky, explaining that Buckwheat was tan with white spots while Bucky was Bucky Badger, her favorite mascot.

We all sat and were served Cornish pasty from the Red Rooster. The doctors had never eaten anything like it, even though Teddy Wedgers, in Madison, was famous for it. Conversation turned to what we had seen in the morning and how impressed both doctors were by what we had accomplished and what our goals were. We hadn't mentioned the next phase as we thought it would be too much for one morning.

As we were eating, Dr. Patel realized she had accidently put the sensor gloves in her purse and took them out. Mela looked at them and thought it was strange to have gloves, when it was summer. I tried to explain they were a special kind of glove and with that Mela thought they were magic and put them on. Before anyone could stop her, she pressed the button on the back and felt the prick.

"Ouch!" was all she said.

No one thought much of it as we handed the gloves back to Mark who responded with a sigh of relief.

After lunch, the MadCity boys got into the Suburban and headed back to Madison. Mom and the kids went to House on the Rock which left Amy, Dr. Hsu, Dr. Patel, Tommie, Luke and I to go riding.

Dr. Hsu was an accomplished equestrian, having taken lessons as a child in California. Dr. Patel had never been on a horse before and so, there were a few lessons that needed to be taught about getting Sophie ready and how to handle her, even though Sophie was about as gentle as a kitten.

We all saddled up and went for a slow walk around the property. We went past the family cemetery and I spoke about how the limestone fence had once been the farmhouse and all my ancestors who were buried there. I spoke of George the First's horse named Ed and then my little friend Jake and how they were resting with the other members of my family, as they had been family members too.

As we neared the forest, we stopped and I detailed all that had happened to George the First and how we fought for the land and about Great Grandfather. We tied the leads to the trees and progressed into the woods. It was as if we were entering a church as everyone was silent and respectful. We stopped at what was left of the school foundation and I explained why the school was built, where it had been and how valuable my ancestors thought education was. I outlined how the kids had to walk a mile to the school every day, regardless of the weather.

We went to the glen where George the First saved Rodney's many greats grandmother's life and how, because of that, I connected with Rodney and Ann, and how Rodney was my best friend. As we were walking towards the springs, Dr. Patel stopped in her tracks. "Someone is here, I can feel their presence," she whispered.

I looked at Luke and he nodded. "I feel it too," he said.

Tommie and Dr. Hsu looked at Dr. Patel and Luke with a degree of trepidation.

"My God, what a strange feeling!" Dr. Patel exclaimed, as we continued on.

As we came to the small obelisk, Luke and Dr. Patel stopped and I saw tears in their eyes. They were feeling what I always felt. They were experiencing what washed over my body and gave me peace. They looked at each other and both knew right then and there, God had brought them together to this spot to meet with the spirit of Great Grandfather so he could remove their loneliness. It was then they both smiled as Great Grandfather's purity was filling their souls with love.

As we walked on, I looked back and Luke and Dr. Patel were waking side-by-side. I just knew it would be that way the rest of their lives. I don't know why, but I knew.

We arrived at the spot where Amy and I had first made love. She squeezed my hand and I hers. This was our special spot that meant so much to the two of us. Luke explained about the convergence of the Ley Lines and the positive energy. He detailed the entire concept of pure water, as I opened the little storage box and took out the tin cups, dipping each one in the cold, clear, water that trickled forth.

"To our success. May we bask in the beauty of healing others!" I toasted as we all drank the cold, clear water.

Dr. Hsu looked at all of us and said "I cannot thank you enough for what you have shown me today, not only at the research center, but with your family." We all just smiled.

We made our way back to the stables and Tommie asked Dr. Hsu if she would like to tour the barn to see the animals. She replied that would be, "cool". I smiled … a recognized expert, with not one but two PHD's, and she said "cool"!

I knew Dr. Patel had no interest in cows and pigs and so I suggested we go into Mineral Point and show her around town. We took the truck while Amy and I, Cecelia and Johnnie, along with Luke and Indira as she asked us to call her, visited fifteen artists stores along with the Ben Franklin in town. I told her the story of Pointer the dog and the beginning of Mineral Point. I outlined how the Ben Franklin store was one of the last ones in America and how it was filled with all kinds of things from days gone by.

As we were heading back to Waldwick, Indira said," What a wonderful little town. How far is it to Madison?"

"52 miles," I responded.

"What a neat place. I wouldn't mind living here."

We made it back just as Tommie and Hsu, as she wanted us to call her, were finishing their farm tour. Tommie had relaxed and was actually smiling. Hsu, had a slight grin on her face as she was in her domain, amongst the animals she had dreamt of caring for her entire life.

It was nearly five when mom and the kids got back from House on The Rock, to which Mila had to tell us all about the "magical musical instruments that played all by themselves, with no one around."

We sat in the gazebo and had steaks for dinner along with salad made from fresh vegetables from mom's garden … spinach, carrots and cucumbers, all covered with mom's homemade hot-bacon dressing.

"No, they were not," was all Tommie said to Hsu, with a smile on his face, as she looked at the steak in front of her.

It was a traditional farm meal…steak, green beans and baked potatoes from mom's garden. When we were all stuffed, Tommie offered to go and get dessert from the house. Hsu asked if he needed help and the two of them walked into the house together. I remember thinking, it wouldn't be the last time they ever did that and had a smirk on my face as my wife was reading my mind.

In a couple minutes, the duo brought out three pies mom baked the day before … apple, blueberry and raspberry, all made from fruits picked on the farm, that mom had canned the year before.

Tommie also brought a quart of fresh cream and had a smile on his face.

"Who wants ice cream on their pie?" he asked.

The kids were excited and the adults looked at him like he was nuts until he brought out a small canister of liquid helium. As he poured the cream into a platter, he added some vanilla extract and then shot it with the liquid helium to make ice cream in front of our eyes. The kids were amazed.

We sat and ate homemade pie with homemade ice cream, which came from our farm and our cows. Amy and I had eaten in the finest restaurants in the world and no one ever had a dessert that tasted better. While everyone sat back in stuffed splendor and let the food settle, we talked about Wisconsin, the farm and the research.

Indira asked Amy if her mother was Dr. Marie Williams and Amy said, "Yes".

"I have had the honor of attending symposiums where your mother has spoken about new treatment options and how she is an advocate of affordable health care for everyone. She is quite a doctor and person." Indira replied.

Amy nodded and shyly smiled saying, "Thank you," adding, "We hope to help bring down the cost of health care and open preventive medicine to everyone. That's what our mission is all about."

It was getting pretty intense and so I interjected. "We have a tradition here on the farm when we have guests." I paused for effect and announced … "We have a bonfire!" to which Mela jumped up and down with excitement.

"Do we get to make Smores?" Mela asked.

Hsu and Indira both had frowns on their faces and so Mela had to explain. "You take a mushmillow and put it on a magic stick and put it over the fire and it turns brown just like Grandma Marie. Then you take it off the stick and put it on a grain cracker with a Hershey square and pop it in your mouth. It's my favoritist food in the whole wide world!" to which everyone laughed.

We made our way to the fire pit on the hill where George the First and Elizabeth would sit every night and watch the sun go down. Tommie had placed blocks in a circle which could seat twelve and we all sat as Tommie started the fire. My MadCity Boys had developed ultra-sonic speakers that were buried outside the fire pit ring which they promised would keep our state bird … the mosquito, away. Sure, enough, it worked, as we all sat and watched the fire and talked about our families, where we were from and what we enjoyed doing.

I had Amy on one side, with the boys next to her. Mela was sitting next to Hsu with Tommie on Hsu's other side. Next to Tommie was Luke and then Indira and finally mom, Cecelia and Johnnie, who was sitting next to me. We watched the fire burn and listened to it crackle and pop as darkness fell. It was about nine when I noticed the kids were getting tired. I phoned Andrew and asked if he could come and pick us up, as he had gone back to Madison to have dinner with his wife.

Tommie looked at me and the kids and then said, "Why don't Luke and I drive Hsu and Indira back to Madison? That way you can take the kids directly home."

I looked at Amy and she had a slight smile on her face.

"It's up to our guests" I said.

Hsu looked at Indira and they both nodded as Hsu said, "Your kids are getting tired and you can go straight home."

"If you don't mind," Amy said.

"Not at all!"

I called Andrew and told him to change the flight plan. We would be heading directly back to Hartland. Within what seemed like a few minutes, we heard the rush of the helicopter blades and it was time to leave.

"I hope you see how sincere we are about what we are doing." I said to the two doctors.

Indira spoke first. "I was reluctant on coming, but would have profoundly regretted it had I known what this was all about. Your family, the farm, Mineral Point and your project are all wonderful. Thank you".

Hsu added, "Please count me in."

Mom slipped into the house and came out with two small boxes. Amy and I both knew what was inside, as the ladies opened them and found copies of *'Waldwick'* and *'Hocak'* inside.

"I hope you find time to read about our family," mom said.

Both Hsu and Indira thanked us for the wonderful day as we headed for the chopper and mom to her truck. I don't know when the foursome let the fires burn down, but I do know it was a day everyone marked on their calendar as one that would always be remembered.

The Report:

"Now" refers to the present moment, the point in time that is currently occurring. It is the immediate instance between the past and the future, constantly shifting as time progresses. Philosophically, "now" can be seen as the only real moment, as the past exists only in memory and the future only in anticipation.

In life, each day has a way of blending into the next until they become nothing more than a blur. Every now and then, a day will come along … both good and bad … that you will never forget. The following Monday was one of those days. I was sitting in the office when Cecelia came in with a worried look on her face.

"What's going on?" I inquired.

"I just got a call from Mark," Cecelia replied.

"And?"

"He wanted to know who, besides Doctor Hsu and Dr. Patel, had the gloves on?"

I thought for a moment and remembered dinner and Mela.

"Mela, why?"

Cecelia sat down across from me. "They were running tests on the computer and downloaded all the glove data that had been acquired."

"Ok?"

Cecelia continued with a look of fear on her face, "Simon ran the numbers and they didn't come back as they should."

Terror ran through my body. "What do you mean?" as my hands went to my cheeks in fear.

"I don't know how to tell you this."

"What?"

"According to the report, someone might have leukemia."

My heart sank. The marker Amy and I had feared, appeared. Amy's malady, which had killed her grandmother, had potentially arisen in our daughter. Our worst nightmare was coming true.

"Oh my God!" was all I could say, as I collapsed back into my chair.

I took a deep breath and thought of my little girl. My mind raced, hoping it was mistake. What could I do? Who should I call? Amy? Her mom? Mark, to double check the numbers? I closed my eyes, as tears rolled down my cheeks.

I never shared Amy's battle with anyone. That was her wish, when she was cancer "cured". As Ceclia and I sat there, I let out all my emotions, feeling bad I hadn't shared it with her previously. I reported, "When Amelia was going to college, she was diagnosed with acute lymphocytic leukemia or (ALL) which is a cancer that affects a type of white blood cell which helps your body fight infection,".

I took a deep breath and continued. "Doctor Roberts and I had a long conversation when Amy and I were dating and I took some notes. She indicated, research had shown that ALL was directly related to a specific gene mutation that could be inherited. While it normally is only found in Caucasian males, the mutation is part of Amelia's genetic footprint that probably started with some of her ancestors, who were of European lineage."

I added, "ALL killed Amelia's grandmother! It skipped her mother, but affected Amelia. Our hope was that it wouldn't be prevalent in our kids. However, it looks as if Simon determined our dreams might not have come true."

Cecelia was sitting with her hands in her lap and a sorrowful look upon her face. "Perhaps it's an error," she said trying to console me and minimize the fear.

My tone was becoming more clinical as the initial shock and emotional devastation was beginning to wear off and I continued, "When Amy got sick, she went to John Hopkins in Baltimore, who put her on a chemo program that wasn't working very well. Amy said they did their best and were really great. Amy's mom once told me that the outcome of cancer treatment depended on multiple interactions between metastatic cells and stable cells. For this reason, the John Hopkins treatment of metastasis wasn't only aimed at Amy's specific cancer cells, but against host factors, as well, which contributed to the support, growth and survival of the metastatic cancer cells."

I looked at Ceclia and added, "This is why Amy and so many people get so sick when they go through chemotherapy and why people, including Amy, lose so much weight after their chemo rounds."

Cecelia sat shaking her head almost in disbelief. Like everyone else, she thought wealth and power meant things like health were never an issue as I continued, "Needless to say, the Williams were frantic, especially after losing Derrick. With resources and medical knowledge, Amelia's mom learned about an experimental drug which was having some success in Madison and Dr. Williams was able to get Amelia in the clinical trial. At the same time, the oncologists suggested T-cell therapy, where T-cells are removed from the blood, genetically modified to enhance their cancer-fighting abilities and reintroduced back into the patient's body. In tests done, more than 90% of those who were terminally ill went into remission, including Amy."

"Amy and I spent a lot of time studying the drug, as we both wanted to know what it did and what were the consequences. We found out her drug restored the normal cellular life cycle in those who have the gene mutation by blocking the protein lifeline to the cancer cells. In so doing, the malignant cells end up committing suicide. When combined with the T-cell therapy, the combination returned Amelia to a healthy state, but the costs were incredible, both physically and financially, as the process was a five-year ordeal with monthly 'cleansing' of Amelia's blood, along with harvesting T-cells, plus the administration of the test drug. The total cost for just Amy exceeded a million dollars."

I took a deep breath and looked in Cecelia's eyes and continued, "I met Amy when she was three years into the program and witnessed how difficult the entire procedure was. Each month meant a day having all of her blood drained and put back in. The next day or two, she would suffer from nausea and acute cramps, which were debilitating. Amy was a trooper at twenty-four years old. I don't know how difficult it would be for a four-year-old to endure."

"Other than her doctors, parents, Rodney, Ann, you, me and Amy, no one else knows she had ALL and will always be on medicine to prevent its recurrence. Everyone thinks she is cured and while we celebrated her 'survivor' anniversary, there is always doubt and fear. While the current medication is working, there are no guarantees it will keep going long term and one of the key ingredients regarding its return is stress. Even though money has never been an issue and Amy is totally dedicated to her jobs as a mother and leader, I don't really know if she could handle the stress of both, especially if it means taking care of her sick child, who has inherited a disease from her."

I sat back in my chair and listened to the deafening silence of regret. Not that Mela was there, as she was the light of my life; not that she might have the same malady that her mother had; but that my wife might have to endure the pain and suffering again that she had before, but only through the life of her daughter. How do you tell a little girl who appears happy and healthy, she has a terrible disease which will require years of treatments? My God, the mountain from which I must depart and the valley into which I must traverse was so profound and so incredibly steep, I only asked for guidance and forgiveness that I had not cherished each moment more than I did.

Cecelia stood and came around my desk and gave me a big hug. It was a motherly hug of love and compassion. It was a hug to tell me she cared and would always be there for us. It was a hug of love, for which I was deeply grateful.

As Cecelia left, I stood and walked to the cedar chest in the corner of my office. It had been a very long time since I sat upon its surface … too long … and I slowly pulled the last vestige of a man so great away from the wall, put my hands to my face, sat down and began to cry, with the tears dropping onto the glass case with the two white eagle feathers in it.

Dinner:

I texted Amelia and suggested dinner. She sent back a note saying fine and asking if the kids should come. I replied, I thought it should just be the two of us. I think she knew something was wrong.

We met at the Five O'clock Club on the east end of Pewaukee Lake. On any Friday at their fish fry, the wait could be hours. It was Monday and I got there first and sat at a table out on the deck and ordered a beer. Amy arrived a few minutes later and knew something was wrong by the expression on my face. I breathed deep and let it slowly exhale.

"What's wrong?" she asked.

"Remember when we were at the farm and Dr. Patel mistakenly put Mark's sensor gloves in her purse?"

"Yes," Amy replied.

"Remember when she put them down on the table?"

"Sort of."

"Remember who slipped the gloves on?"

"Mela?"

"Yes!" I replied

A look of terror came across Amy's face as I continued, "The gloves did their analysis of everyone who had worn them and the data was transferred to the lab. The boys finished the correlation software and integrated the collected information into Simon to run a beta test to determine how he would function in terms of diagnostics and prescription."

I looked at Amy, then at the ground and then back at Amy. "The results came back, stating Mela or someone, may have the ALL gene".

Amy's hands went to her mouth and tears welled in her eyes. "Oh my God, no!" My Amelia thought back to her own ordeal and the lesson learned that, even the innocent can be caught and crushed by life's unfairness, leaving an indelible mark about what really matters.

"That's all I know for right now. It could be an error or it could be Mela or someone has the gene and needs to be watched." I didn't want to overly concern my wife.

Amy sank down in the chair and closed her eyes and shook her head.

"I need to talk to mom," she whispered.

"I know. Do you want to wait until tomorrow?"

"I want to see the report."

Before leaving the office, I had assumed she would and brought it with me. She looked at the numbers and tried to make sense of them.

"Can we go see mom now?"

"Of course!" I said, as we stood. I gently grabbed Amy's arm. "We'll get through this, I promise!" as I put a twenty-dollar bill on the picnic bench and walked to Amy's car.

"Do you want to call your mom and make sure she's home?"

"I was talking with her on my way here. I know she's home."

We got into her car in almost total silence and drove to Amy's parent's house. The gate was closed and Amy called and the gate swung open.

As we got to the front door, Dr. Williams was there and could tell by our expressions, there was something wrong. I took another deep breath and walked in the house as Amy began outlining the entire day and how the test results had come back.

Dr. Williams took the report and scoured the data and took a deep breath. "Her vitals are fine, which is a good sign. Her blood level is right on the edge, but there's something going on."

This was like sticking a dagger in my heart. I thought it was just that Mela was susceptible. Dr. Williams was making it sound more urgent. As she was talking, The Duke came into the living room.

"Doug, it's Mela". Dr. Williams said. "There might be a problem".

"What?" The Duke inquired.

"Same thing!" Dr. Williams replied as the Duke sat down and slid back in his chair. I saw fear in his eyes for the first time ever.

"Oh my God!" was all he could say.

"We will need to run some tests to confirm. I'll make the arrangements."

With that, Amy began to cry. "It's all my fault!" Her guilt complex was coming into play.

"We'll get through this dear," Dr. Williams responded.

Tests:

How do you go home and tell a four-year-old she might have a lethal disease? How do you explain she might die? How do you tell her there could be months or years filled with hospitals, tests, drugs and pain and all the dreams she has of being a princess might end? What a terrible nightmare! Peaks and valleys! Peaks and valleys!

Amy and I drove home in deafening silence, stopping only to pick up my car at the Five O'Clock Club. In our separation, our minds must have been running on the same tracks as arrival home met with complete agreement … minimize, and let the awareness of the malady take hold in a gradual manner, instead of one profound catastrophe. It was agreed, we needed confirmation and affirmation before any form of treatment.

While other parents would have been overwhelmed by the profound dichotomy that comes from the abject differences between fairy tales and the aesthetic world of medicine, once again, we were blessed by a transitional phase, as the doctor in charge was Amelia's mother. Instead of Mela visiting with strangers who poked and prodded and did all kinds of things she wasn't prepared for, Mela would be gradually introduced to a world of tests and treatments, equipment and procedures, that were never found in children's books about dragons and princesses.

A timetable was developed and, because of who Dr. Williams was and what people thought of her, we knew only the best treatment would be provided. The first phase consisted of acclimation. To this end, Amelia took Mela to "visit" grandma where she worked. Mela was all excited about going to visit grandma and meeting new kids her age until she got there and realized they were all sick.

"Mommy, that girl doesn't have any hair." Mela whispered to Amy as they walked through the pediatric cancer ward.

"I know" Amy replied. "She has one of the new hairstyles. What do you think? Would you like to try that someday?"

"I think my head would get cold and other kids would laugh at me," Mela replied.

"They wouldn't laugh and you could wear your favorite stocking cap all year long." Amy answered.

After the tour of the hospital, Amy and Mela made it to Doctor Williams' office. Mela was excited to see grandma.

"Grandma, you get to wear a white coat like all those other people!" Mela said.

"That's because I'm a doctor, too," Doctor Williams said.

"Do you help mommies get babies out of their tummies?" Mela asked.

"No, I help little girls and boys grow up so they can become mommies and daddies, like yours."

That seemed to suffice the inquisitive one.

"Today, Mela we want to play some games. Do you mind doing that?" Dr. Williams asked.

"No Grandma. You know I like games."

"Well here is what the game is. We're going to spray some funny smelling stuff on your arm and then wrap a big rubber band around it. Then, we're going to poke you with a very small needle, but you won't feel it."

"Will it hurt?"

"Not at all, sweetie! Then when we're done, you get to pick out a funny face to put over the spot. Is that all right with you?"

"OK, Grandma."

The technician sprayed the numbing agent on Mela's arm and waited a few seconds before adding the tourniquet.

"Does that hurt?" Dr. Williams inquired.

"Nope! I'm a big girl and I promise I won't cry."

The aide inserted the small butterfly needle and blood ran through the tube.

"Is that my blood?" Mela asked as her eyes widened in amazement.

"Yes, it is!" Grandma Williams replied.

When three vials were filled, the needle was removed from Mela's arm.

"You did great!" Amelia said.

"Did grandma ever stick a needle in you, Mommy?" Mela asked.

"Not grandma, but other people have." Amelia replied.

"Did you cry?"

"Sometimes!"

"So, I'm braver than you?"

"Yup! You're my brave Mela!" Amelia answered, almost choking up.

"Well, Grandma's got to get back to work. If you open my desk drawer, there's a present in there just for you." Dr. Williams noted.

Mela's eyes widened again as she pulled open the drawer and saw a small, plush, Bucky Badger stuffed animal.

"Oh Grandma, Bucky Badger! He's my favorite!"

Dr. Williams looked at Amy and said, "Lab work should be back tomorrow. I'll call you as soon as I know."

Amelia and Mela walked out of the hospital with Amy praying there would be no reason to come back for a long, long time. When Amy got to her car, she called and detailed all that happened. I asked her to put me on the speaker phone and I told Mela how proud I was of her. She told me all about her special bandage and Bucky Badger. I told her I couldn't wait to see them both when she got home.

That night and the following morning, were the longest of my life. I wanted to go to the forest, but didn't want to leave Amelia. Around two, the phone rang and it was Dr. Williams.

"I've got some very good news." Doctor Williams reported to a collective sigh of relief. "All of Mela's blood work came back normal. The sample either came from someone else or the computer doesn't work."

I looked at Amy and she at me and tears of relief were in both of our eyes. We hugged each other and shook our heads. Our worst nightmare was over.

After a collective sigh, I called Luke and reported the news, along with the conclusion. Either the gloves or the computer didn't work, or they were someone else's vitals.

Luke responded. "George, the issue isn't the test or gloves were wrong, it's just that we haven't uploaded the initial genetic and fingerprint tracers and so the computer doesn't have the identity of who the person is."

I sat and shook my head and thought "Of course! No one who tried on the gloves had their identity put into the database and so it could be anyone."

I looked at Amy and explained and she raised the palms of her hands into the air as if to totally agree.

Amy and I sat and went through all the people who had worn the gloves...Dr. Hsu, Dr. Patel and Mela were the only ones who came to mind. But there could have been so many more. Twenty minutes later the phone rang. It was Luke. The MadCity boys had learned the sample had determined that the test results could be from males or females of Caucasian, African and Asian descent. In other words, almost then entire world!

We sat perplexed. Caucasian? That could be anyone in the lab, including me. Central Asian? Dr. Hsu was the only person we could think of until it hit me ... Rodney! Rodney put the gloves on and we had shown him how they worked.

Because it was just a casual demonstration in his office, no one thought the data might be transmitted via the Ho-Chunk WIFI network to Simon. Because, the MadCity boys didn't know about the demonstration in Black River Falls, they assumed the only Asian data came from Doctors Hsu and Patel and hadn't gone any further in their confirmations. Luke said the boys were feeling terrible about the false alarm and the trauma they put us through.

I sat for a minute, took a deep breath and asked Great Grandfather for guidance. Once he told me all people make mistakes and if they recognize them, admit them and learn from them, to forgive them and move on. "Luke, tell the boys mistakes happen. Also, please tell them, in the future, double check whenever something as major as a life-threatening disease appears."

In our relief, we had forgotten one thing. My best friend. My big brother could be sick and didn't know it.

Details:

While we were profoundly relieved, I also knew I needed some advice on how to tell Rodney and Ann. Amy suggested we have dinner with The Duke and Dr. Williams and get some guidance. I suggested it be with Dr. Roberts and her husband as they were experts in the field. When you donate millions of dollars to their research, you should be able to expect something.

We suggested meeting in Madison at Paisan's, because they had outside seating. The Roberts were more than amenable and the next night we met and sat out on the deck and ordered our pizza. While there was relief, there was also concern and I asked Dr. Roberts to fill me in on adult Leukemia.

Dr. Roberts looked out at Lake Monona and outlined the basics. "At all times, our bodies are being invaded by foreign matter they need to fight off. This matter can either be bacterial in nature, viral or fungal. The first line of defense are the white blood cells. Within the white blood cells, the body creates what are called granulocytes, which are white blood cells that have small granules or particles in them. These granules contain numerous proteins which are responsible for helping the immune system fight off viruses and bacteria. When granulocytes leave the bone marrow, they circulate through the bloodstream and respond to signals from the immune system. Their role is to attack foreign substances which cause inflammation or infection."

Dr. Roberts continued, "When everything is working properly, you have just the right number of cells to keep you healthy. When the system is imbalanced, you can have too few or too many white blood cells and this is called leukemia, of which there are four different classes depending on which type of cell is imbalanced."

Dr. Robert's husband was a noted oncologist at UW Hospitals and so his input was also welcomed as he said, "The first type is called Acute Lymphocytic Leukemia or ALL, which mostly occurs in children and the type Amelia had. There are about 6,000 new cases diagnosed annually in the U.S. and the five-year survival rate is 68.2 percent which, fortunately, has been climbing rapidly."

"While we all live in fear that we have sent a genetic time bomb to our children, ALL can be found in approximately 5% of all babies born and is what is called a transcription error, which is a mutation of the gene. Fortunately, of the 5% of children who are born with the transcription error, only one in two-thousand have the gene mutate into ALL. When this happens, the person becomes quite susceptible."

The doctor paused for a moment to collect his thoughts and then continued, "Before age twenty, when nature appears to wipe the mutation clean, a seemingly minor infection must happen, which can be anything as insignificant as the flu. The infection triggers further genetic mutation that activates the malignant potential of the first two factors and ALL begins with the production of immature lymphocytes, which spin out of control, which is what happened to Amy. Because the diagnoses may be for Rodney, who is an adult male in his late 30's, we can assume he is not suffering from ALL."

Dr. Roberts added, "The next type is called Chronic Myelogenous Leukemia or CML, which affects mostly adults. About 9,000 new cases of CML are diagnosed annually. The five-year survival rate for CML is 66.9 percent. The third type is called Chronic lymphocytic Leukemia or CLL and is most likely to affect people over the age of 55, who have a genetic pre-disposition. It's very rarely seen in children and about 20,000 new cases of CLL are diagnosed in the U.S. annually. The five-year survival rate for CLL is 83.2 percent."

Doctor Roberts added. "The fourth and most probable type is Acute myelogenous leukemia or AML, which involves myeloid cells, which are immature blood cells normally associated with what is called the innate immune system. Myeloid cells provide immediate defense against foreign substances and cause inflammation or infection."

"AML can occur in children and adults and is caused by abnormalities in the DNA, which controls the development of cells in bone marrow. Researchers at the Carbone lab have studied proteins in DNA called the GATA family and how mutations in the DNA that code these proteins give rise to blood cancers. One single mutation, in just one site of the DNA appears to cause AML. This happens because a person who has inherited the deficiency, lacks the ability to efficiently regenerate the blood system. It's not exactly clear what causes the DNA mutation. Some doctors believe it may be genetic, others feel it is related to exposure to certain chemicals, radiation and even the drugs used for chemotherapy."

The doctor continued, "If a patient has AML, their bone marrow creates countless white blood cells that are immature. These abnormal cells eventually become leukemic white blood cells, called myeloblasts, which build up and replace healthy cells. This causes bone marrow to stop functioning properly, thereby making the person's body more susceptible to infections."

The doctor looked at me and then at Amy and added, "There are about 21,000 new cases of AML diagnosed annually in the United States and is the most common form of adult leukemia. The average age for a person with AML is about 67 and is more common in men than women. While there are treatments for the other types of the malady, at this time, there are only a very few drugs being tested and there is little that can help someone with AML."

Doctor Roberts paused for a moment and then continued, "While a blood test, like the one from the glove you explained, may help determine whether there's a problem, a bone marrow test or biopsy is needed to diagnose AML definitively. Some doctors do a spinal tap or lumbar puncture, which involves withdrawing fluid from the spine with a small needle, but I normally don't do this."

"What about treatments" I asked.

Dr. Roberts continued. "What treatment there is for AML involves two phases. The first is called remission induction therapy which uses chemotherapy to kill the existing leukemia cells in the patient's body. Most people stay in the hospital during treatment because chemotherapy also kills healthy cells, raising their risk for infection and abnormal bleeding.

If the disease is still in the patient's body after the induction phase, the doctor may give prescribe a second treatment phase called *consolidation therapy* using what is called Rydapt that works by blocking the signals that help certain cells grow and divide. This can be done, either in the hospital or as outpatient therapy.

"So there is some form of treatment?" Amy inquired.

Doctor Roberts continued, "RYDAPT is only for adult patients, who are newly diagnosed with AML and have what is called the FLT3 genetic mutation. After the initial AML diagnosis, the doctor will order a test for FLT3. If the test is positive, the doctor may prescribe RYDAPT, in addition to chemotherapy."

Looking directly at me, Dr. Roberts added, "AML is a disease that can get worse very quickly. Unfortunately, at this time, the five-year survival rate for AML is just 26.9 percent and a person's risk of developing AML increases with age and most doctors start the treatment right away." This meant, we really needed to solve the riddle as quickly as possible.

The Long Ride to Black River Falls:

I called Rodney and asked to see him. I didn't want to tell him why, but did indicate it had to do with the computer and running tests using volunteers from the Ho-Chunk Nation. A date was set and I boarded the chopper and took the longest ride of my life. How do you tell your best friend he might be critically ill?

We landed behind the parking lot and big brother was standing at the back door waiting for us, as always, with his great big, infectious smile.

"Heh little brother, good to see you!" Rodney hollered over the still swirling helicopter blades.

"You too!" I said, as I hugged him.

We walked into his office and he sat behind his desk.

"What's up?"

I could never play poker because something was written all over my face.

"Remember when I was here and you put on the medi-gloves?"

"Sure!" Rodney responded.

"Remember pressing the button on the back and asking what it was for?"

"Yah!" Rodney said with shrugged shoulders.

"Well, the gloves took your vitals and they were transmitted via your server, back to our computer."

"Yah?"

"Well, there's a chance you might have leukemia."

"What?" Rodney said as he slumped forward in his chair, incredulous.

"We're not sure because we didn't have the fingerprint and DNA markers in the database and so we're not certain who all tried on the gloves, but we need to rule out, it's not you. We've already run tests on virtually everyone else including Mela, Amy and me and they have come back clear and we're running out of people we can remember who tested the gloves."

I could see the fear brewing in Rodney's mind, but who wouldn't be if they heard the words "You've got cancer?" ...Words that are spoken nearly 5,000 times each day in America that scares the shit out of those who are told it's them, even though, there are over sixteen million cancer survivors in the United States today.

I needed to soften the blow and added. "It might not be you, but I, no...we, want to make absolutely sure that, if it is, all steps are taken to begin testing and treatments as soon as possible."

Rodney's face turned completely somber. I now knew what it was like to be a doctor and have to tell someone they might have a fatal disease.

Rodney let out a deep sigh. "You came all the way up here to tell me face-to-face?"

"Yes, big brother, I did."

"This is why you are my best friend. You are showing your love for me. What do I need to do?"

"I've made arrangements for a complete physical at University Hospital in Madison."

"When?"

"The chopper is waiting."

"I need to call Ann."

"Amy just called her."

Rodney shook his head and looked at the floor and got very serious. "Let me tell the people in the office there is a small emergency and I need to go to Madison."

"Agreed!"

With that, Rodney went and told everyone he had a personal emergency in Madison and we ducked out the back door and into the chopper where Ann was already sitting. Rodney looked at Ann and she at him and then she squeezed his hand as tears trickled down her cheeks.

The ride to Madison seemed to take forever. We had clearance for the helipad at University Hospital, landed, and quickly exited, as Andrew lifted the chopper off the emergency pad and out to Truax. We went in through the emergency doors and Dr. Roberts and two doctors met us, along with Dr. Patel. Rodney looked at them and then at me and gave me a big hug saying, "Thank you, Little Spirit!"

Ann and I went into the waiting room and sat in stone silence. Time seemed to freeze, as each glance at the clock hardly saw any progress. One hour! Two hours! Nearly three hours later Rodney walked in with Dr. Patel at his side and a huge grin on his face.

"Not me!" he whispered. Ann slumped back in her chair in total relief. I looked at the ground first and then at my best friend in total embarrassment. I had scared the ever-loving shit out of him saying, "I'm so sorry!"

"For what? For scaring me or for caring about me so much you came and brought me here?" Rodney replied. "I told you long ago, how I was going to die." A shy smile came across my face as his old joke rattled around in my brain while Rodney laughingly said, "At age 95, I'm going to be shot by a jealous twenty-five-year-old husband," which got a quick punch in the ribs from Ann and a huge guffaw from Rodney.

Andrew brought one of the cars and we headed back towards Truax. "Can I at least buy you dinner?" I asked. We went to the square and I hopped out and brought the Teddywedger's back to the car and we ate them as Andrew drove us to the airport.

I sighed a deep sigh of relief. First Mela and now Rodney. Fear, apprehension and heartbreak, superseded by profound relief and the joy of life. Then the trepidation set in. If not Mela, Amy, Rodney or me, who?

We made it back to Black River Falls and dropped off Rodney and Ann and headed for home. I closed my eyes and thanked God for His blessings, as my head shook from side-to-side wondering whether this was a wild goose chase or was someone out there living on borrowed time.

Andrew dropped me off at home and I walked slowly into the house. Amy saw me coming up the driveway, rushed to the front door and gave me a big hug. She knew I was relieved. She also knew I was tormented. Was our marvelous machine really wrong?

The next morning, I went to the office and Cecelia asked how I was doing. I told her the emotional roller coaster was almost too much to bear. Perhaps I wasn't cut out for the world of medicine. Cecelia looked at me and squinted as she pointed her finger at me and said, "George Terrill, I don't know another person who doesn't belong in the world of medicine, as much as you. You are caring and compassionate and, above all else, generous to a fault, not only of your money, but of yourself and you are one of the finest people I've ever known." Next, Cecelia did what she had rarely done before, she stood and gave me a hug … a long, generous, hug telling me she cared. After a long pause, she stood back and quietly said, "Little Spirit, ask for guidance!"

With so much going on, I had overlooked the one place where there was a point of respite and it was sitting in my office. I pulled up the old chest and asked Great Grandfather to come to me and give me peace. The silence was deafening. Was this a test of my will or was he gone from my life forever?

Searching:

It was as if I'd lost something, I was trying to find. I retraced our steps and all those I knew who had worn the gloves. I wrote a timeline and worked backwards to the day Mark walked through the door with the gloves. I thought of all the meetings and people who had slipped them on and was about to give up when I looked at the two white feathers and remembered who had also last called me Little Spirit.

I picked up the phone and called Amy.

"I think I've solved the riddle."

"Who?"

I reiterated my first meeting with Mark and how excited we were. I explained, we made a call and invited someone to come and see what had been developed and how that person said the invention would help make the world a better place.

There was a long silence on the other end and then I heard the sobs ... "Mom!"

Tears rolled down my cheeks, as reality set in. I hoped and prayed we were wrong, but every other possible person had been tested and came back negative.

I didn't want to alarm anyone, but also knew we needed to inform Dr. Williams. I thought long and hard and finally got up the courage to call The Duke. "Hi, dad!"

"Hi, son!" The Duke replied in a pleasant, but surprised manner.

"Dad, we need to talk. Can I come and see you?"

"Sure! When?"

"I'll be there in about an hour, if it's all right."

I was certain, by the tone of my voice, he knew it was serious. I told Cecelia I needed to go see The Duke and to hold all my calls. She surmised right away that I had put the last piece of the puzzle in place and shook her head and looked down at the floor, not wanting to make eye contact, as I walked out the door.

The drive to the lake took forty-five minutes and the security gates were open. Dad was expecting me. As I walked up the steps, he opened the front door. For the first time ever, he looked like an old man and not an icon.

"What's up, son?"

I explained the project, even though he already knew every detail. I outlined the gloves and what they did, even though he also knew that. I then explained how we hadn't set up the fingerprint, DNA cross-checking system and that, even though we had concerning medical results, we didn't know who they came from, because we weren't registering anyone during beta testing. I outlined how we had double and tripled checked all the people who had tried on the gloves and explained how I had gone to Black River Falls and taken Rodney to University Hospital, where he came out clear. I outlined how we put together the entire sequence and the only person left who hadn't been cross-checked was Doctor Williams.

Dad Williams looked at me and then at the floor and then back at me. "Amy's mother already knows she has AML leukemia. She just wanted to keep it from you kids as long as possible and make certain no one else has it, especially Mela. We didn't know about Rodney being suspected or we would have told you sooner. This is the reason why I retired, son. I wanted Marie to retire too, but she wants to work as long as she can."

My mouth dropped open as my head shook in disbelief. "Did she look at all the medical options?"

"We've checked with the finest doctors in the world and all of them give her months to live." The Duke responded and then added." Son, you can have all the money in the world and even all the love, but what good are they, if you don't have your health?"

"How long?" I asked.

"We don't know! Until God calls her home. She's ready when he does! She told me she wants to be with Derrick!"

I took a deep breath and slowly exhaled.

"What can we do?" I asked

"What can anyone do? Hope, pray, live life and make certain she is made to feel wanted, needed and loved."

"Oh my God, so much so, you can never imagine," I responded.

"I can imagine son. I see it in your face. I feel it in the warmth and love you have for Amelia and the grandchildren. Now that you know, you must keep one promise."

"What's that?"

"No one is to know except Amelia. That's how Marie wants it."

On my way home, I broke my promise to Dad Williams and called Peter and filled him in. We knew who had the malady, we had her DNA and knew she was 62 years old. Why not ask Simon for advice?

When I got home, Amy was waiting and I looked at her through teary eyes and she at me. We held each other tight and I told her I had already broken my promise and asked Peter to have Simon run the data and see what he could come up with.

"What about Doctors Roberts, Hsu and Patel?" Amy asked. I shook my head in agreement. Three experts in the field made sense.

In a matter of minutes, we went from grieving, to making plans to see if we couldn't be of assistance. Amy's mother was not going to just give up if we had anything to do with it.

Initially, I called Dr. Roberts, but got his answering service.

I then called Luke and asked him to see when it would be convenient to meet with Dr. Patel.

Luke said, "Just a minute, I'll ask her." In a matter of seconds Dr. Patel was on the phone and offered to meet whenever it could be arranged. I told her I would get back to her as I wanted Dr. Hsu involved, as well. Dr. Patel responded Dr. Hsu was with Tommie, down at the farm. I called Tommie's cellphone and he picked up on the third ring.

"Tommie, Dr. Patel said Dr. Hsu is there. Here's what's going on…" with that, I explained the whole situation.

Tommie told me to hold on and he would get Dr. Hsu and so I repeated everything to her. Instead of playing telephone tag, I asked if we could have a conference call and gave Tommie the number, called Luke back and did the same. In fifteen minutes, we had everyone, Doctors Patel and Hsu, Peter, Tommie, Luke, Amy and I on a call.

I explained what was going on and said we needed to harvest data to confirm Dr. Williams prognosis and validate her treatment that would maximize her fight. Peter said he had already called the MadCity boys and they would run the scan that night and have all the data in the morning. It was agreed we would re-convene at the same time the next day.

The next twenty-four hours were pure hell as we waited for the results. I got an e-mail from Luke saying Doctor Williams' results came back and she definitely had AML, as the doctors had determined. Simon had run a sweep and harvested all the pertinent information on the malady and there were over five-thousand pages of data, which was fed into Watson, who condensed the information and paralleled it to the DNA and blood sample from Dr. Williams.

Simon concluded Dr. Williams had a rare form of AML called promyelocytic leukemia and confirmed that anti-cancer drugs, such as arsenic trioxide or all-trans retinoic acid could not be used to target specific mutations in the leukemia cells. Simon also noted that, in normal AML cases, these drugs had the potential of killing the leukemia cells and stopping the unhealthy cells from dividing. However, things would be difficult as Dr. Williams cell mutations were extremely rare.

Dr. Hsu spent the day doing research and concurred with what Dr. Roberts had said, "Consolidation or post-remission therapy, is crucial for keeping AML in remission and preventing a relapse.

This is because, the goal of is to destroy any remaining leukemia cells."

Dr. Hsu added, "Patients may require a stem cell transplant for consolidation therapy and it is my recommendation the process be implemented as soon as possible."

Dr. Patel added, "Stem cells are often used to help the patient's body generate new and healthy bone marrow cells. The stem cells may come from a donor or be harvested and remain cryogenically frozen until needed. Either way, once the patient with AML is in remission, the cells are then re-inserted in a process called autologous stem cell transplant. In 1998 the FDA approved a drug that inhibits what is called the HER2 protein for treating metastatic gastric cancer, which some researchers believe could also impede the expansion of cancer in other parts of the body."

I must have had another of my all-too-familiar, "huh?" moments as Dr. Patel continued. "While there are many causes of cancer, some of them can be correlated to genetic mutations within the body. Some genes that have been implicated develop what are called somatic mutations, or alterations that occur in the cancer cells themselves. To determine this, doctors examine genetic test samples of the tumor that are designed to detect whether the tumor has a gene abnormality that causes the overproduction of what is called HER2, which is a protein that promotes the development and spread of cancer. The problem here is that there is no tumor, as the cancer is in Dr. Williams blood."

"My recommendation would be to have Simon run a complete diagnostic on Dr. Williams DNA if that hasn't already been done, and then one specifically on her spinal fluid to compare the differentials. From this, we would know if the cancer is genetic or not which will also allow for a higher level of awareness in Amelia and your kids."

I shuddered to think that this could be the feared inherited trait.

Because Dr. Williams' cancer was in an advanced stage, Dr. Hsu concurred with Simon that the course of action was chemo, and the stem cell addition right away couldn't hurt. "You normally need to be in remission for the stem cell transplant method." Dr. Hsu added.

Dr. Patel continued, "Getting stem cells from a donor has more risks than getting a transplant made up of your own stem cells. A transplant of your own stem cells, however, involves a higher risk for relapse because some of the old leukemia cells may be present in the sample retrieved from your body."

Dr. Patel continued, "Beyond the type of leukemia, there is another classification, which is how fast it appears. The onset of AML leukemia can be fast, which is called acute or sudden onset. When the Leukemia appears gradually, it is called chronic or slow onset. In acute leukemia, cancer cells multiply quickly. In chronic leukemia, the disease progresses slowly and early symptoms may be very mild. In this case, it appears that Dr. William's Leukemia is quite aggressive and means we need to initiate treatment as soon as possible."

One thought was the stem cell transplant and Amy was asked to put on the glove again, as she would be the closest genetic match to her mother. In a matter of minutes, her complete work-up was done. Her vitals were submitted to Simon who came back and indicated that, while she was a close match, the fact she had suffered from the same malady meant there would be a high risk that the stem cells could carry some cancer cells that would exacerbate Dr. Williams condition and actually do more harm than good.

To Amy's relief, Simon did note, "With early-phase detection and prompt treatment, remission is highly likely in many patients. Once all signs and symptoms of AML have disappeared, a patient is considered to be in remission. If they are in remission for more than five years, they are considered cured of AML."

At first, we all were perplexed until Dr. Hsu asked if Dr. Williams had any siblings. Right away, we thought of Aunt Julia. We agreed, we needed to see if she would be a match. We knew we couldn't break the promise of secrecy, especially to Aunt Julia and time was of the essence. This meant a blood test and lab work which would take too long. I suggested to Amy, we make it a long weekend and go to St. Martin and have Aunt Julia put on the gloves.

St. Martin Redux:

Amy thought it was a great idea, cleared her calendar, made certain the kids would be with the nanny and the next morning Andrew flew us down to Phillipsburg on Amelia II. We made our plans on the way as to what to say to Aunt Julia and Uncle Frank and how to get Aunt Julia to put on the gloves and press the button. We needed to make certain we were in an area with Wifi and the gloves were programmed to transmit, which meant staying at The House-On-The-Hill.

Uncle Frank met us at the plane. "You staying long?" he inquired, somewhat surprised by our spur-of-the-moment visit.

"No, just through Sunday. We needed a break and I miss you guys so much," Amelia responded.

"Your Aunt Julia will want to see you."

"I want to see her. In fact, we'd like to have you come to dinner tomorrow night at the house." Amelia replied.

"We can go out to dinner!" Uncle Frank offered.

"No, we want it to be a quiet evening with just the two of you. We never really did get to thank you for the engagement ring upgrade."

Uncle Frank took the bait and agreed. The next morning, we went to Cost-U-Less and bought food and wine to made certain everything was just the way Amelia wanted it.

"Do you want to walk down on Orient Beach?" I asked.

Amelia had a sad look on her face as she shrugged her shoulders. "It's not the same," she replied.

"I know," I said. "Perhaps walking the beach will do us both some good"

We went down to where Pedro's had been and parked the car. We saw the devoted nudists where Orient Beach Club had been. Their numbers were far fewer and they were sequestered at the east end of what had once been a sprawling property.

Amy had referenced the stone demarcation between the area where she would be judged as wearing too little for going topless and too much for wearing anything at all and it was nothing more than a few boulders almost buried in the sand with green concrete steps butting out like forlorn, jagged teeth into the ocean.

As we walked past the spot where Pedro's had been and the famous "plage naturiste" sign existed, there was simply nothing as if to reflect that the time of innocence was also long gone. All that remained of the famous sign were a few million pixels on photos buried in memories of visitors all over the world.

The beach had been repeatedly buffeted in the 1990's with hurricanes and yet the people were always able to quickly re-build, planting sea grapes and palm trees that sequestered the beach from the hotels behind it. Irma was different! She was massive, mean and above all else, had been a surprise. Not that she was coming, but by her ferocity. I sat shaking my head, looking at the results of the devastation. All that existed was a broad swatch of sand. The water was still crystal clear, but the deafening silence of solitude was broken only by the soft sound of the waves coming ashore.

"This is where daddy's stores were!" Amelia said, as we walked, adding, "This is where we met Rodney and Ann when they were on their honeymoon!" on the now-vacant spot where Le' String once stood. "This is where Kon-Tiki stood and next-door Ka-Kao," Amy said as she shook her head looking at one lone couple nestled beneath an umbrella stuck in the vacant sand.

We walked even further, past a concrete slab. "This is where Bikini Beach stood," Amy reflected as we slowly made our way towards Mont Vernon. There had always been an issue with seaweed on the west end that was removed every morning. With no one walking the beach, the idea of cleaning it up was long forgotten, so that the smooth soft sand was littered with the carcasses of detached and rotting seaweed, piled so deep we couldn't keep walking.

Amy stopped and looked at me with tears in her eyes. "One storm! One giant storm washed away hopes and dreams and memories!" With that she began to sob and I held her tight. All of her pent-up emotions flowed like the torrents of Irma as she convulsed in profound sadness.

We paused to allow Amy to get her emotional bearings and then walked back to the road to where "Good Morning" bakery had been where I would come at sunrise and get croissants. It had re-opened and that gave us both a glimmer of hope. The restaurants in the cul-de-sac had also re-opened and Le Piment was one of them. We saw tables and chairs promised ourselves to come back that night.

It was nearly three when we got back to The House-On-The-Hill and I took a swim while Amy took a nap. I came in and looked at the photos of her when she was sick and realized it could be her mother in a very few months and cringed.

I lay down beside my wife and we held each other and said nothing. Our hearts beat a syncopated rhythm of life, acceptance, love and trust. We lay thinking the same thing and sadly understanding the realization that the dark clouds on the horizon could mean a profound level of sadness was about to make its way into our existence.

I gently kissed Amy on the forehead and whispered, "I love you." Amy nuzzled her chin into my chest and we both fell into a deep sleep awakening as the sun was setting over the hill. There was to be no intimacy, just husband and wife, living life together.

We got up and showered and went back down the hill to Le Piment. What used to be packed every night saw about half the tables occupied. The wounds of the wind were hard to heal!

The owner came over and had a smile of recognition on her face. "Amelia, it is so good to see you!" she said.

"Thank you," Amelia responded, reflecting the same polite, smile.

"Are you here for long?" the owner asked.

"Just until Sunday," came the reply.

"Let me make you a very special meal."

"That would be nice," Amy responded.

With that, the owner was gone. As I peered across the courtyard, my eyes locked on whom I thought I would never see again. I was hoping it wasn't her and yet it was. There stood Sydney and she saw us. She was working as a waitress at Cote Plages, wearing her short shorts under a small black apron.

Sydney went to someone and said something and began coming our way. As she began walking towards us, a smile came across her face, while I sat in trepidation. What would the consequence be? When she was about twenty feet away, I began to notice her features. The years had not been good to her. Too much sun! Too much booze and too many parties had aged her extensively. She had lost weight and was extremely thin. She was still trying to live the dream and yet reality was rudely awakening her.

"Bonjour!" was all she initially said in her French accent.

Amy turned and saw her and withdrew, politely responding "Hi".

"It's been a long time!" Sydney said. "How are you feeling?"

"Fine," Amy responded, shaking her head from left to right in direct contradiction to her thoughts and words.

"That's wonderful news. Is this your husband?"

"Yes!"

Sydney eyed me and realized we'd met before when Amy and I came to pick up Rodney and Ann and responded, "Magnifique! Do you have children?"

"Yes, we have three…twin boys age six and a daughter who's just about to turn five." I replied.

"Oh, how wonderful!" Sydney politely answered.

"Thank you and how about you?" Amy inquired nodding towards Sydney.

"I'm fine thank you." Sydney replied in a polite manner and continued. "After Hurricane Irma, I went back to Paris, but missed my friends and thought I could come back and help people get their lives back together. It has been very difficult" she almost whispered, as she sighed deeply with her head tilted down, to allow her to look forlornly at the ground. After a short pause, she continued, "We were all so innocent back then! We thought the world was ours and yet it belongs to God and he can do whatever he wants."

I was about to ask Sydney to join us when Amy spoke in a very professional tone. "Sydney, I never got to thank you for all your help when I was sick. I have never forgotten how much you meant to me. Without you, I don't think I would have made it."

There was a long pause and then, turning to French, Amy added. "Mon mari ne parle pas français et donc, nous pouvons parler librement. Tu m'as toujours manqué, ainsi que nos moments passés ensemble. Je chéris ces moments et la douceur de tes baisers. Cependant, ma vie a changé et moi aussi, mais je serai toujours reconnaissante pour ton amour."

Sydney shook her head and replied. "Mon corps et mon cœur seront toujours ouverts pour toi. Notre passion était si grande. Notre plaisir si intense. Notre joie d'amoureux n'a jamais été remplacée. Aujourd'hui encore, je rêve de sentir ton corps à côté du mien et le doux contact de tes lèvres pendant que nous faisions l'amour."

"Je comprends et j'accepte ta nouvelle situation. Cependant, je sais aussi que lorsque nous étions ensemble, c'est toi qui m'as ouvert tant de portes... des portes qui ne peuvent pas être fermées... même si tu penses qu'elles le sont."

I had no idea what was said but was pleased with the emphasis on the word "then" as I believe was Amy's way of saying it was completely over.

After a long pause, Sydney responded in English. "It was nothing."

"It was everything!" Amy responded as she stood and hugged Sydney, not in a physical way, but as an expression of gratitude and then quickly backed off. "It was so nice seeing you. I hope all your dreams come true!"

This was a signal to Sydney, it was time for her to go. I slowly rose from my chair and hugged Sydney as well, feeling her shoulder bones and back ribs, while saying, "Thank you for saving Amy's life. She will never forget you and I will always be grateful." With that, there was closure. The final curtain had come down, as Sydney walked into the darkness and, like Orient Beach, was washed away, into yesterday.

Amy and I quietly ate our dinners and headed back to The House-On-The-Hill. Not a word was spoken that night about Sydney or ever again. As we drove back to the house, my mind reflected on that day so long ago, when I offered Amy her freedom and told her that if she needed, I would share her with other women. I remembered saying, *"All I want is for you to be happy and if that means sharing you, I will, or, if you would be happier, give you up."*

Regrets? Certainly! When one offers words that become actions, they can come back to haunt you. Yet I believe, because of our love for each other and the bond we re-established, Amy accepted her role as wife and mother and put those above all else and what was, would stay that way ... buried in the past ... forever adrift upon the sea of memories.

Dinner:

The following day, we spent getting ready for dinner and going into Phillipsburg to see Aunt Julia. As always, Aunt Julia was gracious and gregarious and made us feel welcome. The lines which creased her face had not been there before, as the stress and strain of sadness, had etched themselves deeply into her soul. The staff of friendly folks in her jewelry store were gone. With them, all the really expensive pieces of jewelry had been replaced by costume knock-offs that could be quickly sold. Aunt Julia worked alone, hoping the tourists would stop by and make her day. We didn't stay long, only to say hello and affirm our dinner.

As we walked back to the car, reflections of the palm shaded promenade that once existed, ricocheted off my mind as I stared at the bare sand strewn between the concrete slabs which had violently replaced tranquility. My God, Irma had come from hell and the wounds she made were so deep, the scars would last forever.

Dinner was set for seven and right-on-time, the doorbell rang. Amy had soft music playing and the lights down respectfully low. Candles flickered on the dinner table as Uncle Frank and Aunt Julia marveled at the setting. It had probably been months since they had eaten anywhere but home. Things were just too expensive and they were too proud to take family money.

After casual family chit-chat, Amy brought up that I was heading up the company foundation and my team had a new invention called Medi-glove. I explained what they did and pulled out the samples. I offered them to Aunt Julia and asked her to put them on. I wanted to show her a demonstration. Not knowing the consequences, she abided, as I pushed the activation button on the back and sent signals first to my laptop and then, immediately to Simon. Mission accomplished!

Aunt Julia was amazed that simply wearing a pair of gloves had given her a look at her vitals which, thank God, were all looking good. I outlined how our goal was to help all living beings around the world improve the quality of their lives. Uncle Frank thought it was a noble deed and I saw a soft side of him, I had never seen before.

Dinner was quiet and cordial and by ten, I could see they were both ready to head home. It had been a wonderful evening, albeit devoid of the joy and laughter, which had been prevalent the other times we had been together. It's amazing how twenty-four hours of weather hell can change not only the physical landscape, but the emotional and financial ones, as well.

As soon as they were gone, I called Peter and got the news. I sat dumbfounded and quietly hung up the phone. Looking at Amy I said. "There is no genetic match! Your mother and Aunt Julia are not related."

Amy was incredulous. "How can that be?"

"I don't know. Peter said they double-checked the DNA and it came back that your mother and Aunt Julia are not genetically related."

Amy looked at me with a perplexed stare. "Mom and Aunt Julia aren't sisters?"

I just shook my head, realizing we had reached a dead end, when it came to compatible stem cells. Amy's couldn't be used because of her battle with Leukemia and Aunt Julia and Amy's mom weren't sisters. Amy must have been thinking the same thing as tears came into her eyes and her mouth made an upside-down sadness smile which broke my heart.

As we were clearing the table, the phone rang and it was Peter. He and the MadCity boys had a plan. Peter knew how to break into virtually any secure website and thought if they could get into the databases for all the companies who were selling genetic ancestry information from people who submitted their DNA, they could look for a close match. It was illegal, but they were willing to try.

I was concerned about getting caught, but was assured by the boys that, with Simon as fast as he was, he could be in and out of any database in the matter of seconds, copying all the data and gone before he was detected. The boys added they would develop an artificial tracker in case the invaded system attached itself, that would go to a bogus site in Russia. Peter added that we would not only be able to double check for compatible DNA, but have any close match's name, age and address.

I asked Amy what she thought and she said it was our last hope. I gave Peter permission to proceed, asking how long it would take. He noted breaking in would take longer than harvesting, but felt they could have results in 48 hours, or by the time we got home.

We spent the rest of the weekend simply resting, trying to erase some of the torment and pressure that had been building up. I think it did us both good to be away, even if it meant we did not accomplish our goal. I could see the stress on Amy's face and hoped and prayed it would not lead to a relapse of her "situation" as she called her bout, so long ago.

Andrew called and asked what time we wanted to leave, as he needed to submit a flight plan. Amy wanted to be home in time to put the kids to bed and so we called a cab and left House-On-The Hill at three. The plane ride home was quiet and subdued. Amy brought her laptop and worked. I watched a Brewers game and took a nap. We made it home in time to say goodnight to the kids

As I was tucking Mela in, she looked at me and gave me a big hug. "Daddy, do you know I love you?" What more could any father ask for?

Trouble on the Horizon:

The following morning, I called Peter and asked for an update. He said all the data had been harvested. However, due to the myriad of different races Dr. Williams' DNA contained, they were having a difficult time finding a close match. Damn!

I was going through the past few days e-mails when Ceclia walked into my office with a troubled look on her face.

"What's wrong?" I asked.

"There are two FBI agents here and they have asked to see you."

I swallowed hard and told her to let them in. I'd seen enough actors portray FBI agents in movies not to be surprised, but quickly realized they were just the way they were portrayed … clean cut, suits and no smiles.

"Gentlemen, come in," I offered rising from behind my desk and extending my hand for them to shake, which, of course, they did not. Instead, almost in unison, they showed me their badges.

"What can I do for you?" I asked, as I sat and offered them the chairs across from my desk.

"Are you Mr. George Terrill?"

I nodded in the affirmative.

"Do you head up the Derrick Williams Foundation?"

Again, I nodded in the affirmative.

"Did your foundation recently purchase a quantum computer and several IBM Watson computers?"

Again, I nodded in the affirmative.

"Do you have an employee by the name of Peter Kennison?"

"Yes," I answered.

"Are you aware Mr. Kennison has been using your computer to sweep the entire internet?"

"Yes"

"Are you aware that, in so doing, he has harvested secure and sensitive data?"

"No, I am not. We set up the computer, we call Simon, to scan for medical information and harvest data for medical research.

"Are you aware Mr. Kennison is a convicted felon?"

"Yes! A brilliant man, who made a mistake as a kid, went to prison, where he not only attained his high school diploma, but set up computer and chess classes for other inmates and was paroled after serving three years of a five-year sentence for good behavior."

"Are you aware of what Mr. Kennison was doing when he was arrested?"

"Yes, he was involved in computer programming games which challenged individuals to not only see if they could break into secure databases, but how fast they could get their computer to operate."

"Are you aware Mr. Kennison broke into the database of the National Security Administration?"

"Yes, for which he was convicted and served his time."

"Are you aware Mr. Kennison also broke into several banks and transferred several thousand dollars into his own account?"

"Yes, for which he was convicted and served his time, to which all banks have been reimbursed with interest."

"Are you aware Mr. Kennison is forbidden from working for the US Government, any banking institution and not allowed to gamble, as part of his parole?"

"Yes, that's why he's working for me." I was getting pissed.

"Mr. Terrill, the FBI believes Mr. Kennison has used your computer to break into several business databases in the past 48 hours and in so doing, has broken federal law."

I tried to hide my emotions and lied. "No, I did not."

"Do you know where Mr. Kennison currently is?"

Once again, I sort of lied, rationalizing I didn't know precisely where Peter was and said I didn't know, hoping Cecelia was texting him as we spoke, but afraid we were all under surveillance.

"We won't take up any more of your time, Mr. Terrill, but, the US Government frowns deeply on convicted felons being allowed the opportunity to take sophisticated equipment such as your quantum computer and use it for the purposes you have indicated. We have blocked your satellite dish located in Waldwick, Wisconsin and will scramble any signals which come or go out of that facility until further notice."

Now, my Minnie Point dander was now up. "You mean because we have the financial capability to purchase sophisticated equipment, which is equal to that of the government, and use it for medical research that MIGHT, and I say MIGHT, infringe on some of the data harvesting the NSA does on a daily basis, I cannot have Mr. Kennison work for me?"

"That's correct, sir!"

"Gentlemen, this meeting is now over! Any further communication will need to come through our legal department." I hollered out to Cecelia, "Cecelia, would you please escort these gentlemen out of my office and provide them with a business card for our law firm?"

"That won't be necessary, sir. We already have that address. And, by the way, how was your trip this weekend to St. Martin?"

This was their way of telling me we were under surveillance. It was my way of knowing there was about to be war.

Cecelia walked into my office as they left the building.

I told her, "Use your personal cellphone and get hold of security and have our offices swept right away. Call Raskin and tell him to meet me at Copps at four this afternoon and I'll fill him in. Get Senator Fitzgerald's Washington office on the phone and tell them I need to see the Senator as soon as possible. Better yet, call them and tell them that Amelia One will be waiting for the Senator tomorrow morning at six at Reagan and I need him for the day."

Fifteen minutes later she came back and said Peter was notified and went camping. I smiled. She said Raskin would meet me, but she had trouble with the Senator's office, as they said he was in a meeting and couldn't be disturbed.

I motioned with my hand for Cecelia's cellphone and hit redial for the Senator's office.

"Senator Fitzgerald's office," some young girl on the other end answered.

"This is George Terrill and I need to speak with Tom right away." I barked.

"Sir, Mr. Fitzgerald is in an important meeting and can't be disturbed."

"Once again, this is George Terrill of the Wilco Corporation. My company provides $200,000 per month in campaign contributions to Senator Fitzgerald and I really don't care who he is meeting with or about what, I need to talk to him right now."

"Sir, the Senator is a very busy man!"

"Young lady, I am asking you for the last time, to put the Senator on this line or tomorrow, you WILL be working for someone else. Do you understand?"

Another voice came on the phone. "This is Phil Reznick, Senator Fitzgerald's administrative aide. What seems to be the problem?"

"This is George Terrill of Wilco and I need to speak to Tom Fitzgerald. It's an emergency!

"Mr. Terrill, does the Senator know you?"

"OK, Mr. Reznick, let's do it this way! My name is George Terrill, my wife's name is Amelia and her father is Douglas Williams, who Senator Fitzgerald calls The Duke. If you stick your head in the Senator's office and say The Duke's son-in-law is on the phone and it's an emergency, watch what happens."

"But, Mr. Terrill!"

"I am out of patience! Either get him on the phone NOW or the $200,000 per month in campaign contributions we provide, will be stopped. Do you understand?"

There was a pause and then the phone picked up again. "George, it's Tom Fitzgerald, what's the problem."

"Tomorrow morning at 5:00 AM, there will be a limo outside your house to pick you up and take you to Reagan. You will be flying to Milwaukee and then meeting me at our research facility. Clear your schedule and I will see you in the morning."

"But!"

"Listen Senator, I need to see you tomorrow. I'm tired of all the bullshit from your little office girl and your aide. This is extremely important and this is what The Duke and I need."

"But!"

"One last time. We don't ask for much, but when we do, we expect it to be done. Now clear your schedule and I will see you tomorrow!"

I hung up the phone, leaned back in my chair and looked at Cecelia.

"Well?" I asked.

Cecelia smiled and applauded.

"One last thing, Cecelia!"

"Yes, Mr. Terrill."

"I'll need the Fitzgerald black file on a thumb drive. Have someone from security deliver it to my house tonight. Tell security to send me the operating code, but have the security numbers reversed. You only get one chance to unlock the code and I don't want anyone to see what's in the file except the Senator and me."

Cecelia knew black files were kept on all politicians and included anything and everything we had that could balance things in our favor. The information was kept on a special server, which required two codes to be simultaneously typed in. The material would be downloaded onto a thumb drive and prepared for the meeting. It could include all kinds of materials which could break any person's career, marriage or livelihood. We didn't use the information often, but when we did, it could be quite devastating to the person who witnessed their own indiscretions.

Once done, the thumb drive would have acid poured on it so there was no trace of its contents and no way for anyone to see what we had in our files. The laptop would then be given to the "guest" as a token of our meeting with the Wilco logo etched on the surface.

Was it, dirty pool? You bet it was! Dr. Williams life was at stake and I wasn't going to let the U.S. Government or anybody, stand in my way of doing everything possible to keep her alive.

The Senator:

I was up early the next morning and the chopper was waiting to take me to Waldwick. We were taking the beloved Senator to our ballpark, where we could play by our rules. I would be there and prepared. He was in for a little, no make that, a big surprise.

I arrived at 7:30 and around 8:30, I heard the chopper land. The boys met the Senator at the landing pad and brought him to the compound. He wasn't too pleased that Reznik, his administrative aide, was left behind in Washington, but that wasn't my problem.

From the get-go, I hadn't liked the guy. He always seemed greasy. I hadn't seen him since our wedding and he was all bluster there. I think fifteen years in office had covered him in Teflon and it showed. He was upset he had to walk all the way from the landing pad to the compound and complained about the mosquitos.

After a brief handshake, with no smile on either side, we began.

"This had better be important," the Senator said.

"If it wasn't important, you wouldn't be here," I replied.

"Where in hell, are we?" he asked.

"You're at our research facility in Waldwick, Wisconsin." I answered.

"Research? What type of research?"

"Until yesterday, medical research."

"You put a medical research facility in the middle of farmland?" he said incredulously.

His comments were both insulting and derogatory but I held my tongue, politely replying, "The farmland, upon which you are standing, has been in my family for nearly 200 years. It is adjacent to property co-owned by the Ho-Chunk Nation and me and is sacred grounds for both of us."

"What's so sacred about it?" the Senator inquired, shaking his head.

My God, this jerk was pissing me off, but I kept my composure and replied, "My ancestors saved the life of an Indian girl about fifty yards from here. That Indian girl grew up and had children and one of her descendants is CEO of the Ho-Chunk Nation and my best friend."

The Senator seemed unimpressed as he kept looking at his own reflection in the window.

I continued, "Between that spot and here are the remains of a foundation which once held a single-room school house, where my ancestors were educated."

Again, no positive response. I was quickly learning why I disliked the son-of-a-bitch.

"You brought me all the way here to show me a school house and talk about dead Indians?" The Senator inquired, showing his disdain and contempt for me, my family and what we believed in .

I gritted my teeth and politely answered, "No, I brought you here because we have a problem and **you** need to fix it," I responded in a very direct way, literally pointing my finger up his nose, which was much better than where I really want to shove it

"Well, this better be good. I cleared my entire schedule for you," our beloved Senator replied, exposing an arrogance, I hadn't experienced since me college days.

I looked him in the eye and said in a monotone, "As I noted yesterday, Senator, we give you a lot and only ask for a few small favors in return. However, when we ask, we expect them to be provided."

He didn't like the answer.

Tough shit! I thought. My ballpark, my game and MY rules! He wasn't in Washington D.C. with all his cronies. He was on my turf. However, I realized, I needed to calm down and quickly changed the subject, as we entered the research center. "First, I want to introduce you to our technical team who will take you on a tour of the facility."

The Senator could have cared less, as I introduced Luke and the MadCity boys. He was used to having his ass kissed and these boys were too smart, too talented and way to indifferent to allow any elected official come in and wow them. They knew what the goal was and yet, they also understood that this guy made all the difference in the world between them working and not working on what had become the passion of their life.

Peter was camping somewhere for his and our own protection and it was made clear who was and wasn't present as the boys took the Senator on a fifteen-minute tour and outlined what Simon was programmed to do and how we used the Watsons to take inputted information and decipher it down into comprehensive data for the participating researchers.

Most politicians give you a phony "wow" but even Fitzgerald seemed impressed as he said "Impressive, but where do I fit in?" as he returned to the conference room.

I responded, "Yesterday, I had a visit from two FBI agents. These gentlemen, noted that our key programmer, Peter Kennison had been in jail for using his brilliance as a kid to hack into the NSA database, along with several banks and was a convicted felon. I noted Peter had been found guilty, was sentenced to five years in prison, was a model prisoner who taught computer programming while incarcerated, paid back the stolen money with interest and was paroled in forty-two months."

"So? They got one right for a change," the Senator replied in a condescending manner.

I continued, "It seems someone considers Peter to be a threat to national security and wants to stop him, and subsequently us, from continuing our medical research. To do so, they are jamming our satellite so we can't harvest data from the internet and our researchers can't continue with their work."

"And?"

"We need to have this stopped immediately," I answered.

"I can't go against the NSA!" the Senator replied.

"Sure, you can," I responded. "We placed you on the Appropriations Committee and, without your approval there will be no funding for all their clandestine little tricks, such as this one."

"What do you mean, placed me on the committee?"

"We have several friends in Washington and made certain you were placed where we needed you," I answered, to which he simply shook his head as if to say 'bullshit'.

"What you want, can't happen until we begin budgetary hearings in the Fall," the Senator replied.

"We can't wait until then. We need it done in the next three days," I answered.

"Impossible!" the Senator replied as he arose from his chair. "Take me back to Washington"

"Sit down, Senator!" I coldly instructed.

"Gentlemen," I said looking at the assembled team, "Will you please excuse us and leave the Senator and I alone?" It was time to light the blow torch and put it on the Senator's ass.

I swung my chair around until I was looking directly at the Senator. "Back in the 1890's Mark Twain wrote that America had the best politicians money could buy and some of them were even honest."

The Senator's upper lip curled in anger as I continued, "We put you in office and have helped keep you there so that when we needed small favors like this, they took place. We are not asking for financial favors! We are not asking for anything illegal! All we are asking is for you to use your authority and political leverage to get this done and have it done quickly."

"I'm an elected official who has served the State of Wisconsin for the past fifteen years. I built my following based on my reputation of honesty, integrity and value. I'm not going to sit here and have some young little shit like you, tell me what I'm going to do," the Senator responded.

Needless to say, the gloves came off as I slid back in my chair and stared at the Senator. "Let me begin with what we have done for you!"

"We? We? Where do you get this, we bullshit?" the Senator snarled. "Duke Williams has supported me because he believes in me and what I stand for and the only reason I am here is because you are his son-in-law. Now, don't make me angry, little boy or this whole god damn … facility … our whatever it is, will be permanently shut down."

My anger was reaching the Minnie Point badass mode as I turned on the computer and the screen came to life with a financial chart.

"Senator, **MY** foundation provides $200,000 PER MONTH to your campaign fund. This is **MY** decision and no longer my father-in-law's." With this, a screen appeared with a summary of how much money we had contributed throughout the years.

Next, I pulled up a photo of his Washington residence. "The house you rent in Washington is owned by our company and the $1500 per month rent you are **supposed** to pay, is one-fourth what we can get if we put it on the market. Unfortunately, you are currently nearly one year past due."

"Are you threatening me, Mr. Terrill?" the Senator recoiled.

"No, I'm just reminding you that you are on a monthly lease basis, which can be broken at any time."

Next, I pulled up a photo of his Lexus. "You are leasing this vehicle from our dealership in Silver Spring, Maryland for $100 per month. The general lease agreement for this vehicle is $750 per month. I don't believe you are reporting the differential on your income taxes Senator."

"The accident you had in February, when you were driving drunk, not only saw us have your ticket 'temporarily lost,' but required $7500 in repairs, which we have yet to bill you for."

"This is blackmail!"

I continued, "Politics is a dirty business and you, sir, are a prime example of what I sincerely feel is wrong with our government today. You live in America's version of Versailles, which is just as sick as the palace of the French royals. Fortunately for us, you do so without the rouge and powdered wigs. You have learned to play the game where you don't bear the cost of corruption.

In your fifteen years, you have become very good at playing with the rules, not by the rules. Rules, by the way, you help write, which you know how to bend in your favor. Senator you sincerely believe that you are master of the universe capable of getting anything and everything for yourself, whenever you want it."

Fitzgerald was turning beet red as I added, "Let me continue Senator. In our country, local school boards are thwarted by you … the government, who decides what subjects are to be taught in classes. You are a lawyer and not an educator and yet **YOU** make decisions about curriculum. Sadly, Senator, in some cases, your votes are cast according to the whims of cultural, political or religious beliefs and not what students really need to learn. Sometimes, Senator, you do so to the point where those decisions create a very, very difficult situations for many people to accept and yet, we sit helpless because you've got the law and money on your side!" I was pissed and he knew it!

The Senator's head jerked back in disagreement. "Son, we do what needs to be done for the good of all the people, not some of the people."

"Senator, some of the people, can be all of the people, when they are affected in ways which leave them helpless and suppressed by a system run by special interest groups who have their own rewards above those of *all the people,* you a referring to! These special interest groups fund political campaigns and then get people, who just happen to agree with their point of view, nominated or appointed to decision-making positions, which then affect all the people in a way that favors them."

The Senator poked his tongue into the inside of his cheek. He knew he was in a pissing match and didn't want to get his pants wet and was starting to boil, as I continued, "I might be some little shit, but I've got you figured out. Those gentlemen who took you on the tour are naïve because they are not masters of the universe and that's why you and I are here alone. They work morning, noon and night to make the world a better place so that people like you can enjoy your bounty more than ever before and all I've asked is for you to allow them to continue to do so."

I was on a roll. "Senator, there is a cost to political corruption which has nothing to do with whether **you** get special perks! Political corruption is all about what you have taken **from** the people, which is trust … trust in you, trust in government and trust that tomorrow will be better than today. The corruption is not what you get for yourself, it's what **you** are taking from the people."

The Senator stood.

"Sit down, Senator. I'm not done with you, and you are **NOT** dismissed!"

"How dare you talk to me that way!" the Senator barked.

I continued, indifferent to his objections, "These are decent people whose lives are affected. Peter Kennison, is their project leader who is being harassed by the government and it needs to stop, **NOW!"**

"This is bull shit!" the Senator retorted, shaking his head in disbelief.

"Senator, have you ever read *"The Fourth Turning?"* I asked.

The Senator shrugged his shoulders in indifference, as I continued, "The *Fourth Turning* describes a theorized recurring cycle in American history, where events are associated with recurring generational personas called *archetypes*. These archetypes unleash a new era called a *'turning'* in which a new political climate exists. Successive turnings historically last the length of a generation or about twenty years. The eras are then part of a larger cyclical called a *"saeculum,"* which is the average lifespan of a person and therefore between 80-90 years. What *"The Fourth Turning"* states is that … after every saeculum, a crisis recurs in American history, which is then followed by recovery."

Once again, the Senator shrugged his shoulders as if to indicate he really didn't care, raising my ire even more, as I continued, "During this recovery, institutions and community values are strong, such as right after the Viet Nam War. Ultimately, succeeding generational archetypes attack and weaken institutions in the name of autonomy and individualism. These attacks ultimately create, yet another tumultuous, political environment that ripens conditions for yet another crisis, such as the one we are in right now, Senator."

Fitzgerald sat shaking his head in disbelief and profound disagreement as I added, "Our government continues to grow and evolve and mistreat the people they represent, along with others all over the world and will continue to do so until the people respond, at which time the government … namely people like you, will either react or cease to exist."

The Senator was gritting his teeth and I knew it was time to slow the boil. "Senator, there are many of us who believe we are near that point right now … a point of calamity, where those in power have gone too far and taken too much from those who simply want to live their lives in peace. People, like those men out there, who simply want life without interference, without intervention and without the fear that our government will exceed the rights guaranteed by the Constitution."

I had misjudged the Senator's demeanor as there was a slight snicker from my audience. With that, my jaw tightened and the Senator could sense the anger, frustration and apprehension in my voice as I looked him right in the eyes and continued, "Our society cannot and will not survive the continuing extremism and resentment that persists amongst the governing class. This whole concept of us-versus-them that permeates Washington right now, has resulted in **all** of us believing the worst about each other. This permeation stands as the largest single barrier to solving many of the country's social and economic problems. Sadly, there are solutions right now, that could make this country and the entire world a better place, if and I say if, you and your cohorts would only allow it to happen, by simply making the good of the people more important than sustaining your own political power and prestige."

"This is absurd!" the Senator said in a voice raised to a level just below what I would call a holler! "The people of Wisconsin back me and support me in record numbers."

I continued on. "Sir, the people of Wisconsin aren't just unhappy with you and your fellow elected officials, they're unhappy with the media and how everything today is sensationalized. The common folks, worry about the fractured politics you participate in and how social media and twenty-four-hour cable news have turned serious policy debates about how to make America better, into nothing more than verbal wrestling matches where today, only the most extreme voices drive national discussion and ordinary people feel truly left out. Your politics and that of your peers have created this and it has trickled all the way down to the local level, Senator."

Fitzgerald was pissed, but I didn't care. All my anger and frustration had exploded and this son-of-a-bitch was getting both barrels, as I looked him in the eyes and continued in a monotone, as I shook my head, "I see it every day! I see elected officials, who want nothing more than the betterment of their community, who are fighting with each other, degrading, demonizing and insulting each other, simply because the sincerely believe that today, in America, compromise is a **death threat** to their own political existence."

The Senator sat with a smug look on his face, shaking his head and calculating whether what little I had shown him was cause for concern. I could almost read his mind … *"smart ass punk, who married for money, now thinks he can control me!"*

I continued on, "Our foundation has only one only goal Senator, to improve the quality of life for all living beings. There is no financial reward beyond covering our basic costs. We are not here to get rich or put a burden on others. We are here simply to expand knowledge, which we willingly share with those who share the common goal of the betterment of the world. Unfortunately, because we had the funds needed to begin at the technical top, so to speak, our government is suspect of our intent and yet, our objective is nothing more than to help people."

I could sense my message was falling on deaf ears. Fitzgerald wasn't listening and really didn't care. He was too altruistic to understand the concept and beauty of giving instead of getting. I quickly concluded I needed to force him to work with us and decided it was time to put the hammer down. I paused and pressed the button on the computer and the screen showed the Senator leaving a cheap motel with a woman, who was not his wife.

"Where did you get that?" the Senator screamed.

"We cover our bases, Senator."

I pressed the button again and yet another photograph of the Senator with another young lady appeared and then another and another and another. In all, we had seven different photos of our beloved Senator in all sorts of compromising photos with women as young as eighteen.

"Now, let me tell you what I want done," I nearly whispered.

"First, the jamming stops and this is done by tomorrow. Second, you will get a Presidential pardon for Peter Kennison and it will be signed no later than Monday.

"That's absurd! I can't get that." the Senator retorted.

"You have an appointment with the President's administrative assistant tomorrow morning at ten. She has the paperwork completed and all you need do is ask the President to sign it, which he will."

The Senator reeled back in shock. I'm certain he was wondering what we had on the President.

I continued. "Before going back to Washington, you will stop in Madison and present a news conference outlining what we are doing to help mankind and what a tremendous young man Peter Kennison is. Finally, you will point out that … through using the judicial system properly, Peter educated, not only himself, but those in prison and has dedicated his life to medical research."

"And if I don't?" the Senator asked.

"The media will have a field day with you! We both know the media understands what sells and that's called conflict-and-division. Senator, they would love nothing better than taking yet another elected official like you, down. Your career and your life would be worth about twenty-four hours of coverage before they moved on to the next sound bite, leaving you in shambles."

The Senator was getting even more red as I continued. "Half of what was reported would be incorrect or over-stated, but that doesn't matter, now does it? What matters is there would be story for them to cling to, which would entice viewers to tune in to the 'breaking news'".

Fitzgerald was about to stand when I stared him down again and added, "Senator, we both know anger works better than answers in raising people's interest and we have enough information to make certain you would be the headline story on every newscast in the State and twenty-four-hour cable news for days and days and days."

The Senator was fuming as he knew I had hit him right in the gut. I should have stopped, but I was too pissed and continued. "Phase one, the lease on your house will expire next week and you will be evicted for non-payment of rent, with stories in every major newspaper in Wisconsin."

"Phase two, the missing traffic ticket will magically appear and you will be hauled into court for drunk driving, refusal to take a sobriety test and the body cam video of you verbally accosting the police officer. All of which will be provided to the media."

"Phase three, you will be personally sued by the seventy-year-old woman you ran into for damages, pain and suffering."

"Phase four, you will be called in front of the Ethics Committee, who will not only have the photos I've shown, but some, which are much more graphic, and you can explain those to your wife and kids and more importantly, to the morally correct voters of Wisconsin."

The Senator sat completely deflated. He was at profound risk and knew it, as he asked, "What happens if I can't get this done?"

"Phase one!" I said in a very pointed way, raising one finger into the air. "Phase two!" I continued adding a second finger pointed skyward. "Phase three!" I added, with the third finger raised. "Phase four, Goodbye!" I said, lowering two of the fingers, leaving only my middle finger raised."

The Senator sat as a broken man. It was time to rebuild him. I removed the thumb drive and dropped it into a beaker filled with acid as we watched it smolder. As the evaporations dissipated, I booted up the laptop with a highly-complimentary photo with the Senator's face on it and handed it to him and looked deeply into his dark eyes and said, "What has been said and what has been shown is only between you and me. What happens from now on is totally up to you."

The Senator closed the cover to the laptop and saw the Wilco emblem on it, as I continued, "Senator, we want you to remain in office and will continue to provide support. However, if you ever double-cross me or impinge my authority again, your career will abruptly end."

I stood to indicate the meeting was over and pressed a button, which opened the doors. I invited the Senator to take a walk with me to the forest where I showed him where George the First had saved Rodney's so-many-great Grandmother's life. We walked to the obelisk, where I explained the crossed feathers and my love and respect for Great Grandfather.

I mentioned the crossing of the three Ley lines. Sadly, there was no response at all. For some, the effects of their convergence are profound. For others, the positive energy has no effect. I had learned the human heart emits an electromagnetic field which changes according to emotions. This could explain why the radiation from the Ley Lines and those from one's heart affect some and not others. I simply did not know. I tried to give the Senator the benefit of the doubt. Perhaps it was the anger! Perhaps the frustration! Perhaps the Teflon he had acquired from so many years in Washington, shielded his ability to care.

We continued to the springs where I took the two tin cups and filled them with water, handing one to the Senator in the form of a toast. "To our mutual trust, mutual respect and mutual success."

The Senator knew I held all the cards and this was the easiest way out, but then, that's what politicians always do … take the easy way out. All I could do was make certain he followed through.

We stopped for a moment and the Senator said, "Son, you're one tough son-of-a-bitch. Don't ever go into politics."

I looked him straight in the eyes and replied, "I would never make it in your world. I can't stand the battles you fight, always, us-versus-them! Instead of common good, politics is where people try to see who can get the advantage and leverage needed to sustain themselves and provide that next fix … that narcotic, called power and prestige you folks crave. I don't need it! Never have! Never will! However, I've been blessed with the resources needed so we can have people like you to rely on. It's a trade-off Senator, from which we both can benefit."

I believe he finally understood, as we walked back through the forest and the tensions lifted. By the time we were in front of the facility, all was calm and there were smiles on everyone's faces. Photographs were taken in front of Simon, with the Senator wearing the infamous Medi-gloves.

"Here's your news release. At the press conference, all you need do is explain your trip and how excited you were to see first-hand, the future of medical research and how wonderful it was that this project is located in Waldwick, Wisconsin."

The Senator was informed that our PR team would be with him. The team had media kits already prepared regarding what he had seen, along with photographs of him with the Medi-gloves on and his speech, including how he worked so diligently with Wilco in creating, developing and supporting our endeavor.

"What about the media?" he inquired.

"Trust me, they'll be there. Your press conference has already been announced and our advertising division has contacted the primary media member's and reminded their account executives, we are spending millions of dollars with each of them in advertising."

"What would have happened if I said no?"

"There still would have been a press conference." He got my drift.

We walked to the waiting chopper and, as the Senator was about to board, I presented copies of Waldwick and Hocak, explaining they were gifts from Rodney Whitehorse, who couldn't be with us due to a prior commitment and me.

The Senator looked me in the eye and announced to the entire group, "You have my total support. I will do everything in my power to assist you in every possible way". I simply nodded and smiled. The Duke had trained me well.

At 2:00 PM, the Senator provided exactly what was written and did so on the steps of the Capitol in Madison, facing State Street.

At 4:00 PM, Mark called and said the communication system was up and running. The following Monday, a Presidential pardon was signed and Peter Kennison returned from a camping trip with Cindy, to learn his criminal record had been expunged and was no longer limited in his endeavors.

That afternoon, the phone rang. It was The Duke, "Heard you really hammered him!"

"I hope I wasn't too strong." I replied.

"Might have been a little rough on the guy, but I'll take care of it," The Duke responded.

"Sorry" I replied.

"Nothing to be sorry about. However, always remember, he doesn't work for us and will only be loyal as long as he thinks he needs us. The day he believes we can't provide something he needs, whether it's power or money or the political connections he doesn't have that we do, you will have an enemy and will need to watch your back."

"Thanks, dad, for the advice."

"By the way, he left both books you gave him on the floor of the helicopter," The Duke interjected.

There was a lesson learned.

That night, Mrs. Terrill and I went out to dinner and simply smiled, knowing we had knocked down one the barricades and were a step closer to helping Dr. Williams survive. Behind my smile was the profound sense of fear I had stepped across the line, been too powerful and created an enemy from someone who should have been an ally. The lesson learned was, don't over-react and work on changes gradually. Perhaps I was so used to controlling everything that, when I move to the next level, I need to understand that power comes in many forms and needs to be balanced against the level of power of the other person.

The folks at the genetic testing companies never caught on that we had the names and addresses of every person who ever sent in a saliva test and Simon was searching for a match. The next day, our hopes were dashed again as the genetic results came back indicating there was only one person with a close link and she had lived in Guatemala but had abruptly departed. We all knew what that meant. Our only genetic hope, walked across Mexico and either slid into the U.S. illegally or was buried along the way. Whatever the reason, she was gone and we knew there would be no way to ever find her.

While we had won the battle, I felt we were losing the war. The agents who came to see me were pissed because we got Peter off. The Senator was pissed because I threatened him and, for all intents-and-purposes, blackmailed him. The government was pissed and a long way from having the entire issue resolved regarding Simon. I just didn't know to what extreme the NSA would go to stop us and this really concerned me. Farm boys from Wisconsin aren't used to being considered threats to national security.

The Senator was right. "Don't ever go into politics George Terrill IV!"

The Battle:

Amy's mom shared with us that she had investigated chemotherapy, radiation and other existing treatments and none of them had been deemed appropriate based on her prognosis. She agreed to begin putting the Medi-gloves on every day so Simon could read her vitals. Simon reported that, in the week since her last Medi-glove evaluation, Dr. Williams cancer was worse and quickly progressing. Action was needed as soon as possible. While different than Amy's leukemia, Simon noted that implementing the same Car-T Cell Therapy Amy had in her treatment was one option, albeit with only a very slim chance of working.

Dr. Hsu reported there were about 2,500 cases of ALL in the U.S. each year of which 600 children didn't respond to standard treatments. As had been the case with Amy, we looked for experimental treatments and learned of a drug that took a patient's white blood cells and genetically modified them in the lab, which were then infused back into the patient.

Dr. Patel told us the procedure was quite simple. Blood was drawn from the patient and laboratory technicians inserted a form of the desired T-cell receptor-encoding gene sequence, called a 'vector' into the patient's own T-cells, via an inactive virus. Dr. Patel explained inserting the vector caused the T-cells to express what were called "express receptors" on their surfaces. This enabled them to find and fight the antigen associated with the patient's cancer. The modified cells would then multiply into the hundreds of millions, which would then be put back into the patient's blood stream.

Once they were injected, they would seek out the cancer cells and kill them by piercing their membrane and putting a chemical called granulysin in the cancer cell's center. The entire process was similar to what Amy had been through, except her modified blood cells were frozen and stored in case they were ever needed. We had hope!

The drug company said the entire process, from harvesting to re-insertion, took 22 days. We called and asked if the process could be expedited and they noted it could not, because the T-cells needed to multiply and the incubation took that long. We realized that even if we could get approval from the FDA due to the political power and virtually unlimited resources we had, we couldn't speed up the process and yet we had to try.

The Duke called someone, somewhere and applied a little pressure and the FDA re-classified drug with "breakthrough therapy" status. We had to be careful as any political pressure could backfire and so, the whole political aspect was done through one of our investment companies.

The new status provided some positive news, which we all needed. With that glimmer of hope we applied for approval to begin treatment, which was denied. The FDA responded with a form letter indicating the test had only approved the drug for patients up to age twenty-five and not a 62-year-old woman. We challenged the ruling and received another form letter stating it was common for immediate complications to arise following the T-cell infusions, which might result in a range of symptoms from fever and nausea to liver failure and cardiac arrest.

We responded that Dr. Williams was willing to sign a waiver releasing any and all parties from liability and her life was in danger. The FDA took its time, responding with a third form letter indicating, even though the drug had been fast-tracked, not enough testing had been done on adults to allow the process to begin.

Dr. Hsu and Patel responded back to the FDA, asking for permission to use Dr. Williams as a test patient. We contacted people we knew at UW Hospital and they concurred and wanted to test the procedure on Dr. Williams, as well.

Two weeks later, the FDA responded with a personal letter indicating the request would need to go through a variance committee, which wouldn't meet for three weeks. We requested that the process be accelerated, but were told it wouldn't be fair to others asking for a variance. We had a person's life at stake and they were worried about protocol.

It had been six weeks of dealing with the FDA and we were watching Amy's mom simply deteriorate. She lost a great deal of weight and had the pallor that only comes when death is at the door. Dr. Williams stopped working and The Duke set up a hospital bed at home, with twenty-four-hour nursing care. The dark circles under his eyes, told me he wasn't sleeping and I was concerned about both of them.

Even though it had only been a few days, we went to visit Dr. Williams. The Duke and I walked out on the patio and looked at Lake Michigan. "I've called everyone I know," The Duke said. "All my favors! All my support! All my efforts for all these years and all I ask in return is that Marie be given the opportunity to take a chance to see if the procedure will work. They say there are no alternatives to the drug and the company cannot bend their rules for fear of having the FDA fine or penalize them."

I looked at him and put my hand on his shoulder. "What can I do to help?" I asked.

"Son, you've done everything you can."

"Sir, Simon is reporting things aren't looking very good!" I said, not wanting to be the bearer of bad news, but simply stating the obvious.

"I know son! I know!"

"Would you mind if Peter and the MadCity boys try one last thing?"

"What's that?" the Duke asked.

"Breaking into the FDA computer and changing the test parameters?" I replied. "We're getting nowhere and the responses we are getting are virtually form letters. If we change the parameters, we might get approval."

"What happens if you get caught?"

"We will probably need the entire Wilco legal team to defend us. In addition, I also have to make certain Peter isn't directly involved by giving him an alibi. The last thing we, or Peter, need is to have problems after just getting his pardon" I responded.

The Duke shook his head and shrugged his shoulders and said, "Why not?"

I called Peter and told him to gather the MadCity boys at Paisan's in Madison where we could talk and make certain no one was listening. I certainly didn't believe what we were saying or doing wasn't being carefully watched by someone in the government.

Amy and I took Dr. Williams' car and had security scan it to make certain it didn't have a tracking device on it or our conversations weren't being recorded. I dropped Amy off at home, kissing her goodbye and telling her I loved her.

It took just over an hour to get to Paisan's. The time provided the opportunity to finalize my plan. I entered the restaurant and got a table in the fireplace room. It was nearly 7:30 and the dinner crowd had already departed and our group was alone. I explained to the boys what I thought we needed to do and outlined my concern for Peter.

Peter responded that Dr. Williams was worth the risk. I told him that he could direct, but could not be directly involved, in the project. All the blame was to fall on one set of shoulders ... mine!

The MadCity boys were reluctant and yet they understood. I proposed having Peter and Cindy go to China on vacation, which would require a Visa to prove they were there. Because they were visiting, when all that was about to transpire, they couldn't be blamed, especially when there was no communication back to the States from either of them.

It was agreed, Peter and Mark would create the protocol and teach me how to use it. I would go to Waldwick and program Simon to break into the FDA network, change the code and have the test parameters modified.

The boys said it would take two days to set everything up. During that time, we got Peter and Cindy China visas and made flight arrangements on United flight #661 to Shanghai. This would prove they were out of the country.

Simon was reporting Dr. Williams' vitals were abnormal, but stable, giving us hope. The MadCity boys wanted to come with me to Waldwick. I told them no. Instead, we made certain that the night I was at the facility, they were out partying with friends who could testify they were together all-night long.

The day came and I went to the Hartland dealership and picked up one of our loaner cars and began driving to Waldwick. At exactly, 6:05 PM, Cecelia went to our house and delivered my cellphone, which Amy plugged in to be charged. As for me, I was alone and went directly to the facility. Even Tommie and Dr. Hsu didn't know I was coming, as I opened the office and went to the control panel for Simon.

"Come on buddy, let's work a little magic," I whispered to Simon punching in the code, which was hand written on a sheet of paper. In an instant, I was at the FDA's website instructing Simon to look for a way to breach their security, which took longer than it did for Simon to break in. I went to where all the test protocols were stored and found the Car-T file and changed the maximum age from twenty-five to seventy-five with one keystroke. Bango, it was over. Simon was instructed to cover his trail by dropping gibberish on his tracks and we backed out of the system, while Simon went into the sleep mode. The entire process had taken less than three minutes.

"Good boy, Simon!" I whispered. I took the hand-written instructions to the shredder and then took the confetti and burned it, mixing it with the Earth.

There was no trail electronically or physically, which could be followed. With that, I locked up and headed for home using a disposable phone to call Amy and giving her the code … "mission accomplished", which consisted of three rings, followed by me hanging up and then three more rings. No call! No trace! Just in case! With all the robo-calls who follow the three-ring procedure, anyone scanning our home phone would assume it was simply yet another invasive, intrusion into one's privacy.

Visitors:

The next morning, I was in the office when the two FBI agents came again.

"Mr. Terrill, where were you last night?"

"Home with my wife, why?"

"We'll ask the questions, if you don't mind."

"Do you know the whereabouts of Peter Kennison?"

"Yes, he's on vacation in China with his girlfriend."

"Can you document where in China?"

"Not really! He is an employee on vacation, does your boss document where you go on vacation?"

"Mr. Terrill, do you know who operated the computer you call Simon last night?"

"No, I don't, but then Simon is programmed to automatically do his work on a regular basis. But then you already know that don't you, because you're tracking everything we do."

"Do you know the whereabouts of your computer programmers last night?"

"Yes, I do. They had a birthday party for Mark in Madison. One of them called this morning and said they were at the Pub on State Street until it closed and were all hung over."

"Can you verify that?"

"Sir, I can't verify it because I was home with my wife. However, knowing the boys, I'm certain they ran up a huge bar bill and, wait a minute, let me check my text, as they said they would send me pictures."

I turned on my phone and went to the text and there were the boys in a group photo with a Miller High Life sign with a clock showing 9:30 pm on it.

"Here are the boys last night at the Pub on State Street in Madison," I responded. "What's this all about?"

You know what it's about, Mr. Terrill. Someone programmed your computer to break into the FDA website. Fortunately, they didn't get past the security system."

This had me worried, but I knew better than to show any facial expressions, and responded, "And so there really wasn't any crime committed, correct?"

The agents didn't like my answer and so I continued. "I walk up to my local bank and pull on the front door and it is locked. Did I try and break in? Did I do anything illegal?"

Agent McConley responded, "That's a different situation."

I continued. "If someone attempted something and failed, you're saying it's a crime?"

McConley continued, "If that person, or persons, attempted to exfiltrate data, then yes, it is."

"And you think I had something to do with this?"

"We wouldn't be here if we didn't."

I shook my head in disbelief and replied, "One of the true conundrums of our era is the advancements of our government that are not only making it more powerful, but more vulnerable. Our researchers are all about doing good and not about creating malware or spyware. In fact, we are probably more innocent than any other group of people you have come in contact with, including your own agency."

This did not go well, as I continued. "We're trying to help the world, not rule it, destroy it or profit from it!" I added, "I know you are still upset because Peter Kennison was given a Presidential pardon and you didn't get your "kill". I know you believe that we used our political clout to accomplish this. I understand you consider us to be suspects and, yet, Peter is in China, the programmers were in Madison and I was at home all night with my wife." I could tell they didn't believe the last part.

I called out, "Cecelia, can you please contact WilServ and ask for video footage from our grounds last night? Gentlemen would you like some coffee or tea as this might take a few minutes?"

Neither man moved until Ceclia came in and nodded. I turned on the monitor and it showed our front gate with a time stamp beginning at 5:30 PM the previous day showing Amelia arriving home. Five minutes later, our nanny was seen leaving. At 6:02 PM, I'm seen driving in the driveway and stopping to get the mail. We then fast forwarded it with no changes, except the time stamp showing 7:05 this morning, when I'm seen picking up the newspaper and carrying it back in the house.

"Gentlemen, as you can see, I arrived home at 6:02 last night and didn't leave until this morning."

"Why did your cellphone go dead at 6:15 last night?" McConley asked.

"Because the battery went dead and needed charging," I replied.

"Who else has access to your facility in Waldwick?"

"No one!" I answered.

"Is the facility under video surveillance?"

"Yes."

"Locked into the same system?"

"Yes."

"Can we see last night's video?"

"Certainly."

Cecelia called and we watched in the fast-forward mode, with the time stamp beginning at 6:00 pm, until this morning, with nothing showing except a raccoon nosing around the front door.

"Perhaps, he's your culprit." I said sarcastically.

Both agents slid back in their chairs, took deep breaths and realized everyone had an alibi. Little did they realize we had moved the time clock ahead one day on the security system at both the house and Waldwick. The raccoon was a surprise.

"Thank you for your time, Mr. Terrill."

As the agents got up to leave I wanted to ask one question, but thought I'd better not … "What would you do to save the life of someone you love?" Instead, I simply said, "Thank you for stopping by."

When they were gone, there was a collective sigh of relief by both Cecelia and me.

The Last Hope:

We re-submitted our request to the FDA, who took three days to respond. This time, the form letter they issued indicated their approval. We called the drug company representative and indicated we had certification. He didn't believe us and said he would need to double check with the FDA. We asked how long it would take and he asked for a day. Time was precious, as Simon was reporting Dr. Williams' vitals were diminishing.

The next day the pharmaceutical representative called and indicated the test had been approved, but needed proof of payment of $475,000. I told him to come by the office and a certified check would be ready. I think he was shocked!

Because Dr. Williams was at home, we arranged for the entire harvesting procedure to take place at the Williams' residence. It took four hours and the drawn blood was flash frozen. Dennis had a plane ready and it was rushed to the test facility. All we could do was wait and hope Dr. Williams could hang on long enough to have the re-worked blood put back into her system.

We counted the days and prayed. At 6:30 AM on the nineteenth day, The Duke called and said Dr. Williams was feeling a little better and asked if she could visit Simon. I was shocked by the request, but happy at the same time.

I called Andrew and asked if the chopper could land on the Williams' front lawn. He thought it could. I explained what was going on and fifteen minutes later, a flight plan was submitted to the FAA ... Milwaukee-to-Waldwick, Wisconsin. I called Tommie and told him what was going on, as Amelia and I drove to the Williams' house. No need for two stops. The trip was going to be difficult enough as it was.

When we got to the house, there were two nurses, The Duke and Dr. Williams. Adding Amelia and I, along with the nurses, meant we had too many people for the chopper. Dr. Williams told the nurses to take the morning off; she would be fine. I was concerned, but didn't let it show.

We boarded the chopper and put the doctor's wheelchair in the back. The forty-minute flight was without incident and when we landed, Tommie and Hsu were there waiting with one of the Suburbans. The Mad City boys had all driven down and were at the compound, as we assisted Dr. Williams into the facility.

The boys took her on the official tour and watched the doctor's weak smile as she realized they were on the cusp of making a medical breakthrough that could change the world. I watched as Amy looked at her mother with the realization her time was near.

Doctor Williams spoke. "Did you ever put that path into the forest?"

"Yes" I replied.

"Can we go there?" Doctor Williams asked.

"Are you up to it?" The Duke inquired.

"Doug. I want to go. It's really important to me." She replied.

We all looked at each other and nodded. Amy slowly pushed her mother's wheelchair down the cinder path with the only sound that of the crunching the small crushed stones.

I watched as the doctor breathed the pure country air, deep into her lungs as yet another smile came across her face.

"I love it here," She whispered. "It is so peaceful. Don't ever let anyone take it away."

We made it to Great Grandfather's memorial and Amy stopped as Dr. Williams raised her hand.

"I feel his spirit," Dr. Williams mentioned, as her eyes peered at the twin feathers on the brass plate.

"Should we turn back?" The Duke asked.

"Oh, heavens no!" the doctor responded. "Can we continue to the springs where George and Amy were married?"

The path had been laid, but was a little rougher and so Amy pushed a little slower.

"Doug, I think you need to get new shock absorbers on this wheelchair!" the doctor joked.

As we came to the springs, Dr. Williams bowed her head for a moment and then looked to the sky while a broad smile spread across her face.

"Would you like some water?" I asked.

"That would be nice," She replied.

I got one of the small tin cups and filled it with the fresh spring water and handed it to Amy who helped her mother slowly drink it.

"I'm ready to go home now," Dr. Williams commented with a soft smile parting her lips. To this day, we do not know if she meant back to Milwaukee or not.

At three-thirty the next morning, Simon notified us he was no longer getting a reading from the Medi-gloves. We hoped someone had taken them off or the batteries were dead. Instead neither was the case.

Amy and I got dressed and went to the Williams' house. Dennis was already there, as the van was outside. We walked in and I looked in the living room. While the bed and all the medical equipment was still there, Dr. Williams was gone. Dad Williams told me later, she wanted it that way.

I took a deep breath and held Amy's hand as we walked into the kitchen. The Duke was sitting at the kitchen table with a cup of coffee before him. Dennis stood behind him as if to protect him from further pain. One of the most powerful men in Wisconsin had turned old before our eyes. The power was gone! The dynamic personality withered like a fallen leaf! Instead, a little old man with stooped shoulders sat staring at a cold cup of coffee unable to speak, unable to move and unable to do anything but stare.

Amy walked to her dad and sat down next to him, holding his hands. Not a word was said. He looked at her through blurry eyes, as tears rolled down his cheeks. His best friend! His confidant! The love of his life had departed and his only wish was to be with her.

I looked at the two of them and then looked away with tears streaming down my face. Death is so final and yet there was a profound sense of peace. Dr. Williams' battle was over. All the pain! All the suffering! All the frustrations were erased and replaced by a complete level of silence enveloped in a sea of tranquility.

I stood and watched as the first vestiges of a brilliant sunrise splashed across the calm Lake Michigan waters. For many, it was just another day. For us, it would be a day etched in our hearts forever. Dr. Williams had left a note. Amy read it and set it on the table. I picked it up and read it to myself. It was dated two weeks before this day.

Dear All:

My doctors tell me their best estimate is that I have only a few weeks to live. This is the final verdict. My fight is over. I wish to thank my doctors and caregivers whose efforts have been magnificent. My family and dear friends, who have given me a lifetime of memories and whose support has sustained me through these difficult months.

I also wish to thank my colleagues and especially my husband and daughter, Amelia, and son-in-law, George, who made my career possible and have given consequence to my life. I sincerely believe in the pursuit of a better world for all, where the right ideas allow for progress towards a better tomorrow. I am grateful to have played a small part in assisting the efforts of so many others and pray I have helped guide the world of medicine to greater heights, that rewarded me by providing my extraordinary destiny.

I leave this life with no regrets. It was a wonderful life — full and complete with the great loves and great endeavors, which made it worth living. I am sad to leave, but leave with the knowledge, I lived the life I intended.

Dr. Marie Williams

Alone:

At 8:00 AM, Dennis, The Duke and Amy went to the funeral home as I stayed at the house. Amy needed to say goodbye. I sat in the now-silent mansion, where dreams of tomorrow once flourished and wondered what it was like to die. Did we really go to heaven or was that just a fairytale? Death was now so definite, so absolute, so profoundly permanent, taking away what is, so that all that's left is yesterday.

I walked out on the patio and peered at Lake Michigan and wondered what my last thoughts would be when it was my turn. Looking up at the morning sky, I closed my eyes and felt a single tear silently meander its way down, across my cheek. I bowed my head in reverence to Dr. Williams, simply praying that, when my time did come, my final thoughts would be of the family I loved more than life itself.

I had to be the strong one. This was my duty. I caught myself and took a deep breath, escaping the grasp of being immersed in the cauldron of remorse.

I punched in the numbers I knew so well, calling Wilco to report the news. They already knew! I requested someone from capital goods come immediately and remove all the medical equipment. I wanted it out of the house before Amy and her dad returned.

Four employees were there in fifteen minutes. Quietly, they went about removing what had been, speaking no louder than a whisper, only nodding to say goodbye. I, in turn, nodded back, in appreciation, unable to speak, as they departed.

The living room was back the way it had always been in less than an hour, as if nothing had ever transpired. Time stood still, while the flickering embers of the battle between life and death, vanished before my eyes. Death had won again, as it always had and will always be. Without death, life would have no meaning.

I returned to the patio, where I stood and watched the world go by. Cars moving, boats sailing, planes flying, realizing that no matter who we are or what we do, we all leave footprints in the sand marking those with whom we have come in contact. I finally understood those footprints aren't created by big houses or fancy cars, expensive clothes or fabulous vacations, but by the people whose lives we touch.

Like those who walked upon the moon, I also realized all of us leave some evidence of our presence. For some the steps will be small and shallow. For others, like Dr. Williams, those steps will be giant leaps, which will leave indelible marks on all mankind. With tears in my heart, I finally, truly accepted what Great Grandfather had instructed … the footprints I would leave, would depend upon what I chose to do with my life.

I now accept there is no one noble profession. What is noble is not our title, but our passion for life, for living and for each other. Through my wife, I learned it is only the true goodness of heart that differentiates us from the masses! It is only the smile upon our face and those we touch that will be etched in the minds of those we leave behind and this made me happy in a time of great sadness.

Regardless of my own footprints … whether they will be great or small … I can only hope that I touch another life and make it better. If I have succeeded, then I too will bask in the warmth of being truly wanted, needed and loved. Feelings and emotions that only come if I have acquired those four critical characteristics that the Medicine Man spoke of … humility, generosity, compassion and forgiveness.

If I succeed, when it is my turn to join Dr. Williams, I will be granted one last, profound wish … that when I am gone … I, too, will be fondly remembered and truly missed, because that's what life is REALLY all about!

I Love You:

Doctor Marie Williams was called home that day. She died with dignity, with the man she loved at her side. Dr. Williams asked that she be cremated and her ashes spread upon the waters surrounding St. Martin. To grant her wish, The Duke, Amy and I went "home' on Amelia X. The Duke put Dr. Williams' urn in her favorite seat, on her favorite plane, for her last ride.

We landed at Princess Juliana Airport and met Uncle Frank and Aunt Julia. Uncle Frank had one of our boats moored near the airport and we went out into the ocean to say goodbye. Slowly, we made our way past Marigot and St. Louis and then past Happy Bay. As we rounded the point, Uncle Frank cut the engines and dropped anchor. To the south was a small inlet called Baie Maria.

Speaking to everyone and also to no one, Aunt Julia pointed towards the shore said, "This is what your mother was named after, Baie Maria or Marie Bay and was her favorite spot. We grew up in Grand Case and our momma would walk us down here to swim in the ocean and watch the sun go down. We had no money and so this was our form of entertainment and tranquility."

"You probably don't know this, but your mother and I really weren't sisters. My mother and father died when I was a baby and your grandmother raised me as if I was her own. Your mother always considered me to be her sister and she will always be mine. She was kind and gracious and, above all else, generous, not only of money, but her love for life and for you, Amelia, and I know this is where she wants her soul to be."

With that, Uncle Frank opened the urn and we each took a small scoop of what had been one of the finest women we had ever known and poured the ashes into the ocean as I quietly began whispering, "The Lord is my shepherd; I shall not want".

The Duke, who had remained quiet the entire trip, and had never once led me to believe he was religious, quietly whispered as we listened.

"He maketh me to lie down in green pastures: he leadeth me beside the still waters.

He restoreth my soul: he leadeth me in the paths of righteousness for his name's sake.

Yea, though I walk through the valley of the shadow of death, I will fear no evil: for thou art with me; thy rod and thy staff they comfort me.

Thou preparest a table before me in the presence of mine enemies: thou anointest my head with oil; my cup runneth over.

Surely goodness and mercy shall follow me all the days of my life: and I will dwell in the house of the Lord forever."

I looked at Amy and she at me as we closed our eyes and I whispered, "Ashes-to-Ashes, dust-to-dust, may you rest in peace and peace be with you."

As quickly as we started, we were done. Uncle Frank started the boat's engines and asked The Duke if he wanted to go to The House-On-The-Hill. The Duke politely said "No". All he wanted to do was go home. We were in St. Martin less than three hours. It was a gut-wrenching time to say the least.

As we flew over the gulf, the plane was saturated in silence. The only sound was that of the wind against the wings, blowing away the pain, invading our sadness. After we landed in Houston for customs and were airborne again, the solitude was broken and it came from The Duke.

Looking not at us, but at the half-empty urn sitting on the seat across from him he said, "We spent our entire life building, building, building, creating something from nothing and yet, the time together these past few weeks has been the most valuable and I wouldn't trade it for all the rest of time."

The Duke looked at me and said, "Money is only a way of keeping score and I would have given every single dime I have for one more day, one more hour or one more moment with my Marie."

Turning to Amy, The Duke continued, "Your mother knew she was going to be with Derrick and there was peace in her heart, accepting what we all must accept. When she was up to it, we talked about anything and everything and how wonderful our lives had been together and most of all, our love for each other and for our children. We reflected on all we had done and all we wanted to do, but never got around to doing. We talked about happiness and sadness and she mentioned the birth of you and your brother as the happiest days of her life and the loss of Derrick as her saddest."

The Duke looked at me and continued. "I thought I really knew my wife of thirty-three years and yet, it was those final days when I really got to know her, understand her and realize just what an incredible person she really was. As a doctor, her passion was for life and living, who fought to save children. Her deepest regret was when one of her patients passed away and never had a chance at life."

The Duke turned to Amy and continued. "Your mother and I talked about living and dying and accepted the fact that these are the two things we all have in common ... rich and poor, black and white, meek and powerful, and there is **nothing we can do** except, accept death and make certain those we leave behind are filled with the love we had for them."

The Duke stared towards the front of the plane and continued, "My greatest regret is that I was too busy for too many years and things which should have come first, came last. As your mother and I were sharing our memories, she asked me to open her Bible and read it to her. It had been her mother's and she cherished it above all else. In it weren't only the scriptures she had heard and felt, but memories of her childhood, as her mother would read to her and Aunt Julia every night."

The Duke looked at both of us and added, "Marie asked me to read Revelation to you when it was all over," opening the old Bible with the red cloth marker, I had seen on the table at the House-On-The-Hill.

With a now-sturdy voice, as if preaching to the choir, The Duke began.

"I saw a new heaven and a new Earth, for the first heaven and the first Earth had passed away, and there was no longer any sea. I saw the Holy City, the new Jerusalem, coming down out of heaven from God, prepared as a bride, beautifully dressed for her husband."

"I heard a loud voice from the throne saying, "Look! God's dwelling place is now among the people and he will dwell with them. They will be his people and God himself will be with them and be their God. He will wipe every tear from their eyes. There will be no more death or mourning or crying or pain for the old order of things has passed away. He who was seated on the throne said, "I am making everything new!" Then God said, "Write this down, for these words are trustworthy and true and said to me: "It is done. I am the Alpha and the Omega, the Beginning and the End. To the thirsty I will give water without cost from the spring of the water of life. Those who are victorious will inherit all this, and I will be their God and they … will … be … my … children."

The Duke looked at Amy, put the book on his lap and continued. "When I finished reading this to her, your mother looked at me and gently squeezed my hand, mouthing the words, too weak to whisper… "I love you!" … and then she was gone."

Amy's eyes filled with tears as we sat in somber silence, oblivious to the fact Amelia X had landed in Milwaukee.

The Duke took the urn home and placed it on a table in the living room next to Dr. Williams' picture and her favorite red vase from our wedding.

Dr. Williams departed on a Wednesday and every Wednesday from then on, The Duke drove to the florist alone and bought one white rose, which he brought home, put in the vase, and whispered *"I love you, too."*

Postscript:

There was nothing we could do to save Amy's mother. However, we began using our political connections to make certain it wouldn't happen to others by working with the Goldwater Institute in passing the "Right-to-Try" legislation that followed legislation already in place in thirty-eight states. Right-to-Try, affords terminally ill patients the right to use experimental medications, which have not yet been approved by the Food and Drug Administration and give them one last chance.

Pharmaceuticals in the United States are regulated by the FDA. When a drug company develops a new compound intended for patient use, the medication goes through three phases of clinical trials that often take years to complete. The first phase requires a company to prove the drug is relatively safe for humans. Phase one trials are often conducted on as few as 30 patients. In later phases, the clinical trials then test to see whether the drug is effective at treating the condition for which it is intended without side effects. It is at this stage that the vast majority of drugs fail to pass approval, because many drugs turn out to be ineffective or cause severe side effects. Right-to-Try legislation authorizes doctors to administer drugs that have cleared the first phase, but have not completed the later human clinical trials. By doing so, the legislation gives terminally ill patients the right to use potentially lifesaving medications without the rigorous testing and years of waiting for the drugs to become commercially available.

Unfortunately, Right-to-Try legislation grants no rights. It merely grants permission for a patient to attempt to acquire experimental medication from a pharmaceutical company. Sadly, nothing in the legislation makes it mandatory for pharmaceutical companies to provide these medications.

Even though Right-to-Try simplifies federal regulation, patients must still convince the pharmaceutical industry to provide drugs outside of trials and patients must still bear the costs for these experimental treatments, which remain out of reach for almost all Americans. We must all hope and pray that someday, we can do what we need to do to improve the quality of life for everyone and not just a few.

As our world continues on a frenetic pace towards what could be our own oblivion, we must all examine both the quantitative and qualitative aspects of our own existence. We too will join those who came before us. We too will have those who fought for us. We too will be grieved that our day has come. Yet in the end, is it the fact that we are all just "visiting" that gives life value where our only goal should be to feel wanted, needed and loved and then when it's our turn next, we are fondly remember and truly missed for the way we touched the lives of others.

Today will be yesterday, tomorrow.
And with it,
Will go another bit of our future,
Slowly slipping into the past.

I cannot remember each today,
And some I wish I could forget.
I only know that all today's must turn to yesterdays,
And slip slowly into the past.

Yesterdays ... Once so near, slowly slip beneath our today's
That were once tomorrow's,
Before they too
Slipped slowly into the past.

Soon, all of our tomorrow's become yesterdays.
Making today's today and tomorrow's today's,
Nothing more than yesterday.

The Waldwick Series: The ten-book series spans nearly 200 years and are independent yet intertwined in several ways including, characters, location and thematic objectives that examine current social issues from different perspectives. Regardless of the time period or the characters in question, the core component - judging people by who they are instead, of what they are, remains paramount.

Waldwick addresses the subject of physical, social, economic and political oppression in the 1800's. Set in Cornwall, England, Virginia and Southwestern Wisconsin, *Waldwick* frankly discusses what one family was willing to do to overcome oppression, as told through the eyes of the narrator, George Terrill. *Waldwick* then summarizes what happens when the oppression is removed and opportunity arises. Integrated into the story line are actual events and people and how the main characters are affected by their existence and their interaction with these people and events. Above all else, *Waldwick* is a love story … love of the land, love of one another and the love of freedom, woven in a tapestry of acceptance, tolerance and justice. *Award Winner*

War of My Brothers examines America of the early 20th century and how and why it changed as seen through the eyes of Hank Terrill, great grandson of George Terrill from the original Waldwick. Ride along as Hank witnesses World War I, the Spanish Flu, the 19th Amendment, that gave women the right to vote, the Great Depression, World War II, Korean War and Viet Nam and how life changed, people changed and those who govern changed, as well. Experience the traumas of life and the joys of the living as you thank God that it didn't happen to you.

The King of Hearts has been reviewed as "*ambitious, extensively researched and deeply engrossing*"…a story that traces the actual Terrill family through 60 generations as it learns the consequence of wealth, power and prestige over 700 years only to have it all collapse around them. Using a blend of magic realism, lyrical prose and imagery *The King of Hearts* weaves a complex tapestry of a family's history from 65 BCE through sixty generations. Beneath it all, the book is about friendship and the deep, mutual bond between people based on trust, support, and genuine connection that goes beyond just companionship—it's about understanding, loyalty, and being there for each other through life's ups and downs.

Little Spirit Based in contemporary Wisconsin, *Little Spirit* examines the concept of eminent domain and the taking of land and dignity, first from the Indian's perspective and then today, as seen through the eyes of George Terrill IV a descendant of the original George Terrill. Using flashbacks through a 94-year-old, blind, Ho- Chunk Indian elder, named Great Grandfather, George learns about the feelings and challenges of the Ho-Chunk nation and the taking of their land and also how contemporary America hasn't changed that much in terms of citizen rights.

Driftless revisits George and his wife fifteen years into their marriage. Reflecting on the challenges they face when their marriage becomes mundane while examining the profound question of which is worse… having nothing or everything. As the mystery of the Forest is revealed *Driftless* examines the consequence of technology and the power of special interest groups to control the status-quo for their financial gain, while addressing the issue of individual rights in time of personal need, where the one thing all people have in common is … time!

The Hayflick Limit addresses the challenges of parenthood, while discussing a person's rights to live and die. When affected by an incurable malady the question becomes *"Would you choose five-to-seven years of normal mental acuity, at which time you would abruptly expire, or risk everything and allow for the slow, gradual decline with hope that a different, longer-lasting cure might come along?" The Hayflick Limit* addresses the role of government in establishing the validity of the Hippocratic Oath?

Let Go examines the consequence of bullying as Melia Terrill is affected by the verbal onslaught and her commitment to the only friend who has shown her the beauty of acceptance for who she is. The books examines the perks and perils of extreme wealth, the solitude of loneliness and frustration of achieving one's goals only to realize that all dreams can become nightmares when one risks everything for perhaps nothing as it delves into thoughts, emotions, joys, sorrow and consequences of being a captive of one's own past and fleeting fame.

Survivor…How Death Saved My Life looks at the consequence of an altered set of priorities and how it can take a near-death experience to "right the ship". Totally immobilized for six days, George Terrill examines his life and it's mistakes and vows, if he survives, to make things right. *Survivor* addresses the psychology of fear, the challenges of being told you have less than a 5% chance of living three hours and what you think about when you sincerely believe you're going to die.

Greed is a thought-provoking literary tale of ambition gone awry, exposing how the pursuit of wealth can fracture family relationships. This intense novel, explores the intricacies of human nature and the pursuit of meaning. It serves as a critique of modern society's obsession with wealth and status that challenges readers to reconsider what success truly means, making this book not just an exhilarating journey but a profound reflection on the human condition.

And/Or Using Newton's Third Law as a lens to explore relationships where every action sets off a chain reaction, *And/Or* journeys in ways no one can predict or control while asking difficult questions about resilience, identity, and redemption. As such, it ponders deep philosophical reflections and existential questions by drawing sharp connections between science and human nature, asking such profound questions as…Is it possible for a person to truly recover from betrayal? Can love survive after it's been broken? And when one loses everything, what's left? *And/Or* is a gripping, thought-provoking read that will linger long after the final page.

Disclaimer: This book and all the Waldwick Series books are works of fiction. Some of the events and experiences detailed herein are true and have been faithfully rendered as researched by the author to the best of his abilities. The information contained in this book is intended to provide helpful and informative material on the subjects and events addressed and written as an interpretation of his learning. No part of this text may be reproduced, transmitted, downloaded, decompiled, reverse-engineered, or stored in or introduced into any information storage and retrieval system, in any form or by any means, whether electronic or mechanical, now known or hereafter invented, without the express written permission of the author.

The author is a descendant of miners from Cornwall. There is a town called Mineral Point, Wisconsin, where his childhood was filled with magical moments and marvelous memories. There is a village called Waldwick that remains nearby and is the birthplace of his grandmother and mother. There are many Terrills living in the area who are his relatives, and he hopes and prays that he's done the family name justice by what he has written, for they are the kindred spirit upon which our country was created. There is no reality to the names used as they are all of consequence.

If the tale he weaves meets your fancy and your interest is piqued, he highly recommends visiting the wonderful area just southwest of Madison, Wisconsin. The scenery is spectacular and is only exceeded by the honor, dignity, and warmth of the people who reside there.

He's written this book as a tribute to his grandmother who was a Terrill and from whom, he learned the value of integrity and honesty and the joy of acceptance that only comes from an open heart and a profound sense of decency that she emanated with each breath.